Frances Power Cobbe

The Collected Works of Theodore Parker

Vol. X. Critical writings - Vol. 2

SALZWASSER
VERLAG

Frances Power Cobbe

The Collected Works of Theodore Parker

Vol. X. Critical writings - Vol. 2

Reprint of the original, first published in 1865.

1st Edition 2022 | ISBN: 978-3-75258-995-5

Verlag (Publisher): Salzwasser Verlag GmbH, Zeilweg 44, 60439 Frankfurt, Deutschland
Vertretungsberechtigt (Authorized to represent): E. Roepke, Zeilweg 44, 60439 Frankfurt, Deutschland
Druck (Print): Books on Demand GmbH, In de Tarpen 42, 22848 Norderstedt, Deutschland

THE

COLLECTED WORKS

OF

THEODORE PARKER

MINISTER OF THE TWENTY-EIGHTH CONGREGATIONAL SOCIETY AT BOSTON, U.S.

CONTAINING HIS

THEOLOGICAL, POLEMICAL, AND CRITICAL WRITINGS, SERMONS, SPEECHES, AND ADDRESSES, AND LITERARY MISCELLANIES.

EDITED BY

FRANCES POWER COBBE.

VOL. X.

CRITICAL WRITINGS.—VOL. II.

LONDON:

1865.

CRITICAL WRITINGS.

BY

THEODORE PARKER.

VOL. II.

LONDON

1865.

CONTENTS OF VOL. II.

CRITICAL WRITINGS.

ESSAYS.

THE HEBREW MONARCHY.

A History of the Hebrew Monarchy from the Administration of Samuel to the Babylonish Captivity. London: 1847. 1 vol. 8vo, pp. xii. and 372.

THE Hebrew nation seems never to have had a genuine historical spirit. It is certain they have left us no pure historical compositions in the scanty records of their national literature. Perhaps none of their historical books preserved in the Old Testament are wholly authentic and free from fiction. In the early ages of the world it was natural that mythology should take the place subsequently occupied by philosophy, and that events should be referred directly to God which come only by the usual mediation of finite causes. An intelligent reader would be surprised to find Mr Bancroft referring the war against King Philip to the direct counsel of God miraculously given to the governor of Massachusetts, but he will not be at all surprised to find similar events referred directly to the counsels of God miraculously given to Moses, or to Agamemnon, in the poetic writings of an earlier day. He would be surprised at the absence of such phenomena. We should be astonished if we did not find a mythology among the Hebrews in their earlier history, as well as among the Greeks and Hindoos. The earliest historical works of the Greeks which have come down to us are poems, not histories, and are of course mythological and not philosophical. At length we find a genuine historical literature in which the attempt is seriously made to relate historical facts in their natural historical order, referring human events to human and obvious causes; to tell a round, unvarnished tale. But such a genuine historical literature is scarcely found in the Hebrew records; all are more or less tinged by this mythological character. The books which treat of the earliest periods are, as it is natural, most strongly tinged with it.

Let any impartial man undertake to study the rise and progress of the nations of western Asia by the help of the Hebrew literature alone, and he would arrive at very remarkable results if he treated his documents as purely historical, and placed implicit confidence in their authority. Let us take the first work—Genesis. We shall not speak of the omissions, nor of ordinary mistakes, which are natural and unavoidable, but of the fact that an attempt seems studiously made to blacken the characters of the numerous nations hostile to the Hebrews, by pointing out some bend sinister on their escutcheon, or some enormous fault in their early progenitors—thus ascribing to them an infamous descent. At the same time an attempt equally studious seems made to dignify and elevate the original stock of the Hebrews, referring that nation to ancestors the most celebrated and unimpeachable.

Abraham is regarded as the common father of many nations in western Asia who speak substantially the same language, and have many customs and traditions in common. The curious traditions respecting him may easily be seen in D'Herbelot and elsewhere. The Book of Genesis traces the descent of the Hebrews directly to Abraham. He is descended from Shem, the oldest son of Noah, and is but the tenth removed from that patriarch, deriving his lineage through nine generations of oldest sons. Abraham marries a wife, Sarah, of the same stock, she being his half-sister. They dwell in Ur, the land of the Chasdim, or Chaldees, but emigrate thence at the command of Jehovah. Now, the patriarch has also other wives of an inferior rank, but the Hebrews are descended from Sarah, the first wife, who is of superior rank, and also of the same illustrious birth with Abraham himself.

That is not all. Isaac, the son of Abraham, from whom the Hebrews originate, is born under peculiar circumstances; in the old age of his mother, born, too, miraculously, in fulfilment of a promise made directly to Abraham and by Jehovah himself—a promise which seemed ridiculous even to the mother, and notwithstanding the dignity of the Being who made the promise. Other promises likewise are made; his posterity are to possess the territory of ten distinct tribes or nations,—all the land from the Euphrates to Egypt. When the miraculous child is born, God commands the father to sacrifice the new-born son, but the offering is miraculously prevented. The son grows up to manhood; a wife must be found for him. But she must not be a woman of ordinary descent, coming from the nations of his own neighbourhood. She must come from the classic and distant land whence Abraham himself had emigrated; must be of the same lineage as her husband. So Rebekah, the daughter of a wealthy and conspicuous man, is found, and becomes the wife of Isaac. Jehovah takes a special care of the son, not less than of the sire. Rebekah bears two sons, twins,—Esau and Jacob. One of these, Jacob, is the ancestor of the Hebrew race. He is the younger of the two, but for a trifle buys the rights of the first-born from his elder brother, and gains in consequence a blessing from his father, which for ever entails upon him and his posterity all the favours that Jehovah had promised to bestow upon the children of Abraham. Jacob is thus represented as born of most illustrious ancestry, having a lineage spotless and august, and is heir of the promises formerly made by God.

When he also grows up to manhood, a wife must be sought for him, but not among the women of the neighbourhood. To keep the race pure and unmixed, he must return to the native land of his grandparents, and take a partner from the celebrated family which had already given to the world an Abraham, a Sarah, and a Rebekah. Jehovah watches over Jacob with the same speciality of affection he had formerly bestowed on Isaac and Abraham. He visits Jacob by night, gives counsel by day—instructing him in the art of over-reaching his wives' father, and cautioning that father against interfering. To Jacob are born twelve sons and two daughters. The family are the special objects of Jehovah's care.

In this way a genealogy is made out which no ancient herald would find fault with. The Hebrews are the noblest of the noble, descended from the prime nobility of the earth. It is true, the character of Jacob is base and treacherous, when measured by the Christian standard of modern times; but in the estimation of the author of the narrative, the characteristic vices of the supplanter were doubtless virtues, and seem to be related as if in themselves deserving praise. Had it seemed otherwise to him, he probably would have represented Jehovah as interposing to punish Jacob, or to prevent the birthright from descending to his posterity.

Now, as if this illustrious descent were not enough to dignify the Hebrew nation withal, a corresponding and parallel effort is made to cast a cloud over the origin of the other races most immediately in contact with them. Many of them, it is said, are descended from Ham, the second son of Noah, a mythological person held in high veneration by many of the Oriental races. But it is said that Ham committed an infamous offence which demanded the severest chastisement on the part of his father. Accordingly Noah curses Canaan, the youngest son of Ham. The Canaanites were the special objects of hatred to the Hebrews, in the early part of their history. The latter conquered and gradually "absorbed" the territory of the former, expelling the inhabitants or reducing them to bondage. So the author of Genesis, after relating the crime of Ham twice in a single paragraph, mentions the fact that Canaan is the son of Ham. The patriarch curses Canaan for his father's fault, and the curse is repeated three times in a single paragraph.

Thus, according to the ethnography of Genesis, one third of the human race are disgraced by the act of their great progenitor, Ham. His descendants are the numerous nations of Caucasian descent in the south and west of Asia, and the north of Africa—the Ethiopians, Philistines, and the Egyptians. But though the disgrace must be shared equally by all the children of Ham, yet the curse falls specially upon Canaan. His posterity—taking the names from the common version of the Old Testament—are the Sidonians, the Hittites, the Jebusites, the Amorites, Girgashites, Hivites, Arkites, Sinites, Arvadites, Hamathites, the Phœnicians, and the Syrians, with many others. These are the nations with whom the Hebrews are so often at war, and who were unworthy to furnish wives for Isaac and Jacob.

In language, manners, and institutions, some of the Arabian tribes were more closely allied to the Hebrews than the Canaanites, as it appears. This fact must be accounted for in the Hebrew history and ethnology. Accordingly they are derived from Abraham. But they also are polluted in their origin. They are not allowed to be descended from Sarah, the honourable and well-born wife of the great patriarch, but from Hagar, a secondary wife, or concubine, and also a slave in Abraham's family, whom Sarah once drove out of doors on account of her insubordination. In addition to this reproach, Hagar is herself an Egyptian woman, and therefore disgraced by her descent from the infamous family of Ham. However, after her expulsion from Abraham's household she returns, bears a son called Ishmael, and remains there until after the birth of Isaac, till Ishmael has nearly attained the age of manhood, as it appears. Then, at the instigation of Sarah, the slave-mother is turned out of doors and her son with her. God himself approving of the expulsion, Ishmael must not be a joint-heir with Isaac, nor inherit the land or the promises. Still, as he also is Abraham's son, he must have a blessing and become a nation; but when Ishmael's posterity are enumerated, pains are taken to add that he was the son of a female slave and she an Egyptian, a daughter, therefore, of the race of Ham.

Other kindred nations are also said to have been descended from Abraham, but having for their mother only an obscure woman, Keturah, whom the author of the Chronicles seeks to degrade still more, calling her by a bad name,—calumniating Abraham while he blackens the origin of a hostile neighbour.

The Edomites, or Idumeans, had likewise a strong national resemblance to the Hebrews in many respects; they therefore must be referred to the same original. Accordingly they are descended from Esau, the twin-brother of

Jacob. But Esau had shown himself unworthy of his privilege of primogeniture, and had shamefully sold the promises entailed upon the first-born. Thus the ancestry of the Idumeans is disgraced at an early period of the family history. But that is not enough; Esau marries against his parents' consent, makes a shameful *mésalliance,* taking two wives, both of them Hittites, descendants, therefore, of the infamous family of Ham, and still more, of Canaan, the most infamous of that family, and inheritor of a special curse. Pains are taken to enumerate the descendants of this unfortunate marriage; but we need not follow the children of Esau further than to show that the Edomites and Amalekites, powerful enemies of the Hebrews, were traced back to that original.

There remain yet two other nations often at war with the Hebrews, the Ammonites and the Moabites. The most intense national hatred appears to have existed between them and the descendants of Jacob, which continued long after the establishment of the monarchy. To these nations, so formidable and detested, an origin yet more disgraceful is assigned: they are the children of Lot and his own daughters—the sons of incest and drunkenness at the very beginning. When the birth of Moab and Ben-ammi is recorded, the author diligently adds that they are the parents of the Ammonites and Moabites. Thus the early and most important enemies of the Hebrews are disposed of, and referred to some disgraceful original. An ingenious man might put all these things together, and, considering also what nations are not thus traduced, might give a shrewd guess at the date of the Book of Genesis itself.

The other four books of Moses, as they are called, are not more precisely historical than the first, equally legendary and mythical in the portions which relate to history, and marked by the same intense nationality, which is at times ferocious. Of the historical inaccuracies of Deuteronomy, the last of these, and of the apparent mode in which it was composed, we shall speak in a subsequent part of this article.*

The Book of Joshua is in many respects like its prede-

* See also De Wette, *Introduction to the Old Testament,* Vol. II. pp. 144—164.

cessors. It is mythical, full of historical inaccuracies and contradictions.

The Book of Judges is less artificially constructed than Deuteronomy, and free from the peculiarly sacerdotal spirit which pervades that book; but it is also legendary, mythological, and by no means a historical document on which any certain reliance can be placed.*

The Books of Samuel and Kings have a more authentic and historical character. All the outlines of the period they treat of are sketched by the hand of contemporary prose writers. State records seem to have been kept from the time of David downwards. The originals seem often to have been in the hands of the authors of Samuel, Kings, and even Chronicles. The mythological spirit is much diminished in its intensity. But the author of the work named at the beginning of this article treats of their character, and we will presently give his opinion upon the subject. His aim is to write a political history of the Hebrews, but he treats also of their religious affairs, for "the whole value of Hebrew history to us turns upon the Hebrew religion." To this end he uses the Hebrew documents with the same critical freedom that Niebuhr and Dr Arnold show in their treatment of the Roman documents. He does not scruple to point out the inconsistencies between the Books of Kings and Chronicles, nor to reject a statement which is absurd, nor to set down a fiction under its appropriate name. "As we have to deal with human fortunes, guaranteed to us by the evidence of documents which bear plentiful marks of the human mind and hand, we cannot dispense with a free and full criticism of these. And in criticizing, we have no choice but to proceed by those laws of thought and reasoning which in all the sciences have now received currency. We advance from the known towards the unknown. We assume that human nature is like itself; and interpret the men of early ages by our more intimate knowledge of contemporary and recent times, yet making allowance for the difference of circumstances. Much more do we believe that God is always like Himself, and that whatever are His moral attributes now and His consequent judgment of human conduct, such were they then and at all times. Nor ought we to

* See De Wette, ubi supra, pp. 166—174.

question that the relations between the divine and the human mind are still substantially the same as ever, until we find this obvious presumption utterly to fail in accounting for the facts presented to our examination. We explain all the phenomena by known causes, in preference to inventing unknown ones; and when one anomaly after another is found gradually to be cleared up by patient research, and a world of reality to evolve itself before the mind, fresh confirmation is added to the grand principles of modern philosophy, which experience proves alone to lead to self-consistent, harmonious results."

The author has not the common superstitious reverence for the Bible, and does not take the Jewish letter to strangle the Christian spirit with. He shows everywhere a large, humane, and Christian spirit. He is aware that his way of treating the Hebrew documents is not usual with his countrymen, and says,—

"A thoughtful and conscientious reader will probably meet here many things which have before passed across his mind, but have been rejected under the idea that if they were true, they would surely be well known to professed divines. But let him be assured there is not the same apathy and ignorance concerning the Old Testament, in the German as in the English Universities. If the Hebrew history has hitherto been nearly as a sealed book to us, it is because all the academical and clerical teachers of it are compelled to sign thirty-nine Articles of Religion before assuming their office. It is *not* easy to conceive how little we might know of Greek history, if, from the revival of Greek studies, test-articles had been imposed with a view to perpetuate the ideas of it current in the fifteenth century; but it is *very* easy to assure ourselves that neither Thirlwall nor Grote could have produced their valuable works under such a restriction. Until the laity strike off these fetters from the clergy, it is mere hypocrisy in them to defer to a clergyman's authority in any theological question of first-rate importance. We dictate to the clergy from their early youth what they are to believe, and thereby deprive them of the power of bearing independent testimony to it in their mature years. True religion consists in elevated notions of God, right affections and a pure conscience towards Him, but certainly *not* in prostrating the mind to a system of dogmatic history. Those who call *this* religion are (in the writer's belief) as much in the dark as those who place it in magical sacraments and outward purifications. But while utterly renouncing both these false and injurious representations, he desires his book to carry on its front his most intense conviction, that pure and undefiled religion is the noblest, the most blessed, the most valuable of all God's countless gifts; that a heart to fear and love Him is a possession sweeter than dignities and loftier than talents; and that although the outward Form of truths held sacred by good men is destined to be remodelled by the progress of knowledge, yet in their deeper essence there is a Spirit which will live more energetically with the development of all that is most precious and glorious in man."—pp. v—vii.

This book must be regarded, we think, as the most valuable contribution ever made in the English language to our means of understanding that portion of Hebrew history and the biblical books which relate to it. Only two writers in the English tongue, Dr Geddes and Dr Palfrey, so far as we know, have ever treated the historical books of the Old Testament with the same freedom and courage. Mr Norton has made a highly valuable contribution to the study of the Old Testament, but as he starts with the gratuitous assumption that "Christianity has made itself responsible for the fact that the Jewish religion, like itself, proceeded immediately from God," his critical and philosophical progress is impeded by a foregone conclusion.*

The work before us is sufficiently learned, but a little more copious reference to other writers would enhance its value. The author appears to be familiar with the works of the best German writers who have treated the subject—even the most recent. In writing a history he has written at the same time a good historical commentary on the Books of Kings and Chronicles, and sheds light, also, on contemporary passages in the prophetic works. He agrees with the most profound of modern critics, that "the five books of Moses" were written long after the time of David; that the Hebrew code of laws, like all others, was formed part by part during a considerable period of time, and that

* *Evidences of the Genuineness, &c.*, Vol. II., Note D, p. xlviii. et seq.

the establishment of the Levitical priesthood is of later date than the monarchy itself. He thinks the Books of Kings were compiled during the Babylonian exile, and those of Samuel a little earlier.

We will not give an analysis of the whole work, but only of parts which appear of most value. The political aim of the Hebrew institutions was to constitute a people of small independent land-owners; the most remarkable law was that which forbade the sale of land beyond the year of Jubilee. This was the Mosaic law of entail, which aimed directly to keep land in each family, and therefore, indirectly to prevent accumulation of large masses of landed property. The practical result was, that no permanent aristocracy could exist. But he admits that the law of Jubilee rested on usage and traditionary feeling rather than on any statute or positive enactment.

He thinks that Samuel may be called a second Moses; that the results of his ministry were greater and his instructions more permanent than those of Moses himself. But we see not how this can be, unless he assign to Samuel and not to Moses the first introduction of the worship of ONE GOD to the Hebrew nation. The Hebrew creed, he thinks, "was not monotheistic, in the sense of denying the *existence* of other gods. It rather degraded them into devils." Samuel preached against idolatry as John Huss and John Knox in Bohemia and Scotland preached against "Popish idolatry and foreign tyranny." The brief dissertation on the Prophets (pp. 31—37) is perhaps the best account of those remarkable men in the language. With all their excellences they were not free from various tinges of fanaticism; they often worked themselves into a religious frenzy. In the administration of Samuel, and during the reigns of the early kings, there were two great parties in the land; one favoured the exclusive worship of Jehovah, the other allowed also that of Baal and other deities. A sign or monument of each of their tendencies may be noticed in the proper names of persons and places. Some are compounded with *El*, some with *Baal*, others with *Jah* or *Je*, for *Jehovah*. In the family of Saul there is a singular mingling of these names; but after his time the names derived from Jehovah predominate. Samuel and the prophets favoured the Jehovistic party. Saul's policy was to foster the worshippers of foreign deities as a counterpoise to the influence of the prophets.

A parallel to the barbarity of David's treatment of the Philistines is found in the conduct of the North American Indians and other savage tribes. His "ecclesiastical proceedings were not modelled according to the Pentateuch." His public cruelties and his private sins are not excused by this author, but looked at with a clear, cool, human eye. He says,—

"The complicated baseness involved in his murder of Uriah so casts his honour in the dust, that thenceforth we rather pity and excuse than admire him. All the brilliancy, alike of his chivalry and of his piety, is sullied, and cold minds suspect his religious raptures of hypocrisy. If Nathan had been wise and bold enough to slash open the monarch's conscience, before the wen of wickedness had swelled into a carbuncle, most happy might it have been; but we cannot wonder that it was so very hard to rebuke a despotic and victorious prince. David was not indeed an Antoninus, an Alfred, or a Saint Louis; yet neither was he one of the vulgar herd of kings. The polygamy in which he indulged so injuriously must in part be laid to his personal weakness, when we observe how restrained (in comparison) was his predecessor Saul. Nevertheless, as a man, he was affectionate and generous, sympathetic and constitutionally pious: as a king, his patronage of religious persons was highly judicious, and his whole devotional character of permanent importance to the best interests of his people and of mankind; as a warrior, he taught Israel a mutual confidence and common pride in Jehovah their God; and first elevated his countrymen into a ruling and leading race, whose high place it was to legislate for and teach the heathen around. His career may serve to warn all who are wanting in depth of passion or enlarged knowledge of human nature, that those on whose conduct society has relaxed its wholesome grasp are not to be judged of by their partial outbreaks of evil, but by the amount of positive good which they habitually exhibit. Compared with the great statesmen of the educated nations of Europe, David's virtues and vices appear alike puerile; but among Asiatics he was a truly great man; and of his own posterity, though several, who were happily subjected to greater restraints, were far more consistent in goodness, there is none who more attracts our interest and our love than the heroic and royal Psalmist." —pp. 112, 113.

Solomon built the temple from mingled motives of policy, ostentation, and piety. The splendour of the building, the gorgeousness of the ceremonies performed there three times a year, led the people to assemble there partly from curiosity, partly for business, and in part for religious purposes. Thus a custom was established which helped consolidate the nation. To this circumstance the author attributes a good deal of the superiority which Judah had over Israel in later times. In Solomon's time "the strange awe of the dangerous Ark appears to have evaporated. . . . The Ark was opened, and in it were found neither the rod of Aaron which budded, nor the golden pot of manna, but only two tables of stone." Yet it is not certain that the successive high-priests dared examine them and compare the inscription with the copy in their books.

The author finds a remarkable disagreement between the two copies of the Decalogue, "which is uniformly overlooked by divines." We give his version of the Decalogue as found in Exodus xxxiv., only remarking that he has abridged the first, third, and sixth commandments.

" [First Table ?]

I. Thou shalt worship no other god than Jehovah; for Jehovah, whose name is Jealous, is a jealous God.

II. Thou shalt make thee no molten gods.

III. The feast of unleavened bread shalt thou keep, and dedicate all firstlings unto me: but the firstborn of thy sons thou shalt redeem. None shall appear before me empty.

IV. Six days shalt thou work, but on the seventh day thou shalt rest: in ploughing time and in harvest thou shalt rest.

[Second Table ?]

V. Thou shalt observe the feast of Weeks, the Firstfruits of Wheat-harvest, and the feast of Ingathering at the year's end.

VI. Thrice in the year shall all your males appear before the Lord Jehovah, the God of Israel.

VII. Thou shalt not offer the blood of my sacrifice with leaven.

VIII. The sacrifice of the feast of the Passover shall not be left to the morning.

IX. The first of the firstfruits of the land shalt thou bring into the house of Jehovah thy God.

X. Thou shalt not seethe a kid in his mother's milk."

During the latter part of Solomon's reign, through the influence of his seraglio, the party opposed to the worship of Jehovah came again into favour, and Abijah, a popular prophet, appealed to Jeroboam, an eminent man, for redress of the wrongs which the nation was suffering. This was the beginning of the revolution which finally separated the kingdom. But the pious design of the prophet was by no means accomplished. Jeroboam is painted in black colours by the Hebrew writers, and, as our author thinks, mainly because he did not favour the Levitical priesthood. "The grand quarrel was a ceremonial one." But the prophets made no real opposition until the reign of Ahab.

The author relates the counter-revolution which took place in favour of the monotheistic party, in which the descendants of Ahab were so cruelly slaughtered by Jehu, "a tiger of a man."

"Such is the train of atrocities which Elisha's message entailed on both the Hebrew kingdoms. A third time was the royal house of Israel extirpated, and now likewise that of Judah. That Jewish writers can gloat over such funereal events, so deadly to their own people, is sufficiently wonderful. That men called Christians can read them with calm approbation, is still more melancholy; for this is the training of mind which steeled all Europe to cruelty under the name of religion. This has lit up hell-fires in Christendom; this has perpetrated perfidious massacres unknown to Paganism; this has bequeathed, even to the present age, a confusion of mind which too often leads those who are naturally mild and equitable, to inflict hardship, vexation, degradation, and loss on the professors of a rival creed. Until men learn that Jehovah neither does, nor ever did, sanction such enormities as Elisha commanded and Jehu executed, they will never have a true insight into the heart of Him who is the God of the Pagan as well as of the Jew."—p. 210.

The account of the development of the priesthood is ingenious and valuable. The *priestly* system was complete, while that of the Levites was in its infancy; the sacerdotal caste included the professional or learned men. By frequent intermarriages they became almost an hereditary caste, and thus the idea of a tribe of priests, descendants of Levi, gradually grew up. Then the regular priests became exclusive. Books were written by them, or under their influence; facts were suppressed or distorted to suit their purposes, and insertions made. Some books are thus strangely marked by a Levitical spirit. This appears eminently in Deuteronomy and in the Chronicles, not to mention other books. Sometimes the priests furnished an important check to the fanaticism of the prophets. This was particularly the case in Judah and Jerusalem.

"It is undeniable, that in the Israelitish prophets, as in the Scotch Reformers, the pugnacious principle was too much in the ascendant. There was earnestness and deep conviction, noble ends proposed, and unshrinking self-devotion to them; but nothing of the meekness of wisdom; no gentleness and sensitiveness as to other men's equal rights, and far too little scruple to combine with bad men and commit their good cause to wicked means. . . . The forty days' fast of Elijah, his journey to the solitary Horeb, the stormy wind, the earthquake, and the fire, in which Jehovah was not; with the still small voice in which Jehovah was found,—are a noble poem. But Elisha, sitting in Samaria, and miraculously revealing the plans of Benhadad's campaign and the words which he speaks in his bed-chamber, is far less dignified, and reminds us of tales of magic. When Elijah twice calls down fire from heaven, and slays two bands of fifty soldiers sent to arrest him, he is severe and terrible; but when Elisha curses a troop of young children in the name of Jehovah, and brings two bears out of the wood, who devour forty-two of them, because they mocked at his bald head, he is ludicrous as well as savage. Elijah, who assembles the prophets of Baal, and after vanquishing them in a public trial of miracles, incites the spectators to slay them all, commits a semi-heroic crime; but Elisha, who by proxy incites a captain with an army at his back to kill his wounded and confiding master, and make away with Ahab's children and little grandchildren, besides being barbarous, is cowardly and deceitful. Elijah appears before Ahab face to face, to threaten him bitterly for the murder of Naboth; but Elisha, when the king is angry with him, and seeks his life, has supernatural intimation of it, and gives orders to shut the door in the messenger's face, while others arrest him outside. Elijah predicts a drought to Ahab, and again predicts rain, in simple words; but Elisha, when about to spell warlike successes to King Jehoash, makes them depend on a piece of luck. He bids him to take his arrows and shoot upon the ground. The youth (who lavishes appellations of honour on the aged prophet) intends to obey, and shoots three times. But Elisha is enraged that he has not shot five or six times, because (as he now reveals) Jehovah had decreed to give him as many victories over the Syrians as the times he should shoot. Finally, when Elijah's hour of removal is come, he is carried up to heaven in a chariot of fire; but when Elisha dies and is buried as other men, his bones have a like virtue to those of a dark-age Saint:—they raise to life a strange corpse, which by accident touches them."—pp. 281, 282.

Our author thinks the Pentateuch was produced about the time of Josiah; that is, about six hundred and fifty years before Christ, or nearly nine hundred after Moses. The first four books of the Pentateuch he regards as a growth and not a composition. They received their final shape and public recognition at that time. We will not repeat his arguments, which have been often given before, but make a single extract.

"The high pretensions made for the Pentateuch are disproved by a topic which cannot be plainly stated without extreme offence, yet which it would be cowardice on that account to suppress. Its prophecies indicate a marked acquaintance with events which preceded Josiah, but nothing at all clear which needs to be referred to later times. The book is familiar with the tribes of Israel and their distribution; with the qualities which characterized Judah and Ephraim, Reuben or Zebulon. It knows well the extent of David and Solomon's empire; the conquest of Edom and its final liberation; the fortunes of the Ishmaelites, and the desert over which they roved. It knows even the numerous wives of Solomon, his wealth, and his importing of horses from Egypt. It foresees the horrible fact of a woman devouring her child in a siege, as in that of Samaria by Benhadad; also the scattering of Israel by piracy and by invasion into many distant lands. It predicts not only the vanishing of Amalek from among the names of nations, but the wide-spread power of *Assyria*, which shall carry the Kenites into captivity. Nay, it is acquainted with the Cyprian force which attacked Esarhaddon from the Cilician coast, and perhaps also declares the final ruin of Assyria. But the *Chaldees* are not named as a conquering nation; nor had they yet become formidable to Judea when the book at length came out. Knowledge thus limited to the era which preceded its publication, cannot be imputed to a divine prescience, nor yet to accident."—p. 336.

He traces in the prophets the growth of a wide and expansive spirit which, extending beyond the Hebrews, embraces the whole world. He finds this especially in Isaiah, and yet more eminently in the anonymous author of the last twenty-six chapters of the Book of Isaiah, whom he calls the younger Isaiah.

"More important it is to observe the softened tone towards *the Gentiles* here pervading. Indeed, the tenderness and sweetness of this prophet is far more uniformly evangelical than that of any other. His very rhythm and parallelisms generally tell of the more recent polish and smoothness. He retains, moreover, all the spirituality of the older school: ceremonial observances are in no respect elevated by him. The *Sabbath* alone is named, and that in a tone the very reverse of formalism, although indicating the same high reverence for that institution which Christians in general have retained. With the exception of the fall of Babylon, which was the immediate means of release to his people, he does not concern himself with Gentile politics; but dilates on the trials, sorrows, and hopes of Zion, and the promises of divine aid to her, in general terms, to which the heart of spiritualized man in all ages and countries has responded."—pp. 366, 367.

After the return from captivity the nation was changed. Those who returned were chiefly persons "over whose minds sacerdotal principles had a commanding influence." The nation became enslaved by the letter of their old law; reverence for the Levitical priesthood became more profound; the exposition of the law became the most important profession.

"It is not intended here to pursue the later fortunes of the Jewish nation. We have seen its monarchy rise and fall. In its progress, the prophetical and the sacerdotal elements were developed side by side; the former flourished in its native soil for a brief period, but was transplanted over all the world, to impart a lasting glory to Jewish monotheism. The latter, while in union with and subservient to the free spirit of prophecy, had struck its roots into the national heart and grown up as a constitutional pillar to the monarchy: but when unchecked by prophet or by king, and invested with the supreme temporal and spiritual control of the restored nation, it dwindled to a mere scrubby plant, whose fruit was dry and thorny learning, or apples of Sodom which are as ashes in the mouth. Such was the unexpansive and literal materialism of the later Rabbi, out of which has proceeded nearly all that is unamiable in the Jewish character: but the Roman writers who saw this side only of the nation, little knew how high a value the retrospect of the world's history would set on the agency of this scattered and despised people. For if Greece was born to teach art and philosophy, and Rome to diffuse the processes of law and government, surely Judea has been the wellspring of religious wisdom to a world besotted by frivolous or impure fancies. To these three nations it has been given to cultivate and develop principles characteristic of themselves: to the Greeks, Beauty and Science; to the Romans, Jurisprudence and Municipal Rule; but to the Jews, the Holiness of God and His sympathy with His chosen servants. That this was the true calling of the nation, the prophets were inwardly conscious at an early period. They discerned that Jerusalem was as a centre of bright light to a dark world; and while groaning over the monstrous fctions which imposed on the nations under the name of religion, they announced that out of Zion should go forth the Law and the word of Jehovah. When they did not see, yet they believed, that the proud and despiteful heathen should at length gladly learn of their wisdom, and rejoice to honour them."—pp. 369, 370.

We thank the anonymous writer for his valuable book, and would gladly see it reprinted here, but as its publication would not favour any sect, we have no reason to expect to see it in an American form, and accordingly have been thus copious in our extracts from its pages. A few works written with the industry, learning, and philosophical discernment so perceptible in this, and above all marked by the same humane spirit of religion, would do much to relieve the Christian world from the incubus of superstition now resting on its bosom, disturbing its sleep with ugly dreams, yet at the same time forbidding it to awake. So long as Christianity is thought responsible for Judaism, so long will the letter of the Old Testament strangle the spirit of the New. The Bible will be appealed to for sanction of slavery, war, formalism, and a thousand abominations; and so long, likewise, will the real spiritual beauty, the hearty piety, the manly faith which fills so many a page of psalmist and prophet, be lost to the world. The modern Christian may say, with the ancient Greek, Give us light: in the darkness only are we afraid.

BALLAD LITERATURE.

The Pictorial Book of Ballads, Traditional and Romantic: with Introductory Notices, Glossary, and Notes. Edited by J. S. Moore, Esq., &c. London: 1847-48. 2 vols. 8vo, pp. vi. and 424, vi. and 428.

The origin of Ballads and Ballad-singers we shall for the present leave to the philosophical antiquaries, and for ourselves confess that we know not whether they claim their descent from Shem, Ham, or Japhet. Neither will we undertake to observe the nice distinctions that have been made between Ballads, Romances, and Legends; and the many other distinctions which have not yet been made, but might easily be if any one would show a difference sufficient to afford a basis for such a distinction—or even without that difference. We take a ballad to be a lyrical narration of some human event real or pretended. It may be a ballad of love, or a ballad of war; it may set forth the feelings of the author, and so far be mainly subjective in its character,—or only the feelings of the persons described in the poem, and so be mainly objective in its character. It may be long or short, good or bad, old or new. To us in either case it may be a ballad. We say all this, lest it should be supposed from what follows that we are not aware of the distinctions above hinted at, and which have been made by critics and criticasters, who, if not very wise, were at least very nice. On the contrary, we are painfully aware of such distinctions, and respectfully would notice such differences,—but at present we bid farewell to both, and address us to the ballads themselves —understanding the word in the wide sense we have given to it. However, let us narrow the signification a little, so as not to include all the narrative poetry in the world, ecclesiastical and secular. As a general rule, the ballad is simple in the structure both of the plot and the language, which has but a slight rhythmical movement; and in this particular, as well as others, it is distinguished specifically from odes, songs, and yet other kinds of lyric poetry. Nobody doubts that the poem called Chevy-Chase is a ballad, and we give the same name to those beautiful lyrical productions which Mr Macaulay has wrought out of the Roman materials. Indeed, he found the materials in Livy almost in the form of ballads, though certainly rude in form and moving with prosaic foot.

We find ballads, in one form or another, in almost every nation which has attained any considerable degree of social development. They differ widely in form, and not less widely in spirit. Taken as a whole they are valuable indications of the spirit of the nations amongst whom they have been produced. Some ballads have been made by regular artists, and are pieces of literary sculpture; others have grown up amongst the people, and are not so much the statues as they are children of the people. The latter are of course the most valuable of all as indications of national thought and feeling, even though they have but inferior poetic merit. They are the field flowers of poetry,—not so rare and exquisitely beautiful as the briefer songs, of love, of religion, which spring up in a poetic people as the water-lily and the fringed gentian, and by no means so nicely framed and finished off as the artistic creations of well-bred poets, the choice garden-flowers and exotics of the greenhouse,—but yet, like the violets, the dandelions, and the wild roses, breaking the monotony of the landscape, and lending a certain charm to the common places of the world.

A collection of all the popular poems which are in the mouth of the people would pretty truly represent the character of that people; at least, at the time when they were collected. The old Greek spirit of the heroic age is reflected in the ballads of the Homeric cycle of poets, as sharp and clear as the mountains and their clouds in the Lake of Geneva, of a still summer day. In the sombre ballads of Spain we find the superstitions, the gloom, and the fire of that nation. Their love, their patriotism, and their jealous sense of personal honour obtain here, perhaps, the fullest expression they have anywhere found in the national literature. The ballads of the Teutonic race express not less fully the peculiar character of the Danes, the Germans, and the English. Had we space, we would gladly pause awhile over the popular poetry—the Volksleider—of the continental portion of the race, and give some specimens thereof, from Volker Babbulus in the tenth century down to the "The Song of the Three Kings of Cologne" in the seventeenth, not neglecting the artistic ballads of Bürger, Uhland, Schiller, and Goethe.

The ballads of the English partake of the characteristic homeliness of the nation; of their manly good sense, their humanity not without a certain admiration of rough strength, of coarse pastimes, of gross eating and drinking. There appears likewise that strong tendency to individual freedom which marks all the movements of the Anglo-Saxon people. Their ballads delight in representing the man of nature as superior to the man of circumstances. All distinction of rank is occasionally broken through, sometimes in the most absurd and impossible manner. This characteristic appears eminently in "The Blind Beggar of Bednal Green," in "King Cophetua and the Beggar-Maid," which under the title of "A Song of a Beggar and a King" was old in Shakspeare's time, for Moth, in the play, says, "the world was very guilty of such a ballad some three ages ago." Then there is a strong moral sense running through the English ballads, as indeed it appears in most songs of the people everywhere. The popular minstrel loves to show how cunning is baffled by simple wisdom, and innocence proves too strong for crime; thus "the unnatural father" in the well-known ballad, falls into trouble, and is delivered by the son whom formerly he had spurned. Poetical justice must be done to the unworthy guardian of "the Children of the Wood:"

"And now the heavy wrath of God
Upon their uncle fell;
Yea, fearful fiends did haunt his house,
His conscience felt an hell:

"His barnes were fired, his goods consumed,
His landes were barren made,
His cattle dyed within the field,
And nothing with him stayed."

If a man is unjustly treated by the powerful, and especially by the government, the bard of the English people loves to tell how the innocent was rescued by force or stealth. The Story of Robin Hood "rescuing the squires three" is of this character.

"Bold Robin Hood ranging the forest all round,
The forest all round ranged he;
O then did he meet with a gay ladye,
She came weeping along the highway.

"'Why weep you, why weep you?' bold Robin he said."

She answers that she weeps for her three sons, for "they are all condemned to die,"—who, it seems, have not committed the most ordinary offences.

"'What have they done then?' said jolly Robìn,
'Come tell me most speedily.'
'O! it is for killing the king's fallow deer,
That they are all condemned to die.'

"'Get you home, get you home,' said jolly Robìn,
'Get you home most speedily,
And I will unto fair Nottingham go,
For the sake of the 'squires all three.'

"Then bold Robin Hood for Nottingham goes,
For Nottingham town goes he,
O there did he meet with a poor beggar-man,
He came creeping along the highway.

"'What news, what news, thou old beggar-man?
What news, come tell unto me.'
'O there's weeping and wailing in Nottingham town,
For the death of the 'squires all three.'

"This beggar-man had a coat on his back,
'Twas neither green, yellow, nor red;
Bold Robin Hood thought 'twas no disgrace
To be in the beggar-man's stead.

"'Come, pull off thy coat, thou old beggar-man,
And thou shalt put on mine;
And forty good shillings I'll give thee to boot,
Besides brandy, good beer, ale, and wine.'

"Bold Robin Hood then unto Nottingham came,
 Unto Nottingham town came he;
Oh there did he meet with great master sheriff,
 And likewise the 'squires all three.

"'One boon, one boon,' says jolly Robìn,
 'One boon I beg on my knee;
That, as for the death of these three 'squires,
 Their hangman I may be.'

"'Soon granted, soon granted,' says master sherìff,
 'Soon granted unto thee;
And thou shalt have all their gay cloathìng,
 Aye, and all their white monèy.'

"'Oh I will have none of their gay cloathìng,
 Nor none of their white monèy,
But I'll have three blasts on my bugle-horn,
 That their souls to heaven may flee.'

"Then Robin Hood mounted the gallows so high,
 Where he blew loud and shrill,
'Till a hundred and ten of Robin Hood's men
 Came marching down the green hill.

"'Whose men are these?' says master sherìff,
 'Whose men are they?' tell unto me.
'O they are mine, but none of thine,
 And are come for the 'squires all three.'

"'O take them, O take them,' says great master sheriff,
 'O take them along with thee;
For there's never a man in fair Nottinghàm
 Can do the like of thee.'"

Sometimes, indeed, this moral feeling, which is cosmopolitan, sinks down into patriotism and is limited to the country of the bard; sometimes it is bounded by men of his own humble rank in life. But this seldom happens in such poetry, except when war or oppression has made wise men mad, bringing out passions which are narrow and hateful. Notwithstanding the English ballads so commonly scorn the authority of circumstances, they yet betray the purely empirical character of the English nation. With the exception of these overleapings of the conventions of life, they contain scarce anything which has not its parallel in actual experience. We look in vain for the signs of that more elevated spirituality so noticeable in the popular poetry of some other nations.

The Americans have produced but little poetry in the simple form of ballads; little which circulates among the people, and that little is destined to a speedy and unlamented burial, as we think. Hitherto circumstances have not favoured the production of original literature. With the perpetual exception of speeches and sermons,—which grow out of the daily wants of state and church,—they from their nature must ever be ephemeral. New-England has always been the most literary part of America; but the fathers of New-England had a form of religion—or rather of theology—perhaps the most unpoetic that was ever developed on a scale so extensive. Calvin was no poet: he dwelt years long on the Lake of Geneva, preaching within sight of Jura and Mont Blanc, with the most beautiful scenery in the world spread out before him, and yet, so far as we remember, there is not in sermon or letter a single allusion to that wondrous beauty wasted on his cold eye,—not a single figure of speech ever is drawn from the scene before him—the lake, the mountain, or the sky. His followers in America had scarce more inclination to poetry than he. Men who are reflecting on the "five points," discoursing of election, reprobation, and the kindred themes, or inwardly digesting the Assembly's Catechism, would not be likely to write war-songs, or to make ballads. They did well in allowing "the nursery rhymes" to be sung to children; in not suffering "unworthy Barbara Allen" to be wholly forgotten. Still further, their outward circumstances were most unfavourable to the production of popular poetry, songs, and ballads amongst the people. They were struggling against poverty, against the wilderness, the wild beasts, and savage men,—not to mention the difficulties which came from the other side of the water. Thus stood the fathers of New-England. On the one side was starvation, and destruction on the other; and the Indians lying in wait and ready to hasten the advance of both. Under such circumstances few men would incline to sing anything very secular, or æsthetic. Besides, to the Puritan "common things" had a certain savour of uncleanness about them, and were thought scarce worthy of being sung. Would a man be merry, he might indeed sing, for there was a scriptural argument for his singing; but it must be —psalms. New-England psalmody is a proverb amongst nations. We speak not of the melodies, so long-drawn and so nasal, but of the substantial words which endure while the volatile melodies have long ago been hushed into expressive silence. We give a verse from an old American version of "the Psalms of David," assuring our readers that it is no invention of ours, but an undoubted original.

"The race is not to them that do the swiftest run,
Nor the battell,
To the peopel,
That carries the longest gun."

Of psalm-singing there was no lack in New-England. But that was not quite enough even for the Puritans. The natural heart of man wanted something a little more epic —some narrative of heroic events in a form slightly poetical, with a tinge of moral feeling, and a minute specification of time, place, person, and all particulars thereto belonging. This want was supplied—so far as we can learn —by the public prayers so abundantly made by the Puritans. They were as narrative as the popular ballads, about as long-winded, equally garrulous, it is said; only the rhythmic element was wanting; and that was supplied, we suppose, by the intonation of the orator, or by the repetition of particular phrases—as a sort of refrain, or "burden." Few men esteem the founders of New-England more than we, but we honour them for what they were, not for what they were not—not so much for their poetry as for their masculine character and unshrinking faith in God.

We have seen many of the early American ballads, but few of any merit. New-England ran to theology, politics, and practical life; not to lyric poetry. Even war, which forced such music from the Greeks and the Spaniards, extorted but little song from the stern men of America,— and that little poor. Of the ballads which belong to the Revolutionary period, there are few which are worth perusing. We insert a portion of one, which seems to us the best. Its date is obvious.

"While I relate my story, Americans give ear;
Of Britain's fading glory you presently shall hear,
I'll give you a true relation, attend to what I say,
Concerning the taxation of North America.

"The cruel lords of Britain, who glory in their shame,
The project they have lit on they joyfully proclaim;
'Tis what they're striving after, our rights to take away,
And rob us of our charter in North America.

"There are two mighty speakers, who rule in Parliament,
Who always have been seeking some mischief to invent,
'Twas North, and Bute, his father, this horrid plan did lay,
A mighty tax to gather in North America.

"He search'd the gloomy regions of the infernal pit,
To find among those legions one who excell'd in wit,
To ask of him assistance, or tell them how they may
Subdue without assistance this North America.

"Old Satan, the arch traitor, resolved a voyage to take,
Who rules sole navigator upon the burning lake;
For the Britannic ocean he launches far away,
To land he had no notion in North America.

"He takes his seat in Britain, it was his soul's intent,
Great George's throne to sit on, and rule the Parliament,
His comrades were pursuing a diabolic way,
For to complete the ruin of North America.

"He tried the art of magic to bring his schemes about,
At length the gloomy project he artfully found out;
The plan was long indulged in a clandestine way,
But lately was divulged in North America.

"These subtle arch-combiners address'd the British court,
All three were undersigners of this obscene report—
There is a pleasant landscape that lieth far away,
Beyond the wide Atlantic in North America.

"There is a wealthy people, who sojourn in that land;
Their churches all with steeples, most delicately stand;
Their houses, like the gilly, are painted red and gay;
They flourish like the lily in North America.

"Their land with milk and honey continually doth flow,
The want of food or money they seldom ever know:
They heap up golden treasure, they have no debts to pay,
They spend their time in pleasure in North America.

"On turkeys, fowls, and fishes most frequently they dine,
With gold and silver dishes their tables always shine,
They crown their feasts with butter, they eat and rise to play,
In silks their ladies flutter in North America.

"With gold and silver laces, they do themselves adorn,
The rubies deck their faces, refulgent as the morn!
Wine sparkles in their glasses, they spend each happy day
In merriment and dances, in North America.

"Let not our suit affront you, when we address your throne,
O king, this wealthy country and subjects are your own,
And you their rightful sovereign, they truly must obey,
You have a right to govern this North America.

"O king, you've heard the sequel of what we now subscribe?
Is it not just and equal to tax this wealthy tribe?
The question being asked, his majesty did say,
My subjects shall be taxed in North America.

"Invested with a warrant, my publicans shall go,
The tenth of all their current they surely shall bestow,
If they indulge rebellion, or from my precepts stray,
I'll send my war battalion to North America.

"I'll rally all my forces by water and by land,
My light dragoons and horses shall go at my command,
I'll burn both town and city, with smoke becloud the day,
I'll show no human pity for North America.

"Go on, my hearty soldiers, you need not fear of ill—
There's Hutchinson and Rogers, their functions will fulfil—
They tell such ample stories, believe them sure we may,
That one half of them are Tories in North America.

"My gallant ships are ready to hoist you o'er the flood,
And in my cause be steady, which is supremely good;
Go ravage, steal, and plunder, and you shall have the prey;
They quickly will knock under in North America.

"The laws I have enacted, I never will revoke,
Although they are neglected, my fury to provoke,
I will forbear to flatter, I'll rule with mighty sway;
I'll take away the charter from North America.

"O George! you are distracted, by sad experience find
The laws you have enacted are of the blackest kind.
I'll make a short digression, and tell you by the way,
We fear not your oppression in North America.

"Our fathers were distressed, while in their native land;
By tyrants were oppressed, as I do understand;
For freedom and religion they were resolved to stray,
And try the desert regions of North America.

"Heaven was their protector while on the roaring tide,
Kind fortune their director, and Providence their guide;
If I am not mistaken, about the first of May,
This voyage was undertaken for North America.

"To sail they were commanded, about the hour of noon,
At Plymouth shore they landed, the twenty-first of June;
The savages were nettled, with fear they fled away,
And peaceably they settled in North America.

"We are their bold descendants, for liberty we'll fight,
The claim to independence we challenge as our right,
'Tis what kind Heaven gave us, who can take away?
Kind Heaven, too, will save us in North America.

"We never will knock under, O George, we do not fear
The rattling of your thunder, nor lightning of your spear:
Though rebels you declare us, we're strangers to dismay;
Therefore you can't scare us in North America.

"To what you have commanded we never will consent;
Although your troops are landed upon the continent;
We'll take our swords and muskets, and march in bright array,
And drive the British rustics from North America.

"We have a bold commander who fears not sword nor gu[n]
The second Alexander, his name is Washington,
His men are all collected, and ready for the fray,
To fight they are directed for North America."

The "Whig songs" of 1840 are still fresh in the recollection of their authors, no doubt, and are pretty fair samples of what America has produced in the form of poetry for the people, and were besides valuable as specific signs of that period.

The work of Mr Moore named at the beginning of this article is intended to supply the want of a book containing all the good, or at least all of the best, ballads in the language. Certainly the want has long been felt, and remains still unsupplied. These volumes contain some pieces unworthy of a place in such a collection,—as it seems to us,—such as the "Story of John Gilpin," Kirk White's "Gondoline," and "The Rime of the Auncient Waggonere." Valuable ballads are omitted to make way for them. We miss, and who would have thought it, "the grand old ballad of Sir Patrick Spence," the "Friar of Orders Grey," the ballads relating to "sweet William" and "fair Margaret," and even those about King Arthur. "Auld Robin Gray" is likewise omitted. The most valuable that he has inserted which are not in the hands of lovers of ballad lore, are "The Luck of Muncaster," "Robin Conscience," "The King and a poore Northerne Man." The last—which seems to be the original of a popular song, "A Farmer there was in the west countrie,"—is supposed to have been written by one Martin Parker, a celebrated author of ballads. We give some extracts from it.

"Come hearken to me all around,
And I will tell you a merry tale
Of a Northumberland man that held some ground,
Which was the King's land, in a dale.

"He was borne and bred thereupon,
And his father had dwelt there long before,
Who kept a good house in that country,
And staved the wolfe from off his doore.

"Now for this farm the good old man
Just twenty shillings a-year did pay.

At length came cruell death with his dart,
And this old farmer he soone did slay;

"Who left behind him an aulde wife then,
That troubled was with mickle paine,
And with her cruches she walkt about,
For she was likewise blinde and lame.

"When that his corpes were laid in the grave,
His eldest sonne possesse did the farme,
At the same rent as the father before:
He took great paines and thought no harme.

"By him there dwelt a Lawyer false,
That with his farme was not content,
But over the poore man still hanged his nose,
Because he did gather the King's rent.

"This farme layd by the Lawyer's land,
Which this vild kerne had a mind unto:
The deele a good conscience had he in his bulke,
That sought this poore man for to undoe.

"He told him he his lease had forfite,
And that he must there no longer abide:
The King by such lownes hath mickle wrong done,
And for you the world is broad and wide.

"The poore man pray'd him for to cease,
And content himselfe, if he would be willing;
And picke no vantage in my lease,
And I will give thee forty shilling.

"Its neither forty shillings, no forty pound,
Ise warrant thee, so can agree thee and me,
Unlesse thou yield me thy farme so round,
And stand unto my curtesie."

The tenant sets off to carry the matter before the King.

"He had a humble staffe [stuffe] on his backe,
A jerkin, I wat, that was of gray,
With a good blue bonnet, he thought it no lacke;
To the King he is ganging as fast as he may."

So he goes to London, and thence to Windsor. He gives the porter a penny and a nobleman a groat to introduce him to the King, who is playing at bowls.

"Loe, yonder's the king, said the Nobleman,
 Behold, fellow, loe, where he goes.
Beleevet hee's some unthrift, sayes the poore man,
 That has lost his money and pawnd his cloathes.

"How hapt he hath gat neere a coate to his backe?
 This bowling I like not; it hath him undone.
Ise warrant that fellow in those gay cloathes,
 He hath his coyne and his doublet won.

"But when he came before the King,
 The Nobleman did his curtesie:
The poore man followed after him,
 And gave a nod with his head and a becke with his knee.

"If you be Sir King, then said the poore man,
 As I can hardly thinke you be,
Here is a gude fellow that brought me hither,
 Is liker to be the King than ye.

"I am the King, his Grace now sayd,
 Fellow, let me thy cause understand.
If you be Sir King, Ime a tenant of yours,
 That was borne and upbrought within your owne lande.

"There dwels a Lawyer harde by me,
 And a fault in my lease he sayes he hath found:
And all was for felling five poore ashes,
 To build a house upon my owne ground.

"Hast thou a lease here? said the King,
 Or canst thou shew to me the deed?
He put it into the King's owne hand,
 And said, Sir, 'tis here, if that you can read.

"Why, what if I cannot? said our King,
 That which I cannot, another may.
I have a boy of mine owne not seven yeares old,
 A will read you as swift as yould run i' th' highway.

"Lets see thy lease, then said our King.
 Then from his blacke boxe he puld it out.
He gave it into the King's owne hand,
 With four or five knots ty'd fast in a clout.

. . . .

"When the King had gotten these letters to read,
And found the truth was very so;
I warrant thee, thou hast not forfeit thy lease,
If that thou hadst felld five ashes moe.

. . . .

"Thoust have an injunction, said our King;
From troubling of thee he will cease:
Heele either shew thee a good cause why,
Or else heele let thee live in peace.

. . . .

"Thoust have an attachment, said our King;
Charge all thou seest to take thy part.
Till he pay thee an hundred pound,
Be sure thou never let him start.

"A, waise me! the poore man saide then;
You ken no whit what you now do say,
A won undoe me a thousand times,
Ere he such a mickle of money will pay.

. . . .

"Thou art hard a beleefe, then said our King:
To please him with letters he was right willing.
I see you have taken great paines in writing,
With all my heart Ile give you a shilling.

"Ile have none of thy shilling, said our King;
Man, with thy money God give thee win.
He threw it into the King's bosome;
The money lay cold next to his skin.

"Beshrew thy heart, then said our King;
Thou art a carle something too bold:
Dost thou not see I am hot with bowling?
The money next to my skin lies cold.

. . . .

"The King called up his Treasurer,
And bad him fetch him twenty pound.
If ever thy errant lye here away,
Ile beare thy charges up and downe.

"When the poore man saw the gold tendred,
For to receive it he was willing.

If I had thought the King had so mickle gold,
 Beshrew my heart, Ide a kept my shilling.

. . . .

"The poore man got home next Sunday;
 The Lawyer soone did him espy.
Oh, Sir, you have been a stranger long,
 I thinke from me you have kept you by.

"It was for you indeed, said the poore man,
 The matter to the King as I have tell.
I did as neighbours put it in my head,
 And made a submission to the King mysel.

"What a deel didst thou with the King? said the Lawyer;
 Could not neighbours and friends agree thee and me?
The deel a neighbour or friend that I had,
 That would a bin sike a daies man as he.

"He has gin me a letter, but I know not what they cal 't;
 But if the King's words be true to me,
When you have read and perused it over,
 I hope you will leave and let me be.

"He has gin me another, but I know not what 'tis;
 But I charge you all to hold him fast.
Pray you that are learned this letter reade;
 Which presently made them all aghast.

"Then they did reade this letter plaine,
 The Lawyer must pay him a hundred pound.
You see the King's letter, the poore man did say,
 And unto a post he sal straight way be bound.

"Then unto a post they tide him fast,
 And all men did rate him in cruell sort;
The lads and the lasses, and all the towne
 At him had great glee, pastime and sport.

"Ile pay it, Ile pay it, the Lawyer said,
 The attachment, I say, it is good and faire;
You must needes something credit me,
 Till I goe home and fetch some meare.

"Credit! nay thats it the King forbad:
 He bad, if I got thee, I should thee stay.

The Lawyer payd him an hundred pound
  In ready money, ere he went away.

"Would every Lawyer were served thus!
  From troubling poore men they would cease:
They 'd either show them a good cause why,
  Or else they 'd let them live in peace.

"And thus I end my merry tale,
  Which shews the plain man's simplenesse,
And the King's great mercy in writing his wrongs,
  And the Lawyer's fraud and wickednesse."

Mr Moore has not inserted any songs in his volumes, as most collectors of ballads have done. We cannot forbear adding a little piece not so well known as it deserves to be, called

"ROSELYND'S MADRIGAL.

"Love in my Bosom like a Bee
  Doth suck his sweet;
Now with his wings he plays with me,
  Now with his feet.
Within my Eyes he makes his nest,
His bed within my tender Breast.
My Kisses are his daily feast,
But yet he robs me of my Rest!
  Ah Wanton—will ye!

"And when I sleep, then percheth he
  With pretty flight,
And makes his pillow on my Knee,
  The live-long night.
I strike the harp, he tunes the string,
He music plays if so I sing,
He gives me many a lovely thing,
But cruel, he my heart doth sting!
  Whist, Wanton, still ye."

Here is a little piece by Anastasius Grün, a German poet of the Swabian school, not without merit. We know not the name of the translator.

"THE LAST POET.

"'When will be poets weary,
And throw their harps away?
When will be sung and ended
The old, eternal lay?

"'When will your horn of plenty
At last exhausted lie?
When every flower is gather'd,
And every fountain dry?'

"As long as the sun's chariot
Rolls in the heavenly blue,
As long as human faces
Are gladdened with the view:

"Long as the sky's loud thunder
Is echoed from the hill,
And, touched with dread and wonder,
A human heart can thrill:

"And while, through melting tempest,
The rainbow spans the air,
And gladden'd human bosoms
Can hail the token fair:

"And long as night the ether
With stars and planets sows,
And man can read the meaning
That in golden letters glows:

"As long as shines the moon
Upon our nightly rest,
And the forest waves its branches
Above the weary breast:

"As long as blooms the spring,
And while the roses blow,
While smiles can dimple cheeks,
And eyes with joy o'erflow:

"And while the cypress dark,
O'er the grave its head can shake,

And while an eye can weep,
And while a heart can break:

"So long on earth shall live
The goddess Poesy,
And make of human life
An endless melody.

"And singing, all alone,
The last of living men,
Upon Earth's garden green,
Shall be a poet then.

"God holds his fair creation
In his hand, a blooming rose,
He smiles on it with pleasure,
And in his smile it glows.

"But when the giant-flower
For ever dies away,
And earth and sun, its blossoms,
Like blooms of spring, decay;

"Then ask the poet—then—
If you live to see the day—
'When will be sung and ended
The old, eternal lay?'"

WILLIAM ELLERY CHANNING.

Memoir of William Ellery Channing; with Extracts from his Correspondence and Manuscripts. In three volumes. Boston. 1848. 12mo, pp. 427, 459, 494.

It is now nearly six years since William Ellery Channing, ceasing to be mortal, passed on to his rest and his reward. We have waited impatiently for the publication of his memoirs, that we might "beg a hair of him for memory." They are now before us—three well-printed volumes, mainly filled up with his own writings, letters, extracts from journals, sermons, and various papers hitherto kept from the press. As a public speaker and a popular writer he was well known before; these volumes show us not merely the minister and the author, but the son, husband, father, and friend. If they reveal nothing new in his character, we have yet in them ample materials for ascertaining whence came his influence and his power. What estimate shall we make of the man, and what lesson draw from his life and works? These are matters worth considering, but, before answering the question, let us look a little at the opportunities afforded him by his profession.

The Church and State are two conspicuous and important forms of popular action. The State is an institution which represents man in his relations with man;—the Church, man in his relations with man and God. These institutions, varying in their modifications, have always been and must be,—as they represent two modes of action that are constant in the human race, and come from the imperishable nature of man. In each of these modes of action, the people have their servants,—politicians, the servants of the State, and clergymen, the servants of the Church.

Now the clergyman may be a priest, or a minister—the choice depending on his character and ability. The same distinctions are noticeable in the servants of the State, where we have the priest of politics and the minister of politics. We will pass over the priest.

The business of the minister is to become a spiritual guide to men, to instruct by his wisdom, elevate by his goodness, refine and strengthen by his piety, to inspire by his whole soul—to serve and to lead by going before them all his days with all his life, a pillar of cloud by day, of fire by night. The good shepherd giveth his life to his sheep as well as for them. The minister aims to be, to do, and to suffer, in special for his own particular parish, but also and in general for mankind at large. He proposes for himself this end: the elevation of mankind,—their physical elevation to health, comfort, abundance, skill, and beauty; their intellectual elevation to thought, refinement, and wisdom; their moral and religious elevation to goodness and piety, till they all become sons of God also, and prophets. However, his direct and main business is to promote the spiritual growth of men, helping them to love one another, and to love God.

His means to this end are, in general, the common weapons of the Church. To him the Sunday is a high day, for it is the great day of work, when he comes into close relations with men, to instruct the mind, to warn in the name of conscience, gently arousing the affections, kindling the religious emotions, and so continuing his Father's work; the meeting-house, chapel, or church, is the great place for his work, and so, like the Sunday, it is holy, to him;—both invested with a certain sanctity, as to the pious farmer or the smith, the plough or the hammer seems a sacred thing. The Bible, the service-books, the traditions he appeals to, the sacramental ordinances he uses, all are means, but not ends, helps to whom they help, but nothing more, their sanctity derivative, not of them but of the use they serve. In our day, the press offers him its aid, and stands ready to distribute his thought among the millions of mankind. By means of that he gradually gets beyond the bounds of his parish, rural or metropolitan, and if God has so gifted him, has whole nations for his audience, and, long after his death, his word will circulate among the nations—a word of power and blessedness.

The minister finds a certain respect paid to the clergyman. This is not a thing that is new, but old, hallowed, and slowly fading out of the consciousness of the nations. This traditional respect gives him a certain position and influence, and enables him at once to anticipate and claim a place which is granted to other classes of men only as the result of long life and faithful work. He finds a pulpit erected for him, an audience gathered, respectful and disposed to listen and gratefully to receive whatever good he has to offer. While the priest uses this position and traditional respect to elevate himself, to take his ease in his inn—to keep men still, the minister uses it to help men forward; not to elevate himself, but them. The pulpit is his place to stand on and move the world. It is not to be denied that even now, in incredulous America, the calling of a clergyman gives a man a good opportunity for power, for a real, serious, and lasting influence, or it gives him the best chance for a sleep, silent and undisturbed, and deep and long.

Such are the general means of the minister towards his great end—means which belong to all clergymen, and vary in efficiency only with the number, the wealth, the talent, and social position of his audience. His particular and personal means are his talents, little or great; his skill, acquired by education and self-discipline; his learning, the accumulated thought which has come of his diligence, as capital is accumulated by toil and thrift; his eloquence,—the power of speaking the right thing, at the right time, with the right words, in the right way; his goodness and his piety,—in a word, his whole character, intellectual, moral, and religious. These are the means which belong to the man, not the clergyman; means which vary not with the number, wealth, talent, and social position of his audience, but only with the powers of the man himself. His general means are what he has as servant of the Church—his special, what he is as a man.

Say what men will, the pulpit is still a vantage ground, an eminence; often a bad eminence, it may be, still one of the places of public power. If a man would produce an immediate effect and accomplish one particular work, let him storm awhile in Congress, if he will. But if he aims to produce a long and lasting influence, to affect men deeply, and in many ways promote the progress of mankind, he may ascend the pulpit, and thence pour forth his light and heat on youth and age, distil his early and his latter rain; he is sure to waken the tender plants at last, and sure to strengthen the tallest and most strong. Yet for all that, say what we may of the power of that position, the man is more than the pulpit, more than the church,—yes, more than all pulpits and all churches, and if he is right and they wrong, he sets them a-spinning around him as boys their tops. Yet 'tis a great mistake to suppose it is the spoken word merely that does all; it is the mind, the heart, the soul, the character, that speaks the word. Words—they are the least of what a man says. The water in some wide brook is harmless enough, loitering along its way, nothing but water; the smallest of fishes find easy shallows for their sport; careless reptiles there leave their unattended young; children wade laughing along its course, and sail their tiny ships. But raise that stream a hundred feet—its tinkle becomes thunder, and its waters strike with force that nothing can resist. So the words of a man of no character, though comforting enough when they are echoed by passion, appetite, and old and evil habits of our own—are powerless against the might of passion, habit, appetite. What comes from nothing comes to nothing. I know IN WHOM I have believed, said the apostle—not merely WHAT.

It is the minister's business to teach men truth and religion, not directly all forms of truth—though to help so far as he may even in that—but especially truth which relates to man's spiritual growth. To do this he must be before men, superior to them in the things he teaches: we set a grown woman to take care of children, a man to teach boys. There is no other way; in mathematics and in morals the leader must go before the men he leads. To teach truth and religion the minister must not only possess them, but must know the obstacles which oppose both in other minds—must know the intellectual errors which conflict with truth, the practical errors which contend with religion, and so be able to meet and confront the falsehoods and the sins of his time. He must therefore be a reformer,—there is no help for it. He may have a mystical turn, and reform only sentiments; a philosophical turn, and reform ideas—in politics, philosophy, theology; or a practical turn, and hew away only at actual concrete sins; but a reformer must he be in one shape, or in all, otherwise he is no minister, serving, leading, inspiring, but only a priest; a poor miserable priest,—not singing his own psalm out of his own throat, but grinding away at the barrel-organ of his sect—grating forth tunes which he did not make and cannot understand.

The minister is to labour for mankind, for the noblest end, in one of the highest modes of labour, and its fairest form. He does not ask to rule, but to serve; not praise, but perfection. He seeks power over men not for his sake, but theirs. He is to take the lead in all works of education, of moral and social reform. If need is, he must be willing to stand alone. The qualities which bind him to mankind for all eternity are qualities which may sever him from his class and his townsmen; yes, from his own brothers, and that for his mortal life. The distinctions amongst men must be no distinctions to him. He must honour all men, become a brother to all—most brotherly to the neediest. He must see the man in the beggar, in the felon, in the outcast of society, and labour to separate that diamond from the rubbish that hides its light. In a great city, the lowest ranks of the public should be familiar to his thoughts and present in his prayers. He is to seek instruction from men that can give it—and impart of himself to all that need and as they need. He must keep an unbroken sympathy with man; above all, he must dwell intimate with God. It is his duty to master the greatest subjects of human thought: to know the nature of man, his wants, appetites, exposures,—his animal nature, his human nature, and his divine; man in his ideal state of wisdom, abundance, loveliness, and religion; man in his actual state of ignorance, want, deformity, and sin. He is to minister to man's highest wants; to bring high counsel to low men, and to elevate still more the aspirations of the loftiest. He must be a living rebuke to proud men and the scorner; a man so full of heart and hope that drooping souls shall take courage and thank God, cheered by his conquering valour.

To do and to be all this, he must know men, not with the half-knowledge which comes from reading books, but by seeing, feeling, doing, and being. He must know history, philosophy, poetry—and life he must know by heart. He must understand the laws of God, be filled with God's thought, animated with His feeling—be filled with truth and love. Expecting much of himself he will look for much also from other men. He asks men to lend him their ears, if he have anything to teach, knowing that then he shall win their hearts; but if he has nothing to offer, he bids men go off where they can be fed, and leave the naked walls sepulchral and cold, to tell him, "Sir, you have nothing to say; you had better be done!" But he expects men that take his ideas for truth to turn his words to life. He looks for corn as proof that he sowed good seed in the field; he trusts men will become better by his words—wiser, holier, more full of faith. He hopes to see them outgrow him, till he can serve them no more, and they come no longer to his well to draw, but have found the fountain of immortal life hard by their own door;—so the good father who has watched and prayed over his children, longs to have them set up for themselves, and live out their own manly and independent life. He does not ask honour, nor riches, nor ease—only to see good men and good works as the result of his toil. If no such result comes of a long life, then he knows either that he has mistaken his calling or failed of his duty.

We have always looked on the lot of a minister in a country town as our ideal of a happy and useful life. Not grossly poor, not idly rich, he is every man's equal, and no man's master. He is welcome everywhere, if worthy, and may have the satisfaction that he is helping men to wisdom, to virtue, to piety, to the dearest joys of this life and the next. He can easily know all of his flock, be familiar with their thoughts, and help them out of their difficulties by his superiority of nature, or cultivation, or religious growth. The great work of education—intellectual and spiritual—falls under his charge. He can give due culture to all; but the choicer and more delicate plants, that require the nicest eye and hand—these are peculiarly his care. In small societies eloquence is not to be looked for, as in the great congregations of a city, where the listening looks of hundreds or thousands would win eloquence almost out of the stones. The ocean is always sublime in its movements, but the smallest spring under the oak has beauty in its still transparence, and sends its waters to the sea. In cities the lot of the minister is far less grateful—his connections less intimate, less domestic. Here, in addition to the common subjects of the minister's discourse, everywhere the same, the great themes of society require to be discussed, and peace and war, freedom and slavery, the public policy of states, and the character of their leaders, come up to the pulpits of a great city to be looked on in the light of Christianity and so judged. With a few hearers, we see not how a man can fail to speak simply, and with persuasive speech; before many, speaking on such a theme as religion, which has provoked such wonders of art out of the sculptor, poet, painter, architect—we wonder that every man is not eloquent. Some will pass by the little spring, nor heed its unobtrusive loveliness,—all turn with wonder at the ocean's face, and feel for a moment awed by its sublimity, and lifted out of their common consciousness.

In the nineteenth century the clergy have less relative power than ever before in Christendom; it is partly their own fault, but chiefly the glory and excellence of the age. It has other instructors. But there was never a time when a great man rising in a pulpit could so communicate his thoughts and sentiments as now; a man who should bear the same relation to this age that Augustine, Thomas Aquinas, and Bernard of Clairvaux bore to their age, so far overtopping men—would have more influence, not less than theirs. Nations wait for noble sentiments, for generous thoughts; wait for the discoverer and organizer. The machinery of the age is ready to move for him,—the steam-horses, the steam-press. His audience has no limit. Even now the position of a minister gives him great advantages. He has a ready access to men's souls, a respectful hearing from week to week, and constant dropping will wear the stones—how much more the hearts of men. The children grow up under his eye and influence.

All ministers stand on the same level, and nothing lifts one above another but his genius, his culture, his character, and his life. In the pulpit, the most distinguished birth avails nothing; the humblest origin is no hindrance. In New-England, in America, everywhere in the world money gives power, never more than to-day; a rich lawyer or merchant finds himself more respected for his wealth, and listened to with greater esteem by any audience. Wealth arms him with a golden weapon. It is so in politics,—power is attracted towards gold. With the minister it is not so. If a clergyman had all the wealth of both the great cardinals Wolsey and Richelieu, did he dwell in a palace finer than the Vatican—all his wealth would not give him a whit the more influence in his pulpit, in sermon, or in prayer. Henry Ware moved men none the less because he had so little of this world's goods. In this way, therefore, the minister's influence is personal, not material. The more he is a man, the more a minister.

In virtue of his position he has the best chance to know men. He overrides all distinctions of life, associates with the humblest man as a brother, with the highest as their equal. If well trained, his education places him in the circle of the most cultivated minds, while his sympathies and his duty attract him to the lowest sphere of rudeness, want, and perhaps of crime. He sees men in joy and in grief, at a wedding and a funeral, and when flushed with hope, when wrung with pain, when the soul bids earth farewell. If a true man, the most precious confidence is reposed in him. He looks into men's eyes as he speaks, and in their varying faces reads their confession, what they could oft conceal, both ill and good,—reads sometimes with astonished eyes. Reader, you have seen an old coin, worn smooth so that there was no mark on it, not a letter; you know not whence it came nor whose it is; but you heat it in the fire, and the stamp of the die is plain as when the coin was minted first; you see the image, read the superscription. So the excitement of a sermon reveals the man's character in his oft-unwilling face, and the preacher, astonished, renders unto Cæsar the things that are his, and unto God His own. Sometimes one is saddened to see the miser, satyr, worldling in his many forms, under a disguise so trim and neat; but oftener, perhaps, surprised to find a saint he knew not of before; surprised at the resurrection of such a soul from such a tomb. The minister addresses men as individuals: the lawyer must convince the whole jury, the senator a majority of the senate, or his work is lost; while if the minister convinces one man—or but half convinces him—he has still done something, which will last. The merchant deals with material things, the lawyer and the politician commonly address only the understanding of their hearers, sharpening attention by appeals to interest; while the minister calls upon the affections, addresses the conscience, and appeals to the religious nature of man—to faculties which bind man to his race, and unite him with his God. This gives him a power which no other man aspires to; which neither the lawyer nor the merchant, nor yet the politician, attempts to wield; nay, which the mere writer of books leaves out of sight. In our day we often forget these things, and suppose that the government or the newspapers are the arbiters of public opinion, while still the pulpit has a mighty influence. All the politicians and lawyers in America could not persuade men to believe what was contrary to common-sense and adverse to their interest; but a few preachers, in the name of Religion, made whole millions believe the world would perish on a certain day, and, now the day is past, it is hard for them to believe their preachers were mistaken!

Now all this might of position and opportunity may be used for good or ill, to advance men or retard them; so a great responsibility rests always on the clergy of the land. Put a heavy man in the pulpit, ordinary, vulgar, obese, idle, inhuman, and he overlays the conscience of the people with his grossness; his Upas breath poisons every spiritual plant that springs up within sight of his church. Put there a man of only the average intelligence and religion —he does nothing but keep men from sliding back; he loves his people and giveth his beloved—sleep. Put there a superior man, with genius for religion, nay, a man of no genius, but an active, intelligent, human, and pious man, who will work for the human race with all his mind and heart—and he does wonders; he loves his people and giveth his beloved his own life. He looks out on the wealth, ignorance, pride, poverty, lust, and sin of the world, and blames himself for their existence. This suffering human race, poor blind Bartimæus, sits by the wayside, crying to all men of power—"Have mercy on me;" the minister says, "What wilt thou?" he answers, "Lord, that I might receive my sight." No man may be idle, least of all the minister; he least of all in this age, when Bartimæus cries as never before.

Dr Channing was born at Newport in Rhode Island, the 7th of April, 1780, and educated under the most favourable circumstances which the country then afforded; employed as a private teacher for more than a year at Richmond, and settled as a clergyman in Boston more than five and forty years ago. Here he laboured in this calling, more or less, for nearly forty years. He was emphatically a Christian minister, in all the high meaning of that term. He has had a deep influence here; a wide influence in the world. For forty years, though able men have planned wisely for this city, and rich men bestowed their treasure for her welfare, founding valuable and permanent institutions, yet no one has done so much for Boston as he—none contributed so powerfully to enhance the character of her men for religion and for brotherly love. There is no charity like the inspiration of great writers. There were two excellent and extraordinary ministers in Boston contemporary with Dr Channing, whose memory will not soon depart—we mean Buckminster and Ware. But Dr Channing was the most remarkable clergyman in America; yes, throughout all lands where the English tongue is spoken, in the nineteenth century there has been no minister so remarkable as he; none so powerful on the whole. No clergyman of America ever exercised such dominion amongst men. Edwards and Mayhew are great names in the American churches, men of power, of self-denial, of toil, who have also done service for mankind; but Channing has gone deeper, soared higher, seen further than they, and set in motion forces which will do more for mankind.

What is the secret of his success? Certainly his power did not come from his calling as a clergyman: there are some forty thousand clergyman in the United States. We meet them in a large city; they are more known by the name of their church than their own name; more marked by their cravat than their character. Of all this host, not ten will be at all well known, even in their own city or village, in a hundred years; perhaps not one. Nay, there are not twenty who are well known in America, now even, out of their denomination—they, perhaps, known by the unlucky accident of some petty controversy, rather than by any real eminence of character and work. Who of them is otherwise known to Europe, or even to England? But Dr Channing is well known in Germany and France; his writings more broadly spread in England than in his native land; his power widens continually, and deepens too.

His eminence came from no extraordinary intellectual gifts born with him. Truly his was a mind of a high order. Yet it is not difficult to find men of far more native intellectual force, both here and everywhere; and throughout all his life, in all his writings, you see the trace of intellectual deficiencies—his deficiencies as a writer, as a scholar, and still more as an original and philosophical thinker. Nor did it come any more from his superior opportunities for education. True, those were the best the country afforded at that time, though far inferior in many respects to what is now abundantly enjoyed with no corresponding result. In his early culture there were marked deficiencies—the results of which appear in his writings even to the last, leading him to falter in his analysis, leaving him uncertain as to his conclusion, and timid in applying his ideas to practice. His was not the intellect to forego careful and laborious and early training; not an intellect to cultivate itself, browsing to the full in scanty pastures, where weaker natures perish for lack of tender grass and careful housing from the cold.

His signal success came from no remarkable opportunity for the use of his gifts and attainments. He was one minister of the forty thousand. His own pulpit was only higher than others, his audience larger and more influential, because he made it so. His clerical brothers in his last years hindered more than they helped him; his own parish gave him no remarkable aid, and in his best years showed themselves incapable of receiving his highest instructions—and in the latter part of his life proved quite unworthy of so great a man.

He had none of the qualities which commonly attract men at first sight. He was little of stature, and not very well-favoured; his bodily presence was weak; his voice feeble, his tone and manner not such as strike the many. Beauty is the most popular and attractive of all things—a presence that never tires. Dr Channing was but slightly favoured by the Graces; his gestures, intonations, and general manner would have been displeasing in another. He had nothing which at first sight either awes or attracts the careless world. He had no tricks and made no compromises. He never flattered men's pride nor their idleness—incarnating the popular religion; he did not storm or dazzle; he had not the hardy intellect which attracts men with only active minds, nor the cowardly conservatism which flatters Propriety to sleep in her pew; he never thundered and lightened—but only shone with calm and tranquil though varying light. He had not the social charm which fascinates and attaches men; though genial, hospitable, and inviting, yet few came very near him.

He was not eminently original, either in thought or in the form thereof; not rich in ideas. It is true, he had great powers of speech, yet he had not that masterly genius for eloquence, which now stoops down to the ground and moulds the very earth into arguments, till it seems as if the stones and trees were ordained his colleagues to preach with him, obedient to his Orphic enchantment;—not that genius which reaches up to the heavens, pressing sun and moon and each particular star into the service of his thought; which proves by a diagram, illustrates by a picture, making the unwilling listeners feel that he had bribed the universe to plead his cause;—not that rare poetic power, which is born Genius and bred Art, which teems with sentiments and ideas, clothes and adorns them with language gathered from letters, nature, art, and common life, grouping his family of thoughts as Raphael in a picture paints the Madonna, Joseph, Baby, Ass, Angel, Palm-tree, those incongruous things of earth and Heaven, all unified and made harmonious by that one enchanting soul. He had not that intellectual, wealthy eloquence, beautiful as roses yet strong as steel. Nor had he the homely force of Luther, who in the language of the farm, the shop, the boat, the street, or nursery, told the high truths that reason or religion taught, and took possession of his audience by a storm of speech, then poured upon them all the riches of his brave plebeian soul, baptizing every head anew—a man who with the people seemed more mob than they, and when with kings the most imperial man. He had not the blunt terse style of Latimer, nor his beautiful homeliness of speech, which is more attractive than all rhetoric. He had not the cool clear analysis of Dr Barrow, his prodigious learning, his close logic, his masculine sense; nor the graceful imagery, the unbounded imagination of Jeremy Taylor, "the Shakspeare of divines," nor his winsome way of talk about piety, elevating the commonest events of life to classic dignity. He had not the hard-headed intellect of Dr South, his skilful analysis, his conquering wit, his intellectual wealth:—no, he had not the power of condensing his thoughts into the energetic language of Webster—never a word wrong or too much—or of marshalling his forces in such magnificently stern array; no, he had not the exquisite rhythmic speech of Emerson, that wonderful artist in words, who unites manly strength with the rare beauty of a woman's mind.

His eminence came from no such gifts or graces. His power came mainly from the predominating strength of the moral and religious element in him. He loved God with his mind, his conscience, his affections, and his soul. He had goodness and piety, both in the heroic degree. His intellectual power seemed little, not when compared with that of other men, but when measured by his own religious power. Loving man and God, he loved truth and justice. He would not exaggerate; he would not undervalue what he saw and knew—so was not violent, was not carried away by his subject. He was commonly his own master. He said nothing for effect; he never flattered the prejudice of his audience; respecting them, he put his high thought into simple speech, caught their attention, and gradually drew them up to his own elevation.

He was ruled by conscience to a remarkable degree; almost demonized by conscience—for during a part of his life the moral element seems despotic, ruling at the expense of intellect and of natural joy. But that period passed by, and her rule became peaceful and harmonious. He loved nature, the sea, the sky, and found new charms in the sweet face of earth and heaven as the years went by him, all his life. He had a keen sense of beauty—beauty in nature, in art, in speech, in manners, in man and woman's face. He loved science, he loved letters, and he loved art; but all of these affections were overmastered by his love of man and God,—means to that end, or little flowers that bordered the pathway where goodness and piety walked hand in hand. This supremacy of the moral and religious element was the secret of his strength, and it gave him a peculiar power over men, one which neither Luther nor Latimer ever had,—no, nor Barrow, nor Taylor, nor South, nor Webster, nor Emerson.

He had a large talent for religion, and so was fitted to become an exponent of the higher aspirations of mankind in his day and in times to come. He asked for truth, for religion. He was always a seeker, his whole life "a process of conversion." Timid and self-distrustful, slow of inquiry and cautious to a fault, always calculating the effect before fraternizing with a cause, he had the most unflinching confidence in justice and in truth,—in man's power to perceive and receive both.

Loving man and God, he loved freedom in all its legitimate forms, and so became a champion in all the combats of the day where rights were called in question. He hated the chains of old bondage, and moved early in the Unitarian Reformation; but when the Unitarian party became a sect, and narrow like the rest—when it also came to stand in the way of mankind, he became "little of a Unitarian," and cared no more for that sect than for the Trinitarians. He could not be blind to the existence of religion in all sects, and did not quarrel with other men's goodness and piety, because he could not accept their theology. He was not born or bred for a sectarian; such as were he did not hate, but pity. He engaged in the various reforms of the day,—he laboured for the cause of peace, for temperance, for the improvement of prisons, for the abolition of imprisonment for debt, for education; for the general welfare of men by elevating the most exposed classes of society. He was an eminent advocate for the abolition of slavery.

We do not mean to say that he committed no errors, that he never faltered. He had his imperfections and weaknesses, which we shall presently consider; sometimes he was over-timid, and seems to have allowed meaner men to prevail over him with their counsels, their littleness, and their fears. A sick body often enfeebled his mind and sometimes his courage. So he never stood in the foremost rank of any reform, speculative or practical. This is partly owing to the causes just hinted at; in part, also, to his want of originality.

He was, we think, the fairest model of a good minister known to the public or his age. He preached what he knew and he lived what he preached. He had a profound confidence in God; not in God merely as an abstraction—the abstract power, wisdom, and love,—but as that abstraction becomes concrete through Providence, and reveals itself in the course of nature, men, nations, and the world. He had also, and accordingly, a profound respect for man and profound confidence in man; not for great men, rich men, and cultivated men alone, but for man as man, for all men: he did not despise the proud, the ignorant, the wicked. He had a deep reverence for God and for man; this gave him eloquence when he spoke—gave him his name amongst men, and gave him his power.

A good deal of his earlier preaching, it is said, related to abstract matters—to ideas, to sentiments, to modes of mind. Men complained that he did not touch the ground. He spoke of God, of the soul, the dignity of human nature; of love to God, to men; of justice, charity, of freedom, and holiness of heart; he spoke of sin, of fear, of alienation from God. Years ago we remember to have heard murmurs at his abstract style of thought and speech—it went over men's heads, said some. But his abstractions he translated into the most concrete forms. Respect for God became obedience to His laws; faith in God was faith in keeping them; human nature was so great and so dignified, the very noblest work of God,—and therefore society must respect that dignity and conform to that nature: there must be no intemperance—and men who grow rich by poisoning their brothers must renounce their wicked craft; there must be no war, for its glory is human shame, and its soldiers only butchers of men; there must be education for all—for human nature is a thing too divine for men to leave in ignorance, and therefore in vice, and crime, and sin; there must be no pauperism, no want—but society must be so reconstructed that Christianity becomes a fact, and there are no idle men who steal their living out of the world, none overburdened with excessive toil, no riot, no waste, no idleness, and so no want; there must be no oppression of class by class—but the strong are to help the weak, the educated to instruct the rude; there must be no slavery—for that is the consummation of all wrongs against the dignity of human nature. So his word became incarnate, and the most abstract preacher in the land, the most mystical in his piety, and, as it seemed at first, the furthest removed from practice, comes down to actual sins and toils for human needs.

Then came the same grumblers, murmuring to another tune, and said—"When Dr Channing used to preach about God and the soul, about holiness and sin, we liked him—that was Christianity. But now he is always insisting on some reform; talking about intemperance, and war, and slavery, or telling us that we must remove the evils of society and educate all men: we wish Dr Channing would preach the Gospel." Thus reasoned men, for their foolish hearts were darkened. The old spirit of bondage opposed him when with other good men he asked of Calvinism—"Give us freedom, that we may go in and out before the

Lord, and find truth." But the new spirit of bondage opposed him just as much when he came up with others, and asked for the same thing. Each reform he engaged in got him new foes. The Tories of the Church hated him—because he asked for more truth; the Tories of the State hated him—because he asked for more justice; the Tories of society hated him—because in the name of man and God he demanded more love! Yet he silently prevailed—against all these; new truth, new justice, new love, came into the Churches, into the State, into society, and now those very Tories think him an honour to all three—and claim him as their friend! Such is the mystery of truth!

We have just said he never stood in the van of any reform—his lack of originality, his feeble health, his consequent caution and timidity, hindering him from that: yet there was scarcely a good work or a liberal thought in his time, coming within his range, which he did not aid, and powerfully aid. True, he commonly came late, but he always came and he never went back. He was one of the leaders of new thought in the new world and the old.

How strange is the progress of men on their march through time—a democracy! how few are the leaders! So a caravan passes slowly on in the Arabian wilderness—the men and the women, the asses and the camels. There is dust, and noise, and heat, the scream of the camels and the asses' bray, the shouts of the drivers, the songs of the men, the prattle of the women, the repinings and the gossip, the brawls and the day-dreams, the incongruous murmur of a great multitude. There are stragglers in front, in flank, in rear. But there are always some who know the landmarks by day, the sky-marks by night, the special providence of the pilgrimage, who direct the march, giving little heed to the brawls or the gossips, the scream, or the bray, or the song. They lift up a censer, which all day long sends up its column of smoke, and all the night its fiery pillar, to guide the promiscuous pilgrimage.

The work before us is well named "Memoirs" of Dr Channing. It is not a life—it is almost wholly autobiographical; we learn, however, from the book, a few facts relating to his life not related by himself. It appears, that when a boy he was "a remarkable wrestler," fond of "adventurous sports;" that he once "flogged a boy larger than himself" for some injustice; that in boyhood he was called "little King Pepin," and "the Peacemaker;" that he was distinguished for courage, and once offered to go and sleep on board a ship at Newport which was said to be haunted. He was studious and thoughtful, naturally pious, a lover of truth and justice. At college he was studious, yet mirthful, and excelled in the athletic sports of his companions. He soon became disgusted with the gloomy doctrines of Calvinism.

He early saw some of the contradictions in society. "When I was young," says he, "the luxury of eating was carried to the greatest excess. My first notion, indeed, of glory, was attached to an old black cook, whom I saw to be the most important personage in town." He was grave and reflective, fond of lonely rambles by the sea-shore. His early life was sad, and each year of his course seemed brighter than the last. His character was shaped more by his own solitary thought than the influence of companions. In body, when a child, "he was small and delicate, yet muscular and active, with a very erect person, quick movement, a countenance that while sedate was cheerful;"—"an open, brave, and generous boy." He was eminent at college, and graduated at Cambridge in his nineteenth year, with distinguished honours.

He served for one or two years as a private tutor in a family at Richmond, and lost his health, which he never fully recovered. He seriously set himself about the work of self-improvement at an early age, and diligently continued it all his life. At the age of twenty-three he began to preach. "His preaching at once attracted attention for its power, solemnity, and beauty." On the first of June, 1803, he was ordained as minister of the church in Federal street, Boston,—"a pale, spiritual-looking young man."

At that time he was serious in his deportment to a degree that seemed oppressive.

"He had the air of one absorbed in his own contemplations, and looked care-worn, weary, and anxious. Society seemed distasteful; he joined but little in conversation; took his meals in haste; was retired in his ways; lived mostly in his study; appeared rather annoyed than pleased with visitors; seldom went abroad,—declining, when possible, all invitations; and, in a word, was most content when left uninterruptedly to himself. There was sweetness in his looks and words, however; solemn counsels were gently given, and an atmosphere of holiness threw a winning charm over his conversation and conduct."—*Memoirs*, Vol. I., pp. 175, 176.

He says himself—

"In the early years of my ministry, ill health and a deep consciousness of unworthiness took away my energy and hope, and I had almost resolved to quit my profession. My brother Francis begged me to persevere, to make a fairer trial; and to his influence I owe very much the continuance of labours which, I hope, have not been useless to myself or to others."—*Memoirs*, Vol. I., p. 177.

High expectations were naturally formed of such a man.

"The devoutly disposed in the community looked to him with the hope that he might be a means of fanning once more to flame the smouldering ashes on the altars of piety. The seriousness of his deportment, the depth and sweetness of his voice, the pathos with which he read the Scriptures and sacred poetry, the solemnity of his appeals, his rapt and kindling enthusiasm, his humble, trustful spirit of prayer, his subdued feeling, so expressive of personal experience, made religion a new reality; while his whole air and look of spirituality won them to listen by its mild and somewhat melancholy beauty. The most trifling saw in him a man thoroughly in earnest, who spoke not of dreams and fictions, but of facts with which he was intimately conversant; and the serious gladly welcomed one who led the way and beckoned them nearer to the holy of holies which they aspired to enter. Intellectual people, too, were attracted by the power and grace of his pulpit addresses. He opened to them a large range of thought, presented clear, connected, and complete views of various topics, roused their faculties of discernment by nice discriminations and exact statements, and gratified their taste by the finished simplicity of his style. But the novelty, perhaps, that chiefly stirred his audiences was the directness with which he even then brought his Christian principles to bear upon actual life. With no flights of mystic exaltation, forgetful in raptures of the earth, with no abstract systems of metaphysical theology, with no coldly elegant moral essays, did he occupy the minds of his hearers, but with near and sublime objects made evident by faith, with lucid truths approved alike by Scripture and by conscience, and with duties pressed urgently home upon all as rules for daily practice. He saw, and made others see, that life was no play-place, but a magnificent scene for glorifying God, and a rich school for the education of spirits. He showed to men the substance, of which surrounding appearances are the shadow; and behind transient experiences revealed the spiritual laws which they express. Thus he gathered round him an enlarging circle of devoted friends, who gratefully felt that they drank in from him new life. The old members of the society, too, for the most part simple people of plain manners, took the heartiest delight in his services, while feeling just pride in his talents. And the few distinguished persons of the congregation knew well how to appreciate his rare gifts, and to extend his fame."—*Memoirs*, Vol. I., pp. 205, 206.

"Thus passed the first ten years and more of Mr Channing's ministerial life. They were uneventful, but inwardly rich in results; and many good seeds then planted themselves, which were afterward to bear abundant fruits. Inherited errors, too, not a few, in thought and practice, had been slowly outgrown,—so slowly, that he was perhaps unconscious of the change which had been wrought in his principles. Above all, he had learned the lesson of keeping true to his purest, highest self, or, to express the same fact more humbly and justly, of being obedient to the Divine will, however revealed to his inmost reason. Goodness had firmly enthroned itself as the reigning power in his nature. He lived the life communicated from above. He was becoming yearly and daily more and more a child of God.

"From his very entrance on a public career, he produced upon all who came into his presence the impression of matured virtue and wisdom, and inspired reverence though young. He wore an air of dignity and self-command, of pure elevation of purpose, and of calm enthusiasm, that disarmed familiarity. Careful of the rights of others, courteous and gentle, he allowed no intrusions upon himself. He was deaf to flattery, turned at once from any mention of his own services or position, paid no compliments, and would receive none; but, by constant reference to high standards of right, transferred the thoughts of those with whom he held intercourse from personal vanity to intrinsic excellence, and from individual claims to universal principles. He gave no time to what was unimportant, made demands upon the intellect and conscience of those he talked with, and inspired them with a sense of the substantial realities of existence. In his treatment of others there was no presumption nor partiality. He was deferential to old and young; listened without interruption, and with patience, even to the dull and rude; spoke ill of none, and would hear no ill-speaking; tolerated no levity, but at once overawed and silenced it by wise and generous suggestions; was never hasty, rash, nor impetuous in word or act, and met these weaknesses in others with an undisturbed firmness that disarmed passion while rebuking it. Above all, he recognized in his fellows no distinctions but those of character and intelligence, and, quietly disregarding capricious estimates and rules of mere etiquette, met rich and poor, learned and ignorant, upon the broad ground of mutual honour and kindness. Thus his influence was always sacred and sanctifying."—*Memoirs*, Vol. I., pp. 239, 240.

But we must pass rapidly where we would gladly delay our readers. His health became feebler; he visited Europe in 1822, and was but little better in 1824. A colleague was settled with him; then, freed from the necessity of producing one or two sermons a week, he was enabled to devote more time to other concerns, to direct all his efforts to objects of great importance. Hereafter his position was highly favourable to literary activity and extensive influence. He became "less ministerial and more manly." His interest in the great concerns of mankind continued to increase. All his important works were written after this period. Yet he was still deeply interested in the ministry, though he did not accept the popular views of that profession.

"I consider my profession as almost infinitely raised above all others, when its true nature is understood, and its true spirit imbibed. But as it is too often viewed and followed, it seems to me of little worth to him who exercises it, or to those on whom it ought to act. But when taken up for its respectability, for reputation, for a support, and followed mechanically, drudgingly, with little or no heartiness and devotion, or when seized upon fanatically and with a blind and bigoted zeal, I think as poorly of it as men of the world do, who, I grieve to say, have had too much reason for setting us ministers down among the drones of the hive of society.

. . . . . .

"My mind turns much on the general question, what can be done for the scattering of the present darkness? I think I see, more and more, that the ministry, as at present exercised, though, on the whole, a good, is sadly defective. What would be the result of a superior man, not of the clergy, giving a course of lectures on the *teaching* of *Jesus*, just as he would give one on the philosophy of Socrates or Plato? Cannot this subject be taken out of the hands of ministers? Cannot the higher minds be made to feel that Christianity belongs to them as truly as to the priest, and that they disgrace and degrade themselves by getting their ideas of it from 'our order' so exclusively? Cannot learned men come to Christianity, just as to any other system, for the purpose of ascertaining what it is?"—*Memoirs*, Vol. II., pp. 257—259.

"At the present day, there is little need of cautioning ministers against rashness in reproving evil. The danger is all on the other side. As a class, they are most slow to give offence. Their temptation is to sacrifice much to win the affections of their people. Too many satisfy themselves with holding together a congregation by amenity of manners, and by such compromises with prevalent evils as do not involve open criminality. They live by the means of those whose vices they should reprove, and thus are continually ensnared by a selfish prudence. Is it said, that they have families dependent upon them, who may suffer for their fidelity? I answer, Let no minister marry, then, unless the wife he chooses have such a spirit of martyrdom as would make her prefer to be stinted in daily bread rather than see her husband sacrifice one jot or tittle of his moral independence. Is it said, that congregations would be broken up by perfect freedom in the ministers? Better far would it be to preach to empty pews, or in the meanest halls, and there to be a fearless, disinterested witness to the truth, than to hold forth to crowds in gorgeous cathedrals, honoured and courted, but not daring to speak one's honest convictions, and awed by the world."—*Memoirs*, Vol. II., p. 269.

"The erroneous views which doomed the Catholic clergy to celibacy are far from being banished from Protestantism. The minister is too holy for business or politics. He is to preach creeds and abstractions. He may preach ascetic notions about pleasures and amusements; for his official holiness has a tinge of asceticism in it, and people hear patiently what it is understood they will not practise. But if he 'come down,' as it is called, from these heights, and assail in sober earnest deep-rooted abuses, respectable vices, inhuman institutions or arrangements, and unjust means of gain, which interest, pride, and habit have made dear, and next to universal, the people who exact from him official holiness are shocked, offended. 'He forgets his sphere.' Not only the people, but his brother-ministers, are apt to think this; and they do so not mainly from a time-serving spirit, not from dread of offending the people,—though this motive too often operates,—but chiefly from false notions about the ministry, its comprehensive purpose, its true spirit, which is an all-embracing humanity. Ministers in general are narrow-minded and superstitious, rather than servile. Their faults are those of the times, and they are more free from these, perhaps, than most of the people. And are they not becoming less and less ministers, and more and more men?"—*Memoirs*, Vol. II., pp. 324, 325.

He continued to preach from time to time during the greater part of his life.

All Dr Channing's most important writings may be arranged in three classes,—Reviews, Essays, and Sermons or Addresses. His Reviews, however, are not so much accounts of books as of men. The articles on Milton, Fénélon, and Bonaparte comprise the most important part of the first class. They were published in 1826 and the three subsequent years, and are valuable specimens of this kind of composition. They established his fame as a writer both at home and abroad. But for ability of thought, for strength and beauty of expression, they will not bear comparison with the best pieces of Carlyle, or even of Macaulay, not to mention other and humbler names. Milton and Fénélon he appreciates justly, and these two articles are perhaps the most finished productions of his pen, when regarded merely as pieces of composition. They indicate, however, no very great depth of thought or width of observation: the style is clear, pleasing, and in general beautiful. The article on Napoleon has certainly great merits; considering the time and circumstances under which it was written, its defects are by no means so numerous as might reasonably have been looked for. In his later years he felt its imperfections, but it is still, we think, the fairest estimate of the man in the English language, though full justice is not done to Napoleon as a statesman and a lawgiver. In some passages the style is elevated and sublime, in others it becomes diffuse, wordy, and tedious. The peculiar charm of these three articles consists in the beautiful sentiment of religion which pervades them all. This, indeed, as a golden thread, runs through all his works, giving unity to his reviews, essays, sermons, letters, and conversation.

His Essays are more elaborate compositions. They treat of the subject of Slavery and its kindred themes, the Abolitionists, Annexation of Texas, Emancipation, the Duty of the Free States in regard to Slavery.* Several of these Essays are in the form of letters. They are his most important and valuable productions. They have been extensively read in America and Europe, and have brought him more enemies than all his other writings. Here Dr Channing appears as a reformer. His biographer says—

> "Temperament and training, religious aspirations and philosophical views, above all, the tendencies of the times, conspired to make Dr Channing a social reformer; although the loftiness of his desires and aims, the delicacy of his feelings, the refinement of his tastes, his habits of contemplative thought, and his reverence for individual freedom, enveloped him in a sphere of courteous reserve and guarded him from familiar contact with all rude radicalism."—*Memoirs*, Vol. III., p. 3.

We shall never forget the remarks made by men of high social standing, at the publication of the Essay on Slavery.

* The date of the first Essay on Slavery is not given in the edition of Dr Channing's works. It was first published in December, 1835.

They condemned both it and its author. He was "throwing firebrands;" "meddling with matters which clergymen had no right to touch;"—as all important matters, we suppose, belong to pettifogging lawyers, who can never see through a precedent or comprehend a principle, or to politicians, who make "regular nominations" and adhere to them; or else to editors of partisan newspapers;—"he will make the condition of the slaves a great deal worse," "and perhaps produce an insurrection." This offence was never forgiven him in Boston, and he continued to increase it till the very period of his death. His anti-slavery views struck a death-blow to his popularity here. His zeal for the poor, the intemperate, the criminal, the ignorant, extraordinary as it was, could be suffered; it was not wholly unministerial, and was eminently scriptural,—but zeal for the slave, that was too much to be borne. The first publication, in 1835, has had a wide influence and a good one. The essay is not very philosophical in its arrangement, but the matter is well treated, with clearness and force,—the wrong of slavery is ably shown. High motives are always addressed in this, as in all his productions. But we have one word of criticism to make on Dr Channing as an abolitionist. In his first essay* and his subsequent writings, he distinctly separates himself from the abolitionists who contend for "Immediate Emancipation." He passed severe censures upon them; censured their motto of "Immediate Emancipation," their method of acting by "a system of affiliated societies," gave countenance to the charge that they were exciting the slaves to revolt. He condemned their "denunciations." This was at a time when the abolitionists were not a hundredth part so numerous as now; when the pulpit, the press, and the parlour rang with denunciations against them; when their property, their persons, and their lives were not safe in Boston. Now we have no fault to find with criticism directed against the abolitionists; no fear of severity. But at a time when they were few in number, a body of men whom many affected to despise because they hated, and hated because they feared; when they were poor and insulted, yet manfully struggling against oppression, equal to either fate; when the Church only opened her mouth to drown the voice of the fugitive

* Works, Vol. II.

crying to God for justice; when the State, which had had but one president who spoke against slavery, and he a man who sold the children of his own body, riveted the fetters still closer on the slave's limbs; at a time when the press of the South and the North, political or sectarian—but always commercial, low, corrupt, and marketable—said not one word for the millions of slaves whose chains the State made and the Church christened; when no man in Congress either wished or dared to oppose slavery therein, and no petitions could get a hearing; when the governor even of Massachusetts could recommend to her legislature inquiries for preventing freedom of speech on that subject; at a time when the abolitionists were the only men that cared or dared to speak; at a time, too, when they were mobbed in the streets; when an assembly of women was broken up by "respectable" violence, and the authorities of the city dared not resist the mob; when a symbolical gallows was erected at night in front of the house of the leading abolitionist of America, "by the order of Judge Lynch," and a price of five thousand dollars set on his head by the governor of Georgia,—why, such criticism was at least a little out of season! Had the abolitionists been guilty of denunciations?—in 1817, when a minister preaching in Boston "actually vilified the character of the Liberal clergy in the most wholesale manner," Dr Channing "directed all his remarks to softening the feelings of those who were aggrieved. . . . . 'I cannot blame this stranger so severely,' said he; 'these harsh judgments never originated from himself. . . . . How sad is controversy, that it should thus tempt our opponents to misrepresent men when they might and should know better.'" * Yet here the difference between the stranger and the Liberal clergy related only to a matter of theological opinion, not to the freedom of millions of men. We dislike denunciation as much as most men, but we wish it was peculiar to the abolitionists; denunciation is the commonest thing in politics, the weapon of Democrats and Whigs; the pulpits ring with its noise; the Unitarians are denounced as "infidels" to this day; and who does not know it is the fashion of whole churches to denounce mankind at large as "totally depraved," "capable of no good thing," "subject to the wrath of

* *Memoirs*, Vol. II., p. 89, et seq.

God," "and deserving eternal damnation." If these terms mean anything they amount to denunciation. If by denunciation is meant violent speech, exaggeration, and ill temper, then it is an infirmity, and is always out of place. Yet such is the weakness of strong men that we meet with it in all the great movements of mankind, in the Christian Reformation and the Protestant Reformation, and in all great revolutions. The American Revolution was the effort of a nation to free itself from tyranny—the very mild tyranny of the British crown. The denunciations, violence, and bloodshed which followed are well known. Yet now, there are none but the abolitionists who think the Revolution was not worth what it cost. But in the case which Dr Channing complained of, a population greater than that of all the colonies in 1775 were entirely deprived of all their rights and reduced to abject slavery, and the abolitionists—ultra-peace men and non-resistants almost all of them—attempted no violence, and used nothing harder than hard words. For our own part we confess their language has not always been to our taste, but we know of no revolution of any importance that has been conducted with so little violence and denunciation. When Dr Channing wrote about Milton and the stormy times of the English commonwealth, he thought differently, and said—

"In regard to the public enemies whom he assailed, we mean the despots in Church and State, and the corrupt institutions which had stirred up a civil war, the general strain of his writings, though strong and stern, must exalt him, notwithstanding his occasional violence, among the friends of civil and religious liberty. That liberty was in peril. Great evils were struggling for perpetuity and could only be broken down by great power. Milton felt that interests of infinite moment were at stake, and who will blame him for binding himself to them with the whole energy of his great mind, and for defending them with fervour and vehemence? We must not mistake Christian benevolence, as if it had but one voice, that of soft entreaty. It can speak in piercing and awful tones. There is constantly going on in our world a conflict between good and evil. The cause of human nature has always to wrestle with foes. All improvement is a victory won by struggles. It is especially true of those great periods which have been distinguished by revolutions in government and religion, and from which we date the most rapid movements of the human mind, that they have been signalized by conflict. Thus Christianity convulsed the world and grew up amidst storms; and the Reformation of Luther was a signal to universal war; and Liberty in both worlds has encountered opposition over which she has triumphed only through her own immortal energies. At such periods, men, gifted with great power of thought and loftiness of sentiment, are especially summoned to the conflict with evil. They hear, as it were, in their own magnanimity and generous aspirations, the voice of a divinity; and thus commissioned, and burning with a passionate devotion to truth and freedom, they must and will speak with an indignant energy, and they ought not to be measured by the standard of ordinary minds in ordinary times. Men of natural softness and timidity, of a sincere but effeminate virtue, will be apt to look on these bolder, hardier spirits as violent, perturbed, and uncharitable; and the charge will not be wholly groundless. But that deep feeling of evils, which is necessary to effectual conflict with them, and which marks God's most powerful messengers to mankind, cannot breathe itself in soft and tender accents. The deeply moved soul will speak strongly, and ought to speak so as to move and shake nations."—*Works*, Vol. I., pp. 23—25.

There are not many things in Dr Channing's life which we could wish otherwise, but his relation to the abolitionists is one of that number. In 1831, Mr Garrison, a printer in the office of the Christian Examiner, at Boston, issued the first number of the "Liberator," making the declaration—"I am in earnest, I will not equivocate, I will not excuse, I will not retreat a single inch, *and I will be heard*." He borrowed the type and press of the office he worked in. He could not get trusted for fifty dollars' worth of paper "because he was opposed to the Colonization Society." So he waited till a negro in Philadelphia sent him that sum. He was obscure and destitute, but "had a determination to print the paper as long as he could live on bread and water, or his hands find employment." He was reviled, insulted, mobbed; a price set on his head; he lived in the same city with Dr Channing, struggling with poverty, obscurity, and honourable disgrace for twelve years, and Dr Channing afforded him no aid, nor counsel, nor sympathy, not a single "God bless you, my brother," and did not even answer his letter! This we find it difficult to understand, as it is painful to relate. We gladly hasten away from the subject, which we could not pass by in silence, but have spoken of in sorrow.

His public sermons and addresses—we speak now only of such as he wished to preserve—treat of a large variety of subjects: Temperance, Education, Christ, Christianity, the Evidences of Religion, the Ministry, and kindred subjects. These are somewhat unequal, but all are marked by the qualities mentioned above, by a profound reverence for man, and most unhesitating confidence in God. None of those sermons indicates a mind of a very high order; as works of intellect they will not compare with the great sermons of the best English preachers; but we know none of which the effect is more ennobling. His analysis of a subject is seldom final, he usually halts short of the ultimate fact; his arrangement is frequently unphilosophical, his reasoning often weak, unsatisfactory, various parts of the argument not well connected, his style diffuse and verbose. We know diffuseness is the old Adam of the pulpit. There are always two ways of hitting the mark, one with a single bullet, the other with a shower of small shot. Each has its advantages; Dr Channing chose the latter, as most of our pulpit orators have done. It is commonly thought men better understand a truth when it is told two or three times over, and in two or three different ways; be that as it may, it is certain that a small quantity of metal will cover the more space the thinner it is beaten, and when a man must write one or two sermons in a week, never to be used again, perhaps he may be forgiven if the depth be less as the surface becomes greater. Dr Channing was not very diffuse for a preacher, but certainly for a great man. His vocabulary was not copious; there is no idiomatic freshness in his style; his illustrations are trite, often commonplace. Neither literature nor nature gets reflected in his style. His thought and feeling are American in the best sense of the word; but the form, the colouring, the tone are wholly destitute of nationality—there is no American image in his temple; no American flowers in his garden. We think this a defect. In all his writings you see that he had lived alone, not much among books, not much with nature you would fancy, but with his own thoughts.

As a speaker his style of eloquence was peculiar. He stands alone. His powers of reasoning were certainly not very great, by no means to be compared to the many able men of his country or his age; he had not that great power of demonstration which at once puts the pointed thought into your mind, and then drives it home with successive blows. He had not that creative force which attracts, conquers, and then directs; nor that energy of feeling, which, making an impression almost magical, carries the audience away with its irresistible tide. He commanded attention by presenting numerous minute particulars—trusting little to the effect of any one great argument. His eloquent warfare was a guerilla war. He carried the hearer's understanding little by little, never taking it by storm. He did not represent a great reason, a great imagination, or a great passion; but a great conscience and a great faith. In this lay the power of his eloquence, the charm of his preaching, the majesty of his character.

As a public speaker, at first sight he did not strongly impress his audience, he did not look the great man; his body was feeble and unusually small; his voice not powerful—though solemn, affectionate, and clear. How frail he seemed! Yet look again, and his organization was singularly delicate—womanly in its niceness and refinement. When closely viewed he seemed a soul very lightly clad with a body—and you saw the soul so clearly that you forgot the vesture it wore. He began his sermon simply, announced the theme, spoke of its importance, glanced over the surface for a moment—then sketched out his plan, as the farmer *lands* out his field which he is to plough up inch by inch. He began simply, calmly, and rose higher and higher as he went on, each thought deeper and nobler than the last. His conscience and his faith went into the audience till he held them breathless, entranced, lifted out of their common consciousness—till they forgot their own littleness, forgot the preacher, soul and body, and thought only of his thought, felt only his feeling.

There was never such preaching in Boston; never such prayers. His word sunk into men as the sun into the ground in summer to send up grass and flowers. Did he speak of sin, the ingenuous youth saw its ugliness with creeping hate;—of the dignity of human nature, you longed to be such a man;—of God, of His goodness, His love, you wondered you could ever doubt or fear. It was our good fortune in earlier years to hear him often, in his noblest efforts; often, too, on the same day have we listened to the eloquence of another good minister, now also immortal, a man of rare piety and singular power in the pulpit—we mean the younger Ware. More sentimental than Channing, more imaginative, with an intellect less capacious and a range of subjects by no means so broad, he yet spoke to the native soul of man with a sweet persuasion rarely equalled. Ware told you more of heaven —Channing more of earth, that you might make it heaven here. It was his conscience and his trust in God that gave him power. What strength there is in gentleness, what force in truth, what magic in religion! That voice so thin and feeble, a woman's word—it was heard above the roar of the street and the clatter of legislation; it went beyond the Alleghanies; it passed over the din of the Atlantic waves, and became a winning and familiar sound in our mother-land; that hand, so thin and ghostly it seemed a moonbeam might shine through—it held a power which no sceptred monarch of our time could wield,—the power of justice, of all-controlling faith; that feeble form, that man with body frailer than a girl's—he had an influence which no man that speaks the English tongue now equals. He spoke not to men as members of a party, or a sect, or tribe, or nation, but to the universal nature of man, and that "something that doth live" everlastingly in our embers answered to his call.

He became conscious of his power. It could not be otherwise when his word thus came echoed back from the heights and depths of society. But this only made him yet more humble. A name in both hemispheres gave him no pleasure but as a means of usefulness and increase of power; but made him more zealous and more powerful to SERVE. Laudations he put aside without reading, and abuse had small effect on him. Did proud men scorn his humanity, and base men affect to pity—it was only the pity which he returned. Yet when a letter from a poor man in England came to thank him for his words of lofty cheer, he could well say "This is honour." When a nursery-man forgot his plants and his customers to express an interest in him, or a retired Quaker family was moved by his presence, then he could say "This is better than fame a thousand times." Forgive him if that made him proud. We remember well his lecture on the Elevation of the Labouring Classes, and the sneers with which it was received by some that heard it at the time; and we shall not soon forget the feelings it brought to our heart, when one day, in a little town in a Swiss valley, we saw in the shop of an apothecary, who was also the bookseller, a copy of that lecture in the German tongue. It was printed at that place, and was the second edition! The word which some sneered at here was gone "to the Gentiles," to comfort the poor labourers under the shadow of the Alps.

We know that men sneer at the pulpit, counting it a low place and no seat of power; we know why they sneer, and blame them not. But if there is a man in the pulpit, with a man's mind, heart, soul, the pulpit is no mean place, it shall go hard if his power is not felt. In Boston there are well nigh fivescore of clergymen: out of these were there fifty like Dr Channing, fifty more in New York, and yet another fifty in the pulpits of Philadelphia; let them be of all ways of thinking,—Catholic, Calvinistic, or Quaker,—only let them love God as much and man as well; only let them love truth and righteousness as well as he, and labour with as much earnestness to reform theology, society, Church, and State: what cities should we have; what churches, what a society, what a State! Would there be the intemperance, the pauperism, the ignorance among the people, the licentiousness—the sheer and utter lust of gain which now takes possession of the most influential men of the nation? Oh no!—there would have been no annexation of Texas for a new slave-garden, no war against Mexico, no "Holy Alliance" in America between Democrats and Whigs to secure the "partition" of our sister republic; there would not be three millions of slaves in the United States, and a slave-holder on the throne of the nation—for 'tis a throne we speak of, and the people only subjects of a base aristocracy, no longer citizens. Did we speak of fifty Channings in Boston?—were there only ten, they would make this city, as we think, too good to hope for. But there are not ten such men,—nay, there are not—but we will not count them. There are still good men in pulpits, here—only rare and few—floating amid the sectarianism, wealth, and pride which swim round in this whirlpool of modern society. They never wholly failed in Boston. Nay, when the oil has run low and the meal was almost spent, some prophet came along to cheer this poor widow of the Church with his blessing, and the oil held out in the cruse, and the meal was not spent, so that her children did not wholly starve and die outright, saying, "Who is the Lord?" True, there has always been some rod, a scion from the tree of life, that held its own amid the drought, and kept obstinately green, and went on budding and blossoming—a memory and a hope; always some sacramental portion of the manna which fed our fathers, a fragrant reminiscence of the old pilgrimage, and a promise of the true bread which shall one day be given from heaven;—at least, there is always some heap of stones to remind us that our fathers passed over Jordan, and, though sorely beset and hunted after, they could yet say, even in their extremity, "Hitherto hath the Lord helped us!" These do not fail—"thanks to the human heart by which we live;" but a powerful ministry in any denomination we have not. Yet the harvest truly is plenteous. How white are all the fields—only the labourers are few, feeble, faint in heart and limb, and while wrangling about names have so long left their sickles idle in the sun that their very tools have lost their temper, and ring no longer, as when of old they cut the standing corn.

Why does not the Church save us from slavery, party-spirit, ignorance, pauperism, licentiousness, and lust of gain? It has no salvation to give. Why not afford us great teachers, like the old and venerable names—Edwards, Chaunceys, Mayhews, Freemans, Buckminsters, Channings? The Church has nothing to teach which is worth the learning of grown men, and even the baby-virtue of America turns off from that lean, haggard, and empty breast, yet cries for food and mother's arms. But there is a providence in all this. Taking the churches as they are, ecclesiastical religion as *it* is, it is well that able men do not stand in the pulpits; well that men of superior ability and superior culture flee from it to law, politics, the farm, and the shop. If the Church has nothing better to teach them than the morality of the market-place and the theology of the dark ages, if she is the foe to pure goodness, pure piety, and pure thought, then parson Log is the best parson. Let us accept him with thankfulness. But it will not always be so; no, not long. A better day is coming, when the real Church shall be the actual; when

Theology, the queen and mother of Science, shall assert her ancient rule, driving off superstition and priestly unbelief; when a real ministry in religion's name shall rebuke that party-spirit which makes a monarch out of a president, a miserable oligarchy out of a republic, and transforms the citizens of New-England into the subjects of slave-holders, and makes our free men only the servants of gain. Pandora has opened her box, sectarianism and party-rage have flown out; see the anarchy they make in Church and State! But there is yet left at the bottom—hope. When the lid is lifted next that also will appear, and a new spring come out of this winter, and we shall wonder at the White-Sunday on all the hills, at the Pentecost of inspiration and tongues of heavenly truth.

But we have wandered from our theme. In the midst of Boston, so penny-wise and so pound-foolish,—worldly Boston, which sent to the heathens more rum and more Bibles than all the States—the one to teach them our Christianity, and the other to baptize the converts, making their calling and election sure; which sent sleek men to Congress, ambassadors to lie in the capitol for the benefit of their party and themselves; in the midst of Boston, where men set up the hay-scales of their virtue, and on one side put their dollars and on the other set patriotism, democracy, freedom, Christianity, while the dollar weighed them all down: in the midst of this stood Dr Channing, liberal, wise, gentle, pious without narrowness, democratic, and full of hope. Shall we wonder that he wrought so little; that he could not get an anti-slavery notice read in his own pulpit, nor the door open to preach a funeral sermon on his anti-slavery friend—the lamented Follen? Rather wonder that he did so preach. No sailing vessel can stem the Mississippi, nor the stoutest steamboat go up the falls of St Anthony, and it takes time to go round.

Here was one great man in Boston who did not seek wealth, nor want place, nor ask for fame; one man who would not sell himself. He only asked, sought, and coveted the power to serve. He was afraid he should give too little and take too much. So he took only his living, and gave men the toil of his genius, his prayers, and his life. There is no charity so great as this. See, now, the effect of such a life;—here in America there is one great man, with broad brows, a colossal intellect, and the most awful presence the world has seen for some centuries, it is said; one who would seem an Emperor in any council, even of the Kings by nature; with understanding so great that Channing's mind would seem but a baby in his arms; a senator, who for many years has occupied important public posts,—and yet in New-England, in the United States, Channing has far more influence than Webster. He was never in his life greeted with the shout of a multitude, and yet he has swayed the mind and heart of the best men, and affected the character and welfare of the nation far more than the famous statesman. In our last number we spoke of that venerable man who breathed his last breath in the capitol: John Quincy Adams had held high offices for fifty years,—been minister to courts abroad, had made treaties, had been representative, senator, secretary of state,—been president; he had lived eighty years—a learned man, always well, always at work, always in public office, always amongst great men and busied with the affairs of the nation,—and yet, which has done the most for his country, for mankind, and most helped men to wisdom and religion, man's highest welfare? The boys could tell us that the effect of Adams and Webster both is not to be named in comparison with the work done for the world by this one feeble-bodied man. Yet there are forty thousand ministers in the United States, and Channing stood always in the pulpit, owing nothing to any eminent station that he filled. In this century we have had two presidents who powerfully affected the nation,—one by his mind, by ideas;—his public acts were often foolish: the other by his will, his deeds, ideas apparently of small concern to him;—we mean Jefferson and Jackson. But, with the exception of Jefferson, no president in this century has ever had such influence upon men's minds as that humble minister. No, not all together—Madison, Monroe, Adams, Jackson, Van Buren and Harrison and Tyler and Polk. Some of them did good things, yet soon they will be gone, all but one or two; their influence, too, will pass away, and soon there will be left nothing but a name in a book—for they were only connected with an office, not an idea,—while Channing's power will remain long after his writings have ceased to be read and his name is forgot; of so little consequence is it where the man stands, if he be but a man, and do a man's work.

The one great idea of Dr Channing's life was respect for man. He was eminent for other things, but preeminent for this. His eminent piety became eminent philanthropy, in all its forms. This explains his action as a reformer, his courage, and his inextinguishable hope. Dr Channing was one of the few democrats we have ever known. Born and bred amongst men who had small confidence in the people, and who took little pains to make them better, he became intensely their friend. The little distinctions of life, marked by wealth, fame, or genius, were of small account to him. He honoured all men; saw the man in the beggar, in the slave. He never desponded; he grew more liberal the more he lived, and seemed greenest and freshest when about to quit this lower sphere. His youth was sad though hopeful; in the middle period of his life he seems saddened and subdued, in part by the restraints of his profession, in part by ill health, and yet more by austere notions of life and duty, imposed by a gloomy theory of religion, but which in his latter days he escaped from and left behind him. He is a fine example of the power of one man, armed only with truth and love. By these he did service here, and spoke to the best minds of the age, giving hope to famous men, and cheering the hearts of such as toiled all day in the dark mines of Cornwall. By these he sympathized with men, with nature, and with God. Hence he grew younger all his life, and thought the happiest period was "about sixty." In 1839 he thus wrote :—

"Indeed, life has been an improving gift from my youth; and one reason I believe to be, that my youth was not a happy one. I look back to no bright dawn of life which gradually 'faded into common day.' The light which I now live in rose at a later period. A rigid domestic discipline, sanctioned by the times, gloomy views of religion, the selfish passions, collisions with companions perhaps worse than myself,—these, and other things, darkened my boyhood. Then came altered circumstances, dependence, unwise and excessive labours for independence, and the symptoms of the weakness and disease which have followed me through life. Amidst this darkness it pleased God that the light should rise. The work of spiritual regeneration, the discovery of the supreme good, of the great and glorious end of life, aspirations after truth and virtue, which are pledges and beginnings of immortality, the consciousness of something divine within me, then began, faintly indeed, and through many struggles and sufferings have gone on. . .

"I love life, perhaps, too much; perhaps I cling to it too strongly for a Christian and a philosopher. I welcome every new day with new gratitude. I almost wonder at myself, when I think of the pleasure which the dawn gives me, after having witnessed it so many years. This blessed light of heaven, how dear it is to me! and this earth which I have trodden so long, with what affection I look on it! I have but a moment ago cast my eyes on the lawn in front of my house, and the sight of it, gemmed with dew and heightening by its brilliancy the shadows of the trees which fall upon it, awakened emotions more vivid, perhaps, than I experienced in youth. I do not like the ancients calling the earth *mother*. She is so fresh, youthful, living, and rejoicing! I do, indeed, anticipate a more glorious world than this; but still my first familiar home is very precious to me, nor can I think of leaving its sun and sky and fields and ocean without regret. My interest, not in outward nature only, but in human nature, in its destinies, in the progress of science, in the struggles of freedom and religion, has increased up to this moment, and I am now in my sixtieth year."—*Memoirs*, Vol. III., pp. 412—414.

His life was eminently useful and beautiful. He died in good season, leaving a memory that will long be blessed.

It remains for us to say a word of the "Memoirs." The work is well done, by a kindred and a loving hand. The Memoirs only are published, however, the Life yet remains to be written. Some things are passed over rather hastily by the Editor; we should have been glad if he had told us more of Dr Channing's relations to the theological parties of his time, especially to his own sect in his later years; if he had shown us more in detail with what caution and slowness he came to his liberal conclusions. As a whole, the picture wants a background, and also shadow. But, on the whole, the work is well and faithfully done, though it does not give us so complete and thorough a view of the man as the Memoir of Henry Ware offered of that lamented and sainted minister. An index would be a welcome addition, but, as one seldom finds that in an American book, we will not make a special complaint.

THE ETERNITY OF GOD.

A HYMN TRANSLATED FROM THE GERMAN.

I.

Thou Ocean-deep of God's Eternity;
Thou, the Primeval Source of Time and Space;
Sole Ground of refuge from a world of storms
Art Thou: Perpetual Presentness Thou art.
The ashes of the Past are but the Germ
Of vast Futurities to Thee. Then what
Is man,—the point we call To-day, the worm,
Born yester-night,—when with Thy greatness weighed?

II.

To Thee, Eternal One, a Universe
Marks but a day, and we in our brief lives

I.

O Meer von Gottes Ewigkeit!
Uralter Quell von Welt und Zeit!
 Grund alles Fliehns von Welt und Zeiten!
Beständ'ge Gegenwärtigkeit!
Die Asche der Vergangenheit
 Ist dir ein Keim von Künftigkeiten.
Was ist der Mensch, der Punkt von heut',
Der Wurm, der sich seit gestern freut,
 Gemessen gegen deine Weiten?

II.

Vor dir, Gott, Ewiger, vor dir
Sind Welten Tage nur; und wir

Are scarcely seconds there. Perhaps the Sun
I now behold is e'en the thousandth Sun,
Dancing 'fore Thee with ever changing years,
And thousands, waiting birth, when strikes their hour
Shall come, at Thine Almighty word moved forth.
But Thou remain'st, nor count'st the vanished Orbs.

III.

The Stars, in all their silent majesty,
And raised on high within unbounded space;—
They who to us discourse the measured time,
And stand before our eyes such myriad years,—
Before Thine Eye, O Lord, shall pass away
But as the Grass in summer's sultry days:
As roses at the noontide blooming young,
But shrunken pale before the twilight hour—
Such is the Wain and Polar Star to Thee.

In unserm Leben kaum Sekunden.
Vielleicht wälzt sich dies tausendste
Der Sonnenalter, die ich seh,
Und tausend sind noch nicht entbunden,
Und kommen, wenn die Stunde schlägt,
Durch deiner Allmacht Wink bewegt.
Du bleibst, und zählst nicht, die verschwunden.

III.

Der Sterne stille Majestät,
In unbegränztem Raum erhöht;
Sie, die uns Jahr' und Monden sagen,
Und uns viel tausend Jahre stehn,
Sie werden, Herr, vor dir vergehn,
Wie Gras an schwülen Sommertagen.
Wie Rosen, die am Mittag jung,
Und welk sind vor der Dämmerung,
Ist dir der Angelstern und Wagen.

IV.

In the Primeval Time when Life, new born
And quickened by Almighty power, struggled
'Gainst chaos still; when Ancient Nothingness
Had scantly left the threshold of that Life;—
Before e'en Gravity had learnt to fall,
And ere the earliest gleam of new-made Light
Had shot upon the grim and desert Dark—
Thou still wert there, wert then, and, spread abroad
Far from thy source as now, didst all things fill!

V.

And when a different breath shall come of Thine
Omnipotence to sepulchre the world
In nothingness, in dead and silent harmonies;
When many a Firmament, far, far away,
Though swarming now with hosts of stars, shall yield
Its Being up, and vanish into Nought—
Creator! Thou art, young as now, untouched
By age, to live for ever future days.

IV.

Zur Urzeit, als durch Allmachtszwang
Mit Nichtseyn noch ein Werden rang,
  Und kaum von neuer Wesen Schwelle
Das alte Unding sich entfernt;
Eh' Schwerkraft fallen noch gelernt,
  Eh' noch des Lichtes erste Helle
Sich auf ein ödes Dunkel goss,
Warst du, der allerfüllend floss,
  Gleich ewig fern von aller Quelle.

V.

Und wenn ein andrer Allmachtshauch
Die Welt in Nichts begräbet auch,
  In todte stille Harmonien;
Wenn mancher ferne Himmel noch,
Obgleich von Sternen wimmelnd, doch
  Wird seinem Daseyn einst entfliehen,
Wirst, Schöpfer, du so jung als jetzt,
Von keinem Alter je verletzt,
  Im ewig künft'gen Heute blühen.

VI.

Compared with Thought—time, wind, and sound,
And wingèd light are tedious and slow;
But Thought—wearied her rapid wing, hung down,
And wearied, too, in vain—Eternal One!
Must bow 'fore Thee, and vainly hope to find
The limit of Thy Might. A million times
In thought the monstrous numbers monstrous sum,
I multiply till Sense and Reason fail:

VII.

Then age to age I add, and world to world.
But when I've builded up that height sublime,
And turn, Eternal One, my wildered eye
On Thee,—the monstrous sight of billion worlds,
Ages, and times, though multiplied by 'tself,
Is all no part, nay not a Now of Thee!
I take them all away, and Thou art still
The same; complete in Thy Eternity!

VI.

Wogegen Zeit und Schall und Wind
Selbst Lichtesflügel langsam sind,
  Die schnellen Schwingen der Gedanken,
Ermüdet stehn sie fruchtlos hier,
Und beugen, Ewiger, sich dir,
  Und hoffen nur vergebens Schranken.
Ich thürme millionenmal
Der Zahlen ungeheure Zahl,
  Und alle meine Sinnen schwanken.

VII.

Ich wälze Zeit auf Zeit hinauf,
Ich thürme Welt auf Welt zu Hauf.
  Wenn ich, der grausen Höh' Erbauer,
Dann richte meinen Schwindelblick,
O Ewiger, auf dich zurück,
  Ist Billionen-Zahlen-Schauer,
Mit sich vermehrt, kein Theil, kein Nu
Von dir. Ich tilge sie, und du
  Liegst ganz vor mir in deiner Dauer.

VIII.

Oh Measure of immeasurable time,
Thy Now is in itself Eternity:
And Thou, Sun of the universe, dost stand
Perpetual noon, with ever equal power;
Nor risest Thou—of circling times the Cause,
Nor from Thy midday height shalt Thou descend!
On Thee, Eternal and Unchanging God,
On Thee, who art, and wert, and art to come,—
On Thee alone doth all Existence hang.

IX.

Aye, now, could Nature's firm and solid power,—
Which, all sustaining, ever new creates—
Sink in some moment back to thee:
In that same hour, with wide and horrid mouth,
Would Nothingness devour the host of Suns,
That transient shine, and drink the wide-spread realm
Of all existing things; yes, Time and e'en
Eternity would sink within that horrid maw,
As Ocean drinks a dropling of the rain.

VIII.

O Maass der ungemessnen Zeit!
Dein Jetzt ist lauter Ewigkeit.
Du Sonne bleibst im Mittag stehen,
In gleicher Kraft. Du gingst nie auf,
Du Grund von aller Zeiten Lauf!
Nie wirst du jemals untergehen.
An dir, der da unwandelbar
Gott ewig ist, und ewig war,
An dir allein hängt Allbestehen.

IX.

Ja wenn des Wesens feste Kraft,
Die allerhaltend ewig schafft,
In dir, Gott, jemals könnte sinken:
Dann würde, zu derselben Stund',
Mit grässlich aufgesperrtem Schlund,
Und ob jetzt Sonnenheere blinken,
Das Nichts, der Wesen-Heere Reich,
Die Zeit und Ewigkeit zugleich,
So wie das Meer ein Tröpflein, trinken.

X.

Thou Ocean-deep of God's Eternity,
Thou the Primeval Source of Time and Space;
Sole Ground of refuge from a world of storms
Art Thou: Perpetual Presentness Thou art.
The ashes of the Past are but the Germ
Of vast Futurities to Thee. Then what
Is man,—the point we call To-day, the worm
Born yester-night,—when with Thy Greatness weighed?

XI.

No! he is more than that brief point—To-day;
More than the worm born yester-night; and may
Himself compare with that Immensity!
For when God founded Earth, and Angel choirs
Proclaimed His praise,—unseen and fondly wrapped
In swaddling garments of primeval Time,
A riddle to myself, I still was there,
Although I could not then therewith rejoice,
Nor see my God establishing the world.

X.

O Meer von Gottes Ewigkeit!
Uralter Quell von Welt und Zeit!
  Grund alles Fliehns von Welt und Zeiten!
Beständ'ge Gegenwärtigkeit!
Die Asche der Vergangenheit
  Ist dir ein Keim von Künftigkeiten.
Was ist der Mensch, der Punkt von heut',
Der Wurm, der sich seit gestern freut,
  Gemessen gegen deine Weiten?

XI.

Nein, er ist mehr als Punkt von heut',
Als Wurm, der sich seit gestern freut;
  Darf messen sich mit jenen Weiten.
Als Gott die Erde gründete,
Ihn Engellob verkündete,
  Schon in den Windeln grauer Zeiten,
Mir selbst ein Räthsel, war ich da,
Wenn ich gleich noch nicht jauchzend sah
  Durch Ihn der Erde Grund bereiten.

XII.

And when yet many a thousand times
New heavenly hosts appear, and as a robe
Worn out and old are laid aside by Thee;—
When other heavenly hosts made by Thy hand,
Come forth in ever new vicissitude,
Yet seem for ever during durance made—
Shall I eternal be as Thou, and, robed
In glory, through the eternal Ocean-deep,
Shall celebrate Thine everlasting Praise.

XII.

Und wenn auch einst viel tausendmal
Noch neuer Himmel Heere all'
  Vor dir wie ein Gewand vergehen;
Wenn andre, Gott, durch deine Hand
Dann treten in den Wechselstand,
  Zu scheinbar ewigem Bestehen,
Dann werd' ich, ewig wie du, Herr,
Durch aller Ewigkeiten Meer
  Verklärt dein ewig Lob erhöhen.

SONNETS.

FROM THE LIBERTY BELL, 1846.

I.

JESUS, there is no name so dear as thine
Which Time has blazon'd on his ample scroll;
No wreaths nor garlands ever did entwine
So fair a temple of so vast a soul;
There every angel set his triumph seal,
Wisdom combined with strength and radiant grace
In a sweet copy Heaven to reveal,
And stamp perfection on a mortal face:
Once on the Earth wert thou before men's eyes,
That could not half thy beauteous brightness see,
E'en as the emmet cannot read the skies,
Nor our weak orbs look through immensity;
Once on the Earth wert thou—a living shrine,
Wherein conjoining dwelt—the Good, the Lovely, the Divine.

II.

OH thou great Friend to all the sons of men,
Who once appear'd in humblest guise below,
Sin to rebuke and break the captive's chain,
To call thy brethren forth from want and woe,—
Thee would I sing. Thy Truth is still the Light
Which guides the nations—groping on their way,
Stumbling and falling in disastrous night,
Yet hoping ever for the perfect day;
Yes! thou art still the Life; thou art the Way
The holiest know,—Light, Life, and Way of Heaven!
And they who dearest hope and deepest pray,
Toil by the Light, Life, Way, which thou hast given.
And by thy Truth aspiring mortals trust
T' uplift their faint and bleeding brothers rescued from the dust.

III.

Dear Jesus, were thy spirit now on earth
  Where thou hast pray'd and toil'd a world to win,—
What vast ideas would sudden rise to birth,
  What strong endeavours 'gainst o'er-mastering Sin!
Thy blest beatitudes again thou'dst speak;
  But with deep-hearted words that scorch like fire,
Wouldst thou rebuke the oppressors of the weak:
  Or, turning thence to Prophets that aspire,
How wouldst thou cheer the men who toil to save
  Their brothers smarting 'neath a despot's rod,
To lift the Poor, the Fallen, and the Slave,
  And lead them all alive to worship God!
Bigots wouldst thou rebuke—that idle stand,
But send thy Gospel-fraught Apostles conquering through the land.

West Rosebury, Mass. U. S. A.

A SONNET FOR THE TIMES.

(From the Liberty Bell, 1851.)

Way-farer, pause! for late there stoop'd and fell
  One of Earth's mightiest, loftiest minds;* and now
  Stain'd and dishonour'd lies that ample brow,
Wherein the nations dream'd there slept a spell,
  To slay the ancient Fiend, who overthrew
Corinth, Athena, and wide-grasping Rome,
With every state where Freedom found a home,
  Digg'd down her altars, and her Prophets slew!
All vainly gazed the Nation on that brow;
  Vainly they ask'd that kingly mind for aid;
  The new Iscariot Freedom's trust betray'd!
Go, passer-by! to men this warning tell:—
The Mightiest, Loftiest Mind, scorning God's Justice, Fell.

Boston, Nov. 1850.

* Daniel Webster.

CHARACTER OF MR PRESCOTT AS AN HISTORIAN.

1. *The History of the Reign of Ferdinand and Isabella the Catholic.* By WILLIAM H. PRESCOTT, &c., &c. Boston: 1838. 3 vols. 8vo.
2. *History of the Conquest of Mexico, with a Preliminary View of the Ancient Mexican Civilization and the Life of the Conqueror, Hernando Cortes.* By WILLIAM H. PRESCOTT, &c., &c. New York: 1845. 3 vols. 8vo.
3. *History of the Conquest of Peru, with a Preliminary View of the Civilization of the Incas.* By WILLIAM H PRESCOTT, &c., &c. New York; 1847. 2 vols. 8vo.

IT is now more than eleven years since our accomplished and distinguished countryman, Mr Prescott, appeared before the world as a writer of history. Within that period he has sent forth three independent historical works, which have found a wide circle of readers in the New World and the Old. His works have been translated into all the tongues of Europe, we think, which claim to be languages of literature; they have won for the author a brilliant renown, which few men attain to in their lifetime; few, even, after their death. No American author has received such distinction from abroad. The most eminent learned societies of Europe have honoured themselves by writing his name among their own distinguished historians. He has helped strengthen the common bond of all civilized nations, by writing books which all nations can read. Yet while he has received this attention and gained this renown, he has not found hitherto a philosophical critic to investigate his works carefully, confess the merits which are there, to point out the defects, if such there be, and coolly announce the value of these writings. Mr Prescott has found eulogists on either continent; he has found, also, one critic, who adds to national bigotry the spirit of a cockney in literature; whose stand-point of criticism is the church of Bowbell; a man who degrades the lofty calling of a critic by the puerile vanities of a literary fop. The article we refer to would have disgraced any journal which pretended to common fairness. We often find articles in the minor journals of America, written in a little and narrow spirit, but remember nothing of the kind so little as the paper we speak of in the *London Quarterly Review,* No. cxxvii., Art. 1. We have waited long for some one free from national prejudice to come, with enlarged views of the duty of an historian, having suitable acquaintance with the philosophy of history, a competent knowledge of the subjects to be treated of, and enough of the spirit of humanity, and carefully examine these works in all the light of modern philosophy. We have waited in vain; and now, conscious of our own defects, knowing that every qualification above hinted may easily be denied us, we address ourselves to the work.

The department of history does not belong to our special study; it is, therefore, as a layman that we shall speak, not aspiring to pronounce the high cathedral judgment of a professor in that craft. The history, literature, and general development of the Spanish nation fall still less within the special range of the writer of this article. We are students of history only in common with all men who love liberal studies, and pursue history only in the pauses from other toils. However, the remarkable phenomena offered by the Spanish nation in the fifteenth and sixteenth centuries long ago attracted our attention and study. Still, it is with reluctance we approach our task; had any of the able men whose business it more properly is, girded himself and applied to the work, we would have held our peace; but in the silence of such we feel constrained to speak.

Before we proceed to examine the works of Mr Prescott, let a word be said of the office and duty of an historian—to indicate the stand-point whence his books are to be looked upon. The writer of Annals, or of Chronicles, is to record events in the order in which they occur; he is not an historian, but a narrator; not an architect, but a lumberer, or stonecutter of history. It does not necessarily belong to his calling to elaborate his materials into a regular and complete work of art, which shall fully and philosophically represent the Life of the nation he describes.

The biographer is to give an idea of his hero, complete in all its parts, and perfect in each; to show how the world and the age with their manifold influences acted on the man, and he on his age and the world, and what they jointly produced. It is one thing to write the Memoirs or Annals of a man, and a matter quite different to write his Life. Mr Lockhart has collected many memorials of Sir Walter Scott, laboriously written annals, but the Life of Sir Walter he has by no means written. In telling what his hero suffered, did, and was, and how all was brought to pass, the biographer must be a critic also, and tell what his hero ought to have been and have done. Hence comes the deeper interest and the more instructive character of a true Biography; Memoirs may entertain, but a Biography must instruct.

The annalist of a nation or a man works mainly in an objective way, and his own character appears only in the selection or omission of events to record, in referring events to causes, or in deducing consequences from causes supposed to be in action. There is little which is personal in his work. On the other hand, the personality of the biographer continually appears. The lumberer's character or the stonecutter's does not report itself in the oak or travertine of Saint Peter's, while the genius of the architect confronts you as you gaze upon his colossal work. Now as the less cannot of itself comprehend the greater, so a biographer cannot directly, and of himself, comprehend a man nobler than himself. All the Oysters in the world would be incompetent to write the Life of a single Eagle. It is easy for a great man to understand the little man; impossible to be directly comprehended thereby. It is not hard to understand the position of a city, the mutual relation of its parts, when we look down thereon from a high tower. Now while this is so, by the advance of mankind in a few centuries, it comes to pass that a man of but common abilities, having the culture of his age, may stand on a higher platform than the man of genius occupied a short time before. In this way the Biography of a great man, which none of his contemporaries could undertake, because he so far overmastered them, soon becomes possible to men of marked ability, and in time to men of ordinary powers of comprehension. At this day it would not be very difficult to find men competent to write the Life of Alexander or of Charlemagne, yet by no means so easy to find one who could do justice to Napoleon. Lord Bacon was right in leaving his "name and memory" "to foreign nations and to mine own countrymen after some time be passed over." We are far from thinking Lord Bacon so great as many men esteem him, but at his death there was no man among his own countrymen, or in foreign nations, meet to be his judge. The followers of Jesus collected only a few scanty memorials of the man, and they who have since undertaken his life are proofs that the world has not caught up with his thoughts, nor its foremost men risen high enough to examine, to criticise, and to judge a spirit so commanding. But after all, no advance of mankind, no culture, however nice and extensive, will ever enable a Hobbes or a Hume to write the Life of a Jesus or even a Plato. It would be hard, even now, to find a man, in England or out of it, competent to give us the Biography of Shakspeare, even if he had all that Annals and Memoirs might furnish.

Now an historian is to a nation what a biographer is to a man: he is not a bare chronicler, to indite the memoirs of a nation and tickle his reader with a mere panorama of events, however great and brilliantly coloured,—events which have a connection of time and place, but no meaning, coming from no recognized cause and leading to no conclusion; he is to give us the nation's life,—its outer life in the civil, military, and commercial transactions; its inner life in the thought and feeling of the people. If the historian undertake the entire history of a nation that has completed its career of existence, then he must describe the country as it was when the people first appeared to take possession thereof, and point out the successive changes which they effected therein; the geographical position of the country, its natural features—its waters, mountains, plains, its soil, climate, and productions—all are important elements which help modify the character of the nation. The historian is to tell of the origin of the people, of their rise, their decline, their fall and end; to show how they acted on the world, and the world on them, —what was mutually given and received. The causes which advanced or retarded the nation are to be sought, and their action explained. He is to inquire what sentiments and ideas prevailed in the nation; whence they came, from without the people or from within; how they got organized, and with what result. Hence, not merely are the civil and military transactions to be looked after, but the philosophy which prevails in the nation is to be ascertained and discoursed of; the literature, laws, and religion. The historian is to describe the industrial condition of the people,—the state of agriculture, commerce, and the arts—both the useful and the beautiful; to inform us of the means of internal communication, of the intercourse with other nations—military, commercial, literary, or religious. He must tell of the social state of the people, the relation of the cultivator to the soil, the relation of class to class. It is important to know how the revenues of the state are raised; how the taxes are levied —on person or property, directly or indirectly; in what manner they are collected, and how a particular tax affects the welfare of the people. The writer of a nation's life must look at the whole people, not merely at any one class, noble or plebeian, and must give the net result of their entire action, so that at the end of his book we can say: "This people had such sentiments and ideas, which led to this and the other deeds and institutions, which have been attended by such and such results; they added this or that to the general achievement of the human race."

Now in the history of each nation there are some eminent men, in whom the spirit of the nation seems to culminate—either because they are more the nation than the nation is itself, or because by their eminent power they constrain the nation to take the form of these individuals; such men are to be distinctly studied and carefully portrayed; for while embodying the nation's genius they are an epitome of its history. In a first survey, we know a nation best by its great men, as a country by its mountains and its plains, its waters and its shores,—by its great characters. Still, while these eminent men are to be put in the foreground of the picture, the humblest class is by no means to be neglected. In the family of man there are elder and younger brothers; it is a poor history which neglects either class. A few facts from the every-day life of the merchant, the slave, the peasant, the mechanic, are often worth more, as signs of the times, than a chapter which relates the intrigues of a courtier, though these are not to be overlooked. It is well to know what songs the peasant sung; what prayers he prayed; what food he ate; what tools he wrought with; what tax he paid; how he stood connected with the soil; how he was brought to war, and what weapons armed him for the fight. It is not very important to know whether General Breakpate commanded on the right or the left; whether he charged uphill or downhill; whether he rode a bright chestnut horse or a dapple gray, nor whether he got dismounted by the breaking of his saddle-girth or the stumbling of his beast. But it is important to know whether the soldiers were accoutred well or ill, and whether they came voluntarily to the war, and fought in battle with a will, or were brought to the conflict against their own consent, not much caring which side was victorious.

In telling what has been, the historian is also to tell what ought to be, for he is to pass judgment on events, and try counsels by their causes first and their consequences not less. When all these things are told, history ceases to be a mere panorama of events having no unity but time and place; it becomes philosophy teaching by experience, and has a profound meaning and awakens a deep interest, while it tells the lessons of the past for the warning of the present and edification of the future. A nation is but a single family of the human race, and the historian should remember that there is a life of the race, not less than of the several nations and each special man.

If the historian takes a limited period of the life of any country for his theme, then it is a single chapter of the nation's story that he writes. He ought to show, by way of introduction, what the nation has done beforehand; its condition, material and spiritual, the state of its foreign relations, and at home the state of industry, letters, law, philosophy, morals, and religion. After showing the nation's condition at starting, he is to tell what was accomplished in the period under examination; how it was done, and with what result at home and abroad. The philosophy of history is of more importance than the facts of history; indeed, save to the antiquary, who has a disinterested love thereof, they are of little value except as they set forth that philosophy.

Now the subjective character of an historian continually appears, colours his narrative, and affects the judgment he passes on men and things. You see the mark of the tonsure in a history written by a priest or a monk; his standing-point is commonly the belfry of his parish church. A courtier, a trifler about the court of Queen Elizabeth, has his opinion of events, of their causes and their consequences; a cool and wise politician judges in his way; and the philosopher, neither a priest, nor courtier, nor yet a politician, writing in either age, comes to conclusions different from all three. A man's philosophical, political, moral, and religious creed will appear in the history he writes. M. de Potter and Dr Neander find very different things in the early ages of the Christian Church; a Catholic and a Protestant History of Henry the Eighth would be unlike. Mr Bancroft writes the history of America from the stand-point of ideal democracy, and, viewed from that point, things are not what they seem to be when looked at from any actual aristocracy. Hume, Gibbon, Mackintosh, and Schlosser, Sismondi, Michelet, and Macaulay, all display their own character in writing their several works. Hume cannot comprehend a Puritan, nor Gibbon a "Primitive Christian;" Saint Simon sees little in Fenelon but a disappointed courtier, and in William Penn Mr Bancroft finds an ideal Democrat.

A man cannot comprehend what wholly transcends himself. Could a Cherokee write the history of Greece? A Mexican, with the average culture of his nation, would make a sorry figure in delineating the character of New-England. If the historian be a strong man, his work reflects his own character; if that be boldly marked, then it continually appears—the one thing that is prominent throughout his work. In the Life and Letters of Cromwell we get a truer picture of the author than of the Protector. The same figure appears in the French Revolution, and all his historical composition appears but the grand fabling of Mr Carlyle. But if the historian is a weak man, a thing that may happen, more receptive than impressive, then he reflects the average character of his acquaintance, the circle of living men he moves in, or of the departed men whose books he reads. Such an historian makes a particular country his special study, but can pass thereon with only the general judgment of his class. This is true of all similar men: the water in the pipe rises as high as in the fountain, capillary attraction aiding what friction hindered; you know beforehand what an average party-man will think of any national measure, because his "thought" does not represent any individual action of his own, but the general average of his class. So it is with an ordinary clergyman; his opinion is not individual but professional. A strong man must have his own style, his own mode of sketching the outline, filling up the details, and colouring his picture; if he have a mannerism, it must be one that is his own, growing out of himself, and not merely on him, while in all this the small man represents only the character of his class: even his style, his figures of speech, will have a family mark on them; his mannerism will not be detected at first, because it is that of all his friends. Perhaps it would make little difference whether Michael Angelo was born and bred amid the rugged Alps or in the loveliest garden of Valombrosa—his genius seeming superior to circumstances; but with an artist who has little original and creative power, local peculiarities affect his style and appear in all his works.

Now within a thousand years a great change has come over the spirit of history. The historical writings of Venerable Bede and of Louis Blanc, the *Speculum Hystoriale* of Vincencius Bellovacensis, so eagerly printed once and scattered all over Europe, and the work of Mr Macaulay, bear marks of their respective ages, and are monuments which attest the progress of mankind in the historic art.

In the middle ages Chivalry prevailed: a great respect was felt for certain prescribed rules; a great veneration for certain eminent persons. Those rules were not always or necessarily rules of nature, but only of convention; nor were the persons always or necessarily those most meet for respect, but men accidentally eminent oftener than marked for any substantial and personal excellence. The spirit of chivalry appears in the writers of that time,—in the song and the romance, in history and annals, in homilies, and in prayers and creeds. Little interest is taken in the people, only for their chiefs; little concern is felt by great men for industry, commerce, art; much for arms. Primogeniture extended from law into literature; history was that of elder brothers, and men accidentally eminent seemed to monopolize distinction in letters, and to hold possession of history by perpetual entail. History was aristocratic; rank alone was respected, and it was thought there were but a few hundred persons in the world worth writing of, or caring for; the mass were thought only the sand on which the mighty walked, and useful only for that end; their lives were vulgar lives, their blood was puddle blood, and their deaths were vulgar deaths.

Of late years a very different spirit has appeared; slowly has it arisen, very slow, but it is real and visible,—the spirit of humanity. This manifests itself in a respect for certain rules, but they must be laws of nature—rules of justice and truth; and in respect for all mankind. Arms yield not to the gown only, but to the frock; and the aproned smith with his creative hand beckons destructive soldiers to an humbler seat, aud they begin with shame to take the lower place, not always to be allowed them. This spirit of humanity appears in legislation, where we will not now follow it; — but it appears also in literature. Therein primogeniture is abolished; the entail is broken; the monopoly at an end; the elder sons are not neglected, but the younger brothers are also brought into notice. In history, as in trade, the course is open to talent. History is becoming democratic. The life of the people is looked after; men write of the ground whereon the mighty walk. While the coins, the charters, and the capitularies —which are the monuments of kings—are carefully sought after, men look also for the songs, the legends, the ballads, which are the medals of the people, stamped with their image and superscription, and in these find materials for the biography of a nation. The manners and customs of the great mass of men are now investigated, and civil and military transactions are thought no longer the one thing most needful to record. This spirit of humanity constitutes the charm in the writings of Niebuhr, Schlosser, Sismondi, Michelet, Bancroft, Grote, Macaulay, the greatest historians of the age; they write in the interest of mankind. The absence of this spirit is a sad defect in the writings of Mr Carlyle;—himself a giant, he writes history in the interest only of giants.

Since this change has taken place, a new demand is made of an historian of our times. We have a right to insist that he shall give us the philosophy of history, and report the lessons thereof, as well as record the facts. He must share the spirit of humanity which begins to pervade the age; he must not write in the interest of a class, but of mankind,—in the interest of natural right and justice. Sometimes, however, a man may be excused for lacking the philosophy of history; no one could expect it of a Turk; if a Russian were to write the history of France, it would be easy to forgive him if he wrote in the interest of tyrants. But when a man of New-England undertakes to write a history, there is less excuse if his book should be wanting in philosophy and in humanity; less merit if it abound therewith.

Mr Prescott has selected for his theme one of the most important periods of history—from the middle of the fifteenth to the middle of the sixteenth century. The three greatest events of modern times took place during that period: the art of printing was invented, America discovered, the Protestant Reformation was begun. It was a period of intense life and various activity, in forms not easily understood at this day. The revival of letters was going forward; the classic models of Greece and Rome were studied anew; the revival, also, of art; Lionardo da Vinci, Pietro Perugino, Michael Angelo, Raphael, were achieving their miracles of artistic skill. Science began anew; new ideas seemed to dawn upon mankind; modern literature received a fresh impulse. The new thought presently reported itself in all departments of life. Navigation was improved; commerce extended; a new world was discovered, and, baited by the hope of gold or driven by discontent and restless love of change, impelled by desire of new things or constrained by conscience, the Old World rose and poured itself on a new continent, and with new ideas to found empires mightier than the old. In Europe a revolution advanced with the steps of an earthquake. The Hercules-pillars of authority were shaken; the serf rose against his lord; the great barons everywhere were losing their power; the great kings consolidating their authority. Feudal institutions reeled with the tossings of the ground, and fell—to rise no more. It was the age of the Medici, of Machiavelli, and of Savonarola; of Erasmus and Copernicus; of John Wessel, Reuchlin, Scaliger, and Agricola; Luther and Loyola lived in that time. The ninety-five theses were posted on the church door; the *Utopia* was written. There were Chevalier Bayard and Gonsalvo "the Great Captain;" Cardinal Ximenes, and Columbus. Two great works mark this period,—one, the establishment of national unity of action in the great monarchies of Europe, the king conquering the nobles; the other the great insurrection of mind and conscience against arbitrary power in the school, the state, the church,—an insurrection which legions of mediæval scholars, no armies, and no Councils of Basil and of Trent could prevent or long hinder from its work.

Writing of this age, Mr Precsott takes for his chief theme one of the most prominent nations of the world. Spain, however, was never prominent for thought; no idea welcomed by other nations was ever born or fostered in her lap; she has no great philosopher—not one who has made a mark on the world; no great poet known to all nations; not a single orator, ecclesiastic or political; she has been mother to few great names in science, arts, or literature. In commerce, Venice and Genoa long before Spain, England and Holland at a later date, have far out-travelled her. Even in arms, save the brief glory shed thereon by the Great Captain, Spain has not been distinguished; surely not as France, England, and even the Low Countries. But her geographical position is an important one —between the Atlantic and the Mediterranean. At the time in question her population was great, perhaps nearly twice that of England, and she played an important part in the affairs of Europe, while England had little to do with the continent. Spain was connected with the Arabs, for some centuries the most civilized people in Europe; hence she came in contact with industry, skill, and riches, with letters and with art, and enjoyed opportunities denied to all the other nations of Europe. For her subsequent rank among nations, Spain is indebted to two events, which, as they did not come from the genius of the people, may be called accidental. One was the connection with the house of Austria, the singular circumstance which placed the united crowns of Castile and Arragon on the same head which bore the imperial diadem of Germany. This accident gave a lustre to Spain in the age of Charles the Fifth and his successor. But the other cause, seemingly more accidental, has given Spain a place in history which nothing else could have done—the fact that when the Genoese navigator first crossed the Atlantic, the Spanish flag was at his masthead.

Mr Prescott writes of Spain at her most important period, at the time when the two monarchies of Castile and Arragon were blent into one; when the Moors were conquered and expelled; the Inquisition established; the Jews driven out; the old laws revised; a new world discovered, conquered, settled, its nations put to slavery, Christianty, or death; an age when Negro Slavery, Christianity, and the Inquisition first visited this western world. Not only has the historian a great age to delineate and great events to deal with,—a new continent to describe, a new race to report on, their origin, character, language, literature, art, manners, and religion,—but, to enliven his picture, he has great men to portray. We will not speak of Ferdinand, Isabella, and Charles the Fifth, who pass often before us in kingly grandeur; but there are Gonsalvo, Ximenes, and Columbus, here are Cortes and Pizarro.

Few historians have had an age so noble to describe; a theme so rich in events, in ideas, and in men; an opportunity so fortunate to present the lessons of history to ages yet to come. The author has this further advantage: he lives far enough from the age he writes of to be beyond its bigotry and its rage. The noises of a city hardly reach the top of a steeple; all the din of battle is hushed and still far below the top of Mont Blanc; and so in a few years the passions, the heat, the dust, the rage and noises of kings and nations are all silenced and lost in the immeasurable stillness which settles down upon the past. If the thinker pauses from his busy thought, and after a year or so returns thither again, how clear it all becomes! So is it with mankind: the problems of that age are no problems now; what could not then be settled with all the noise of parliaments and of arms, in the after-silence of mankind has got its solution. Yet Mr Prescott does not live so far from the time he treats of that genius alone has power to recall the faded images thereof, to disquiet and bring it up again to life. Yet he lives so remote that he can judge counsels by their consequences as easily as by their cause; can judge theories, laws, institutions, and great men by the influence they have had on the world,—by their seal and signal mark. In addition to these advantages, he lives in a land where there is no censorship of the press; where the body is free, and the mind free, and the conscience free—to him who will. His position and his theme are both enviable; giving an historian of the greatest genius scope for all his powers.

To judge only from his writings, Mr Prescott is evidently a man with a certain niceness of literary culture not very common in America; of a careful if not exact scholarship in the languages and literature of Italy and Spain. Perhaps he cannot boast a very wide acquaintance with literature, ancient or modern, but is often nice and sometimes critical in his learning. He is one of the few Americans not oppressed by the *Res angusta domi*, who devote themselves to literature; to a life of study and the self-denial it demands in all countries, and eminently here, where is no literary class to animate the weary man. His quotations indicate a wealthy library—his own fortune enabling him to procure books which are rare even in Spain itself. Where printed books fail, manuscripts, also, have been diligently sought. He writes in a mild and amiable spirit: if he differ from other historians, he empties no vials of wrath upon their heads. He always shows himself a gentleman of letters, treating his companions with agreeable manners and courtesy the most amiable. Few lines in these volumes appear marked with any asperity, or dictated in any sourness of temper. These few we shall pass upon in their place.

Within less than thirteen years eight volumes have appeared from his hand; the first evidently the work of many years, but the last five volumes reveal a diligence and ability to work not common amongst the few literary gentlemen of America. Labour under disadvantages always commands admiration. How many have read with throbbing heart the lives of men pursuing "knowledge under difficulties;" yet such men often had one advantage which no wealth could give, no colleges and guidance of accomplished men supply—an able intellect and the unconquerable will: but Mr Prescott has pursued his labours under well-known difficulties, which might make the stoutest quail. These things considered, no fair man can fail to honour the accomplished author, and to rejoice in the laurels so beautifully won and worn with modesty and grace.

After this long preamble, let us now examine the three works before us, and see how the author has done the high duties of an historian. Treating of this great theme, we shall speak of the three works in their chronological order, and examine in turn the History of Spain, of Mexico, and of Peru, in each case speaking of the substance of the work, first in details, then as a whole—and next of its form. The remainder of this article will be devoted to the History of Ferdinand and Isabella.

To understand what was done by Ferdinand and Isabella, we must know what had been achieved before their time,—must take the national account of stock. This Mr Prescott undertakes in his Introduction (Vol. I. pp. xxix.—cxxiv.), but he fails to render an adequate account of the condition of Castile and Arragon, and of course it is not easy for the reader to appreciate the changes that subsequently were made therein.

To be a little more specific: his account of the condition of the law is meagre and inadequate; the history of the reform and codification of laws poor and hardly intelligible (Part I. Ch. VI.); and though he returns upon the theme in the general account of the administration of Ferdinand and Isabella (Part II. Ch. XXVI.), still it is not well and adequately done. What he says of the Cortes of Castile and that of Arragon does not give one a clear idea of the actual condition and power of those bodies. He does not tell us by whom and how the members were chosen to their office; how long they held it, and on what condition. The reader wonders at the meagreness of this important portion of the work, especially when such materials lay ready before his hands. After all, we find a more complete and intelligible account of the constitution, of the laws, and of the administration of justice in the brief chapter of Mr Hallam's work than in this elaborate history. Nay, the work of Mr Dunham, written for the *Cabinet Cyclopædia,* written apparently in haste, and not always in good temper—gives a far better account of that matter than Mr Prescott. This is a serious defect, and one not to be anticipated in an historian who in this country undertakes to describe to us the ancient administration of a foreign land. With a sigh the student remembers the masterly chapter of Gibbon which treats of the administration of justice and of the Roman law, a chapter which made a new era in the study of the subject itself, and longs for some one to guide him in this difficult and crooked path. With the exception of the *Code of the Visigoths,* the *Fuero Juzgo,* and the *Siete Partidas,* works of Spanish law, or treating thereof, are in but few hands: Marina, Zuaznavar, and Garcia de la Madrid can be but little known in England or America; for information the general scholar must here depend on the historian; considering the important place that Spanish legislation has held, the wide reach of the Spanish dominion on both continents, it was particularly needful to have in this work a clear, thorough, and masterly digest of this subject.

In speaking of the revenue of the kingdom, Mr Prescott does not inform us how it was collected, nor from what sources. (Introduction, Sect. I. and II. and Part I. Ch. VI.) We are told that the king had his royal demesnes, that on some occasions one-fifth of the spoils of war belonged to him, and it appears that a certain proportion of the proceeds of the mines was his—but there is no systematic or methodical account of the revenues. True, he tells us that Isabella obtains money by mortgaging her real estate and pawning her personal property (Part I. Ch. XIV.); afterwards it appears, accidentally, that two-ninths of the tithes, *Tercias,* formed a part of the royal income. (Part II. Ch. I. p. 283.) We are told that the revenues increased thirty-fold during this administration. (Part II. Ch. XXVI. p. 484.) It is mentioned as a proof of sagacity in the ruler and of the welfare of the people—but we are not told whence they were derived, and it appears that in 1504 the single city of Seville paid nearly one-sixth of the whole revenue.* In a note he tells us that the bulk of the crown revenue came from the *Tercias* and the *Alcavalas*. The latter was an odious tax of ten per cent. on all articles bought, sold, or transferred. Mr Prescott tells us it was commuted—but how or for what he does not say. (Part II. Ch. XXVI. p. 438.)

Armies figure largely in any history of Spain, but it is in vain that we ask of Mr Prescott how the armies were raised, and on what principle, the modern or the feudal; how they were equipped, paid, fed, and clothed. He often dwells upon battles, telling us who commanded on the right or the left; can describe at length the tournament of Trani, and the duel between Bayard and Sotomayor—but he nowhere gives us a description of the military estate of the realm, and nowhere relates the general plan of a campaign. This, also, is a serious defect in any history, especially in that of a nation of the fifteenth century—a period of transition. He does not inform us of the state of industry, trade, and commerce, or touch, except incidentally, upon the effect of the laws thereon. Yet during this reign the laws retarded industry in all its forms, to a great degree. Soon after the discovery of America, Spain forbade the exportation of gold and silver, and, as Don Clemencin says, "our industry would have died from apoplexy of money, if the observance of the laws established in this matter had not been sufficient for its ruin." At a later date it was forbidden to export even the raw material of silk and wool. "Spain," says M. Blanqui, the latest writer on the political economy of that country that we have seen—"is the country of all Europe where the rashest and most cruel experiments have been made at the expense of industry, which has almost always been treated as a foe, managed to the death (*exploitée à l'outrance*) instead of being protected by the Government, and regarded as a thing capable of taxation, rather than a productive element." Restrictions were laid not only on intercourse

* Mr Prescott says *near a tenth*. This is probably a clerical or typographical error. The whole amount is given in the authority as 209,500,000 maravedis, of which Seville paid 30,971,096.

with foreign nations, but on the traffic between province and province, and a tax, sometimes an enormous one, the *Alcavala,* was collected from the sale of all articles whatever. "Members of the legal and military profession," says M. Blanqui, "affected the most profound contempt for every form of industry. Any man who exercised a trade was disgraced for life. A noble who ventured to work lost his privilege of nobility, and brought his family to shame. No town accepted an artisan for its alcalde; the Cortes of Arragon, says Marina, never admitted to their assembly a deputy who came from the industrial class. You would think you were reading Aristotle and Cicero when you find in the writers, and even in the laws of Spain, those haughty expressions of contempt for the men who bow their faces towards the earth, and stoop to smite the anvil, or tend a loom."

Mr Prescott does not notice the condition of the people, except in terms the most general and vague. Yet great changes were taking place at that time in the condition of the labouring class. He does not even tell us what relation the peasantry bore to the soil; how they held it, by what tenure; for what time; what relation they bore to the nobles and the knights. In Castile Mr Hallam says there was no villanage. Mr Prescott gives us no explanation of the fact, and does not mention the fact itself. In Catalonia a portion of the peasantry passed out of the condition of vassalage,—Mariana calls them Pageses, others Vassals de Remenza,—to that of conditional freedom, by paying an annual tax to their former owner, or to entire freedom by the payment of a sum twenty times as large. This was an important event in the civil history of Spain. Mr Prescott barely relates the fact. From other sources we have learned, we know not how truly, that no artisan was allowed in the Cortes of Arragon, that only nobles were eligible to certain offices there, and no nobles were taxed.

In all this History there are no pictures from the lives of the humble,—yet a glimpse into the cottage of a peasant, or even at the beggary of Spain in the fifteenth century, would be instructive, and help a stranger to understand the nation. Much is said, indeed, of the wealthier class, of the nobles, and of the clergy, but we find it impossible from this History alone to form a complete idea of their position in the kingdom; of their relation to one another, to the people, or the crown; of the number of the clergy, of their education, their character, their connection with the nobles or the people, of their general influence—he has nothing to tell us. He pays little regard to the progress of society; to advances made in the comforts of life, in the means of journeying from place to place. Now and then it is said that the roads were in bad order, and so a march was delayed; even at this day the means of internal communication are so poor, the roads so few and impracticable, that some provinces lie in a state of almost entire isolation. Says M. Blanqui, "More than one province of Spain could be mentioned which is more inaccessible than the greater part of our most advanced positions in Africa." "Castile and Catalonia differ as much as Russia and Germany, and the inhabitants of Gallicia do not undertake the journey to Andalusia so often as the French that to Constantinople."

A philosophical inquirer wants information on all these subjects, and the general reader has no authority but histories like this. It cannot be said that Mr Prescott feared to encumber his work with such details, and make his volumes too numerous or big. He has space to spare for frivolous details; he can describe the pageant afforded by the royal pair in the camp before Moclin, in 1486; can tell us that "the queen herself rode a chestnut mule, seated on a saddle-chair embossed with gold and silver;" that "the housings were of a crimson colour, and the bridles of satin were curiously wrought with letters of gold;" that "the Infanta wore a skirt of fine velvet over others of brocade; a scarlet mantilla of the Moorish fashion, and a black hat trimmed with gold embroidery," and that the king "was dressed in a crimson doublet with *chausses* or breeches of yellow satin. Over his shoulders was thrown a cassock or mantilla of rich brocade, and a sopra vest of the same material concealed his cuirass. By his side, close girt, he wore a Moorish scymitar, and beneath his bonnet his hair was confined by a cap or head-dress of the finest stuff. Ferdinand was mounted on a noble war-horse of a bright chestnut colour." (Part I. Ch. XI. p. 401 et seq.)

The account of the Inquisition is eminently unsatisfactory. No adequate motive is assigned for it, no sufficient cause. It stands in this book as a thing with consequences enough, and bad enough, but no cause; you know not why it came. Mr Prescott treats Catholicism fairly. We do not remember a line in these volumes which seems dictated by anti-Catholic bigotry. He has no sympathy with the Inquisition; he looks on it with manly aversion; but he treats the subject with little ability, not showing how subtly the Inquisition worked, undermining the Church and the State, and corrupting life in its most sacred sources. Who made the Inquisition; for what purpose was its machinery set a-going; what effect did it have on the whole nation?—these are questions which it was Mr Prescott's business to answer, but which, as we think, he has failed to answer. Whosoever brought it to pass, there is little doubt but it gained Ferdinand and Isabella the title of Catholic. But our historian does not like to lay the blame on them; they are the heroes of his story. Ferdinand may indeed be blamed,—it were difficult in this century to write and not blame him; but Isabella must not be censured for this—her heroism is to be spotless. The spirit of chivalry in our author is too strong for the spirit of humanity. He thinks Ferdinand may have had political motives for establishing the Inquisition, but Isabella only religious motives for its establishment in Castile. (Part I. Ch. VII. p. 246.) Certainly there was a great blame somewhere: it falls not on the people, who had neither the ability nor the will to establish it; nor on the aristocracy of nobles and rich men,—they had much to lose, and little to gain; it was always hateful to them. The priests, no doubt, were in favour of the Inquisition, but they could not have introduced it; nay, could have had little influence in bringing it about if the crown had opposed it. Ferdinand and Isabella were no slaves to the priesthood; they knew how to favour the interests of the Church when it served their turn; but no forehead was more brazen, no hand more iron than theirs, to confront and put down any insolence of sacerdotal power. Isabella did not favour the old Archbishop of Toledo; she abridged the power of the priests; nay, that of the Pope, and easily seized from him what other monarchs had long clutched at in vain. She allowed no appeals to him. (Part I. Ch. XII. p. 4; Ch. XV. p. 84. Part II. Ch. XXVI. pp. 435—437.) The Pragmaticas of Isabella tended to restrict the power of the clergy and of the Pope within narrower limits than before. Ferdinand and Isabella are the very parties to be blamed for the Inquisition: if so enlightened above their age, the more to be blamed; if cool-headed and far-sighted, they deserve more reproach; if Isabella were so religious as it is contended, then the severest censure is to be pronounced against her. It was only thirty-six years before the Reformation that she introduced the Inquisition to Castile. It is idle to lay the blame on Torquemada (Part I. Ch. VII. p. 247 et al.); we profess no great veneration for this genuine son of Saint Dominic, but let him answer for his own sins, not his master's. We cannot but think history is unjust in painting Isabella so soft and fair, while her inquisitor-general is portrayed in the blackest colours, and she, with all her intelligence, charity, and piety, puts the necks of the people into his remorseless hands. Ferdinand and Isabella were not fools, to be deluded by a priest, however cunning. It seems to us that the Inquisition must be set down to their account, and should cover them both with shame; that as James the Second is to be blamed for Jeffries and the bloody assizes, so are Ferdinand and Isabella for Torquemada and the Inquisition. Mr Prescott admits the most obvious and pernicious cruelties thereof, but has not the heart to trace the evil to its source. It is the fashion of certain writers to dwell with delight on every fault committed by the masses of men. What eloquent denunciation have we heard on the "horrid crimes of the old French Revolution:" "horrid crimes" they were, and let them be denounced; but when the writers come to butcheries done by the masters of mankind, they have no voice to denounce such atrocities. Yet both equally proceed from the same maxim—that might is right. Llorente may be wrong in the numbers who suffered by the Inquisition; perhaps there were not 13,000 burned alive at the stake, and 191,143 who suffered other tortures. Suppose there were but half that number—nay, a tenth part; still it is enough to cover any monarch in Europe, since the twelfth century, with shame. Grant that Torquemada projected the scheme; the fact that Isabella allowed it to be executed shows that she was of soul akin to her infamous ancestor, Peter the Cruel, and deserves the sharp censure of every just historian.

We come next to speak of the Moors and Jews. At the time of Ferdinand and Isabella, there were in Spain two distinct tribes of men. On the one side were the descendants of the Visigoths, one of the new nations who had appeared in history not many centuries before, and united with the existing population of Spain, as the Romans had formerly united with the settlers they found there; on the other side were two nations, descended, as it is said, from Abram, the mythological ancestor of numerous tribes of Asia, the Moors and the Jews. Both of these nations had been for centuries distinguished for their civilization; they had long dwelt on the same soil with the Spaniards, and if we may believe the tale, few families of the Spanish nobility were quite free from all Moorish or all Hebrew taint. A philosophical historian would find an attractive theme in the meeting of nations so diverse in origin, language, manners, and religion, as the sons of the East and the West. It would be curious to trace the effects of their union; to learn what the Hebrews and the Moors had brought to Spain and what they established there; how much had been gained by this mingling of races, which, as some think, is a perpetual condition of national progress. The Jews were not barbarians—they are commonly superior to the class they mingle with in all countries. The Moors were amongst the most enlightened nations of Europe: they had done much to promote the common industrial arts, the higher arts of beauty; they had practised agriculture and the mechanic arts with skill and science, for unlike the Spaniards, they were not ashamed of work; they had fostered science and letters; on their hearth had kept the sacred fire snatched from the altar of the Muses before their temple went to the ground, and still fed and watched its flame, in some ages almost alone the guardians of that vestal fire. The English reader familiar with Gibbon's account of the Arabian race, —a chapter not without its faults, but which even now must still be called masterly,—looks for something not inferior in this history, where the occasion equally demands it. But he looks in vain. The chapter which treats of the Spanish Arabs (Part I. ch. VIII.), though not without merit, is hardly worthy of a place in a history written in this age of the world.

After the two chief monarchies of Spain were practically united into one, it was not to be expected that the Catholic sovereigns would allow so fair a portion of the peninsula to remain in the hands of the Moors. They had only been there on sufferance, and seem never to have recovered from their terrible defeat in 1210. Spanish sovereigns, with the spirit of that age, would wish to subdue the Moors—Christians, the "Infidels;" and when such feelings exist an occasion for war is not long to seek. The conquest of a rich kingdom like that of Granada with a high civilization, is an affair of much importance; the expulsion of a whole people, in modern times, though still meditated by men whom the chances of an election bring to the top of society in Republican America, is an unusual thing, and in this case it was barbarous not less than unusual.

Mr Prescott does justice to the industry, intelligence, skill, and general civilization of the Moors; while he points out defects and blemishes in their institutions with no undue severity, he has yet just and beautiful things to say of them. But he glozes over the injustice shown towards them, and averts the sympathy of the reader for the suffering nation by the remark, that "they had long since reached their utmost limit of advancement as a people;" "that during the latter period of their existence, they appear to have reposed in a state of torpid and luxurious indulgence, which would seem to argue that when causes of external excitement were withdrawn, the inherent vices of their social institutions had incapacitated them from the further production of excellence." Then he puts the blame—if blame there be—on Providence, and says, "in this impotent condition, it was wisely ordered that their territory should be occupied by a people whose religion and more liberal form of government . . . qualified them for advancing still higher the interests of humanity." (Part I. Ch. xv. p. 105 et seq.) Mr Prescott elsewhere speaks with manly and becoming indignation of the conduct of Ximenes, who burnt the elegant libraries of the Moors; yet he has not censure enough, it seems to us, for the barbarous edict which drove the Moors into hypocrisy or exile.

. . . . .

The expulsion of the Jews is treated of in the same spirit: the blame is laid in part on the priests, on Torquemada, and in part on the spirit of the age. Both were bad enough, no doubt, but if Ferdinand and Isabella, as represented, were before their age in statesmanship, and the latter far in advance of its religion, we see not how they can be shielded from blame. It is the duty of an historian to measure men by the general standard of their times,—certainly we are not to expect the morals of the nineteenth century from one who lived in the ninth; but it is also the historian's duty to criticise that spirit, and when a superior man rises, he must not be judged merely by the low standard of his age, but the absolute standard of all ages. Such a judgment we seldom find in this work. Many acts of these princes show that they were short-sighted. Allowing Isabella's zeal for the Church, which is abundantly proved, it must yet be confessed that she possessed its worst qualities—bigotry, intolerance, and cruelty—in what might be called the heroic degree. Ferdinand cared little for any interest but his own. We doubt, after all, if it was love of the Church which expelled the Moors and the Jews, and think it was a love yet more vulgar; namely, the love of plunder. He hit the nail on the head who declared that uncounted numbers of Jews were richer than Christians—*innumeri [Judæorum] Christianis ditiores*. The Jews displayed their usual firmness in refusing to pretend to be converted, but their resolution to adhere to the faith of their fathers and their conscience meets with but scanty praise from our author, living under institutions formed by religious exiles, though he calls it "an extraordinary act of self-devotion."

Mr Prescott's defence of Isabella does little honour to his head or heart, but is in harmony with the general tone of the history. The Catholic sovereign thus struck a deadly blow at the industry of the nation. The Moors had almost created agriculture in Spain; they had founded the most important manufactures—that of silk, wool, leather, and of tempered steel. They were ingenious mechanics and excellent artists. Since that time foreigners have braved the national prejudice against manual work. It was the Flemish and the Italians who re-established the manufacture of tapestry, of woollen goods, and of work in wood; and more recently the English and French have engaged there in the manufacture of linen, cotton, and mixed goods. In the time of Louis XIV. more than seventy-five thousand Frenchmen had gone to settle in Spain.

Mr Prescott's account of the literature of Spain has been much admired, not wholly without reason. The chapters (Part I. Ch. xix. and xx.) which treat of the Castilian literature were certainly needed for the completeness of the work. Everybody knows how much Mr Schlosser adds to the value of his Histories, by his laborious examination of the literature, science, and art of the nations he describes. To know a nation's deeds we must understand its thoughts. "It will be necessary," says Mr Prescott, "in order to complete the view of the internal administration of Ferdinand and Isabella, to show its operation on the intellectual culture of the nation. . . . . It is particularly deserving of note in the present reign, which stimulated the active development of the national energies in every department of science, and which forms a leading epoch in the ornamental literature of the country. The present and following chapter will embrace the mental progress of the kingdom, ... through the whole of Isabella's reign, in order to exhibit as far as possible its entire results." (Part I. Ch. xix. p. 184 et seq.)

The education of Isabella was neglected in her youth, and, at a mature age, she undertook to supply her defects, and studied with such success, says one of her contemporaries, that "in less than a year her admirable genius enabled her to obtain so good a knowledge of the Latin tongue that she could understand without much difficulty what was written or spoken in it." She took pains with the education of her own children, and those of the nobility. She invited Peter Martyr and Marinæo Siculo to aid in educating the nobility, which they readily did. Mr Prescott mentions the names of several noblemen who engaged zealously in the pursuit of letters. "No Spaniard," says Giovio, "was accounted noble who held science in indifference." Men of distinguished birth were eager, we are told, to lead the way in science. Lords, also, of illustrious rank, lent their influence to the cause of good letters: one lady, called La Latina, instructed the Queen in the

Roman tongue; another lectured on the Latin classics, at Salamanca, and a third on rhetoric, at Alcala. Yet, spite of all this royal zeal, this feminine and noble attention to letters, Mr Prescott confesses that little progress was made in the poetic art since the beginning of the century. One cause thereof he finds in the rudeness of the language, which certainly had not become more rude during the progress of so much Latinity and rhetoric;—and another, "in the direction to utility manifested in this active reign, which led such as had leisure for intellectual pursuits to cultivate science rather than abandon themselves to the mere revels of the imagination." (p. 229.)

Let us look at this subject a little more in detail, and see what opportunities Spain had for intellectual culture, what use she made of them, what results were obtained, and how Mr Prescott has described "the mental progress of the nation."

The Arabians, as we have twice said before, were for some time the most enlightened nation in the world: they cultivated arts, the useful and the elegant, with singular success; they diligently studied physics and metaphysics; they pursued literature, and have left behind them numerous proofs of their zeal, if not of their genius. There was a time when the great classic masters of science were almost forgotten by the Christians, but carefully studied and held in honour by the disciples of Mahomet. Men of other nations sought instruction in their schools, or sat at the feet of their sages, or studied and translated their works. By means of their vicinity to the Moorish Arabs, the Spaniards had an excellent opportunity to cultivate science and letters, but they made little use of those advantages. Robert and Daniel Morley, Campano, Athelhard, Gerbert of Aurillac (afterwards Sylvester II.), and others, learned from the Arabian masters; but there were few or no Spaniards of any eminence who took pains to study the thought of their Mahometan neighbours.

It seems to us that Mr Prescott a good deal overrates the literary tendency of the Spaniards under Ferdinand and Isabella. It is true, at that time a great movement of thought went on in the rest of Europe. The capture of Constantinople drove the Greek scholars from their ancient home; the printing-press diffused the Scriptures, the ancient laws, the old classics, spreading new thought rapidly and wide. Literature and philosophy were studied with great vigour. This new movement appeared in Italy, in Switzerland, in Germany, and France—even in England. But in Spain we find few and inconsiderable traces thereof. Mr Prescott cites Erasmus for the fact that "liberal studies were brought in the course of a few years, in Spain, to so flourishing a condition, as might not only excite the admiration but serve as a model to the most cultivated nations of Europe." (p. 202.) But it deserves to be remembered that Erasmus made this statement in a letter to a Spanish professor at the University of Alcala, and besides, founds his praise on the religion as much as on the learning of the country. In a former letter he had said that the study of literature had been neglected in Germany to such a degree that men would not take learning if offered them for nothing,—"nobody was willing to hear the professors who were supported at the public charge." But elsewhere Erasmus knows how to say that in Germany their "schools of learning were numerous as the towns." But this is of small importance.

It is certain that Ferdinand and Isabella did something to promote the literary culture of their people; yet it had not been wholly neglected before the University of Huesca (Osca) was certainly old. Plutarch, in his Life of Sertorius, informs us that the Roman general founded a school there, and some one says that Pontius Pilate was a "Professor Juris"—utriusque juris, we suppose—on that foundation; Spaniards may believe the story. The University of Seville was founded in 990; that of Valencia in 1200, or about that time; that of Salamanca in 1239,—though some place it earlier and some much later; universities had been founded at Lerida and Valladolid in the fourteenth century. This statement may read well on paper, but it is plain that universities had done little to enlighten the nation,—otherwise Cardinal Ximenes had never celebrated that *auto da fe* with the Arabian libraries.

Queen Isabella, we are told, encouraged the introduction of printing into Spain, and caused many of the works of her own subjects to be printed at her own charge; that she exempted a German printer from taxation, and allowed foreign books to be imported free of duty. But more than twenty years elapsed after the discovery of the art before we hear of a single printing-press in the kingdom; and during the whole of the fifteenth century we cannot find that four hundred editions were printed in all Spain, while during that period the press of Florence had sent forth five hundred and fifty-three, that of Milan six hundred and eighty-three, that of Paris seven hundred and fifty-seven, Rome nine hundred and fifty-three, Venice three thousand one hundred and thirty-seven. The little city of Strasburg alone had published more than the whole kingdom of Spain. About fifteen thousand editions were printed in the last thirty years of that century. The character of the works printed in Spain is significant;—first of all comes a collection of songs in honour of the Virgin, setting forth the miraculous conception. It is true, a translation of the Bible into the Limousin dialect was printed at Valencia in 1478, but during the fifteenth century we do not find that a single edition of the Vulgate, or of the Civil Law, was printed in all Spain, though no less than ninety-eight editions of the Latin Bible came forth from the presses of Europe.

Mr Prescott professes to describe the mental progress of the nation. To accomplish this, the historian must tell us the result of what was done in law—in the study of the Roman, the National, and the Canon Law, for all three have been important elements in the development of the Spanish nation; what was done in physics; in metaphysics, including ethics and theology; and in general literature. Now Mr Prescott, in this examination, passes entirely over the first three departments, and bestows his labour wholly upon the last. It is true, he treats of the alteration of the laws in his last chapter, but in a brief and unsatisfactory style. Yet he had before told us that the attention of studious men was directed to science, and it is elsewhere asserted that much was done in this reign for the reformation and codification of the laws. It would be interesting to the mere reader, and highly important to the philosophical student who wishes to understand the mental progress of Spain, to know how much the Roman Law was studied, how much the Canon Law, and what modifications were made thereby in the national institutions themselves—by whom, and with what effect. After all that has been written of late years, it would not be difficult, certainly not impossible, to do this. The publication of *Las Siete Partidas* for the first time in 1491, twenty years after the accession of Isabella to the throne, was an important event; the legal labours of Alfonso de Montalvo deserved some notice; the celebrated *Consolato del Mare,* which has had so important an influence on the maritime laws of Europe and America, and first got printed during this reign, certainly required some notice, even in a brief sketch of the intellectual history of that reign. In all Catholic countries the study of the Canon Law is of great importance, but during the fifteenth century, though more than forty editions thereof got printed in other parts of Europe, we do not find one in Spain.

In science, including the mathematics and all departments of physics, the Spanish did little. Yet circumstances were uncommonly favourable: the conquest of Granada put them in possession of the libraries of the Moors, which were destined only to the flames; under the guidance of Columbus, they discovered new lands and had ample opportunities to study the geography, zoölogy, and botany of countries so inviting to the naturalist. But nothing was done. It is true, Andres, with his national prejudices, undertakes to mention some names that are illustrious in medicine—but Piquer and Lampillas, Monardes, Christoforo da Costa, Laguna, "the Spanish Galen," and the rest that he mentions, may be celebrated throughout all Spain and even in La Mancha: we think they are but little known elsewhere. In the departments of geography and astronomy the Spanish accomplished nothing worthy of mention.

In metaphysics and ethics there are no Spanish names before the sixteenth century—few even then; scholastic philosophy, which once prevailed so widely in the West of Europe, seems not to have found a footing in the Peninsula. In the tenth century Gerbert went to Spain to learn philosophy of the Arabs; in the eleventh, Constantinus Africanus communicated its doctrines to the world; in the twelfth and thirteenth, Athelhard of Bath, called Athelhard the Goth, Gherard, Otho of Frisingen, Michael Scott, and others, filled Europe with translations of Arabian authors. But Spain did nothing.

In theology the Spaniards have but one work to show of

any note, which dates from the period in question. The *Complutensian Polyglot* was a great work; but to achieve that nothing was needed but great wealth and the labours of a few learned and diligent men. The wealth was abundant, and flowed at the Cardinal's command; the treasures of the Vatican and of all the libraries of Europe were freely offered; the manuscripts of the Jews in Spain were at Ximenes' command; the services of accomplished scholars could easily be bought. Learned Greeks there were in the South of Europe seeking for bread. Of the nine men who were engaged in this undertaking, one was a Greek and three were Jews—of course converted Jews. Artists came from Germany to cast the types for the printing. Mr Prescott exaggerates the difficulty of the undertaking: the scholars could be had, the manuscripts borrowed or bought; indeed, so poorly was the matter conducted, that some manuscripts, purchased at great cost, came too late for use. Mr Prescott says, "There were no types in Spain, if indeed in any part of Europe, in the Oriental character," but only three alphabets were needed in the Polyglot—the Roman, the Greek, and the Hebrew. The two first were common enough, even in Spain; and in various parts of Europe, before the end of the fifteenth century, no less than thirty-nine editions had been printed of the whole or a part of the Hebrew Bible. The *Complutensian Polyglot* is indeed a valuable work, but at this day few men will contend that in the Old Testament it has a text better than the edition at Soncino, or that the Complutensian New Testament is better than that of Erasmus. Indeed, we hazard nothing in saying that Erasmus, a single scholar and a private man often in want of money, did more to promote the study of the Scriptures and the revival of letters than Cardinal Ximenes and all Spain put together,—and never burnt up a library of manuscripts because they were not orthodox.

All these matters, except the Polygot, Mr Prescott passes over with few words in his sketch of the mental progress of Spain in her golden age. While France, Germany, Italy, and England made rapid strides in their mental progress, Spain did little—little in law, little in science, in theology little. But Mr Prescott writes in a pleasing style about another portion of the literature of Spain, which is, after all, her most characteristic production in letters—her ballads and the drama. The *Redondilla* is the most distinctive production of the Spanish muse. The ballads of Spain are unlike those of England, of Scotland, and of Germany, in many respects, yet bear the same relation to the genius of the people. They grew up in the wild soil of the Peninsula; no royal or ecclesiastical hand was needed to foster them. Beautiful they are,—the wild flowers of the field,—but under the eye of Isabella they began to droop and wither; no new plants came up so fair and fragrant as the old. Why not? The life of the people was trodden down by the hoof of the priest whom Isabella had sent to his work. The language was rude, says Mr Prescott. That hindered not; Burns found a rude speech in Auld Scotland, but the verses he sung in "hamely westlin jingle" will live longer then the well-filed lines of Pope. Rudeness of language hindered not the genius of Chaucer, of Hans Sachs. Mr Prescott had small space to note the alteration of laws, the change of social systems, or the progress of civilization in Spain, but he has some twenty pages to bestow upon the drama, and gives us an analysis of the "Tragicomedy of Celestina, or Calisto and Melibea," spending four pages upon such a work. A philosophical reader would consent to spare all mention of Encina, Naharro, Oliva, Cota, and even Fernando de Roxas, if in the place which they but cumber there had been an account of the real thought, manners, and life of the nation. Far be it from us to complain of the time and space allotted to the popular literature of Spain,—the chapters are the best of the work; but one familiar with that delightful growth laments that the historian made no better use of his materials to indicate the life, character, and sentiments of the people.

Mr Prescott overrates the excellence of Queen Isabella. The character of Ferdinand was so atrocious that it admits of no defence. Shall it be said the age was distinguished for fraud, double-dealing, perfidy, and hypocrisy? It affords no good defence, for it was in these very qualities that Ferdinand surpassed his age. He was a tyrannical king; a treacherous ally; a master whom no servant could trust; a faithless husband in the life of Queen Isabella, and false to her memory after her death. Few will deny that he had some ability and some knowledge of kingcraft, though we think his powers and political foresight have been somewhat overrated. The great men of the realm he used as his servants, but when they acquired renown he endeavoured to ruin them; cast them off neglected and covered with dishonour. His treatment of Columbus, Gonsalvo, or of Ximenes, would have been a disgrace to any prince in Christendom. He was no friend of the nobility, and quite as little the friend of his people; he did not favour commerce or the arts; no, nor letters and science. His zeal for religion appears chiefly in the expulsion of the Moors and the Jews. Isabella had some natural repugnance to the establishment of slavery in America, but Ferdinand had none. Mr Prescott, who is not blind to his faults, says truly, "His was the spirit of egotism. The circle of his views might be more or less expanded, but self was the steady, unchangeable centre."

Mr Prescott censures Ferdinand, but it seems to us for the purpose of making a contrast with Isabella, quite as much as in reference to the unchangeable laws of morality; the effects of his character on the institutions of his country and the welfare of his people he does not point out in a manner worthy of an historian. Let us turn to Isabella. "Her character," he says, "was all magnanimity, disinterestedness, and deep devotion to the interest of the people." (Vol. III. p. 398.) "Isabella, discarding all the petty artifices of state policy and pursuing the noblest ends by the noblest means, stands far above her age;" "she was solicitous for everything that concerned the welfare of her people." This is high praise; but laying aside the rules of chivalry let us look in the spirit of humanity. The great political work of this reign was the establishment of national unity of action. Spain had been divided into many kingdoms; the separate provinces of each had been united by a feeble tie; the power of the king was resisted and diminished by the authority of the great barons, and thus the nation was distracted, and its power weakened. Under these sovereigns the different kingdoms were formed into one; the several provinces were closely united, the great barons were humbled and brought into dependence upon the throne; and thus national unity of action established by the might of a great central power. To accomplish this work, the first thing to be done after the marriage of Ferdinand and Isabella, was to diminish the power of the nobles. The same problem was getting solved in other countries at the same time. In some countries, as the nobles lost power, the cities, with their charters, gained it; the communes, the guilds, in short, the people, in one form or another, got an increase of political power. But in Spain it was not so. As power receded from the nobles it fell into the hands of the king. The people only gained domestic tranquillity, not practical political power, or the theoretic recognition of their rights. Ferdinand and Isabella were both jealous of the Cortes. Once, when Isabella wanted the Cortes of Arragon to declare her daughter their future sovereign, and they refused, she exclaimed, "It would be better to reduce the country by arms at once than endure this insolence of the Cortes." (Part II. Ch. II. p. 362.) After Isabella's death Ferdinand for a long time neglected to convene the Cortes. (Vol. III. p. 284.) Once he obtained a dispensation from the Pope, allowing him to cancel his engagement with the Cortes. (Ibid. p. 393, note 53.) In the first two years of her reign, Isabella called three meetings of the Cortes—of the popular branch alone. The motive was plain: she wanted to reduce the power of the nobles, and the commons were the appropriate tool. After this work was done, the sessions became rare. She made the Hermandad take the place of the Cortes, to the great detriment of popular liberty. But in 1506 the foolish Cortes, either incited by the court or stimulated by the Spanish desire of monopoly, complained that the right of representation was extended too far. Both Ferdinand and Isabella "were averse to meetings of the Cortes in Castile oftener than absolutely necessary, and both took care on such occasions to have their own agents near the deputies to influence their proceedings" (Part II. Ch. XXVI. p. 444, note 34), and to make the deputies understand that they had not so much power as they fancied. If Isabella had all the superlative qualities which Mr Prescott and others also ascribe to her, the result must have been different.

We will not deny that Isabella did much for the nation—much to establish internal tranquillity; much to promote the security of property and person. The first thing mentioned by Don Clemencin—the restoration of the currency from its debased condition—if taken alone, was highly important. She elevated men of worth to high stations, though they were men of mean birth; doubtless this was done in part to show the nobles that she could dispense with them in places which they had long monopolized; still she knew how to distinguish between the accidents and the substance of a man, and chose her counsellors accordingly. Her management of the affairs of the Church displayed no little skill and much energy. She kept the Church from the incursions of the Pope,—a task not so difficult as it would have been a century or two before, for the papal power was visibly on the wane; still, on the whole, we must confess that she did little to elevate the religious character of the clergy or the people.

Did she encourage letters and establish printing-presses? few great works were published in Spain: the Lives of Saints, treatises in honour of the Virgin, books of "Sacred Offices," and fulminations against Moors, Jews, and heretics; Papal Bulls, and the works of Raymond Lully—such were the books which the Spaniards printed and devoured in the fifteenth century. The works of Sallust were the most important works issued from the press of Valencia in that century. Did she encourage science? it bore no fruits which the nation has aspired to gather from the Spanish tree; poetry? little was brought to pass which could rival the best works of former days. In theology, with the exception of the Polyglot and the publication of the Bible in the Limousin dialect, certainly a surprising event in that age, little was done—nothing worthy of note. Under a hand so despotic, and under the eye of the Inquisition which Isabella had established, what could a Spaniard effect? It must be confessed that Isabella did not foster the greatest interests of the nation. The publication of proclamations which had the force of law (pragmaticas), so frequent in her reign, shows plainly enough her desire to rule without the advice of the people whose constitution she thereby violated. It matters not that they purport to be made at the demand of the Cortes, at the request of corporate cities, or of prominent men. Even in America we could find here and there a man in the Senate of the United States who would recommend a powerful President to do the same—perhaps a city or even a state to advise it. Those proclamations were the passing-bell of popular freedom. Even if they did not, as Mr Prescott assures us, intrench on the principles of criminal law, or affect the transfer of property, they not less undermined the liberty of Castile. The Cortes of Valladolid, foolish as it was in other respects, was right in remonstrating against those pragmaticas. Mr Prescott mentions several causes which contributed to increase the royal power at the expense of the people: the control of the military and ecclesiastical orders; the pensions and large domains; the fortified places; the rights of seigneurial jurisdiction; the increase of power over the Moors; the acquisition of territory in Italy, and the discovery of a new continent; but he omits the one cause which gave force to all these—the selfish disposition that counted political power as a right, which the monarch might use for her own advantage, not a trust which she must administer by the rules of justice, and for the good of all her subjects. This was the cause which enfeebled the people after it had broken their noble tyrants to pieces. The rights of the people were continually abridged. In 1495, the nobles and the representatives of the cities complained that the people were without arms. Mr Prescott thinks this fact a proof that they were in a fortunate condition, not remembering that in such an age an armed people was what the Constitution is to America; what the British Parliament and acknowledged law are to England—the one great barrier against the incursions of the crown. She found the people burthened with an odious tax, imposed for a temporary emergency, and continued through the inertia of the Cortes and the tyranny of the crown. Isabella had conscientious scruples about this tax, but continued it. Monopolies were established by this queen, who is represented as so far before her time: goods must not be shipped in foreign vessels when a Spanish bottom could be had; no vessel must be sold to a foreigner; even horses were not allowed to be exported; gold and silver must not be sent out of Spain on pain of death. Yet when she forbade the exportation thereof by her commercial policy, by sumptuary laws she forbade their use at home. There are four things which will long continue as the indelible monuments of her reign: the establishment of the Inquisition for the torture and murder of her subjects; the expulsion of the Jews and the Moors; the enslaving of the Indians in America, and the establishment of Negro Slavery there. With this we leave her and her memory, to speak on the general form and style of this work.

It is no part of our plan to criticise the account of civil and military transactions; but so far as we have examined his authorities, Mr Prescott is remarkably accurate. Some errors will always escape the vigilance of an author; in this case they are rare and unimportant. The whole work is divided into three portions: an Introduction; a History of the Domestic Policy of Ferdinand and Isabella (Part I.), and a History of their Foreign Policy, their Discoveries and Conquests (Part II.). The main division is a good one, the minuter division into chapters is judicious, and the chapters well arranged. In separate chapters the author treats of various subjects, so as not to confuse the reader. But we notice several defects in the matter and style of the work. There is no description of the large towns; no account of their history, the growth or decline of their population; of their relation to the villages and hamlets; of the political tendencies of their inhabitants. A brief description of Madrid, Toledo, and Seville, of Barcelona and Valencia, would be of great value to one who wished to understand the age; the materials for this are not wanting.

Again, his portraits of distinguished men are not good; they often lack distinctness and specific character. We have a right to demand a careful analysis of the character of such men as Columbus, Gonsalvo, and Ximenes; an historian never does his duty completely until he gives us a picture of each prominent man of the times he describes. Portraits of men like Torquemada, Fonseca, Carillo, and Mendoza,—the Archbishops of Toledo and Seville—of Bayard and Foix, of the monarchs of those times, and of the other eminent foreigners who come upon the stage, ought to have a place in a work like this.

The author does not present himself to his readers as a philosopher who knows man scientifically, and therefore has an *à priori* knowledge of men; nor does he appear as a man of the world, who knows men by a wide practical acquaintance with them. In consequence of this twofold defect the reader finds neither the careful judgment of the philosopher uor the practical judgment of the man of affairs. Both of these defects appear frequently in this work;—for example, in his general review of the administration of Ferdinand and Isabella, which is not written in the spirit of the statesman, or the spirit of the philosopher, but of an amiable gentleman of letters filled with the spirit of chivalry.

The book lacks philosophy to a degree exceeding belief. The author seems to know nothing of the philosophy of history, and little, even, of political economy. He narrates events in their order of time, with considerable skill, but the causes of the events, their place in the general history of the race, or their influence in special on the welfare of the nation, he does not appreciate. He tells the fact for the fact's sake. Hence there are no pages in the book, perhaps no sentences, which the reader turns back to read a second time, to see if the thought be true; here are the facts of history without the thought which belongs to the facts. It would be difficult to find a history in the English language, of any note, so entirely destitute of philosophy. Accordingly, the work is dull and inanimate; the reading thereof tiresome and not profitable. Thus lacking philosophy, and having more of the spirit of chivalry than of humanity, it is impossible that he should write in the interest of mankind, or judge men and their deeds by justice—by the immutable law of the universe. After long and patient study of his special theme, Mr Prescott writes with the average sense of mankind, with their average of conscience—and his judgment, the average judgment of a trading town, is readily accepted by the average of men, and popular with them; but he writes as one with little sympathy for mankind, and seems to think that Spain belonged to Ferdinand and Isabella; that their power was a right and not a trust, and they not accountable for the guardianship which they exercised over their subjects. The style of the work is plain, unambitious, and easily intelligible. The language, the figures of speech, the logic, and the rhetoric are commonplace; like the judgment of the author, they indicate no originality, and do not bear the stamp of his character. There is a certain mannerism about them, but it is not the mannerism of Mr Prescott,—only of the class of well-bred men. His metaphors, which usually mark the man, are commonplace and poor; rarely original or beautiful. Here are some examples: To "spread like wildfire;" to act "like desperate gamblers;" to run "like so many frighted deer;" to extend "like an army of locusts;" to be "like a garden." He calls womankind "the sex;" not a very elegant or agreeable title. There is a slight tendency to excess in his use of epithets; sometimes he insinuates an opinion which he does not broadly assert, rhetorically understanding the truth. In his style there is little to attract, nothing to repel, nothing even to offend; he is never tawdry, seldom extravagant; never ill-natured. If he finds an author in error, he takes no pleasure in pointing out the mistake. Everywhere he displays the marks of a well-bred gentleman of letters; this is more than can be said of the Reviewer we have alluded to before. After long study of this work, we take leave of the author, with an abiding impression of a careful scholar, diligent and laborious; an amiable man, who respects the feelings of his fellows, and would pass gently over their failings; a courteous and accomplished gentleman, who, after long toil, has unexpectedly found that toil repaid with money and with honours,—and wears the honours with the same modesty in which they have been won.

PRESCOTT'S CONQUEST OF MEXICO.

History of the Conquest of Mexico. With a Preliminary View of the Ancient Mexican Civilization, and the Life of the Conqueror, Hernando Cortés. By WILLIAM H. PRESCOTT, author of the "History of Ferdinand and Isabella," &c. &c. In three volumes. New York. 1844.

AFTER Mr Prescott had finished his History of the Reign of Ferdinand and Isabella, noticed in the previous article, several important subjects seemed naturally to claim his attention: these were the Discovery of America, and the Reign of Charles V. But the first of these had already been described by the graceful pen of Mr Irving, adorning what it touches; the second had been treated by Dr Robertson in a work of great though declining celebrity, and rendered attractive by a pleasing style, which often conceals the superficiality of the author's research, the shallowness of his political philosophy, and the inhumanity of his conclusions. Few men would wish to enter the literary career, and run the race with such distinguished rivals. A broader field yet remained, more interesting to the philosopher and the lover of mankind; namely, the Conquest and Colonization of America by the Spaniards. On this theme Mr Prescott has written two independent works, of wide popularity. Of the first of those we now propose to speak, only premising what we said before in respect to the office and duty of an historian.

The new world was discovered in the reign of Ferdinand and Isabella; its islands and continents, though not for the first time,* laid open to the eye of civilized Europe. The greater part of America was found to be thinly peopled by a single race of men, different in many respects from the inhabitants of the eastern hemisphere. A large part of the new world was inhabited by tribes, not only not civilized, but not even barbarous; the nations were eminently savage, though most of them were far removed from the lowest stage of human life, still represented by the Esquimaux, the New-Hollanders, and the Bushmans of South Africa. The French, the English, and the Dutch, in their North American settlements, came in contact with the barbarous portion of the nations, who had a little agriculture, it is true, but subsisted chiefly on the spontaneous products of the forest and the flood. But some tribes had advanced far beyond this state: some had ceased to be barbarous. There was an indigenous and original civilization in America. Attempts have often been made to trace this civilization to the old world; to connect it now with the Tyrians, now with the Egyptians, and then with the Hebrews or roving Tartars. Sometimes the attempt

* *Massachusetts Quarterly Review*, No. VI. Article III.

has been guided by philology, which makes language the basis of comparison; sometimes by physiology, and scientific men have sought in the bodies of the red Americans to discover some trace of the stock they sprung from; sometimes by theology, which seeks the affinity indicated by kindred forms of religion. But commonly inquirers have started with the theological prejudice that all men are descended from the single primitive pair mentioned in the Hebrew myth, and have bent philology, physiology, and theology to conform to their gratuitous assumption. Hitherto these attempts have been in vain. Even the lamented Mr Prichard, who had this theological prejudice in the heroic degree,—small for an English theologian, indeed, but great for a philosopher, as he certainly was, a prejudice which appears throughout his researches into the physical history of mankind,—fails to connect the American civilization with that of any other race. We therefore take it for granted, in the present stage of the inquiry, that it was original and indigenous. Geologists inform us that the western continent appears older than the eastern. If it be so, perhaps the American aborigines are the oldest race now in existence, and may look down on the bearded and pale Caucasians as upstarts in the world. If this be true, the red man has not advanced so rapidly in civilization as the white: this seems owing to the inferior organization of the former, and also to the absence of swine, sheep, horses, oxen, and large animals capable of being tamed, which in the eastern continent have so powerfully aided the progress of civilization. The man who would tame the sheep and the ox, must tame also himself. The domestication of animals, those living machines of an earlier age, once promoted the progress of civilization as much as the invention of machinery at this day. The camel, the ship of the desert, and the steamboat, the ship of the sea, have each something to do in ferrying man out of barbarism.

After the discovery of America, the Spaniard soon came in contact with the more advanced tribes of red men, contended with and overcame them, partly in virtue of his superior development, but partly also through the aboriginal and organic superiority which marks the Caucasian race in all historical stages of their progress, and appears in every conflict with any kindred race. This indigenous American civilization had two centres, or mother-cities, mainly independent of one another, if not entirely so—Mexico and Peru. The chief seats thereof were soon reached by the Spaniards, and conquered; the advanced tribes reduced to subjection, to slavery, or to death. The European brought there two things, wholly unheard of before—the doctrines of Christianity and a sword of steel, each thought to be the ally of the other in the conqueror's hand.

Here is a theme more important, and therefore more profoundly interesting, than the Lives of Columbus and his followers, or the Reign of Charles the Fifth, though both of those bring great events before the thinker's eye;—certainly the biography of Columbus, of Amerigo, Cabot, and Verrazzani, would offer an attractive field to a thinking man. A philosophic historian would delight in a land newly discovered. Its geography, botany, and zoölogy were all new to the eastern world; there were tribes unheard of before, with a peculiar physical structure, language, literature, manners, arts, laws, institutions, and forms of religion unlike the old. It were a noble task for the naturalist to describe this virgin America, as she appeared in the fifteenth century, when she first stood unveiled before the European eye.

In ages before the historical period, the Caucasian race had taken possession of the fairest portions of the ancient world. Now, for the first time during many ages, on a grand scale it encounters another race. For the first time in human history, the white man and the red man fairly meet. These two families, so dissimilar in natural character, so unlike in their development, now join in war, in wedlock, and at length mingle in political union. Ethnographers of this day somewhat obscurely maintain that the mingling of tribes, if not races, is an essential condition of progress. It would be instructive to pause over the facts, and consider what influence in this case each race has had on the other, and their union on the world. Never before in the historical age had two races thus met, nor two independent civilizations, with modes of religion so dissimilar, thus come together. In the great wars which the classic nations engaged in, the two parties were commonly of the same stock. Even in the expeditions of Sesostris, of Xerxes, and of Alexander, it was Caucasian that met Caucasian. The same is true, perhaps in its full extent, of the expeditions of Hannibal and of the Moors. In all the wars from that of Troy to the Crusades, the heroes on both sides were of the same stock. The nations that we meet in history, from Thule to the "fabulous Hydaspes," all are Caucasians—differing indeed in development and specific character, but alike in their great, general peculiarities. Other races appear only in the background of history, among the classic, the Shemitish, or the East-Indian nations; but seldom even there, and not as actors in the great drama of human civilization.

The Spanish colonies afford the best known example of the mingling of men of different races. The Anglo-Saxon is eminently Caucasian: he also met the red men. But the Saxon, though like other conquerors forgetting his dignity in loose amours, will not mix his proud blood, in stable wedlock, with another race. There seems a national antipathy to such unions with the black, or even the red, or yellow races of men—an antipathy almost peculiar to this remarkable tribe, the exterminator of other races. In New-England more pains were taken than elsewhere in America to spare, to civilize, and to convert the sons of the wilderness; but yet here the distinction of race was always sharply observed. Even community of religion and liturgical rites, elsewhere so powerful a bond of union, was unable to soften the Englishman's repugnance to the Indian. The Puritan hoped to meet the Pequods in heaven, but wished to keep apart from them on earth, nay, to exterminate them from the land. Besides, the English met with no civilized tribe in America, and for them to unite in wedlock with such children of the forest as they found in North America would have been contrary, not only to the Anglo-Saxon prejudice of race, but to the general usage of the world—a usage to which even the French in Canada afford but a trifling exception. The Spaniards had less of this exclusiveness of race, perhaps none at all. They met with civilized tribes of red men, met and mingled in honourable and permanent connection. In Peru and Mexico, at this day, there are few men of pure Spanish blood.

All the historical forms of religion which have prevailed in Europe, and the parts of Asia inhabited by the Caucasians, seem to have sprung from a common stock. Perhaps this is not true, but at least their resemblances may often be accounted for by reference to some actual union, to their historical genealogy; not wholly by reference to human nature; their agreement is specific, not merely generic. But the forms of religion that prevailed in America seem to have no historical element in common with those of the eastern world. When they agree, as they often do, and in their most important features, the agreement is generic, referrible to the identity of human nature acting under similar conditions; it is not specific, or to be explained by reference to history, to community of tradition. It is the same human nature which appears in all races, and accordingly many, especially religious, institutions have a marked likeness all over the world, but the individual peculiarity of each race appears also in those institutions. The civilization of the Caucasian tribes in the eastern world, powerfully affected by their religious institutions, seems to have been propagated by offsets and cuttings from some primeval tree, and only modified by circumstances and degrees of development; so there is an historical element common to all those nations. It appears in their manners, dress, and military weapons; in their agriculture, from the east to the west, where the same staple articles of culture appear, and the same animals—the cereal grasses, the sheep, the goat, the swine, the horse, and the ox; in their arts, useful and beautiful; in their politics, their morals, their forms of religion; in their literature, and even in the structure of their language itself, so deep-rooted is the idiosyncrasy of race. In America, to judge from the present state of ethnographic investigation, it seems that another seed, independent and likewise aboriginal, got planted, came up, grew, and bore fruit after its kind. This also was propagated by cuttings and offsets, so to say; its descendants had spread from the land of the Esquimaux to Patagonia. Here, as in the other hemisphere, the race became specifically modified by external circumstances, and the degree of development. Still there is a generic element common to all the tribes of America, running through their civilization, and apparent in their institutions. The idiosyncracy of race appears here also, conspicuous and powerful as there.

This diversity of race and the analogous difference between the two civilizations brought into such close connection, renders the history of the Spanish settlements in America exceedingly interesting to a philosophical inquirer: the English colonies are interesting on account of the ideas they brought hither and developed, and the influence those ideas have had on the world; the Spanish settlements are chiefly interesting on account of the facts they bring to light. Under these circumstances, it becomes the duty of the historian, who will write a book worthy of his theme, to note the effect of this mingling of races and of civilizations; he is not merely to tell who was killed, and who wounded, on which side of the river each one fought, and how deep the water was between them, or how bloody it ran; he is to describe the civilization of the nations, giving, however briefly, all the important features thereof, and then show the effect of the meeting of the two.

More than three centuries have passed by since the Mexican conquest was complete. During that time great revolutions have taken place in the world,—theological, political, and social. A great progress has been made in the arts, in science, in morals and religion,—in the subjective development thereof as piety, the objective application to life in the form of practical morality. But the Spanish-Americans have but a small share in that progress; they seem to have done nothing to promote it. They have not kept pace with the Anglo-American colonies; not even with the French. It is pretty clear that the population of Spanish North America—continental and insular—is less numerous now than when Columbus first crossed the sea. The condition of the Americans in many respects is improved. Still it may be reasonably doubted if the population of Mexico is happier to-day than four hundred years ago. What is the cause of this: have the two races been weakened by their union; were the Mexicans incapable of further advance; or were the Spaniards unable to aid them? The Europeans gave the Indian most valuable material helps to civilization—cattle, swine, sheep, goats, asses, horses, oxen, the cereal grasses of the East, iron, and gunpowder; ideal helps also in the doctrines of Christianity;—the machinery of the old world. In another work, Mr Prescott declares the Moorish civilization incapable of continuing, as it had in its bosom the causes of its ruin. Is the same thing true of the Spanish civilization? Surely it cannot stand before the slow, strong, steady wave of the Anglo-Saxon tide, which seems destined ere long to sweep it off, or hide it in its own ample bosom. The consequence is always in the cause; there but hidden. The historian of the conquest of Mexico, writing so long after the events he chronicles, while those consequences are patent to all the world, might describe to us the cause; nay, the history is not adequately written until this is done. Without this, a work is history without its meaning—without philosophy. We must complain of Mr Prescott's work, in general, that he has omitted this its most important part. True, he was only writing of the conquest of the country and the immediate colonization; but this is not adequately described until the other work is done.

Not only has Mr Prescott an attractive theme—obvious facts and glittering deeds, to attract all men and satisfy the superficial, and larger, more general facts of a profound significance, to pause upon and explain—but the materials for his work are abundant. There are the narratives of men personally engaged in the expeditions they write of—men like Bernal Diaz and Gomara; official documents like the letters of Cortés; early histories, as that of Solís; works on the antiquities of Mexico, like that of Clavigero, and the magnificent volumes published by Lord Kingsborough. Then there are works written by men themselves descended from the Mexicans. In addition to printed volumes, Mr Prescott has richly supplied himself with such manuscript treasures of Spanish history as few American eyes ever behold. He has at his command about eight thousand folio pages of the works of Las Casas, Ixtlilxochitl, Toribio, Camargo, Oviedo, and others. Public and private collections abroad have been opened to him with just and scholarlike liberality.

If we divide Mr Prescott's work according to its substance, it consists of three parts:—the first relates to Mexico, its inhabitants and their civilization; the second to the conquest of Mexico; and the third to the subsequent career of Cortés. In respect of its form, the volumes are divided into seven books, treating respectively of the Aztec civilization, of the discovery of Mexico, the march thither, the residence there, the expulsion thence, the siege and surrender of the city, and the subsequent career of Cortés. A valuable appendix is added, and a copious index, the latter quite too uncommon in American books.

This history has been so much admired, so widely circulated in America and Europe, and so abundantly read, that, as in the former article, we shall take it for granted that our readers are familiar with the work, and spare them our analysis thereof. We shall also presuppose that the well-informed reader is sufficiently familiar with the writings of Diaz and Solís, with the printed works of Las Casas, with Clavigero, Herrera, and the original accounts published at Madrid, a hundred years ago, in the collection of "Historiadores primitivos."

We now propose to examine this history of the conquest of Mexico somewhat in detail, and to say a word of each of the three grand divisions of the subject. We will speak first of the civilization of the Aztecs. Mr Prescott's account of the geography of Mexico, with his description of the country, is attractive and graphic. It seems to be sufficient; we only regret the absence of a more extended map. With only the ordinary maps the reader is often puzzled in trying to make out the exact position of a place, and accordingly he cannot always understand the account of a battle or the description of a march. The two small maps (in Vols. I. and II.) are of great service, and were prepared with much care, but are not adequate to render all parts of the text intelligible: thus Itztapalapan (Vol. III. p. 6) is said to stand "on a narrow tongue of land which divides the waters of the great salt lake from those of the fresh," while on the map no such narrow tongue exists, and the reader must seek it in Clavigero or elsewhere. But this is a trifle.

In Mexico Mr Prescott finds four important tribes, or "races." The most conspicuous of these are the Toltecs, who came from the North before the end of the seventh century, and in the eleventh century "disappeared from the land as silently and mysteriously as they had entered it;" the Chichemecs, a numerous and rude tribe who came from the North-west in the twelfth century, and were soon "followed by other races of higher civilization, perhaps of the same family with the Toltecs;" the most noted of these tribes were the Aztecs, or Mexicans, and the Acolhuans, or Tezcucans. The civilization of the Toltecs was communicated to the Tezcucans, and by them to the Chichemecs.

Of these four tribes—Toltecs, Chichemecs, Tezcucans, and Aztecs—the latter have become the most celebrated. They are the Mexicans, and by that name we shall designate them in what follows. After encountering various fortunes in the land, they came to the valley of Mexico in the year 1325, A.D., according to Mr Prescott, where they subsequently built Tenochtitlan, the city of Mexico. The Mexicans were a warlike people, and in less than two centuries their empire extended from shore to shore. This rapid enlargement of their power proves the martial vigour of the tribe, and their skill in forming political organizations — though Mr Prescott seems to doubt their political ability. But as the Mexican empire was composed of several nations recently conquered and united almost entirely by external force, it is plain it contained heterogeneous elements which might easily be separated. Like the old Roman and all other states thus formed, it was a piece of carpentry, artificially held together by outward circumstances, not a regular growth, where the branch grows out of the bole, that out of the root, and all are united by a central principle and partake of a common origin and history.

Mr Prescott devotes four chapters to the civilization of Mexico, and one to Tezcuco. His materials are derived chiefly from Torquemada, Clavigero, Sahagun, Gama, the works which have appeared in France and England on the antiquities of Mexico, the writings of Boturini and Ixtlilxochitl. Of these authors Clavigero is the best known to general readers. Notwithstanding the advantage which Mr Prescott has in coming sixty years after the work of Clavigero was published, we must confess that on the whole the earlier writer has given the more satisfactory account of the matter. It is true, Clavigero had space to be minute and curious in particulars,—for nearly two of his four quarto volumes are devoted to the subject,—but his general arrangement is better, though by no means perfect or philosophical,—following an inward principle,—and his account of the Mexican institutions is on the whole more distinct as well as more complete. Yet in some details Mr Prescott surpasses his predecessor.

Mr Prescott gives an account, sufficiently lucid, of what may be called the Constitution of Mexico; he speaks intelligently of the royal power, which was both legislative and executive. He gives a good description of the judicial power, certainly a very remarkable institution for such a nation, and in many respects a very wise one. But his account of the nobles, of their power and position, is meagre and unsatisfactory. He does not tell us how the distinction of nobility was obtained.

What he says of the penal laws is still less satisfactory, or complete. The only punishments he mentions are death, slavery, reduction of rank, and confiscation of property. Clavigero adds confinement in prison and banishment from the country. Prisons as houses of punishment generally indicate a higher civilization than the penalty of death, or exile.

Clavigero has given the fuller and more satisfactory account of the Mexican system of slavery. He mentions also one important provision of the penal law omitted by Mr Prescott, that kidnapping was punished with death.

Mr Prescott's account of the manner of collecting the revenue is full and clear. The same must be said of his account of the military establishment of Mexico. Still the reader would be glad to know whether the soldiers were volunteers or conscripts, how they were fed, and, when successful in war, what share of the booty belonged to them. Clavigero mentions a significant fact, that there were three military orders, called Princes, Eagles, and Tigers (Achautin, Quauhtin, and Ocelo). Since the two last are titles of honour, as well as the first, they furnish an important monument of the ferocity of the nation.

The civilization of the Mexicans has been sometimes exalted above its merit; still it is plain they had attained a pretty high degree of culture. Yet it differed in many respects from that of the eastern nations: it was a civilization without the cereal grasses; without wine, milk, or honey; without swine, sheep, or goats; without the horse or the ass, or any beast of burthen; civilization without iron. Mexico seems to have been the centre of refinement for all North America. Agriculture, one of the earliest arts, seems to have travelled northward; the three great staples thereof among the natives of North America in the temperate zone—maize, beans, and various species of the pumpkin or squash—had journeyed from the Gulf of Mexico to the Bay of Fundy, and extended inland to the Rocky Mountains, covering a great extent of country where they were not indigenous, and could not exist but for the care of man.

In Mexico, the fundamental law or constitution was fixed and well understood. The monarchy was elective; though, by law or custom, the choice must be made from a certain family, still the chief was chosen for his personal qualities. Montezuma was distinguished as a soldier and a priest—compatible titles in many a land not otherwise very barbarous—before he was elected king. Throughout North America there seems to have been a general custom of choosing the ruler among the nephews rather than among the sons of the former chief.

The judicial power was carefully separated from the executive. The judges were appointed by the king or chosen by the people, and held their office for life or during good behaviour. The laws seem to have been well administered. Property was so secure that bolts and bars were not needed. Life, liberty, and the honour of women were carefully guarded, and seem to have been more secure than in Scotland at the same time. Lands were held in severalty and by a certain tenure. Almost all men held real estate in their own right. In the most densely peopled regions there was little land not improved; far less than at the present day, as we judge. The law of descent was fixed, and well understood. The right of testament was universal.

Historians tell us that the laws were written, and published to the people. We think they exaggerate the extent of a written law, and the power of the Mexicans to record laws with their imperfect mode of writing. Perhaps Mr Prescott with others has fallen into a slight error in this particular, though we do not say this with much confidence.

Slavery prevailed in a mild form. Men became slaves by judicial sentence, as a punishment for crime, by selling themselves, or from being sold by their parents. The slave could hold property, real or personal, and devise it to whom he would; he could own other slaves. This was not a privilege which the master might revoke, but a right at common law. The slave's life was, theoretically, sacred as the free man's. His children were all free. Nobility was hereditary, while slavery was merely a personal affair, and did not attaint the blood. Indeed, the slave was only a vassal, bound to render certain services to his feudal lord. This fact shows that the nation had emerged from that state where man is so lazy that only the slave can be made to endure continuous toil, and where Slavery is the chief handmaid of Industry.

The penal laws were severe; capital offences were numerous. Theft was punished with death, as it was until lately in England, if the property stolen exceeded five shillings in value. Imprisonment, fine, exile, and social degradation were legal punishments for certain crimes. The revenues of the nation were collected in a regular and constant form. As in most despotic countries, the taxes were enormous; but there seems no reason for supposing that they were so excessive as they have been for many years in the kingdom of Naples; perhaps they were not proportionately so great as in England at this day. Some of the nobles were exempt from taxation, but we know not whether this exemption was the reward of some extraordinary service, or, as in France before the Revolution, came purely from the selfishness of that class who had the power to withdraw their necks from the common yoke.

War was conducted in a systematic manner; regularly declared and commenced in a formal style. The arts of diplomacy were well known, and the rights of ambassadors respected. The military code was minute in its provisions. The arms of the Mexicans were well made and destructive. They used shields of wood, and body armour of quilted cotton. They had embattled fortifications of stone, well situated and constructed with skill. There were military hospitals for the sick and wounded soldier—institutions unknown to the Eastern world till long after the time of Christ; hospitals better than the Spanish, and supplied with surgeons more faithful.

Their cities were numerous and large, supplied with

water by aqueducts. There were many towns containing thirty thousand inhabitants; the capital contained at least three hundred thousand. In his second official letter, Cortés says that Tlascala was larger and much stronger than Granada when taken from the Moors; that it had more fine houses, and was better supplied with provisions. Thirty thousand persons were daily in its markets, to buy and sell. He says the exterior aspect of Cholula is more beautiful than any town in Spain. From a single temple (Mezquita) he counted four hundred other temples with towers. Houses were built of wood, of sun-dried bricks, and of stone. While in Spain labour was a disgrace, in Mexico it was held in honour. The calling of a merchant was honourable, and he sometimes rose to distinction in the State, a very remarkable circumstance in a nation so warlike. Trading in slaves seems to have been as respectable among the Catos of Mexico as of Rome. Agriculture was held in high and deserved esteem. The harder work in the fields was performed by the men; only the light work fell to the lot of women. Great pains were taken with the cultivation of flowers: ornamental gardening was better understood in Mexico than in Europe. In some places the land was artificially watered, as among the Moors in Spain. There were floating gardens on the lake of Mexico. In the large cities there were public gardens of great extent and beauty. Yet, though blessed with maize and potatoes, the Mexicans lacked the valuable staples of Eastern agriculture—the more useful grains, the vine, and the olive; they had no aid from the ox or the horse—not even from the humbler servant of the plough, the ass.

The mechanics wrought with adroitness and good taste, in wood, in stone, and in feather-work. Their earthen ware, says Cortés, was equal to the best in Spain. Cotton was manufactured and dyed with taste and skill. Gold and silver were abundant, and wrought with a dexterity which rivalled the best works of Venice and Seville, astonishing the artists of Europe. They used also copper, lead, and tin. It has been said—we doubt if correctly—that they did not know the power of fire to render metals more pliant under the hammer. Iron was unknown: in its place their cutting instruments were made of obsidian (itzli), a stone which takes a keen edge, though it is easily blunted.

For money they used gold-dust, bits of tin, and bags of cacao.

The public roads excited the admiration of the Spaniards, and were probably better than they left at home. Runners went with such speed, that despatches were carried one or two hundred miles in a day. Buildings were erected along the road side for their accommodation. Indeed, couriers went with such rapidity, that fish were caught in the Gulf of Mexico, and in twenty-four hours were two hundred miles off, in the kitchen of Montezuma.

There were botanic gardens in several Mexican cities, where the plants were scientifically arranged. Cortés mentions one two leagues in circumference; it contained an aviary,—for Mexico is the country of birds, as Africa of beasts,—and basins stocked with numerous varieties of fish. At that time such gardens were unknown in Europe.

The Mexicans had attained a considerable proficiency in science. They had a peculiar system of notation, counting by scores and not by tens:—first they took the five digits of one hand, then of the next, and in like manner the ten digits of the feet. They had made a measurement of the year more exact than that of the Greeks and Romans. Their week consisted of five days; four weeks, or twenty days, made a month. There were eighteen months in the year, and then five days were intercalated that belonged to no month. Thus their common civil year consisted of three hundred and sixty-five days. But in every one hundred and four years, it is said, they intercalated twenty-five days which belonged to no year. Thus their calendar was exceedingly exact, and in many years there would be no important difference between actual and calculated time. Their day was divided into sixteen hours; they had sundials for time-pieces; they understood the causes of an eclipse, and knew the periods of the solstices and the equinoxes.

Women shared in social festivities with the men. Polygamy was allowed, as throughout all North America, and as with the Hebrews before Christ; wealthy men, and especially kings, had many wives; yet the custom seems limited to such, as indeed it must have been everywhere.

The languages of the various nations of Mexico were remarkable for that peculiarity called agglutination by philologists, which characterizes all the dialects of America, with perhaps but a single exception, and forms the linguistic distinction of the American race. Their language was copious, regular, and comprehensive. The Mexicans had a rude mode of writing, by pictures and symbols, which enabled them to record events, to transmit and preserve information. By means of this help they recorded their laws, their judicial transactions, and wrote their civil history. They wrote poetry in the same manner. We would speak with becoming diffidence in this matter, which we certainly have not been able to investigate to our own satisfaction, and modestly express our fear that the art of writing among the Mexicans has been a good deal overrated. We doubt that an ordinary poem could be recorded in Mexican characters. Still, this art of writing seems to have been more perfect than the Egyptian in the time of the pyramids, as indeed their language was more copious and better developed, though greatly inferior to that of the Chinese.

There were schools for the education of the children. Elderly women, serving also as priestesses, took charge of the girls; the priests instructed the boys. The former learned various feminine employments, were taught to be modest, and to pay "entire obedience and respect to their husbands." Boys were taught to work and to fight; they were instructed in the art of writing; they learned the traditionary lore of their country, and studied such sciences as the Mexicans knew; they learned the principles of government, and were taught to hate vice and love virtue—to practise the duties of natural religion. To this, of course, was added an acquaintance with the national mythology, and the rites of the popular worship. This education was no doubt rude, and limited to a comparatively small portion of the people. There was a general Board of Education, called the Council of Music. All this, we suspect, is a good deal more complete on paper than it was in fact;—but Diaz informs us that Montezuma intended to keep some of the Spaniards, whom he hoped to conquer, for schoolmasters, and employ them in teaching the people.

In their religion the Mexicans were polytheists. It is not easy to get at the facts respecting this matter, for the authors we depend upon seem unconsciously to have lent a colouring to what they describe, and much of the Christian tradition or doctrine has got mingled with the opinions of the natives. But it is said that they believed in one supreme Creator; they addressed him as "the God by whom we live;" "invisible, incorporeal, one God, of perfect perfection and purity;" "under whose wing we find repose and a sure defence." There were other gods beside him; the most popular was their God of War, for the Mexicans were a ferocious people, and this peculiarity appears also in their mode of religion. In common with almost every nation of the earth, and perhaps with all, they believed in the immortality of the soul and the doctrine of future retribution. In the Mexican heaven there were two degrees of happiness, of which the warrior had the higher. The Roman poet had got beyond this. There were three degrees of punishment in hell. "Eternal damnation," it has been said, "is not learned by the mere light of nature, but is one of the truths of revelation;" so we suppose the Mexicans were indebted to their Spanish conquerors for this article of the creed. The priests were a distinct class, numerous and respected, and, as in nearly all countries, the best educated class. They served God with an abundance of forms, rites, ceremonies, fasts, and mortifications of the flesh,—according to Mr Prescott's quotation, "In hope to merit heaven by making earth a hell." However, in this respect their conquerors taught them many devices which the simple Mexicans did not know before. The Mexicans do not appear to have practised any ritual mutilation of the body as the Hebrews and Mahommedans do to this day. The priesthood was not hereditary, or even heritable, as it seems. It did not necessarily last for life. There was only a movable priesthood, not a caste perpetuating its traditions and its rites in a single family from age to age. The chief priest was elected, though it does not appear by whom. Some elderly women served as priestesses. The Mexicans had some rites which strangely resembled the Christian:—they baptized their children by sprinkling; the priests heard confession and gave absolution from sin, and, what is remarkable, this absolution not only was thought to save a man from future torment, but actually held good and gave deliverance in a court of justice on earth. There was a Mexican goddess, Cioacoatl was her name, who seems closely related to mother Eve; she was "the first goddess who brought forth;" she "bequeathed the sufferings of childbirth to women;" and by her "sin came into the world." There was also a Mexican Noah, Coxcox, who survived a deluge, and has often been taken for the mythical patriarch of the Hebrew legend.

There is much that is revolting in the worship of savage nations; some of the disgusting features thereof remain long after civilization has swept away civil and social monstrosities. The most hideous thing connected with the Mexican worship was the sacrifice of human beings. Human sacrifices have been common with all nations at certain stages of their development. The custom was well known among the Greeks and Romans: the story of Abraham is a lasting monument of its existence among the Hebrews. But in no country did this abomination prevail to so great a degree. To render the ghastly sacrifice still worse, the worshippers devoured the flesh of the victims. Cannibalism was solemnly practised throughout Mexico. Human blood was the holiest sacrament. The number of victims is variously stated: one authority mentions more than eighty thousand in a single day—an extraordinary occasion; others but fifty in a year, the estimate of Las Casas. Mr Prescott thinks it safe to admit that thousands were sacrificed each year. Diaz declares that there must have been more than a hundred thousand skulls of these victims in a single place, and Gomara relates that two companions of Cortés counted one hundred and thirty-six thousand in a single edifice. No apology can be attempted for such an abomination;—but the same thing is called by different names in different places. In thirty-five years King Henry VIII. put to death seventy-two thousand of his subjects by the hands of the public executioner; many thousand Moors were butchered by the Spanish soldiers, after resistance was over, in the time of Ferdinand and Isabella; a great number were put to death with more terrible torments by the most holy court of the Inquisition. A Mexican would write that all these were sacrificed to

God. Human sacrifices in Mexico excited the just horror of Cortés and his companions, while the butcheries in Spain perhaps did not disturb them at all. Few things can be conceived of more abhorrent than the human sacrifices and cannibalism of the Mexicans: their civilization deprived them of the excuse which shelters the Fiji and New Zealander. Yet these men-slaughterers endeavoured to mitigate the sufferings of their victims. Mr Prescott shows a just and hearty horror of this unnatural mode of worship. But one of their gods, Quetzalcoatl, it is said, taught "a more spiritualizing religion, in which the only sacrifices were the fruits and flowers of the season."

We come next to the conquest of Mexico by Cortés. He first heard the name of Montezuma about Easter, in 1519; on St Hippolytus' day, August 12th, 1521, the Spaniards carried the capital by assault, and the Mexican empire lay at their disposal. Montezuma had died a captive; Guatemozin, his successor, was in their hands. Yet Cortés invaded this powerful empire with but a handful of soldiers. When he left Cuba, February 10th, 1519, he had one hundred and ten mariners, five hundred and fifty-three soldiers, ten heavy guns, four falconets, and sixteen horses; he had also about two hundred Indians. Two horses were subsequently added, and eighteen men; fifteen men were sent away from the expedition, and there were other but inconsiderable losses. He actually began his march into Mexico with about four hundred foot, and fifteen horse, and seven pieces of artillery, such as it was. At the same time, he had also thirteen hundred Indian warriors and one thousand Tamanes or porters, men of burthen. The number of Indians was soon increased to three thousand. When he first entered Mexico against the will of the vacillating monarch, his whole force was less than seven thousand men; but four hundred of these were Spaniards. After he had been driven from the city, and had been reinforced by others of his countrymen who joined the expedition, when he reviewed his forces at Tezcuco, he had eighty-seven horse, eight hundred and eighteen foot, of whom one hundred and eight were arquebusiers and crossbowmen, three large field-pieces of iron, and fifteen smaller guns of brass.

Such were the forces with which Cortés invaded and

finally conquered a country containing more inhabitants, to say the least, than the kingdom of Spain, at that time, with a capital as large and populous as Seville and Cordova united, or twice as great as Milan. Certainly the most daring enterprise of ancient times becomes tame in comparison with this. True, there were some circumstances which favoured the enterprise. Had there been no dissensions in the Mexican empire, his attempt would have been in vain; without his Indian allies he would soon have been cut off. Then he was aided by the superstition of the times. There was a prophecy current among the Mexicans which Cortés was thought to fulfil. There was a story of Quetzalcoatl, a mythical person worshipped as a god; he had taught the Mexicans agriculture, the use of metals, and the arts of government, and opposed human sacrifices which he could not prevent; he had a fair complexion and a flowing beard, the patriarch of the golden age of Mexico; he had left the country, embarking for Tlapallan, the Mexican Eden, or Atlantis, but the prophecy said he would return and resume the possession of the empire. The Mexicans saw Cortés, and said: "This is Quetzalcoatl returned from Paradise." The Spaniards were "white gods." Montezuma himself seems to have shared this opinion. This "random shot of prophecy," as Mr Prescott calls it, seems to have hit the mark, and prepared the nation for conquest.

Then the Spaniards were Caucasians, and had the organic superiority of that race; besides, they were far in advance of the Mexicans in the art of war. They had horses, steel, ships, gunpowder, muskets, and cannon; they understood the value of concerted action, and of well-ordered movements on the field of battle; they had weapons of offence and defence far superior to those of their opponents. If Boston could be invaded by an army that should land at Provincetown, ascend in balloons, and from a single position reconnoitre the whole state of Massachusetts, and from the extremity of Cape Cod should bombard this city, levelling whole blocks of houses at a single shot; if they had swords which could pierce through a ploughshare as easily as silk or cotton cloth, and fire-arms which shot through the most solid walls of brick and stone as readily as a rifle-ball goes through a glass window; if they had animals trained to war, ten times larger than the elephant, as heavy as the largest locomotive steam-engine, swifter than that, and more difficult to encounter—beasts of war that trod down horse, foot, and dragoons, trampling the artillery itself into the ground; if, in addition to this, the invaders were clad in armour bullet-proof, were each stronger than ten common men, had a skill, a foresight, a daring, and a patient courage proportionate to their instruments of destruction, and a cruelty not inferior to their courage; and if, still more, it was currently believed that the Book of Revelations had predicted that they should come and conquer the land; if whole countries were ready to help the invaders,—then we should be confronted with foes which would bear about the same relation to us that the Spaniards bore to the Mexicans. Considering all these things, the success of the conquerors, marvellous as it appears, is less remarkable than the courage and patience with which the Mexicans resisted the attack. Had the Spaniards known the full extent of the difficulty, even the iron heart of Cortés must have failed within him.

But we must ask, What RIGHT had the Spaniards to invade Mexico and possess themselves of its soil? Mr Prescott examines this question in an unsatisfactory manner, and, we are sorry to say it, gives an unjust answer, but in accordance with the spirit in which his three historical works have been written. An unprejudiced man must say the Spaniards had no claim to Mexico, but that of the stout and well-armed highwayman to the purse of the undefended traveller; the right of the pirate over the unprotected ship of the merchant. It is true, the Spanish monarch had a conveyance from the Pope, which in reality gave no better title, and was worth no more than the compendious transfer offered by the tempter in the Bible—"all these will I give thee if thou wilt fall down and worship me." Neither Pope nor Satan could alienate and convey what he did not possess. We think it cannot be maintained in natural law that a savage tribe has a right to arrest civilization in any given spot, to keep a continent for a hunting-field dwelt in by a few wild beasts and wild men. It is commonly, perhaps universally, conceded that a nation has eminent domain over the lands of the individual, and allows him to hold them in individual severalty for his private welfare when not adverse to the general good of the State; even to bequeath them to his successor, subject to the same condition. So the human race has eminent domain over the lands of each particular nation, allowing it to hold in national severalty for the nation's welfare, when not adverse to the universal good of mankind. As there is a solidarity of the nation, so is there of the race, and rights and duties, national or universal, thence accruing. But when the nation takes the lands of the individual, which he has a good natural title to, they must fully indemnify that individual for his lands, else it is robbery; and robbery by a nation, and for the sake of the greatest majority of its citizens, is no better in itself than if done by one man in his own name,—it is still robbery, spoliation contrary to natural law. The same holds good between any one nation and mankind, between the savage and the civilized who may assume to represent the consciousness of mankind. This idea seems to have been in the mind of the settlers of New-England; if not in their mind, they acted as if it were. The pilgrim and the puritan knew that the naked savages of Massachusetts had no natural right, adverse to the welfare of the human race, no right to keep the land a wilderness and shut civilization out of it for ever; but they knew, also, that though the civilized man represented the higher consciousness of mankind, and, so far as that went, represented the human race, still he had no right, whatever necessity compelled him, to take from the savages, against their will, all that they had or anything that they had, without returning them a complete equivalent therefor. So these settlers of New-England did not rely on the grant of the English king for their title to the Indian land; they bought it of the Indians, took a deed, recorded the transfer, and honestly paid for it—a small consideration, but enough to extinguish the title, and more than it was worth to the Indians themselves. But in New-England no Indian owned land in severalty, more than wind and water, excepting the spot his wigwam covered, and the little patch subjected to the rude tillage of his wife. These were the only spots with which he had mixed up his labour. There was enough for all, and therefore personal and exclusive appropriation had hardly begun. At the merest caprice, the Indian left his place to whomsoever might take it, and himself sought another—as free as the beaver or the wild-cat, who like him respected the appropriation of another. This tract belonged to the Narragansetts, that to the Pequods. There was appropriation by the tribe, not by the individual. The title of the Narragansetts was good as against the Pequods, or any other tribe, but each man of that tribe took any of the national lands not previously appropriated, as freely as he took the air and the water which was not in another man's mouth. The chief of the tribe seems to have acted as trustee, and in that capacity gave his quitclaim deed to the chief of the white men, acting in behalf of the rest, and conveyed away the title of the tribe. The Indian parted with his land for a "good consideration," for "value received."

In Mexico the case was quite different. Almost all the valuable land was owned in severalty; individuals had mixed their labour with the soil, owning it as much as they owned the fish-hook they had made, or the ear of corn they had grown; owned it as completely as a man can own the soil. The Mexicans were a civilized people; the lands in the valley of Mexico were as well cultivated as the lands in Granada, the garden of Europe; the natives had not stopped in their progress, as Mr Prescott thinks the Moors had done in Spain, and their land therefore could not be claimed as a derelict of civilization; on the contrary, they seem to have been in a state of rapid advance, as much so as the Spanish nation itself. The superior culture of the Spaniard gave him no right to these lands without indemnifying the individual owners,—no more than the English have to China, or the Dutch to Turkey; no more than the New-Englanders would have to seize Spain and Italy at this day. The Spaniard could not plead necessity, like the pilgrims,—poor, persecuted, and just escaped from the ocean,—who took a fish and some corn in their extremity, when they landed on Cape Cod, and carefully paid for both when, months afterwards, they found the owners! Oppression never planted a single Spaniard in America. The Moors were not allowed to migrate thither, under the administration of Ferdinand and Isabella. The Spaniards did not attempt or pretend to buy a title to the land. Their claim was the claim of the pirate. It is true, the Pope, as head of the human race, trustee for all mankind, and vicegerent of Almighty God, gave a title to America. Could Cortés and the others hold under that? Mr Prescott thinks they could satisfy their own consciences in that way, and though the conveyance were worthless in itself, they would be subjectively in the right. But the Pope gave a grant of lands subject to this condition: the heathen must be converted. If that were not done, the title failed through breach of covenant. We shall see how this was attended to.

Mr Prescott says the desire of converting the natives was "paramount to every calculation of personal interest in the breast of Cortés." (Vol. II. p. 32 et al.) We are amazed at a statement so gratuitous and irreconcilable with the facts of the case; we should say that the calculation of personal interest was always paramount to the desire of converting the natives. Mr Prescott says, "There was nothing which the Spanish government had more earnestly at heart than the conversion of the Indians." (Vol. I. p. 269.) We wish there were some facts to sustain the assertion. It is true, a pretence was often made of a desire to Christianize the Indians. Velasquez instructs Cortés "to bear in mind, above all things, that the object which the Spanish monarch had most at heart, was the conversion of the Indians;" he was, however, to impress on them the grandeur and goodness of his royal master, and to invite them "to give in their allegiance to him, and to manifest it by regaling him with such comfortable presents of gold, pearls, and precious stones, as, by showing their good will, would secure his favour and protection." Imagine, oh gentle or simple readers, imagine the American board of foreign missionaries sending out their servants to China with such instructions, asking for "comfortable presents" of silks, and Sycee silver, and tea! Imagine, also, the admiration of the Castilian court, if Cortés had believed that "the conversion of the Indians" was "the object which the Spanish monarch had most at heart," and had converted the whole of Mexico, overturned every idol, sending them all as trophies to his "most noble, powerful, and catholic prince, invincible emperor, and our sovereign lord," planted the cross on every *teocalli*, but the Spanish flag nowhere, and had not sent home a single ounce of gold, nor gained an inch of land! Imagine the honours, the triumphal processions, that would have been his welcome home to old Castile! Mr Prescott, in the very teeth of facts, maintains that Cortés took this part of his instructions to the letter, and with him that the conversion of the natives was paramount "to every calculation of personal interest." His "first object," says Mr Prescott, "was to reclaim the natives from their gross idolatry, and to substitute a purer form of worship. . . . He was prepared to use force if milder means should prove ineffectual." (Vol. I. p. 269.) He felt "he had a high mission to perform as a soldier of the cross." Cortés comes to St Juan de Ulloa, as it is now called, and invites the natives "to abandon their cursed idols, abolish human sacrifices, and abstain from kidnapping." Everybody knows the fable of the Fox turned Preacher; it is less remarkable than the historical and kindred fable of Cortés turned missionary.

This confessor of the faith, this missionary of the Lord, this great first apostle to the Gentiles of Tenochtitlan, comes to Tabasco, full of war and Christianity, resolved, as Mr Prescott confesses, to build

> "his faith upon
> The holy text of pike and gun."

The natives opposed the entrance of armed strangers, as the Dutch or the Portuguese would have done. Cortés made proclamation, and assured them that "if blood were spilt, the sin would lie on their heads." They answered with shouts of defiance and a shower of arrows. He took the town, and two days after had a severe battle with the inhabitants of the country. Of course the Spaniards were victorious, and the Indians suffered great loss: some say one thousand were slain, some thirty thousand. The battle was fought on Lady Day, the day of the miraculous conception of the mother of God. The battle was a good type of the "annunciation" brought by this new Gabriel to the American Virgin. As the primitive Christians, it is said, had miraculous assistance in wielding their spiritual weapons, so these devout heralds of the faith, "soldiers of the cross," and "followers of the Lamb," had aid from on high —a celestial champion "mounted on his grey war-horse, heading the rescue, and trampling over the bodies of the fallen infidels!" Cortés thought it was his own tutelary saint,—Saint Peter, a patron not wholly unsuitable for such a client,—"but," says Pizarro y Orellana, "the common and indubitable opinion is, that it was our glorious apostle, Saint James, the bulwark and safeguard of the nation." After the battle the Indians were "converted," and the event celebrated on Palm Sunday. "Behold thy King cometh unto thee meek" must have been sung with great unction that sabbath morn, and the lesson for the day, "Come unto me, ye that labour and are heavy laden," must have delighted Saint Peter and Saint James, heard "in this connection!" A city was afterwards built on the battle-field; its name commemorates the day, the deed, and the Christianity of these apostles—Saint Mary of Victory!

At Cempoalla Cortés tried his hand at the delightful work of conversion; the Indian monarch, however, declared his own gods were good enough for him, and he could not comprehend how the Creator of the universe "could condescend to take the form of humanity, with its infirmities and ills, and wander about the earth, the voluntary victim of . . . . those whom his breath had called into existence." Poor benighted heathen! To Cortés this was easy as drawing his sword. However, the nation was converted—at least the temples. Here, though not for the first or last time,—for "the things that are seen are temporal" and require to be renewed,—these devout apostles received a foretaste of their reward, in the form of "eight Indian maidens, richly dressed, wearing collars and ornaments of gold, with a number of female slaves to wait on them." The chief requested that they might become wives to the Spanish captains. "Cortés received the damsels courteously," such was his zeal for Christianity, "but told the cacique they must first be baptized." "*Porque manera no era permitido à hombres, hijos de la Iglesia di Dios, tener commercio con idolatras!*" Similar comforters were frequently "added to their number." Bernal Diaz, a very plain-spoken old soldier, who cared not over much for the souls of the heathen, mentions these things oftener than Mr Prescott. Cortés himself, in virtue of his apostolic dignity, we suppose, or as head of the new church, took the right "to lead about" the celebrated Marina,—not without other helpmeets, we think,—an Indian woman who was of great service in the expedition.

This band of missionaries went to Cholula, and massacred the inhabitants, who had been previously assembled in a narrow place convenient for the slaughter. A portion of the town was burnt, and, as Cortés himself says, three thousand of the inhabitants put to death. Herrera makes the number six thousand, and others yet greater. Mr Prescott is far from justifying the deed, yet he endeavours to excuse the conduct of Cortés: these were heathens; religious infidelity was thought a sin to be punished with fire and faggot in this life, and eternal suffering in the next. But if it is believed that death sends a man to eternal torment, a "soldier of the cross" would hesitate a little before butchering six thousand men. Las Casas adds that he burnt alive more than one hundred caciques whom he had craftily got into his hands, and that while the city was on fire, it was said that Cortés repeated a snatch of poetry, comparing himself to Nero looking down from the Tarpeian rock on the burning of Rome, and caring not for the screams of the children and the old men. This story seems less probable to Mr Prescott than to us. After thus introducing himself to the Cholulans, Cortés "urged the citizens to embrace the cross" and abandon their false gods.

When Cortés had his first interview with Montezuma, he told the monarch that the Christians had come to snatch his soul and the souls of his people from the flames of eternal fire. The Mexican king must have thought them remarkable men for such a mission. When about to advance to the siege of Mexico, Cortés tells his soldiers that "the conversion of the heathen is the work most acceptable in the eye of the Almighty, and one that will be sure to receive his support;" that without this the war would be unjust, and all they might gain by it, robbery. When a new king was established at Tezcuco, Cortés placed several Spaniards about him, ostensibly to instruct him in their language and religion, but really as spies to watch over his conduct and prevent his correspondence with the Mexicans.

The Spanish apostles had one mode of distinguishing their converts and catechumens from such as had not fallen into their hands which we do not find practised by the evangelists of other nations: *they branded their captives with a hot iron.* The letter G was thus indelibly burnt upon them, to denote that they were the spoils of war (*guerra*). Diaz mentions the branding of the captives a great deal oftener than Mr Prescott; on several occasions it was done to "a vast number of the inhabitants," and again, "great numbers were led away into slavery and marked *in the face* with a red-hot iron." (Cap. 130, 154, et sæp.) This hateful torment was burned upon the women as well as the men; even upon the faces of the women who were to serve as temporary "wives" to the conquerors, who, it seems, were not always so anxious to ensure their baptism as their branding.

The motive of the conquerors was love of conquest and plunder. This is plain enough in the despatches of Cortés. Diaz makes no concealment of the fact: he wished the land to be divided as follows: one-fifth for the king, one-fifth for the church, and the rest among the conquerors, according to their rank and merits. (Cap. 169.) As the conquerors who survived the conquest could not have been more than five or six hundred, they would have been pretty well paid for two or three years' service. But what would be left for the converted natives? Heaven in the next life and slavery in this.

The design of the conquerors is made plain by the invasion itself, by their conduct during the war, and by the institutions they established after it was over: they wanted the property and the persons of the Mexicans. They took both, perhaps with as little ferocity and as much decorum as any nation could rob and enslave another. The plea of a desire to convert the Indians is a poor defence, and unworthy of an historian like Mr Prescott. It would be better rhetoric, as well as truer and more honest, to say: these were hard, iron men, with rather less than the average intelligence, morality, and piety of their nation; they went to Mexico, led thither by love of adventure, love of fame, of power, or of gold; they only pretended to care for the souls of the men whose property they plundered, whose daughters they debauched, whose persons they stole or slew!

Certainly they were very remarkable heralds of Christianity. By steel and gunpowder they subdued kingdoms, wrought unrighteousness, obtained promises. They wandered about in steel caps, dragging their artillery after them, impoverishing, afflicting, tormenting. They routed armies; cities they overthrew and turned upside down; captives they took and branded in the name of God. As an earnest of their reward, they had female slaves without number, the first-fruits of them that believe, and having satiated their avarice and their lust, and obtained a good report through the blood of their victims, they received the promises, the heritage of the heathen; yea, such was the reward of all those blessed apostles—of whom the world was not worthy—horse, foot, and dragoons.

Some conquerors have a great idea, and for the sake of that do deeds which revolt the moral sense of mankind. Such men have some excuse for their violent dealing with the world, in the service they render; they esteem themselves men of destiny, and in behalf of their idea go forth through seas of blood of their own shedding. Smiting with the sword, it is not for themselves they smite. Thus there is some defence for Alexander, Hannibal, Cæsar, and Charlemagne; for Napoleon and for Cromwell; even Frederic the Great was not a mere fighter. But Cortés cannot be put in this class. He had no idea in advance of his age; in all but courage and military skill he appears behind his times. No noble thought, no lofty sentiment seems to have inspired him; none such breathes in his words or deeds. Mr Prescott says he was not a "mere fighter," but we see nothing else that can be said to distinguish him from the rest of men. He was one of the most vulgar of fighters; he loved the excitement of adventurous deeds; he sought vulgar fame, and vulgar wealth and power, by vulgar means for vulgar ends. Few distinguished conquerors were so ignoble. He came among the red men of America; they began by calling him a god, and ended with hating him as the devil. In the hot region of Mexico he was treated with great kindness; his companions "experienced every alleviation that could be desired from the attentions of the friendly nations." They made more than a thousand booths for the Spaniards, and freely gave provisions for Cortés and his officers. Montezuma sent to learn who we were, says Diaz, and what we wanted for our ships; we were only to tell what we wanted, and they were to furnish it. The Indians who attached themselves to his standard were faithful; of the Tlascalans only Xicotencatl proved untrue. But Cortés was crafty, insidious, and deceitful. He fomented discontent; he encouraged the disaffected nations to rely on his protection, "as he had come to redress their wrongs," while he came to steal their possessions and their persons. He told his own soldiers they were to fight against rebels who had revolted from their liege lord; against barbarians, the enemies of Christianity; to fight the battles of the cross, to obtain riches and honour in this life and imperishable glory in heaven.

He was unjust to his own soldiers, seizing more than his share of the booty. Diaz complains of this oftener than Mr Prescott; even the food was sometimes unjustly divided. (Diaz, Cap. 105 et al.) Did the soldiers complain, Cortés made a speech full of "the most honeyed phrases and arguments most specious" (*palabras muy mellifluas, ... razones muy bien dichas*). Some he bribed into silence with gold, others with promises; some he put in chains. Were the captives to be divided, he not only selected first the king's fifth thereof and his own, but the finest of the women were secretly set apart, so that, as one of these missionaries complains (Diaz, Cap. 135), the common soldiers found only "old and ugly women" left for them. After the spoil was divided in this unjust fashion, he would not always allow the soldiers to keep their scanty share, but once demanded one-third of it back again, and insisted that if it were not restored, he would take the whole. Under pretence of loans, he extorted a good deal from his own soldiers—a circumstance which injured him much, says Diaz. Mr Prescott thinks such occasions were "critical conjunctures which taxed all the address and personal authority of Cortés. He never shrank from them, but on such occasions was true to himself." (Vol. II. p. 207.) But truth to himself was falseness to his soldiers. He would violate his word to them for the sake of more plunder. Much as they honoured and feared him, few loved him much, and in one of his most trying times, says the same old soldier we have often quoted, they all grudged him a handful of maize to stay his hunger. (Cap. 156.)

Cortés was needlessly cruel; this appears in the slaughter at Tabasco, and in the massacre at Cholula, which even Mr Prescott thinks a dark stain on the memory of the conquerors. His punishments often appear wanton:—he orders a man to be killed for stealing a pair of fowls, another for speaking angrily to Montezuma; he has the feet of his pilot chopped off for some offence; he took fifty Tlascalans who came to his camp as spies, cut off their hands, and sent them home. The friendly Indians were curious to see the Spaniards, and came too near the lines of their encampment, and Cortés coolly relates that fifteen or twenty of them were shot down by the sentries. Mr Prescott excuses this: the "jealqusy of the court and the cautions he had received from his allies . . . seem to have given an unnatural acuteness . . . to his perceptions of danger." (Vol. II. p. 59.) After the conquest an insurrection took place and was speedily put down; four hundred chiefs were sentenced to the stake or the gibbet, "by which means," says Cortés, "God be praised, the safety of the Spaniards was secured." He burnt alive some of Montezuma's officers, who were guilty of no offence but that of obeying their king; at the same time he punished Montezuma for giving them the order. He tortured the members of Guatemozin's household, putting boiling oil upon their feet. This great apostle to the Gentiles put Guatemozin himself and the cacique of Tacuba to the torture—not exactly to save his soul, "so as by fire," but to get his gold. Afterwards, on a groundless suspicion, he treacherously hung them both. Mr Prescott shows little horror at these cruelties, little sense of their injustice; nay, he seems to seek to mitigate the natural indignation which a man feels at such tyranny of the strong over the weak. We confess our astonishment that an historian who thinks the desire of converting the heathen was the paramount motive in the breast of Cortés, has no more censure to bestow on such wanton cruelties, so frequently perpetrated as they were. The soldiers of the cross, going on their mission of mercy, to snatch the Indians from the fires of hell, dress the wounds of their horses with melted fat cut from the bodies of the natives they were to convert (Diaz, Cap. 34); Mr Prescott makes no comment. Cortés has the slaves branded with a hot iron in the cheek. Diaz mentions this more than ten times; Mr Prescott but twice, and then has no word to say—more than if they had been baptized with water.

The massacre at Cholula was terrible as it was needless and wanton. "More than three thousand of the enemy perished in ten hours," says Cortés. Mr Prescott confesses this has "left a dark stain on the memory of the conquerors," that he does not intend to vindicate their cruel deeds, and then undertakes to excuse this very cruelty. We confess our astonishment at such an excuse. (Vol. II. pp. 29—36.)

The massacre at Mexico, after the capture of the city, was terrible. We will not dwell upon it, nor recount its bloody details. Cortés had destroyed town after town; army after army had he swept off. It is within bounds to say that half a million men had been put to the sword since the Spaniards came thither, desirous above all things to convert their precious souls; now the mighty capital—the centre of civilization in North America, whose influence had been felt from the Mexique Gulf to the Bay of Fundy, along either shore of the continent—has fallen; Guatemozin is captured; the wide rich empire lies submissive at his feet; Cortés himself—all iron as he was and smeared with guiltless blood—is moved with compassion; the nation is to be blotted out. But Mr Prescott has no sympathy with the Mexicans; nay, he pauses to avert the sympathy of other men, interposing his shield of ice between the victim and the compassion of mankind. He says:—

> "We cannot regret the fall of an empire which did so little to promote the happiness of its subjects or the real interests of humanity." "The Aztecs were emphatically a fierce and brutal race, little calculated, in their best aspects, to excite our sympathy and regard. Their civilization, such as it was, was not their own, but reflected, perhaps imperfectly, from a race whom they had succeeded. . . . It was a generous graft on a vicious stock, and could have brought no fruit to perfection. They ruled over their wide domains with a sword instead of a sceptre. They did nothing in any way to ameliorate the condition or in any way promote the progress of their vassals. Their vassals were serfs, used only to minister to their pleasure." (Vol. III. pp. 215, 216.)

"The feeble light of civilization," he says, "was growing fainter and fainter." He gives not a single fact to warrant this latter statement, but even if it were true, the

Spaniards did not mend the matter by overturning the candlestick and putting their bloody heel on the flickering torch. He attempts to remove any little compassion which may linger in his reader's heart: the Mexicans were guilty of human sacrifices; they also were cannibals. True, and it is a horrible thing to think of; but think of the butcheries committed by the Spaniards, also in the name of God; try each nation by its light, and which is the worse—the cannibal or the Christian? Mr Prescott tries to excuse the barbarities of the conquerors: when any of the inhabitants fell into their hands, "they were kindly entertained, their wants supplied, and every means taken to infuse into them a spirit of conciliation." The sad shades of Montezuma and Guatemozin—what will they say to that? Diaz informs us of the "means taken" in many an instance. They were reduced to slavery, branded with a hot iron in the cheek. This was the kindly entertainment they met with from those Christian missionaries, who held their lands on condition of converting the natives. We might naturally look for justice from an American writer, with no national prejudice to blind him. But no, his sympathy is wholly with the conquerors; the spirit of chivalry is mightier with him than the spirit of humanity. Bustamente, however, spite of the Spanish blood in his veins, writing on the spot made famous by the deeds of Cortés and his followers, wishes a monument might be erected to Guatemozin, on the spot where he was taken captive, and an inscription thereon to "devote to eternal execration the detested memory of those banditti." The work is needless; themselves have erected a monument "more lasting than brass," telling of their power and their prowess, but also of their more than heathen cruelty, their tyranny, and their shame. The rhetoric of Mr Prescott cannot hide them from the justice of mankind.

We have little to say of the subsequent career of Cortés. He made a bold and desperate expedition to the southern part of North America, enduring wonderful hardships, fighting with his usual skill and courage. Mexico was settled by hungry Spaniards, the natives mainly reduced to slavery. Cortés became rich and powerful. He was accused before the Emperor, and defended himself. He received great honours in Spain, when he returned thither.

He settled down on an estate in Mexico. He died at length in Spain, but in his will expresses doubts "whether one can conscientiously hold property in Indian slaves." Mr Prescott writes the eulogy of his hero, which we have not space to criticize. But there are two ways of judging such a man: one is that of humanity. Here the inquirer looks over the whole field of history, impartially weighs the good and ill of a man, allows for his failings if they belong to his age, and detracts from his individual merits if they also are held in common with the mass of men, but judges the age and its institutions by the standard of absolute justice. This is the work of the philosophic historian. The other way is that of personal admiration of the hero. We are sorry to say that Mr Prescott has taken the latter course. Crime is one thing; but the theory which excuses, defends, justifies crime is quite a different thing, is itself not to be justified, defended, or excused. We are sorry to add the name of Mr Prescott to the long list of writers who have a theory which attempts to justify the crime against mankind, the tyranny of might over right. We are sorry to say of this work in general, and on the whole, that it is not written in the philosophy of this age, and, still worse, not in the Christianity, the wide humanity, which is of mankind. We know this is a severe judgment, and wish we might be mistaken in pronouncing it, but such are the facts.

Mr Prescott has little sympathy with the natives. Marina, unmarried and a captive, becomes the concubine of Cortés, a married man and a conqueror. Her religion allowed the connection, it was not uncommon; his religion forbade it, and he was living "in mortal sin." She seems to have loved him truly and with all her heart. To him she was a useful instrument, personally as his concubine, politically as his interpreter and diplomatic agent. Mr Prescott says, "she had her errors, as we have seen." (Vol. I. p. 297.) The only error he alludes to was her connection with Cortés, not held unlawful, against nature or custom, there; but no censure is passed on Cortés, though he had a wife at Cuba. When his wife dies, Marina might be lawfully married to him, if he would; she had borne him a son, the unfortunate Don Martin Cortés. But he did not want an Indian woman for his wife, whatever might be her services, her love for him, or the connection between them, or the children she had borne him. He must wed one of the titled dames of Spain, daughter of the Count de Aguilar, beautiful and "much younger than himself," and Cortés "gave Marina away to a Castilian knight, Don Juan Xamarillo, to whom she was wedded as his lawful wife," says Mr Prescott, who makes no comment on this transaction, and does not even mention it as one of the "errors" of his hero!

Mr Prescott takes sides with the Spaniards, passes over much of their cruelty in silence, and often apologizes for what he relates, suggesting some idle circumstance which takes off the edge of indignation from the reader, careless, superficial, and requiring a moral stimulus from his instructor. In his narrative he degrades the Mexicans fighting for their homes and the altars of their gods, not less fondly cherished than the homes and the faith of Christians. The Spaniards are brave, chivalrous, heroic. Their victims, he tells us, "filled the air with wild cries and howlings like a herd of *ravenous wolves disappointed of their prey.*" (Vol. III. p. 117.) In the attack on Mexico, a Spanish ensign narrowly escaped falling into the hands of his foe: "*The barbarians,*" says Mr Prescott, "*set up a cry of disappointed rage.*" (P. 146.) Again, at sight of the enemy and of the sacrifice of prisoners going on in the temple, the Mexicans "*like vultures maddened by the smell of distant carrion, ... set up a piercing cry.*" (P. 155.) The efforts of Guatemozin to defend his capital were "*menaces and machinations*" (p. 162); the Mexicans "*raged with impotent anger,* as they beheld their lordly edifices, their temples, all they had been accustomed to venerate, thus swept away." (P. 171.) If we remember aright, the Jews mourned a little when Zion was trodden under foot of the nations, but we should not envy the heart of the historian who should say of the Jeremiahs of that time, that they "raged with impotent anger." Even Cortés thought it a sad sight (*Que era lástima cierto de lo ver*), "but we were forced to it." When driven to despair, some Mexicans, valiant as Leonidas,

> "in the public breach devoted stood,
> And for their country's cause were prodigal of blood."

They would not ask for mercy; Mr Prescott says they

"*glared on the invaders with the sullen ferocity of the wounded tiger,* that the huntsman has tracked to his forest cave." (P. 176.) Even the heroism of Guatemozin is only a "*haughty spirit.*"

The Spaniards established a form of slavery worse than that of the heathens. If the Mexicans did little for their vassals—what did their conquerors do? Mr Prescott passes over the horrors of the slavery established there; excuses the founders for their offence: Columbus had done the same! "Three Hieronymite friars and an eminent Jesuit, all men of learning and unblemished piety," were sent out to investigate the condition of the natives. They justified slavery: the Indians would not work without compulsion; unless they worked, they would not be connected with the whites, and without that connection would not be "converted," and of course not "saved." Slavery, therefore, was their only road to escape damnation. We must confess our amazement that a man of liberal culture, in the midst of a Christian country, writing of such cruelties as the Spaniards practised on their victims, reducing millions of freemen to such a condition, should have no more condemnation for such atrocities. How shall we explain the fact? Can it be that the commercial atmosphere of Boston had stifled the natural and nobler breath of the historian? We know not.

There was one Spaniard who steadfastly opposed the enslaving of the Indians—the Dominican Las Casas, a man who all his life sought continually one great end, the welfare of the Indians. Mr Prescott bestows well-deserved encomiums upon him; often praises him; yet we think he is the only author of all whom Mr Prescott quotes that can complain of the smallest injustice at his hands.

It now remains to speak briefly of the form of the work. The division into books and chapters is sufficiently good. The style is clear and simple, though a little less carefully laboured than in his earlier work. The references are abundant, and, so far as we have examined them, distinguished by the same accuracy which we noticed in the former history. Occasionally there is a little harmless pedantry. Thus (Vol. I. p. 287) in the text, he says, that Cortés told his men to aim at the faces of the foe, and in the margin quotes Lucan, to remind us that the veterans of Cæsar hit the dandies of Pompey's army in the same way. But such things are rare, and by no means disagreeable.

He often refers events to Providence which other men would be content with ascribing to human agency. Thus he says, "it was beneficently ordered by Providence that the land [of the Mexicans] should be delivered over to another race, who would rescue it from the brutish superstitions that daily extended wider and wider." (Vol. I. p. 85.) But in the same manner "it was beneficently ordered by Providence" that merchant ships should be delivered over to Admiral Drake or Captain Kidd; that the Indians of Massachusetts should butcher the white men at Deerfield, and the whites should carry the head of King Philip on a pole into Plymouth and sell his family into slavery. Again, speaking of Cortés, he tells us "Providence reserved him for higher ends," and that he was "the instrument selected by Providence to scatter terror among the barbarian monarchs of the western world, and lay their empire in the dust." (Pp. 236, 260.) Montezuma "was the sad *victim of destiny*." (Vol. II. p. 351.) But all this providential action is in behalf of the invaders. *Causa victrix placet diis.*

The figures of speech are commonplace; we do not remember one that is original, except that already quoted, in which the Mexicans are compared to "vultures *maddened* by the smell of distant carrion." Few of them are elegant or expressive enough to deepen the impression of the simple statement of the fact. One figure, to "*spread like wildfire,*" which is a favourite in the History of Spain, appears also and frequently in this work. Others are poor and common:—to crowd "like a herd of deer," or a "*herd* of wolves;" to be "pale as death;" to "rush like a torrent;" to swarm "like famished harpies," and to be led "like sheep to the slaughter." They add little to the freshness or beauty of the style, and do not impress us very forcibly with the originality of the author.

Here we take leave of the historian, for the present, with the same impression as that left on us by the former work.*

* See previous article, *ad finem*.

THE ADMINISTRATION OF THE LATE MR POLK.

The administration of Mr Polk took place at an important period in the affairs of the nation; it is connected with some of the most remarkable events which have happened in America since the adoption of the Constitution—events which will deeply and long affect the welfare of the people. The time has not yet come when the public, or any person, can fully appreciate the causes then put or kept in action. But the administration was so remarkable, the events connected with it so new in our history, and so important, that it seems to us worth while to pause a moment and study this chapter in American politics, with such light as we now possess. It becomes the more important to do this just as a new Congress is about to assemble, while the government is connected with a new President not very well tried in political affairs. In judging the contemporary events of our country it would be ridiculous in us to pretend to the same coolness and impartiality which it is easy to have in studying the politics of times a thousand years gone by; still, we think we have no prejudice against Mr Polk or his administration, or in favour thereof; certainly we do not look through the partisan eyes of a democrat, or a Whig, or a free soiler, but are ready to praise or blame an idea, a measure, or an act, on its own account, without asking what political family it belongs to.

The materials for the history of this administration are abundant and accessible. We make no pretensions to a knowledge of the secrets of either party; they would be of small value if known. The volumes of private and confidential letters of some New York politicians, of which so much talk was made a few years ago, contain much matter for gossip, some even for scandal, little for history, and for political philosophy nothing at all. We neither seek nor welcome information from such quarters. In politics, as in all science, the common and obvious facts are of the greatest value. With the secret history of the Baltimore Convention, of the Congress, or the Cabinet, we have nothing to do, only with their public acts. Our information will be drawn chiefly from public documents.

We have nothing to say of the personal character and private motives of the distinguished actors in the political drama. Politicians are as honest as the majority of men would be, exposed to the same temptations, under the same circumstances. The misdeeds of other men are done on a small scale or in an obscure way, while the private character of a politician becomes public, his deeds appear before the sun. If the transactions of State-street and Wall-street were public as the acts of Congress, men would not think more highly, perhaps, of mercantile honour than now of political integrity. A little acquaintance with political doings shows a looker on, that while each party is, consciously or blindly, led forward by its idea, and so helps or hinders the progress of mankind, under similar circumstances, the one has about as much patriotism and political honesty as the other. In point of deeds the party that has been long in power is certainly more corrupt than the opposite party, who are limited by their position to longings and intentions. So the apples which have long been exposed for sale in a huckster's basket get bruised with the huckster's attempts to show only their fair sides, and with frequent handling by the public, and begin to rot sooner than other apples from the same branch, but kept out of sight in the barrel, which otherwise resemble them "as much as one apple is like another." The party that is full and the party that is hungry seldom differ much in their political honesty.

In estimating the administration of men like Jefferson and Jackson, men of decided thoughts or decided deeds, the personal character and opinions of the President are important elements to be considered. But Mr Polk was remarkable neither for thought nor action; he had no virtues or vices to distinguish him from the common run of politicians, who swim with the party tide, up or down, in or out, as it may be. His character seems to have had no weight in the public scale, and does not appear to have given the balance a cast to either side. He might follow a multitude, in front or rear—he could not lead. God never gave him "the precious gift" of leading. For his office, no qualities marked him more than a thousand other men in the land. Like Mr Harrison and Mr Tyler, he was indebted for the presidency to "the accident of an accident." So the god Apis was selected from other bullocks for some qualities known only to the priests; though to laical eyes he was nothing but a common stot, distinguished by no mark and likelihood; soon as selected he became a god, and had the homage of his worshippers. The nomination of the Apis might be one "not fit to be made," but when clerically made it always had the laic confirmation, and no Apis was ever found too brute to receive worship.

It was said in 1848, that it was not of much consequence who was President if he were only a Whig; it did not require much ability to fill the office; much acquaintance with the philosophy of politics, nor even much knowledge of the facts of politics; nay, not any eminence of character. Mr Polk was not the first or the last attempt to demonstrate this by experiment.

His private life was marred by no unusual blemish, and set off by no remarkable beauty. He kept the ten commandments very much as other men; was sober, temperate, modest in his deportment; what seems latterly rather unusual for a President, he did not swear profanely. On his death-bed he "professed justifying faith in the Lord Jesus Christ," "relying alone for salvation on the great doctrine of atonement," and "received the ordinance of baptism;" thus he secured a good name in the churches, not yet accorded to Franklin and Washington. Estimating him by the ordinary standard about him, the true way to judge such a man, he has been set down as an exemplary man, using his opportunities with common fidelity. Some official acts of his were purely official. His friends, since his death, claim but little for him. Eulogies are not supposed to limit themselves to telling the truth, or to extend themselves to telling the whole truth. Still they are a good test of public opinion. Burr got none; General Jackson had many; those on Mr Polk were chiefly official, and their temperature, for official panegyrics, was uncommonly low, plainly intimating that little could be made of such a subject. Mr Polk was hardly susceptible of rhetorical treatment after death. While in power he could easily be praised. We shall take it for granted that excepting some of the eminent leaders, almost any prominent man in the Democratic party, if made President under such circumstances, would have done very much as Mr Polk did; would have been merely a portion of the party machine. Last year the Whigs said, also, it was not very important what the personal opinions of the President were.

After eliminating these elements which we do not intend to speak of, the matter becomes quite simple: we have only to deal with the ideas of the administration,—the measures proposed as an expression thereof,—and the acts in which these ideas took a concrete form. These, of course, will be complicated with the adverse ideas and measures of the other party. Such is the theme before us, and such the scheme of this paper.

However, to understand the ideas, measures, and acts of the administration, it is necessary to look a moment at the state of the nation when Mr Polk came to power. In our foreign relations all was serene except in the English and Mexican quarter. In the one the weather seemed a little uncertain; in the other there were decided indications of a storm.

In 1842, Mr Webster, for a short time dignifying the office of Secretary of State, had performed the most valuable public service he has yet rendered his country. He had negotiated the treaty of Washington by which the north-eastern boundary was settled. That was a very important matter, and Mr Webster deserves the lasting gratitude of both nations for the industry, courtesy, and justice with which he managed that complicated, difficult, and vexatious affair. He is often celebrated as the defender of the Constitution, but his services in that work, when looked at with impartial eyes, diminish a good deal, and perhaps will not be much spoken of when a few years have dispelled the mists which hang over all contemporary greatness. It was a real dignity and honour to negotiate the treaty. Certainly there were few men, perhaps not another in the nation, who could have done it. We do not mean to say that a board of civil engineers, or three good, honest men could not as well settle questions in themselves more difficult. But such was the state of feeling in England and America, that none but a distinguished politician could be trusted with the matter, and none possessed the requisite qualities in so eminent a degree as Mr Webster.

There still remained another affair to be settled with England: we refer to the boundaries of Oregon. That question was purposely made difficult by some small politicians who exasperated the public on both sides of the water. The cry was raised "Oregon or fight;" "the whole of Oregon or none;" "54, 40." The legislature of Maine went a little further north, and shouted "54, 49." Some men, whose names are by no means forgotten, made a great outcry, and egged the ignorant headlong towards dangerous measures, threatening "war with England;" men who, like frogs in the spring just escaping from their winter of obscurity, for their own purposes, made a great deal of noise with very little sense. The intrinsic difficulty of the case was very small. England made large pretensions; so did we; both desiring a wide margin of oscillation before they settled down on a permanent boundary. But England was pacific, though firm, and not foolish enough to wish to fight with one whose peace was so profitable. A war between England and America is, on each side, a quarrel with a good customer. That is the mercantile aspect of the case. An administration which should seek honestly to settle the Oregon question would find no difficulty; had Mr Webster remained a year more in the cabinet, we doubt not this affair, also, would have been amicably settled, and the country saved a good deal of wind.

Affairs certainly looked threatening in the neighbourhood of Mexico; there were troubles past, present, and to come. Americans had excited the revolution in Texas; fought her battles, and fomented her intrigues. Texas had just been annexed, or, as the phrase originally was, *re*-annexed. Texas and Mexico had been long at war; though not actively fighting at the time of annexation, the war was not ended. We took Texas with a defective title, subject to the claims of Mexico. If she did not prosecute those claims it was because she was too feeble, not that she had relinquished them. That was not all—we had insulted Mexico, and deeply injured her; not by accident, but with our eyes open, and of set purpose. We had wronged Mexico deeply, and then added new insults to old injuries. What made our conduct worse, was the fact that we were powerful and Mexico defenceless. The motive which lay at the bottom of all makes this accumulated baseness still more detestable; it was done to establish a bulwark for American slavery.

We have on a former occasion spoken of the origin of the Mexican war,* but will now add a few words respecting the scheme of annexation. In 1803, Mr Jefferson purchased Louisiana of France, a vast territory west of the Mississippi, for 15,000,000 dols. He thought he transgressed the Constitution in doing so, and expected an "act of indemnity" by the people, to justify the deed.† The Senate thought otherwise. Slavery was already established in Louisiana. In 1812, the present state of Louisiana was admitted to the Union with a constitution authorizing slavery. In 1820, a new state was formed from what had been the more northern portion of Louisiana. Should it be a slave state, or free? That was the question. The South, "on principle," favoured slavery; the North, "on principle," opposed it. But both parties laid aside their "principles" and made a compromise, such as Mr Clay and Mr Clayton so much admire. Slavery was allowed only south of Mason and Dixon's line, 36° 40′ of north latitude. This was the famous "Missouri Compromise." But only a small part of Missouri lay south of the line. All the new territory, therefore, could make only two Slave States, Louisiana and Arkansas. In 1836, Arkansas was admitted into the Union. Florida territory alone remained to be made into Slave States. Thus the territorial extension of the slave power was at an end, while vast regions were left into which the stream of Northern enterprise continually poured itself; the North rapidly increased in numbers, in wealth, and in the political power which wealth and numbers give; the rapid rise of new states was to the South a fearful proof of this.

The North has always been eminently industrial, particularly eminent in the higher modes of industry, work that demands the intelligent head. The South has always been deficient in industry, especially in the higher modes of industry. The North has an abundance of skilled labour; the South chiefly brute labour. This industrial condition of

* See the *Massachusett's Quarterly Review*, No. I, Article I.

† See his Message of Oct. 17th, 1803, and his letter to Mr Breckenridge.

the South is almost wholly to be ascribed to the institution of slavery, though perhaps something must be allowed for the climate, and something for the inferior character and motives of the original colonists who settled that part of the country. But while the North is industrial, the South is political; as the North sends its ablest men to trade, so the South to politics. The race for public welfare and political power was to be run by those two competitors, "not without dust and heat." After the Revolution, the opposite characteristics of the North and South appeared more prominently than before. The North increased rapidly in numbers, and outpeopled the South. The Revolution itself showed the comparative military power of the "Southern chivalry" and the hardy industry of the North.* After the adoption of the federal constitution, the North increased with still greater rapidity, and began to show a decided superiority to the South. This is partly the result of the industry of the North; but in part the result of our navigation laws, which gave American bottoms a great national privilege. Most of the ships belonged, as they still do, to the North; they were the fruits of her industry. Did the Constitution guarantee slavery to the South, it *protected the ships of the North.* The South got a political advantage, and the North a commercial privilege, whose value in dollars has been greater than that of all the slaves in the United States. In all contests about money, the North carries it over the South; in all contests for immediate political power the South over the North.

Some thirty years later, the nation changed its policy. It had taken pains to encourage commerce, and had a revenue tariff. Now it took pains to restrict trade, and

* "Let us compare a Slave State and a free one, of about equal population. In 1790, South Carolina contained 249,073 persons; Connecticut 238,141. Supposing the population, during the war, only two-thirds as great as in 1790, then South Carolina contained 166,018 and Connecticut 158,760 persons. During the nine years of the war, South Carolina sent 6417 soldiers to the continental army, and Connecticut 32,039. In 1790, Massachusetts contained 475,257 souls; during the Revolution, according to the above ratio, 316,838. While the six Slave States, with their free population of 1,307,549, furnished but 59,336 soldiers for the continental army, and 10,123 militia men. Massachusetts alone sent 68,007 soldiers to the continental army and 15,155 militia. THUS shoulder to shoulder Massachusetts and South Carolina went through the Revolution, and felt the great arm of Washington lean on them both for support."—*Letter to the people of the United States touching the Matter of Slavery,* pp. 99, 100.

established a protective tariff; so the North engaged in manufactures to a greater degree than before. The South could not do this: the slaves were too ignorant, and must remain so as long as they are slaves, otherwise they could not be kept together in the large masses which manufacturing purposes require; the whites were too indolent and too proud. The South continued to increase constantly in numbers and in wealth, but compared with the North, she did not increase. In America political power is the resultant of wealth and numbers; it soon became plain that the political centre of gravity was travelling northwards continually, and with such swiftness that the South before long would lose the monopoly of the Government, which she had long enjoyed by reason of her political character, and which the North cared little for so long as money could be made without it. The prosperity of the North rests on an industrial basis, that of the South on a political basis.

So the South must contrive to outweigh the North. How? Not by industry, which creates wealth directly, and indirectly multiplies men, but by politics. The North works after its kind, and is satisfied with the possession of commerce and manufactures; the South, after its kind, rejoices in Slavery, and thinks to outwit the laws of nature by a little juggling in politics. Behold the results. To balance the North, the South must have new Slave States to give her power in the federal government. New territory must be got to make them of.

Texas lay there conveniently near. It had once been a part of Lousiana, as far west as the Nueces. In 1819, James Long went from Natchez in Louisiana to Nacogdoches in Texas, and, on the 23rd of June, declared the independence of the republic of Texas.* About two years later, Mr Austin and his colony went thither from Mississippi, carrying their slaves with them. In 1826, another insurrection took place, under Benjamin W. Edwards, and another declaration of independence followed. At that time the American government did not interfere nor much covet the territory. Texas was a convenient neighbour, and not a dangerous one; slaveholders could migrate thither with their slaves. But in 1824, the Mexicans forbad

* Speech of Hon. Luther Severance in the House of Representatives, February 4th, 1847, p. 12.

the introduction of slaves, and declared all free soon as they were born; Mexico refused to surrender up fugitive slaves. In 1827, Texas and Coahuila were united into one State with a constitution which allowed no new slaves, born or brought thither, and in 1829 Mexico emancipated all her slaves.

Soon as Mexico made advances toward emancipation, the American government began to covet Texas.* In 1827, under the administration of Mr Adams, an attempt was made to purchase Texas; 1,000,000 dols. were offered. In 1829, Mr Benton desired "the *retrocession*." His reasons are instructive:—we have now "a non-slaveholding empire in juxtaposition with the slaveholding South-west;" and "five or six new slaveholding States may be added to the Union." Yes, "nine States as large as Kentucky." A Charleston newspaper desired it because "it would have a favourable influence on the future destinies of the South, by increasing the votes of the slaveholding States in the United States Senate."† In 1829, in a Virginia convention, Judge Upshur said, the annexation of Texas "would raise the price of slaves, and be of great advantage to the slaveholders of that State;" in 1832, Mr Gholson, in the Virginia Legislature, thought "it would raise the price of slaves fifty per cent. at least." To sharpen the public appetite for Texas, in 1829 the cry was raised that "England wanted Texas; British merchants had offered to loan Mexico 5,000,000 dols. if she would place Texas under British protection." This trick was frequently resorted to, but now it is plain to the public that the apprehension was groundless. The same year, the first of Gen. Jackson's administration, our minister offered 5,000,000 dols. for Texas; the offer was rejected. He then offered a loan of 10,000,000 dols., taking Texas as collateral security; that, also, was rejected. He tried also, but in vain, to obtain a treaty for the surrender of fugitive slaves.‡

* This subject has been ably treated by Judge Jay, in his "Review of the Causes and Consequences of the Mexican War." (Boston. 1849. 12mo, p. 333.) We are indebted to it for several facts. Mr Porter, in his "Review of the Mexican War," &c., &c. (Auburn, N. Y. 1849. 12mo, p. 220), takes a different view, but writes an impartial and valuable book.

† Jay, page 13.

‡ Executive Documents, No. 25, 19th Congress, 2nd Session; also No. 23.

In 1840, considerable talk was made about the annexation. The State of Texas had made large grants of land to various persons, some of which had been brought up by Americans. So in addition to the general desire of the slaveholders, the owners of Texan lands had a special motive to stimulate them. Joint-stock companies were formed in the United States; there were the "Galveston Bay and Texas Company;" the "Arkansas and Texas Company;" the "Rio Grande Company." These had their head-quarters at New York. Then there was the "Union Land Company," and the "Trinity Land Company," and others whose names we remember not. In Mississippi and Arkansas, attempts were publicly made to excite the people of Texas to revolt. In 1830, candidates for Congress in Mississippi were publicly catechised as to their opinion of annexation. The same year Samuel Houston got up his expedition to wrest Texas from Mexico. In 1832, Mexico was obliged to withdraw her troops from Texas, to suppress disturbances in other quarters; emigrants continually went with their slaves from the United States. In 1833, Texas organized herself as a separate State. Mexico refused her assent, and sent troops which were repulsed. As Mr Jay says, "The standard of rebellion was raised. Texan agents traversed the United States, addressing public meetings, enlisting troops, and despatching military supplies to the revolted province. On the 2nd of March, 1836, the insurgents issued their declaration of independence, and fifteen days after adopted a constitution establishing perpetual slavery." "Of the fifty-seven signers to this declaration, fifty were emigrants from the Slave States, and only three Mexicans by birth."* The constitution prohibited the importation of slaves *except from the United States;* but every negro in Texas, or who might come there, was declared a slave!

During the war between Mexico and Texas, the American government took little or no pains to prevent our citizens from aiding the Texans; vessels were openly fitted out in our harbours, and sent to war on a friendly power, yet the Secretary of State had the hardihood to say the President (General Jackson) "took all the measures in his power to prevent it;" Mr Van Buren, in his letter

* Jay, p. 18.

to Mr Hammet, says the same thing. Yet he allowed the Brigadier-General of the Texan army publicly to advertise for volunteers for that army, in the State of North Carolina, and to enlist soldiers. The Mexican minister protested; it was all in vain. The President sent General Gaines with an army to lie on the Texan frontier, ready to further the designs of our citizens against Mexico. He was ordered to advance as far as Nacogdoches, if needful, and Mr Forsyth told the Mexican minister "our troops might, if necessary, be sent into the heart of Mexico." Our government tried to force Mexico into a war with us. American troops were on the soil of Mexico; her minister complained, and requested that they might be withdrawn, the answer is "No." Two days after (Oct 15th, 1936), the Mexican minister demands his passports and goes home.*

Mexico was too feeble to fight. Neither our infraction of a treaty, nor the insults added to that injury, could provoke her to a war. Other measures were to be tried; the American government got up its "claims" on Mexico—fifteen in number. Of these we have not now space to speak.†

On the 1st of March, 1837, the Senate acknowledged the independence of Texas; a minister was sent and one was received. In August, 1837, General Hunt, the Texan minister, proposed annexation. Mr Van Buren was then President: he has been called "the Northern man with Southern principles," though we think he deserves the title rather less than some others not so stigmatized. The offer of annexation was declined: Mexico was still at war with Texas; the Legislatures of New York, Pennsylvania, and all the New-England States had protested against annexation. In regard to Texas Van Buren did not "follow in the steps of his illustrious predecessor." During his administration little was done to promote annexation. Nothing by the government. The third non-slaveholding President did not desire to extend the area of bondage. The consequences we shall presently see.

* See the correspondence between Mr Gorostiza and Mr Forsyth, and Mr Dickens, in Executive Documents, No. 2, 24th Congress, 2nd Session.

† See the correspondence relative to this matter in Executive Documents, No. 139, 24th Congress, 2nd Session, and Executive Documents, No. 3, 25th Congress, 2nd Session, p. 31, *et seq.*, 40, *et seq.*; Nos. 190, 347, 360; also Nos. 75 and 351. See the remarks of Mr Jay, chapters V. VI. IX.—XI.

In 1841, the Whigs came into power with the shout of "Tippecanoe and Tyler too;" as an English traveller has said, "Log cabins with their songs and speeches, their orgies on bacon and hard cider, had more to do with the election of General Harrison, . . . than had less exceptionable means."* The Whigs thus gave the Democrats an opportunity, much needed, to turn themselves out of office. We have nothing to do with the motives which led the Whigs to select Mr Tyler for their candidate for the Vice-Presidency. They are too plain to need comment. The nomination was characteristic of the party. What followed would once have been regarded as "judicial," a "direct intervention of God" to punish an artifice. Mr Tyler, becoming President, was true to his former character and conduct. He set about the work of annexation in good earnest. Commodore Jones was sent with a fleet to lie on the western shore of Mexico—to be ready in case of any outbreak with America. His conduct shows the expectation and design of our government. Mr Upshur, the Secretary of State, is a good exponent of the policy of the administration. In Sept., 1843, he says "few calamities could befall this country [the United States] more to be deplored than the establishment of a predominant British influence [of which there was not the least danger], and the *abolition of domestic slavery in Texas!"* † General Lamar, once President of Texas, had written to his friends in Georgia that without annexation "*the anti-slavery party in Texas will acquire the ascendency . . . and may abolish slavery.*" . . . For "*the majority of the people of Texas are not owners of slaves.*" ‡

On the 11th of October, 1843, Mr Upshur took the initiative and proposed annexation to the Texans; he told them, on the 16th of Jan., 1844, that without annexation "they cannot maintain that institution [Slavery] ten years; probably not half that time." § If Texas is not annexed, he says again, "the people of the Southern States will not run the hazard of subjecting their slave property to the control of a population who are anxious to abolish

* Mackay's Western World, &c. London. 1849. Vol. II. pp. 25, 26.

† Upshur's Letter to Murphy (our Agent at Texas), Sept. 1843. Executive Documents, No. 271, 28th Congress, 1st Session.

‡ Jay, pp. 87, 88.

§ Executive Document, No. 271, 28th Congress, 1st Session, p. 46.

slavery." Mr Upshur was not so crafty as Mr Murphy, his agent at Texas. He says: "Take this position on the side of the constitution and the laws, and the civil, political, and religious liberties of the people of Texas secured thereby (saying nothing about abolition), and all the world will be with you;" say "nothing which can offend even our fanatical brethren of the North; let the United States espouse at once the cause of civil, political, and religious liberty in this hemisphere."* A treaty was made, but "our fanatical brethren of the North" were offended, and on the 8th of June, 1844, the Senate rejected it by a vote of 35 to 16.†

"The immediate annexation of Texas" was now the favourite measure of the slave power. They had little fear that, in the next presidential term, they could repeal the tariff of '42, but felt doubtful of the success of annexation. Mr Upshur feared New-England;‡ had he lived at Boston, and known the influences then controlling New-England, he would have seen there was no reason for present fear. A presidential election was at hand; the Democratic convention was to meet at Baltimore in May. Mr Van Buren was the most prominent candidate of the party. Most of the delegates to the convention had been instructed by the primary assemblies which appointed them, to support him. But he was a Northern man; while President he had *not* favoured annexation; he had lately written a public letter (April 20, 1844), and plainly declared himself hostile to annexation as then proposed.§ Mr Ritchie, "the senior field-marshal of Van Buren's party," forsook and opposed his old friend. Mr Cross, of Arkansas, "would not vote under any circumstances for a man opposed to the annexation of Texas;" Van Buren was "not the proper person for the party to rally around in the coming struggle;" "nine out of ten of our friends think so." The Tyler committee wrote on their card, as for Van Buren, "Texas has destroyed him;" "the last, best, and wisest

* Letter of Sept. 23rd, 1843, and Sept. 24th, *ubi sup.*

† See Mr Tyler's Special Message of April 22nd, 1844, and his Annual Message of Dec. 5th, 1843.

‡ See his Letter to Mr Murphy [No. 14], Executive Document, No. 271, *ubi sup.*

§ See his Letter to Mr Hammet, in Niles' Register, new series, Vol. XVI. p. 153, *et seq.*

counsel of Andrew Jackson was—the annexation of Texas."

The convention assembled; Van Buren got more than a majority, but could not get two-thirds of the votes. Candidates were numerous. There were some that proposed Cass, Calhoun, Buchanan, Tyler, Tecumseh-Johnson; some even thought it best to take again Andrew Jackson—"gallant old Ironsides." Even Commodore Stewart was talked of. When the political tide ebbs clean out of the harbour, strange things appear on the bottom, only seen on such occasions. Men thought it very surprising that such a man should be spoken of—certainly it had no precedent, and he no political experience. Now the nomination would not be at all surprising or irregular. The Commodore's letter looks silly enough now. But who knows, if only elected, that he would not have been as great a man as Mr Polk, nay, as Tyler, or Taylor? He was for "immediate annexation," and would "throw ourselves on the justice of our cause before God and the nations." Valiant Commodore; he might have been as great a man as Mr Polk, had the tide of nomination *served* in his favour.

After all the mountainous labour of the Baltimore convention, there came forth Polk; Mr James K. Polk. Men wondered. "Who the devil *is* James— K—— Polk?" said many Democrats; and when told, they thought it was "a nomination not fit to be made." None of them proved it, by facts and arguments, quite so faithfully as the distinguished author of that phrase did on a recent occasion at Marshfield; they left that for Mr Polk to do (not by logic, but by experiment), and he did—we shall see what he did, in due time. Mr Van Buren was "sincerely desirous for their success," the success of the nominees.* The Whigs were pretty firmly united in support of Mr Clay, "Harry of the West," and "that same old Coon," as he has publicly called himself. He was not, publicly, much opposed to annexation, nor much in favour of it, and in respect to that was a pretty good index of his party. Yet some Whigs were seriously and conscientiously opposed to the annexation of Texas as a slave territory; so were a few Democrats, who constituted the moral element of the party. Both of these minorities have since reported

* Letter of June 3rd, 1844.

their presence in the politics of the land, indications of something yet future. It was a rash movement of the party, this changing their leader and their line on the very brink of battle, under the guns of their opponent, already put in battery and ready to fire; but they were confident in their strength, and were so well drilled that they only needed the word of command to perform any political evolution or revolution.

It is a little curious to look back. On the 3rd of March, 1843, twenty-one members of Congress solemnly declared that "annexation would be identical with dissolution; would be an attempt to eternize an institution and a power of a nature so unjust . . . as . . . *not only to result in a dissolution of the Union,* . . . *but fully to justify it.*" Five of the twenty-one were from Massachusetts. "A good memory is" not so "needful to a" politician, as to another class of persons not named among gentlemen. The protest of March 3rd was not very distinctly remembered at a later date by every one of the signers thereof.

At the other extreme was the State of South Carolina. This is a very remarkable State, and her doings—we mean the doings of her lips—deserve a special notice. Before the Baltimore convention, it was necessary for that Empire State to speak out, her trumpet giving no uncertain sound. So, on the 15th of May, the people of Charleston, who had "forborne to give any public declaration of . . . . opinions and wishes, . . . and patiently waited," at length and solemnly "resolved" that annexation is "an American and national measure, antagonistic to foreign interference ["still harping on my daughter"] and domestic abolitionism;" "if the treaty for the recovery (!) of Texas be defeated because of the increase it will give to the slave-holding States, it will be the denial of a vital right to them."

Even after the convention the danger of the patriarchal institution is so great that there must be "a Southern convention." The "South Carolinian," of May 30th, said, annexation is "a question not of *party,* but of *country,* and to the South one of absolute *self-preservation;*" "under the subtle encroachments of our old enemy of Britain, aided by the traitorous abolitionists at home, . . . her doom is sealed if she does not arise in her might . . . and effect a union with Texas;" "England once firmly seated in Texas, and there is an end of all power or safety for the South, which would soon be made another St Domingo." A convention of Slave States was to be called "to take into consideration the question of annexing Texas to the Union, if *the Union will accept it;* or if the Union *will not accept it,* then of *annexing Texas to the Southern States.*" The convention was to offer the Union this "alternative:" "either to *admit Texas into the Union,* or to proceed *peaceably and calmly to arrange the terms of a dissolution of the Union.*" Annexation must be had at all costs. A meeting "in the Williamsburg district" declared, quite "in the Ercles" dialect of that region, that "the doom of the South is sealed and the dirge of our fair republic will ere long be sung by liberty's last minstrel, if she does not arise in her might and effect a union with Texas."

Here are some of the "sentiments" of South Carolina; the time and place are the 4th of July, and "Marion Court-House:" "The annexation of Texas—the great measure of deliverance to the South—though defeated now by the bitterness and faction of party, come what may we will never give her up." "The protective tariff and abolition—the one, under the form of law, seeks the profits of our labour; the other, under the guise of philanthropy, to wrest our property from us. South Carolina is ready to resist the one and repel the other."

An "unsuspected nullifier" of 1832 came out to assure the people that "the political Moses [to wit, Mr Moses-Calhoun] is neither lost nor dead, but that he is ready to follow the pillar of cloud by day, or fire by night." "True," he says, "there is a Joshua [Mr Joshua-Polk, meaning], full of the spirit of wisdom, for that Moses has laid his hands on him;" but "there is still no prophet in Israel [inuendo the United States of America] like Moses," [to wit, Mr Moses-Calhoun]. But somehow it seemed Moses had been so long talking with *his* Lord, that the Baltimore convention,—sorely to seek for a prophet of some mark and likelihood, for there was no open vision in those days,—could not steadfastly look upon the face of *this* Moses and make him their President; and so as for this Moses, the people of South Carolina wot nct what would become of him, nor even what would become of themselves without Texas. A writer in the *Charleston Mercury* asked, "What is the remedy for the evils which afflict the South?" and is thus replied to by a far-sighted man in the same journal, who does not sign himself "Captain Bobadil," though he is certainly of that military family: "I answer, unreservedly, *Resistance—combined Southern resistance,* if *you can procure it* [if *emphaticum*] ; *if not, then State resistance.*"

A Virginia writer, we forget who, said there was "a big screw loose somewhere in South Carolina;" we shall presently see his mistake. This resistance was seriously meant; South Carolina was apparently arming for the fight, mustering that "small infantry" of hers. How shall we relate her deeds, and in what well-becoming words essay our venturous task? O Muse, author of bombast and of fustian, who, from the heights of Gascony,—where thou presidest over founts of froth and brooks of foam,—didst once descend to inspire the soul of Bavius and of Mævius, bards of vast renown and parents of a never-ending, never-silent line,—come and inspire some of their mighty kin to sing the horrid internecine war, bidding him tell who first, who last, came forth to fight. 'Twas Quattlebum! so is he known to fame. Alas, the muse of Gascony will not again inspire a bard with verse fitting such mighty themes. So let the muse of history record it with pedestrian pen. General Quattlebum, the renowned commander-in-chief, commissioned, epauletted, the admiration of negro slaves, mounted on his war-horse, went round, "sonorous metal blowing martial sounds," full of dignity, state-valour, "reserved rights," and nullification —"an eye like Mars to threaten and command;"—went round to stir up the spirit of fight, "reviewing his regiments." O reader, gentle or simple, this is history which we record; the veracious Niles has registered the deeds. One newspaper says that General Quattlebum addressed every regiment "in a speech for annexation. The men . . . all go for annexation,—right off the reel, now or never." The *Charleston Mercury* exclaimed, "Thus it will be seen that two thousand eight hundred and thirty-two men, with arms in their hands, in the drill-field, have expressed their decided determination to sustain the measure." The "forty-third regiment" resolved "that it would be more for the interest of the States [the South and South-west], that they should stand out of the Union with Texas, than in it without her." This was the thing —"combined Southern resistance if it could be had; if not, then State resistance"—the resistance of South Carolina and her "two thousand eight hundred and thirty-two men with arms in their hands." What if South Carolina had "resolved" not to wait, but to annex Texas at once, leaving her eight-and-twenty sisters to their fate? What would have been the fate of the North? Already does affrighted fancy picture to our eye the South Carolinian general—the terrible Quattlebum, himself a war, his words battles,—his forty-third regiment leading the way, and his "two thousand eight hundred and thirty-two men, with arms in their hands," reaching o'er many a yard of solid ground, and marching north, as when a cloud "with thunder fraught comes rattling o'er the Caspian!" Town after town falls into his hands; State after State; Baltimore is his; Philadelphia has surrendered to Quattlebum; the Palmetto waves over New York; New-England "is not a circumstance" in his way. What avails the memory of Lexington and Bunker Hill? Vain is the skill of General Scott and General Taylor; Commodore Stewart is taken captive; even General Thumb is reduced to despair. Texas would be not merely annexed, but actually spread over the whole land, and the mouths of "our fanatical brethren of the North" literally stopped with Texan dirt. But no —this is fiction, O gentle reader, not fact. There is this peculiarity of South Carolinian valour: it is very valorous before the time of danger and after the time of danger, but in the time of danger, all at once it loses its identity, statical and dynamical, and becomes—DISCRETION. It is the better part of valour. He was a wise man who bid his legs, which were cowards, carry his brave heart out of danger. In the times of nullification in 1832, the great oath of Andrew Jackson laid South Carolinian valour low in the dust; to accomplish that in 1844 it took only the common swearing of John Tyler. It was needless to shoot at such an adversary; it was not worth the shot, for the poor little thing fell of itself and died of the fall. The coast of South Carolina is said to be windy, and the characteristic of the seashore has been communicated to the politicians of the State: her politics, indeed, are like a bag of wind, and we think there was not "a big screw loose" in the State, but only a big string had slipped off. The only aggressive act committed by the petulant little commonwealth, spite of the resolutions of its forty-third regiment, of the "decided determination" of the "two thousand eight hundred and thirty-two men with arms in their hands," and the scheme of "combined Southern resistance," or "at any rate, State resistance,—the only aggressive act of South Carolina was the expulsion of an unarmed gentleman on the 5th of December, who had been sent from Massachusetts to look after her own citizens. Thus was "abolition" repelled. After that the valour of South Carolina flattened away as the wind had blown out, and for a long time all was quiet, not a general stirring. There are noble elements in the State, and some noble men. If ever it becomes a democracy and not an oligarchy, if the majority ever rule there, we shall see very different things, and South Carolina will not be a proverb in the nation.

Mr Polk was elected. On the 25th of Jan., 1845, the Joint Resolution for annexation passed the House of Representatives, by a vote of 120 to 98, and soon after the Whig Senate by a majority of two votes; it was signed by the President on the 1st of March. So the work of annexation was completed before Mr Polk came into power, though by no means without his aid. If this could have been done justly, without extending Slavery, few men at the North would have had cause to complain. We do not blame the Texans for desiring independence, or achieving it; we find no fault with extending the area of freedom over the whole world. We rejoice to extend the institutions of liberty over all North America, and should be glad to see the "honourable Senator" from Labrador or the Lake of the Woods, in the American Congress. We cannot think that Mexico had just cause of war in the bare act of annexation. But when we remember that America colonized Texas for the sake of wresting it from Mexico, who would not sell it; that Americans got up the Texan revolution, and fought it through, and did all this for the sake of getting nine Slave "States as large as Kentucky;" that this was done secretly, fraudulently, with a lie on the lips of the government—we must say the deed itself was a base deed, and the motive base and miserable.

Such was the state of foreign affairs. In all that concerned domestic welfare, the nation was never so well off before. There had been a considerable period of remarkable prosperity. It must be a very bad government which, in four years, can seriously injure a nation like this, where so little depends on the central power. Mr Tyler appealed to the judgment of posterity for his vindication; we have no desire to anticipate the verdict which will be rendered, but certainly no party was sorry when he went out of office.

During the year ending June 30th, 1845, the imports of the United States amounted in value to 117,254,564 dols.; the exports to 114,646,606 dols. The national revenue was 29,769,133 dols. 56 cents; the expenditures 29,968,206 dols. 98 cents. There was a balance in the treasury of 7,658,306 dols. 22 cents. The amount of public debt on the 1st of October, was 17,075,445 dols. 52 cents.

The peculiar and distinctive ideas of the party are set forth in the resolutions of the Baltimore convention—which, having ideas, published its platform—and in the inaugural address of Mr Polk. Some of them were expressed in a negative and some in a positive form.

"It is inexpedient and dangerous to exercise doubtful constitutional powers."

Government has no right "to commence and carry on a general system of internal improvement."

"Justice and sound policy forbid the federal government to foster one branch of industry to the detriment of another, or to cherish the interests of one portion to the injury of another portion of our common country."

"In levying discriminating duties, . . . care should be taken . . . not to benefit the wealthy few at the expense of the toiling millions."

"Congress has no power to charter a national bank." "Such an institute is . . . of deadly hostility to the best interests of the country, dangerous to the republican institutions and the liberties of the people." "Separation of the moneys of the government from banking institutions is indispensable."

"Our title to the whole of Oregon is clear and unquestionable."

The distinctive measures proposed were as follows :—

1. "The separation of the money of Government from banking institutions."
2. "A Tariff for Revenue."
3. "The re-occupation of Oregon."
4. "The re-annexation of Texas."

It is to be regretted that these measures were seldom submitted to a scientific and careful examination. They were abundantly discussed in Congress and out of Congress, but almost wholly in the spirit of party. Some of them were finally carried by a mere party vote; measures, too, on which the welfare of the nation was thought to depend. As we look over the speeches made in reference to the tariff or the subtreasury, we find ability enough; now and then a knowledge of the subject in hand, though that is far enough from common—but fairness which is willing to see good in the measures of a political opponent we almost never find: a man must be a "good Whig," or a "good Democrat," or a "good Free-Soiler;" must favour nothing but the ideas, the measures, the deeds, and the men of his party.

In his first message (Dec. 2nd, 1845), Mr Polk recommended the establishment of a "constitutional treasury . . . as a secure depository for the public money, without any power to make loans or discounts, or to issue any paper whatever as a currency or circulation." In conformity with this suggestion, a bill was reported with a proviso called "the specie clause"—that all payments to or from the government should be made in gold or silver. This bill passed the House by a vote of 123 to 64, the Senate by 28 to 24, and went into operation on the 1st of January, 1847, though the government did not pay specie till the 1st of April following. It is instructive to look at the speeches of eminent men, and the remarks in the leading newspapers, and see how party-spirit can blind the eyes of practical men, otherwise far-sighted. It was thought so much specie would be locked up in the subtreasury that there would not be enough for common business; "the drain would become onerous, indeed, if not insupportable." The *National Intelligencer* of October 10th, 1846, thought it was a "scheme only congenial to despotic governments, and utterly incompatible with the habits, the conveniences, and the whole social structure of free communities;" "every day's experience proves its impracticability, and its mischievous nature, even were it practicable." But before the end of the year Mr Polk could say with truth (Message, Dec. 8th, 1846), "that the amount of gold and silver coin in circulation in the country is greater than ever before." The banks were kept from "inflating" the currency. The measure has proved itself a wise one. Its good effect in retaining coin in the country and thus preventing a suspension of specie payment by the banks during the terrible commercial crisis of 1847—1849, was felt throughout the land, and now pretty extensively acknowledged. The administration deserves the gratitude of the people for this measure. But what Whig journal will venture to do justice to the subtreasury! Mr Gallatin says well: —"the practice . . . to convert every subject . . . into a pure party question destroys altogether personal independence and strikes at the very roots of our institutions. The usages of party . . make every man a slave, and transfer the legitimate authority of the majority of the nation, to the majority of a party, and consequently to a minority of the sovereign people."*

Mr Polk also recommended a "Tariff for Revenue;" Mr Walker, the Secretary of the Treasury, presented his scheme of such a tariff. In due time a bill was reported. The general tone of the discussion in Congress and out of it indicated very clearly the state of the country, and was a good example of the manner in which the most important political matters are investigated. We think there was no impartial discussion of the subject in Congress, or in the newspapers. We doubt that there is a single political or commercial journal in the United States, which would "open its columns" to a free and full discussion of the subject on the merits of the case. Political economy can hardly be considered an exact science as yet; but American politicians, even the most eminent, with here and there an exception, seem ignorant of the conclusions which may be regarded as established. Very few of them seem to study political economy—even to learn the facts on which it is based, still less to learn the natural laws on

* Letter of Feb. 10th, 1846, in the *National Intelligencer*.

which the material prosperity of the nation depends. Why should they? It is a tiresome work to instruct a great nation, and mankind seldom loves its school-masters in their lifetime, while it requires little effort to swim with the tide. In 1827, the citizens of Boston "assembled to take into consideration the proposed increase of duties;" their committee made a long and very able report adverse to that increase, and very justly say:—

> "The success or failure of the candidate for the Presidency, may be of great moment to the country, and still greater to those partisans whose political fortunes are depending on that event; but to the nation at large, the evil or the good which may arise out of the choice of the oue or the rejection of the other, can only be of temporary and limited importance compared with the wise and just disposition of a question on which our whole foreign and domestic policy turns, and which may, in its consequences, affect the stability and happiness of the Union for ages to come."*

In 1789, a moderate protective duty was established, on all imported articles; in 1816, a high protective tariff was for the first time established. Mr Clay and Mr Calhoun were its most important advocates. The tariff was raised in 1818 and in 1822, and was made much higher in 1824. Mr Webster opposed it with his peculiar ability, in a speech not yet forgotten. In 1828, a very high tariff was established by what has been called "the Bill of Abominations." In 1832-3, the tariff relaxed a little, to avert a civil war. Mr Clay got his celebrated "compromise act" established. The compromise lasted about nine years, till 1842. The celebrated tariff of 1842 was passed under the administration of Mr Tyler, and is too well known to require any remarks from us. Mr Webster admitted it had "its imperfections."

Mr Polk came into power with the idea of a Revenue Tariff in his mind. The bill passed the House of Representatives by a vote of 114 to 95, 1 Whig and 113 Democrats voting on that side; 71 Whigs, 18 Democrats, and 6 "Native Americans" voting on the opposite side. It passed

* "Report of a committee of the citizens of Boston and vicinity opposed to a further increase of duties on importations. Boston. From the press of Nathan Hale." 1827. p. 5, *et seq.* See, also, the Proceedings of the Meeting at Faneuil Hall, Oct. 2nd, 1820, in the New-England Palladium of Oct. 3rd, 1820. Also appended to Letters of S. D. Bradford, Esq. Boston. 1846. p. 37, *et seq.*

the Senate by the casting vote of the Vice-President, who was pledged to the measure before his election. A law of this magnitude has seldom passed any modern legislature with such imperfect discussion. In the Senate only a single man, Mr Lewis, spoke in defence of the bill; its friends gave "their thoughts no tongue," they were "checked for silence but never taxed for speech." Certainly we must say the conduct of the friends of the bill was eminently unjust, and the bill itself was carried, not by its merits, but by the power of the party; not by force of mind, but force of numbers.

It is a little painful to see how confident men are when they are so exceedingly short-sighted. We copy some of the remarks of the leading newspapers of the day.

> "The more its details [of the bill] are studied, the more odious is it made to appear;" "it is fruitful of mischief, and of mischief only;" members of Congress must be callous to every principle of justice, to every feeling of humanity, . . . if they can consent to destroy a measure so important as the law of 1842." "The spirit of evil, the exactions of party, the behests of the Baltimore convention, have finally triumphed over the prayers and remonstrances of a betrayed and terrified people. The fatal measure which strikes at the root of all the industry of the country, and at the living of every man in it who earns his bread by the sweat of his brow,—this misshapen and monstrous scheme, . . . this measure so pregnant of evil, has secured the sanction of both houses of Congress;" the specie will be "all drained out of the country in order to pay the balance of trade; . . . . credit will expand to its utmost . . to save the specie. At length, having neither cash nor credit, poverty steps in with its imperative restraints."

Mr Webster made a learned, and in many respects a very able, speech, though he weakened his rhetoric with a little extravagance, unusual with him,—against the new Tariff—against its general principles, and its particular details. He said, in the Senate:*—

> "The Treasury cannot, in my opinion, be supplied at the ratio which has been stated, and is expected, by any possible, I will say passible, augmentation of importations." "Why, the effect of this bill is to diminish freights, and to affect the navigating interests of the United States most seriously, most deeply; and therefore it is, that all the ship-owners of the United States, without an exception, so far

* Speech of July 25th, 1846.

as we hear from them, oppose the bill. It is said to be in favour of free trade and against monopoly. But every man connected with trade is against it; and this leads me to ask, and I ask with earnestness, and hope to receive an answer, at whose request, at whose recommendation, for the promotion of what interest, is this measure introduced? Is it for the importing merchants? They all reject it, to a man. Is it for the owners of the navigation of the country? They remonstrate against it. The whole internal industry of the country opposes it. The shipping interest opposes it. The importing interest opposes it. Who is it that calls for it, or proposes it? Who asks for it? Who? Has there been one single petition presented in its favour from any quarter of the country? Has a single individual in the United States come up here and told you that his interest would be protected, promoted, and advanced, by the passage of a measure like this? Sir, there is an imperative unity of the public voice the other way, altogether the other way. And when we are told that the public requires this, and that the people require it, we are to understand by the public, certain political men, who have adopted the shibboleth of party, for the public; and certain persons who have symbols, ensigns, and party flags, for the people; and that's all. I aver, sir, that is all."

The administration "proposes a new system adverse to all our experience, hostile to everything we have ever learned, different from the experience of any country on the face of the earth."

"It is prohibitory of internal labour. . . It does encourage the labour of foreign artisans over and above, and in preference to, the labour of our own artisans here in the United States."

Before the passage of the bill, Mr Webster presented in the Senate a memorial "signed by every importer of dry goods in the city of Boston, against the bill for the repeal of the Tariff."

What shall be said of the Tariff of 1846;—has it failed to produce a revenue; has it drained the specie out of the country; has it led to a great extension of paper money; has it produced the confusion occasioned by the Tariffs of '16, of '28, of '42? Has it impoverished the nation? The answer is all about us! Still, we admit that by adopting the *ad valorem* instead of *specific* duties, an opportunity has been left for fraudulent invoices, and great fraud has been committed, doing a wrong to the government, and still more to the fair and honourable merchant.

The "re-occupation of Oregon" was also recommended in Mr Polk's first message. Our title "to the whole of

Oregon territory" was "asserted, and, as is believed, maintained by irrefragable facts and arguments;" "to the Oregon our title is clear and unquestionable;" our "claims could not be abandoned without a sacrifice of both national honour and interests," and "no compromise which the United States ought to accept could be effected." He recommended that we should give the British notice of our intention to terminate the period of joint occupancy, as the treaty of 1818 allowed either party to do. Mr Polk, on other occasions, showed himself rather raw in diplomatic affairs; it would seem that he knew little of the matter in hand when he wrote the sentences above. They show him as a mere servant of his party, not as a great statesman, able to mediate between two mighty nations, and distribute justice with an even hand.

A great deal of discussion took place. The minor prophets and the major gave counsel after their kind. The *Union*—the organ of the government at Washington—contended for "the whole of Oregon or none. That is the only alternative as an issue of territorial right." But the *Charleston Mercury* was all at once afflicted with a conscience, and could distinguish between "claims" and "rights." We shall presently see the reason of the difference. In the Senate, Mr Sevier, of Arkansas, said that "war will come;" Mr Breese, of Illinois, would not have the government "grant any position to Great Britain upon any spot whatever of Oregon." Mr Allen, of Ohio, said the "American Government could not recede short of 54, 40." Mr Hannegan, of Indiana, thought that "the abandonment or surrender of any portion of . . Oregon would be an abandonment of the power, character, and best interests of the American people." Mr Cass thought war, "an old-fashioned war," "was almost inevitable;" Great Britain "might be willing to submit the question to arbitration, but the crowned heads whom she would propose as arbitrators would not be impartial, for they would cherish anti-republican feelings." He would negotiate, as Mr Webster very justly said, with the avowed predetermination to take nothing less than the whole of the territory in dispute. In the House of Representatives, John Quincy Adams went in for the territory on religious grounds, and claimed the whole of Oregon on the strength of the first chapter of Genesis. His conduct and his counsels on this occasion can hardly be called less than rash.

The South was not at all anxious to obtain the whole of Oregon. Mr Calhoun was singularly moderate in his desire for re-occupation; nice about questions of title and boundary, and desirous of keeping the peace. The reason is obvious. Mr Hannegan said well, "If it [Oregon] was good for the production of sugar and cotton, it would not have encountered the objection it has done." "I dreaded, on the part of those who were so strenuously in favour of the annexation of Texas at the Baltimore convention,—I dreaded, on their part, Punic faith." Poor, deluded Mr Hannegan, he found it. After Texas was secured, they who hunted after Oregon were left to beat the bush alone; nay, were hindered. This also would once have been considered as "judicial."

> "Here," says he, "we are told that we must be careful and not come in collision with Great Britain about a disputed boundary! But if it were with feeble Mexico that we were about to come into collision, we would then hear no such cautions. There was a question of disputed boundary between this country and Mexico, and those who have a right to know something of the history of that boundary told us that our rights extended only to the Nueces. How did we find the friends of Texas moving on that occasion? Did they halt for a moment at the Nueces? No, sir; at a single bound they cross the Nueces, and their war-horses prance upon the banks of the Rio del Norte. There was no negotiation then—we took the whole; but when Oregon is concerned, it is all right and proper to give away an empire, if England wills it."

In the House, Mr Winthrop suggested that, "in arbitration, reference was not necessarily to crowned heads," but the matter might be left to "a commission of able and dispassionate citizens, either from the two countries . . . or the world at large." Mr Benton was moderate and wise; his speeches on the Oregon question did much to calm the public mind and prepare for a peaceful settlement of the difficulty. The conduct of Mr Webster was worthy of the great man who had negotiated the treaty of Washington. He said in the beginning, "Let our arguments be fair; let us settle the question reasonably."

Congress resolved to terminate the joint occupancy.

The British government was willing to settle the business by arbitration or direct negotiation. America prefers the latter. Britain sends over her proposition to settle on the 49th degree as a general basis. Mr Polk referred the whole matter to the Senate, and asked their advice. He had not changed his opinion; not at all. If the Senate did not take the responsibility and advise him to accept the British proposal, he should feel it "his duty to reject the offer." Thus the responsibility was thrown upon the Senate. The proposal was accepted, a treaty was speedily made, and the only remaining cause of contention with England put to rest for ever. The conduct of Mr Polk, in making such pretensions, and holding out such boasts, on such a subject, was not merely rash, weak, and foolish; it was far worse than that. But for the unexpected prudence of a few men in the Senate, and the aversion of the South to acquire free territory, he would have lit the flames of war anew and done a harm to mankind which no services he could render would ever atone for.

On the 4th of July, 1845, Texas accepted the contract of annexation, and on the 22nd of December, two hundred twenty-five years after the landing of the Pilgrims on Plymouth Rock, the Senate of the United States passed upon the matter finally, and the work was done. However, previous to this event, Mr Polk had proposed to renew our diplomatic relations with Mexico, which had been broken off. Mexico consented to receive "a commissioner . . . with full powers to settle the present dispute." America sent Mr Slidell as a permanent minister plenipotentiary. He was refused *pro causa*.* The instructions given to Mr Slidell have not, we think, been *officially* published, though they were requested by the House. However, a document purporting to contain those instructions was published *un*officially. From that it appears that he was instructed to purchase new Mexico and California; he was allowed to offer 25,000,000 dols. and the American claims on Mexico, amounting, by his estimate, to 8,187,684

* See the *Massachusetts Quarterly Review*, No. I., p. 18, *et seq*. See the correspondence between the various functionaries in Executive Document, No. 60, 30th Congress, 1st Session, p. 12, *et seq*. Unfortunately we have only the translation of the Mexican letters. See, also, Senate Document, No. 337, 30th Congress, 1st Session, p. 18.

dols.* Thus the whole territory of New Mexico and California was thought to be worth 33,187,684 dols.

Soon after the accession of Mr Polk to office, General Taylor was ordered to Texas with an army. On the 15th of June, he was advised by the Secretary of War, Mr Marcy: "The point of your ultimate destination is the western portion of Texas, where you will select and occupy, on or near the Rio Grande del Norte, such a site as . . . will be best adapted to repel invasion. You will limit yourself to the defence of the territory, unless Mexico shall declare war against the United States."† General Taylor took possession on the Nueces at Corpus Christi, "the most western point ever occupied by Texas," but nearly two hundred miles east of the Rio Grande. August 6th, Mr Marcy writes:—‡

"Orders have already been issued to send ten thousand muskets and a thousand rifles into Texas."

August 23rd,

"Should Mexico assemble a large body of troops on the Rio Grande, and cross it with a considerable force, such a movement would be regarded as an invasion of the United States."

August 30th,

"An *attempt* to cross, . . . with such a force, will be considered in the same light. . . . Mexico having thus commenced hostilities, you may . . . cross the Rio Grande, disperse or capture the forces," &c.§

He was authorized to draw militia from five States—Alabama, Mississippi, Louisiana, Kentucky, and Tennessee.‖ Still General Taylor remained at Corpus Christi, not undertaking to commit an act of war by marching into the territory of Mexico. On the 13th of July, 1846, he was ordered to advance and occupy . . . positions on or near the east bank of the Rio Grande."¶ Accordingly General Taylor marches from the Nueces to the Rio Grande, finding no

* Jay, p. 117, *et seq.* See, also, Document No. 2, House of Representatives, 29th Congress, 1st Session, p. 31, *et seq.*, for the correspondence between the government of Texas and the United States, and *Massachusetts Quarterly Review*, No. I., p. 24, *et seq.*

† Executive Document, No. 60, 30th Congress, 2nd Session, p. 81, *et seq.*

‡ See the *Massachusetts Quarterly Review*, No. I., p. 25, *et seq.*

§ Executive Document, No. 60, 30th Congress, 2nd Session, pp. 84, 85, 88, 89.

‖ *Ibid.*, p. 86.

¶ Executive Document, *Ibid.*, p. 90.

Texans or Americans on his way—only "small armed parties of Mexicans," who appeared "desirous to avoid us." He takes his position on the left bank of the Rio Grande, and plants his guns—"four eighteen-pounders"—so as to "bear directly upon the public square of Matamoras, and within good range for demolishing the town."* Behold General Taylor nearly two hundred miles within the territory of Mexico, by the command of Mr Polk—in a district, to use the words of Mr Trist in his letter to Mr Buchanan, which "just as certainly constituted a part of that State [Tamaulipas], and not of Texas, . . . as it is certain that the counties of Acomac and Northampton do now constitute a part of the State of Virginia and not of Maryland."† An interview took place between the American General, Worth, and General Vega on the part of Mexico. "General Vega remarked that 'we' felt indignant at seeing the American flag placed on the Rio Grande, a portion of the Mexican territory." General Worth replied, "that was a matter of taste; notwithstanding there it would remain."‡ On the 12th of April, the Mexican General, Ampudia, very justly said, "Your government . . . has not only insulted, but exasperated the Mexican nation, bearing its conquering banner to the left bank of the Rio Grande del Norte."§

It was plain that America had committed an act of war, still the Mexicans did not commence hostilities. On the 12th of April, Ampudia summoned the American General to "withdraw within twenty-four hours;" he answered the same day that he "should not retrograde." On the 17th he blockaded the mouth of the Rio Grande, thus cutting off supplies from Matamoras, and wrote home that "it will at any rate compel the Mexicans either to withdraw their army from Matamoras, where it cannot be subsisted, or to assume the offensive on this side of the river."‖ Flour rose 40 dols. a barrel, it is said, at Matamoras. Still there was no fighting. But on the 23rd of April, General Taylor thus writes:

"With a view to check the depredations of small parties of Mexi-

* Letter of April 6th, 1846, *Ibid.*, p. 133.
† Executive Document, No. 52, 30th Congress, 1st Session, p. 290.
‡ Executive Document, No. 60, p. 137. § *Ibid.*, p. 140.
‖ Letter of 23rd April, *Ibid.*, p. 143.

cans on this side of the river, Lieutenants Dobbins, 3rd infantry, and Porter, 4th infantry, were authorized by me, a few days since, to scour the country for some miles, with a select party of men, and capture or destroy any such parties that they might meet. It appears that they separated, and that Lieutenant Porter, at the head of his own detachment, surprised a Mexican camp, drove away the men, and took possession of their horses. Soon afterwards there fell a heavy rain, and, at a moment when the party seem to have been quite unprepared for an attack, they were fired upon from the thicket. In attempting to return it, the muskets missed fire, and the party dispersed in the thicket."

Three days later he writes:

"I regret to report that a party of dragoons, sent out by me on the 24th inst., to watch the course of the river above on this bank, became engaged with a very large force of the enemy, and after a short affair, in which some sixteen were killed and wounded, appear to have been surrounded and compelled to surrender.

"Hostilities may now be considered as commenced, and I have this day deemed it necessary to call upon the governor of Texas for four regiments of volunteers."

Here is Captain Thornton's account of the affair:

"I discovered some Mexicans near a house in a large field. I halted the advance guard, and went into the field myself to see them. I had not gone more than a hundred yards when they fled; I turned round and motioned to the advanced guard to come on. In the mean time the main body of the squadron had come up to the advance guard, and, mistaking my order, followed in after them; and while I was questioning a Mexican the enemy appeared. I immediately ordered a charge, in order to cut my way through them; but finding their numbers too large to contend with any longer, I ordered a retreat; and although entirely surrounded, we endeavoured to cut our way through to camp. In the retreat my horse fell upon me, and I was unable to rise.

"As a prisoner of war, I am happy to inform you that attentions and kindness have been lavished upon me; as a proof of which, I will state that upon my reporting to General Arista that a dragoon had treated me rudely, he ordered him immediate punishment."*

Thus it is plain how they "became engaged," and that America not only committed the first act of war, by invading the territory of Mexico, but actually first commenced hostilities. It is true the President of Mexico, on the 18th

* Captain Thornton's letter to General Taylor, April 27th. See, also, Captain Hardee's letter, April 26th, *Ibid.*, pp. 290, 291, *et seq.*

of April, had said "from this day begins our defensive war, and every part of our territory attacked or invaded shall be defended." On the 24th he issued his proclamation declaring that "hostilities have been commenced by the United States, in making new conquests upon our territories within the boundaries of Tamaulipas and New Leon. I have not the right to declare war." * The same day General Arista informed General Taylor that he "considered hostilities commenced, and should prosecute them." † It was on that very day that the two parties "became engaged," as we have shown above.

General Taylor's letter of April 26th, reached Washington on Saturday, May 9th; on Monday, Mr Polk sent a message to Congress and declared that —

> "War exists, and notwithstanding all our efforts to avoid it, exists by the act of Mexico;" "the Mexican government have at last invaded our territory, and shed the blood of our fellow-citizens on our own soil;" "we have been exerting our best efforts to propitiate her good will;" "we have tried every effort at reconciliation." "The cup of forbearance had been exhausted even before the recent information from the frontier of the Del Norte. But now Mexico has passed the boundary of the United States, has invaded our territory, and shed American blood upon the American soil." †

Documents accompanied the message. Mr Winthrop proposed they should be read. No. In a very short time a bill passed the House placing the Army and Navy at the President's disposal, authorizing him to raise 50,000 volunteers, and putting in his hands 10,000,000 dols., for the purpose of enabling him to "prosecute said war to a speedy and successful termination." In the Senate, the same bill passed the next day. The preamble was in these memorable words: "Whereas, by the act of the Republic of Mexico, war exists between that government and the United States." In the House, fourteen voted against the bill, and two in the Senate. Six of the sixteen were from Massachusetts, two were from other parts of New England, and five from Ohio, one of her daughter States. ‡

* Jay, p. 142.

† Mr Polk's Message of May 11th, *ubi sup.*, p. 8. See, also, Porter, *ubi sup.*, chapter VIII.

‡ Here are the names. In the Senate,—*Thomas Clayton*, Delaware; *John Davis*, Massachusetts. In the House,—*John Quincy Adams*, *George Ashmun*, *Joseph Grinnell*, *Charles Hudson*, *Daniel P. King*, of Massachusetts; *Henry*

The history of the war is well known. It was conducted with great vigour; on the whole, with great military skill, and with as much humanity as could be expected. War at best is prolonged cruelty. Still we have read of no war conducted with less inhumanity than this. Some acts of wantonness were certainly committed. The capture of Tabasco is an example. The conduct of the volunteers was often base and revolting.* General Taylor was furnished with a proclamation, to distribute in Mexico, designed to foment discord, to promote hostility between the rich and poor. Their leaders were called "tyrants," and "their real purpose" was "to proclaim and establish a monarchy." Colonel Stevenson was told to make the people "feel that we come as deliverers; their rights of person, property, and religion must be respected and sustained." General Kearney proclaimed: "It is the wish and intention of the United States to provide for New Mexico a free government,—similar to those in the United States." "We shall want from you," says General Taylor's proclamation, "nothing but food for our army, and for this you shall always be paid in cash the full value." ("*y esto os serà siempre pagado en dineros y por su valor entera.*")† But on the 9th of July, General Taylor was told in a "confidential" letter:—

"You will also readily comprehend that in a country so divided into races, classes, and parties, as Mexico is, and with so many local divisions among departments, and personal divisions among individuals, there must be great room for operating on the minds and feelings of large portions of the inhabitants, and inducing them to wish success to an invasion which has no desire to injure their country; and which, in overthrowing their oppressors, may benefit themselves. Between the Spaniards, who monopolize the wealth and power of the country, and the mixed Indian race, who bear its burdens, there must be jealousy and animosity. The same feelings must exist between the lower and higher orders of the clergy; the latter of whom have the dignities and the revenues while the former have poverty and labour. . . . In all this field of division—in all these elements of social, political, personal, and local discord—there must be openings to reach the interests, passions, or principles of some of the parties, and thereby

P. Cranston, Rhode Island; *Luther Severance*, Maine; *Erastus D. Culver*, New York; *John Straham*, Pennsylvania; *Columbus Delano*, *Joseph M. Root*, *Daniel R. Tilden*, *Joseph Vance*, *Joshua R. Giddings*, Ohio.

* See many examples in Jay, p. 223, *et seq.*

† Executive Document, *ubi sup.*, p. 167 and 285.

to conciliate their good will, and make them coöperate with us in bringing about an honourable and speedy peace.

"Availing yourself of divisions which you may find existing among the Mexican people—to which allusion has been made—it will be your policy to encourage the separate departments or States, and especially those which you may invade and occupy, to declare their independence of the central government of Mexico, and either to become our allies, or to assume, as it is understood Yucatan has done, a neutral attitude in the existing war between the United States and Mexico.

"It is far from being certain that our military occupation of the enemy's country is not a blessing to the inhabitants in the vicinity."*

She is told that "to require" supplies "as contributions without paying or engaging to pay therefor" is the ordinary mode; "and you are instructed to adopt it, if in that way you are satisfied you can get abundant supplies for your forces."

It seems that 3,844,000 dols. was thus and in various other ways taken from the Mexicans.† Grave Senators doubted that the President had the right to legislate and levy contributions in Mexico, or elsewhere, without act of the Legislature, but *cedant togæ armis!* Yet Mr Buchanan could say on the 6th of October, 1847, "We have paid fair and even extravagant prices for all the supplies which we have received."‡

The war once begun it was to be prosecuted to a "succesful termination;" that is, to the dismemberment of Mexico. Captain Sloat lands at Monterey, on the Pacific coast of Mexico, on the 7th of July, 1846, issues his proclamation, and declares that, "henceforward California will be a portion of the United States, . . . and the same protection will be extended to them as to the other States of the Union."§ Commodore Stockton sets up his "Ebenezer" at Cindad de los Angelos on the 17th of August, 1846, and says, "I, Robert F. Stockton, . . . do hereby make known to all men, . . . do now declare it [Upper and Lower California] to be a territory of the

* Letter of Mr Marcy, July 9th and Sept. 22nd, 1846, *ubi sup.*, p. 333, *et seq.* and 341, *et seq.* See, also, "more of the same sort," in Executive Document, No. 14, 30th Congress, 1st Session, p. 5, *et seq.*

† Jay, p. 238, and Executive Document, No. 1, 30th Congress, 1st Session, p. 17.

‡ Executive Document, No. 52, 30th Congress, 1st Session, p. 92. See, also, p. 124.

§ Executive Document, No. 60, *ubi sup.*, p. 261.

United States, under the name of the territory of California."* Here is annexation without the least delay; swift enough to satisfy even South Carolina.

One pleasant thing we find in looking through the disagreeable and often hypocritical documents connected with the Mexican war. That is, the instructions sent by Mr Bancroft to Commodore Conner, July 11th, 1845:—

> "This is, perhaps, the largest fleet that ever sailed under the American flag; and while it is sufficient, in case of war, to win glory for yourself, your associates, and the country, you will win still higher glory if, by the judicious management of your force, you contribute to the continuance of peace."†

In his second annual message, Dec. 8th, 1864, Mr Polk said, "the war has not been waged with a view to conquest; but having been commenced by Mexico it has been carried into the enemy's country, and will be vigorously prosecuted there, with a view to obtain an honourable peace, and thereby secure an ample indemnity for the expenses of the war."‡ But in the message of Dec. 7th, 1847, he says, "as Mexico refuses all indemnity, we should adopt measures to indemnify ourselves, by appropriating permanently a portion of her territory." "New Mexico and California were taken possession of by our forces;" "I am satisfied that they should never be surrendered to Mexico." § Some one said to General Pillow, "I thought the object of your movement in this war was a treaty of peace." "True," (replied General Pillow) "that is the object of the *war;* but the object of *this campaign* was to *capture the capital*, and *then* make peace;" ‖ again, "*this* army has not come to conquer *a peace;* it has come to conquer the country;" we will make them *dine* and *sup* on the *horrors of war.*¶ The statements of Mr Polk require no comment. We do not wish to apply to them the only word we know in the English tongue which describes them.

We shall say nothing of the conduct of the administration during the war; nothing of the introduction of Santa Anna

* Executive Document, No. 60, *ubi sup.*, p. 268

† *Ibid.*, p. 232.

‡ Executive Document, No. 4, 29th Congress, 2nd Session, p. 22.

§ See Executive Document, No. 1, 30th Congress, 1st Session, p. 12.

‖ Trist's Letter to Buchanan, in Executive Document, No. 22, 30th Congress, 1st Session, p. 265.

¶ *Ibid.*, p. 275.

into Mexico; nothing of its quarrels with its officers, or their quarrels with one another; nothing of the contracts made with individuals for ships and other things needful in the war. The documents in the margin contain some remarkable things.* The President made the war, and Mr Nicholas P. Trist, "a Secretary in the department of State," made the peace. As the war was begun by Mr Polk without legal authority, so the treaty was made without legal authority. The Senate confirmed it.

There is one valuable provision in the treaty, designed to prevent depredations on private property in case of war, and other gratuitous cruelty.† One or two things in the correspondence of Mr Trist are too remarkable to pass by. June 2nd, 1847, he writes to Mr Buchanan, speaking of a certain boundary:

> "It includes a vast and rich country, with many inhabitants. It is too much to take. The population is mostly as dark as our mulattoes, and nominally free, and would be actually so under our government. The North would oppose taking it lest slavery should be established there; and the South lest its coloured population should be received as citizens, and protect their runaway slaves."

Again, Sept. 4:

> "Among the points which came under discussion was the exclusion of slavery from all territory which should pass from Mexico. In the course of their remarks on the subject, I was told that if it were proposed to the people of the United States to part with a portion of their territory, in order that the *inquisition* should be therein established, the proposal could not excite stronger feelings of abhorrence than those awakened in Mexico by the prospect of the introduction of slavery in any territory parted with by her. Our conversation on this topic was perfectly frank, and no less friendly; and the more effective upon their minds, inasmuch as I was enabled to say with perfect security, that although their impressions respecting the practical fact

* See Executive Documents, Nos. 1 and 60, 30th Congress, 1st Session (correspondence with Generals Taylor and Scott); Nos. 33 and 65 (trial of Lieutenant-Colonel Fremont and Major-General Pillow); No. 29 (contracts under authority of the War Department); and No. 52 (correspondence of Mr Trist and others relative to the negotiation of a treaty with Mexico).

† Articles XXII. and XXIII. of the Treaty, Executive Document, No. 52, 30th Congress, 1st Session, p. 62, *et seq.* The ideas and language thereof are copied from the celebrated Treaty of 1785, between the United States and Prussia. See the treaty (negotiated by Franklin, Jefferson, and Adams, ratified by Congress, May 17th, 1786), in Secret Journal of Congress. Boston. 1821. Vol. IV. pp. 25—43. (Article XXIII., *et seq.*)

of slavery, as it existed in the United States, were, I had no doubt, entirely erroneous; yet there was probably no difference between my individual views and sentiments on slavery, considered in itself, and those which they entertained. I concluded by assuring them that the bare *mention* of the subject in any treaty to which the United States were a party, was an absolute impossibility; that no President of the United States would dare to present any such treaty to the Senate; and that if it were in their power to offer me the whole territory described in our project, increased tenfold in value, and, in addition to that, covered a foot thick all over with pure gold, upon the single condition that slavery should be excluded therefrom, I could not entertain the offer for a moment, nor think even of communicating it to Washington. The matter ended in their being fully satisfied that this topic was one not to be touched, and it was dropped, with good feeling on both sides." *

America had Mexico entirely at her mercy, and wanted "indemnity for the past, and security for the future;" "indemnity for the cost of the war." She took California and New Mexico. The portion of the territory west of the Rio Grande, according to Mr Walker's statement, amounts to 526,078 square miles, or 336,689,920 acres; (Texas, within its "assumed limits," contains 325,529 square miles, or 208,332,800 acres.)† For this the United States are to pay Mexico 15,000,000 dols., and abandon all the celebrated claims which Mr Slidell estimated at 8,187,684 dols., paying to our citizens, however, not more than 3,250,000 dols. Taking the smallest sum—the United States pays Mexico for the territory 18,250,000 dols., and throws in the cost of the war—that being set off, it is likely, against the "imperishable glory" with which the soldiers have "covered themselves." Certainly, we must be in great want of land to refuse to pay more than our "claims," and 25,000,000 dols., and then actually pay the "claims" and 15,000,000 dols., flinging in all the cost of the war, and the loss of 1689 persons killed in battle, or perishing of their wounds received therein, and 6173 who had died by disease and accidents.‡

If England had one of her victims as completely at her feet as Mexico lay helpless at ours, she would have demanded all the public property of Mexico, a complete "in-

* Executive Document, No. 52, 30th Congress, 1st Session, p. 199.
† Executive Document, No. 70, 30th Congress, 1st Session, p. 9.
‡ Executive Document, No. 36, 30th Congress, 1st Session.

demnity for the cost of the war," and a commercial treaty highly disadvantageous to Mexico, and highly profitable to England. Why was Mr Polk so moderate? Had the administration become moral, and though careless of the "natural justice" of the war, careful about justice in the settlement? We wish we could think so. But there were a few men in the land hostile to the war; some because it was WAR, some because it was a WICKED war. These men, few in number, obscure in position, often hated, and sometimes persecuted, reproached by the President as affording "aid and comfort to the enemy," being on the side of the Eternal Justice, had IT on their side. The moral portion of both political parties—likewise a small portion, and an obscure, not numbering a single eminent name—opposed the war, and the government trembled. The pretensions of the South, her arrogance, her cunning, awakened at last the tardy North. Men began to talk of the "Wilmot Proviso;" of restricting slavery. True, some men fired by the instinct for office cried "be still," and others, fired with the instinct for gold, repeated the cry, "be still." There were those who had the instinct for justice, and they would not be still; no, nor will not; never. The slaveholders themselves began to tremble—and hence the easy conditions on which Mexico was let off.

The cost of the war it is not easy, or perhaps possible, at this moment, to make out; * but we can ascertain the sums already paid. The cost of the army and navy for the three years ending 30th June, 1846, was 37,615,879 dols. 15 cents; for the three years ending 30th June, 1849, 100,157,128 dols. 25 cents. The difference between them is a part of the cost of the war, and amounts to 62,541,249 dols. 10 cents. There have been paid for "Mexican War Bounty Scrip," 233,075 dols.; a part of the money obtained from Mexico, say 3,000,000 dols.; 65,000 land warrants, each for 160 acres of land, at 1 dol. 25 cents per acre (by Act of 11th Feb., 1847), 13,000,000 dols., making 16,233,075 dols. more. The whole thus far amounts to 78,774,324 dols. 10 cents. About 25,000 more land warrants, it is thought, will be required, at a cost of 5,000,000 dols. No man can now estimate the sum which will be required for pensions. If we set down

* See, who will, a Sermon of the Mexican War, &c. &c., by Theodore Parker. (Boston. 1848.) pp. 10, *et seq.*, and 17, *et seq.*

the whole direct cost to the nation at 200,000,000 dols., we think we shall not be far out of the way. This is a tax of 10 dols. on each person in the United States, bond or free, old or newly born, rich or poor; like all other taxes, it is ultimately to be paid by the labour of the country, by the men who work with their hands, chiefly by poor men. The twenty-million-headed nation, blindly led by guides not blind, little thought of this when they shouted at each "famous victory," and denounced humble men who both considered the "natural justice" of the war, and counted its cost.

Mr Polk refused his signature to three bills passed by Congress; one making "appropriations for the improvement of certain harbours and rivers," one for the ascertainment and satisfaction of "claims of American citizens" on France before the 31st of July, 1801, a third "for continuing certain works in the territory of Wisconsin, and for other purposes."* It is a little remarkable to find a man who commenced war upon Mexico by invading her territory, seized with such scruples about violating the Constitution while paying an honest debt. The Constitution which can be violated to promote Slavery, can easily afford an excuse for the neglect of justice.

Facile invenit fustem qui vult cædere canem.

Mr Polk found the nation with a debt of 17,075,445 dols. 52 cents, he left it with a debt of 64,938,400 dols. 70 cents. That was the debt on the 4th of March, 1849, including the 2,193,500 dols. of the loan of 1848, subsequently paid in.

Mr Polk has gone to the Judge of all men, who is also their Father. The hurra of the multitude and the applause of an irresponsible party are of no more value than the water which a Methodist minister sprinkled on the head of the dying man. His wealth became nothing; his power and his fame went back to those that gave; at the grave's mouth his friends, and he had friends, forsook him, and the monarch of the nation, the master of negro slaves, the author of a war, was alone with his God. Not a slave in the whole wide world would have taken his place. But God sees not as man. Here let us leave him, not without pity for his earthly history—not without love for a brother man whose weakness,

* See his Special Messages of August 3rd, 1846, August 8th, 1846, and December 15th, 1847.

not his wickedness, wrought for our nation such shame and woe.

Of his administration in general, we would say little. He proved by experiment that his was "a nomination not fit to be made;" not fit to be confirmed after the convention had made it; he demonstrated by experiment the folly of putting a little man into a great man's place; the folly of taking the mere creature of a party to be the President of a nation. It was not the first time this had been done, not the last. Yet such is the structure of government and society in America, such the character of the people, so young, so free, so fresh, and strong—that not even such an administration as Mr Polk's can permanently impede the nation's march. Cattle and corn were never more abundant. Foreigners came here in great numbers, 229,483 in the year ending 30th September, 1848. Our total increase must have been considerably more than half a million a year. Not long ago men sneered at America—a Republic could not hold its own, or only with men like Washington at its head. But in 1848, when the nations of Europe were convulsed with revolutions, whose immediate failure is now the joy of the enemies of mankind, west of the ocean not less than east thereof—America stood firm, though her nominal guide was only James K. Polk. Ours is the most complicated government in the world, but it resembles the complication of the human body, not that of a fancy watch. Our increase in wealth was greater far than our proportionate growth of numbers. When trade is free, and labour free, and institutions for all men, there is no danger that men will multiply faster than bread to fill their mouths. This is God's world and not the Devil's.

We are a new people in a new world; flexible still, and ready to take the impress of a great idea. Shame on us that we choose such leaders; men with no noble gifts of leadership, no lofty ideas, no humane aims; men that defile the continent with brother's blood most wickedly poured out! The President of the Democrats showed himself the ally of the Autocrats of the East who

> "wade through slaughter to a throne,
> And shut the gates of mercy on mankind."

The good things of Mr Polk's administration we have

spoken of and duly honoured; the abomination thereof—whence came that? From the same source out of which so much evil has already come: from Slavery. A nation, like a man, is amenable to the law of God; suffers for its sin, and must suffer till it ends the sin. In the North national unity of action is preserved with little sacrifice of individual variety of action; the union of the people and the freedom of the person are carefully kept secure. Hence each man has as much freedom as he can have in the present state of physical, moral, and social science. But in the South it is not so; there, in a population of 7,334,431 persons, there are 2,486,326 slaves; so if the average amount of freedom in the North be represented by *one*, in the South it will be but about two-thirds;* it is doubtful that the inhabitants of any part of Europe, except Russia and Turkey, have less. Think you, O reader, while we thus trample on the rights of millions of men, we shall not suffer for the crime? No! God forbid that we should not suffer.

There are two things the nation has to fear—two modes of irresponsible power. One is the POWER OF PARTY; one the POWER OF GOLD. Mr Polk was the creature of a party; his ideas were party ideas, his measures party measures, his acts party acts, himself a party man. A party can make a President, as a heathen his idol, out of anything; no material is too vulgar; but a party cannot make a great man out of all the little ones which can be scented out by the keenest convention which ever met. The Democratic party made Mr Polk; sustained him; but no huzzas could make him a great man, a just man, or a fair man. No king is more tyrannical than a party when it has the power; no despot more irresponsible. The Democrats and Whigs are proof of this. One has noble instincts and some noble ideas—so had the other once; but consider the conduct of the Baltimore convention in 1844; their conduct for five years after. Consider the convention of Philadelphia in 1848, and the subsequent conduct of the Whigs! This irresponsible power of party has long been controlled by the South, for various reasons named before.

The irresponsible power of gold appears in two forms,

* $\frac{4,848,105}{7,134,431} = \cdot 661 +$

as it is held by individuals or corporations. The power of gold when vast sums are amassed by a single individual, who owns more property than five counties of Massachusetts, is certainly dangerous, and of an evil tendency. But yet as the individual is transient, it is not presently alarming; a wise law, unwelcome often to the rich man, limits his control to a few years. His children may be fathers of poor men. But when vast sums are held by a corporation, permanent in itself, though composed of fleeting elements, this power, which no statute of mortmain here holds in check, becomes alarming as well as dangerous. This power of gold belongs to the North, and is likewise irresponsible.

Sometimes the two help balance, and counteract one another. It was so in the administration of Jackson and Van Buren. Jackson set the power of party to smite the power of gold. Even Mr Polk did so in two remarkable instances. But this is not always to be expected: the two are natural allies. The feudalism of birth, depending on a Caucasian descent, and the feudalism of gold, depending on its dollars, are of the same family, only settled in different parts of the land; they are true yoke-fellows. The slaveocracy of the South, and the plutocracy of the North, are born of the same mother. Now, for the first time for many years, they have stricken hands; but the Northern power of gold at the Philadelphia convention was subjugated by the Southern power of party, and lent itself a willing tool. Together they have selected the man of their choice, confessedly ignorant of politics, of small ability, and red with war; placed him on the throne of the nation. The slaveocracy and the plutocracy each gave him its counsel. By his experiment he is to demonstrate his fitness, his impotence, or his crime. He is on trial before the nation. It is not ours to judge, still less to *pre*-judge him. Let General Taylor be weighed in an even balance. We trust that some one, four years hence, will report on his administration with as much impartiality as we have aimed at, and with more power to penetrate and judge. We wish there might be a more honourable tale to tell of the first mere military chief the nation ever chose. There are great problems before the nation—involving the welfare of millions of men. We pause, with hope and fear, for the Whigs to solve them as they can.

THE WRITINGS OF RALPH WALDO EMERSON.

1. *Nature, &c.* Boston: 1836. 1 vol. 12mo.
2. *Essays.* By R. W. EMERSON. Boston: 1841. 1 vol. 12mo.
3. *Essays: Second Series.* By R. W. EMERSON. Ibid.: 1844. 1 vol. 12mo.
4. *Poems.* By R. W. EMERSON. Ibid.: 1847. 1 vol. 12mo.
5. *Nature, Addresses and Orations.* By R. W. EMERSON. Ibid.: 1849. 1 vol. 12mo.
6. *Representative Men: Seven Lectures.* By R. W. EMERSON. Ibid.: 1850. 1 vol. 12mo.

WHEN a hen lays an egg in the farmer's mow, she cackles quite loud and long. "See," says the complacent bird, "see what an egg I have laid!" all the other hens cackle in sympathy, and seem to say, "what a nice egg has got laid! was there ever such a family of hens as our family?" But the cackling is heard only a short distance, in the neighbouring barnyards; a few yards above, the blue sky is silent. By and by the rest will drop their daily burden, and she will cackle with them in sympathy—but ere long the cackling is still; the egg has done its service, been addled, or eaten, or perhaps proved fertile of a chick, and it is forgotten, as well as the cackler who laid the ephemeral thing. But when an acorn in June first uncloses its shell, and the young oak puts out its earliest shoot, there is no noise; none attending its growth, yet it is destined to last some half a thousand years as a living tree, and serve as long after that for sound timber. Slowly and in silence, unseen in the dim recesses of the earth, the diamond gets formed by small accretions, age after age. There is no cackling in the caverns of the deep, as atom journeys to its fellow atom and the crystal is slowly getting made, to shine on the bosom of loveliness, or glitter in the diadem of an emperor, a thing of beauty and a joy for ever.

As with eggs, so is it with little books; when one of them is laid in some bookseller's mow, the parent and the literary barnyard are often full of the foolishest cackle, and seem as happy as the ambiguous offspring of frogs, in some shallow pool, in early summer. But by and by it is again with the books as with the eggs; the old noise is all hushed, and the little books all gone, while new authors are at the same work again.

Gentle reader, we will not find fault with such books, they are as useful as eggs; yea, they are indispensable; the cackle of authors, and that of hens—why should they not be allowed? Is it not written that all things shall work after their kind, and so produce; and does not this rule extend from the hen-roost to the American Academy and all the Royal Societies of lierature in the world? Most certainly. But when a great book gets written, it is published with no fine flourish of trumpets; the world does not speedily congratulate itself on the accession made to its riches; the book must wait awhile for its readers. Literary gentlemen of the tribe of Bavius and Mævius are popular in their time, and get more praise than bards afterwards famous. What audience did Athens and Florence give to their Socrates and their Dante? What price did Milton get for the Paradise Lost? How soon did men appreciate Shakspeare? Not many years ago, George Steevens, who "edited" the works of that bard, thought an "Act of Parliament was not strong enough" to make men read his sonnets, though they bore the author up to a great height of fame, and he sat where Steevens "durst not soar." In 1686, there had been four editions of Flatman's Poems; five of Waller's; eight of Cowley's; but in eleven years, of the Paradise Lost only three thousand copies were sold; yet the edition was cheap, and Norris of Bemerton went through eight or nine editions in a quite short time. For forty-one years, from 1623 to 1664, England was satisfied with two editions of Shakspeare, making, perhaps, one thousand copies in all. Says Mr Wordsworth of these facts: "There were readers in multitudes; but their money went for other purposes, as their admiration was fixed elsewhere." Mr Wordsworth himself furnishes another example. Which found the readiest welcome, the Excursion and the Lyrical Poems of that writer, or Mr Macaulay's Lays of Ancient Rome? How many a little philosophist in Germany went up in his rocket-like ascension, while the bookseller at Königsberg despaired over the unsaleable sheets of Immanuel Kant!

Says an Eastern proverb, "the sage is the instructor of a hundred ages," so he can afford to wait till one or two be past away, abiding with the few, waiting for the fit and the many. Says a writer:

"There is somewhat touching in the madness with which the passing age mischooses the object on which all candles shine, and all eyes are turned; the care with which it registers every trifle touching Queen Elizabeth, and King James, and the Essexes, Leicesters, Burleighs, and Buckinghams; and lets pass, without a single valuable note, the founder of another dynasty, which alone will cause the Tudor dynasty to be remembered,—the man who carries the Saxon race in him by the inspiration which feeds him, and on whose thoughts the foremost people of the world are now for some ages to be nourished, and minds to receive this and not another bias. A popular player,—nobody suspected he was the poet of the human race; and the secret was kept as faithfully from poets and intellectual men, as from courtiers and frivolous people. Bacon, who took the inventory of the human understanding for his times, never mentioned his name. Ben Jonson had no suspicion of the elastic fame whose first vibrations he was attempting. He no doubt thought the praise he has conceded to him generous, and esteemed himself, out of all question, the better poet of the two.

"If it need wit to know wit, according to the proverb, Shakspeare's time should be capable of recognizing it. . . . Since the constellation of great men who appeared in Greece in the time of Pericles, there was never any such society;—yet their genius failed them to find out the best head in the universe. Our poet's mask was impenetrable. You cannot see the mountain near. It took a century to make it suspected; and not until two centuries had passed, after his death, did any criticism which we think adequate begin to appear. It was not possible to write the history of Shakspeare till now."

It is now almost fourteen years since Mr Emerson published his first book: Nature. A beautiful work it was, and will be deemed for many a year to come. In this old world of literature, with more memory than wit, with much tradition and little invention, with more fear than love, and a great deal of criticism upon very little poetry, there came forward this young David, a shepherd, but to be a king, "with his garlands and singing robes about him;"

one note upon his new and fresh-strung lyre was "worth a thousand men." Men were looking for something original, they always are; when it came some said it thundered, others that an angel had spoke. How men wondered at the little book! It took nearly twelve years to sell the five hundred copies of Nature. Since that time Mr Emerson has said much, and if he has not printed many books, at least has printed much; some things far surpassing the first essay, in richness of material, in perfection of form, in continuity of thought; but nothing which has the same youthful freshness, and the same tender beauty as this early violet, blooming out of Unitarian and Calvinistic sand or snow. Poems and Essays of a later date are there, which show that he has had more time and woven it into life; works which present us with thought deeper, wider, richer, and more complete, but not surpassing the simplicity and loveliness of that maiden flower of his poetic spring.

We know how true it is, that a man cannot criticise what he cannot comprehend, nor comprehend either a man or a work greater than himself. Let him get on a Quarterly never so high, it avails him nothing; "pyramids are pyramids in vales," and emmets are emmets even in a Review. Critics often afford an involuntary proof of this adage, yet grow no wiser by the experience. Few of our tribe can make the simple shrift of the old Hebrew poet, and say, "*we* have not exercised ourselves in great matters, nor in things too high for *us*." Sundry Icarian critics have we seen, wending their wearying way on waxen wing to overtake the eagle flight of Emerson; some of them have we known getting near enough to see a fault, to overtake a feather falling from his wing, and with that tumbling to give name to a sea, if one cared to notice to what depth they fell.

Some of the criticisms on Mr Emerson, transatlantic and cisatlantic, have been very remarkable, not to speak more definitely. "What of this new book?" said Mr Public to the reviewer, who was not "seized and tied down to judge," but of his own free will stood up and answered: "Oh! 'tis out of all plumb, my lord—quite an irregular thing! not one of the angles at the four corners is a right angle. I had my rule and compasses, my lord, in my pocket. And for the poem, your lordship bid me look at it—upon taking the length, breadth, height, and depth of it, and trying them at home, upon an exact scale of Bossu's—they are out, my lord, in every one of their dimensions."

Oh, gentle reader, we have looked on these efforts of our brother critics not without pity. There is an excellent bird, terrene, marine, and semi-aerial; a broad-footed bird, broad-beaked, broad-backed, broad-tailed; a notable bird she is, and a long-lived; a useful bird, once indispensable to writers, as furnishing the pen, now fruitful in many a hint. But when she undertakes to criticise the music of the thrush, or the movement of the humming-bird, why, she oversteps the modesty of her nature, and if she essays the flight of the eagle—she is fortunate if she falls only upon the water. "No man," says the law, "may stultify himself." Does not this canon apply to critics? No, the critic may do so. Suicide is a felony, but if a critic only slay himself critically, dooming himself to "hoise with his own petard," why, 'tis to be forgiven

> "That in our aspirations to be great,
> Our destinies o'erleap our mortal state."

In a place where there were no Quarterly Journals, the veracious historian, Sir Walter Scott, relates that Claud Halcro, ambitious of fame, asked his fortune of an Orcadian soothsayer:

> "Tell me, shall my lays be sung,
> Like Hacon's of the golden tongue,
> Long after Halcro's dead and gone?
> Or shall Hialtland's minstrel own
> One note to rival glorious John?"

She answers, that as things work after their kind, the result is after the same kind:

> "The eagle mounts the polar sky,
> The Imber-goose, unskill'd to fly,
> Must be content to glide along
> When seal and sea-dog list his song."

We are warned by the fate of our predecessors, when their example does not guide us; we confess not only our inferiority to Mr Emerson, but our consciousness of the fact, and believe that they should "judge others who themselves excel," and that authors, like others on trial, should be judged by their peers. So we will not call this a criticism, which we are about to write on Mr Emerson, only an attempt at a contribution towards a criticism, hoping that, in due time, some one will come and do faithfully and completely, what it is not yet time to accomplish, still less within our power to do.

All of Mr Emerson's literary works, with the exception of the Poems, were published before they were printed; delivered by word of mouth to audiences. In frequently reading his pieces, he had an opportunity to see any defect of form and amend it. Mr Emerson has won by his writings a more desirable reputation than any other man of letters in America has yet attained. It is not the reputation which bring him money or academic honours, or membership of learned societies; nor does it appear conspicuously in the literary journals as yet. But he has a high place among thinking men, on both sides of the water; we think no man who writes the English tongue has now so much influence in forming the opinions and character of young men and women. His audience steadily increases, at home and abroad, more rapidly in England than America. It is now with him as it was, at first, with Dr Channing; the fairest criticism has come from the other side of the water; the reason is that he, like his predecessor, offended the sectarian and party spirit, the personal prejudices of the men about him; his life was a reproach to them, his words an offence, or his doctrines alarmed their sectarian, their party, or their personal pride, and they accordingly condemned the man. A writer who should bear the same relation to the English mind as Emerson to ours, for the same reason would be more acceptable here than at home. Emerson is neither a sectarian nor a partisan, no man less so; yet few men in America have been visited with more hatred,—private personal hatred, which the authors poorly endeavoured te conceal, and perhaps did hide from themselves. The spite we have heard expressed against him, by men of the common morality, would strike a stranger with amazement, especially when it is remembered that his personal character and daily life are of such extraordinary loveliness. This hatred has not proceeded merely from ignorant men, in whom it could easily be excused; but more often from men who have had opportunities of obtaining as good a culture as men commonly get in this country. Yet while he has been the theme of vulgar abuse, of sneers and ridicule in public and in private; while critics, more remarkable for the venom of their poison than the strength of their bow, have shot at him their little shafts, barbed more than pointed, he has also drawn about him some of what old Drayton called "the idle smoke of praise." Let us see what he has thrown into the public fire to cause this incense; what he has done to provoke the immedicable rage of certain other men; let us see what there is in his works, of old or new, true or false, what American and what cosmopolitan; let us weigh his works with such imperfect scales as we have, weigh them by the universal standard of beauty, truth, and love, and make an attempt to see what he is worth.

American literature may be distributed into two grand divisions: namely, the permanent literature, consisting of books not written for a special occasion, books which are bound between hard covers; and the transient literature, written for some special occasion and not designed to last beyond that. Our permanent literature is almost wholly an imitation of old models. The substance is old, and the form old. There is nothing American about it. But as our writers are commonly quite deficient in literary culture and scientific discipline, their productions seem poor when compared with the imitative portion of the permanent literature in older countries, where the writers start with a better discipline and a better acquaintance with letters and art. This inferiority of culture is one of the misfortunes incident to a new country, especially to one where practical talent is so much and so justly preferred to merely literary accomplishment and skill. This lack of culture is yet more apparent, in general, in the transient literature which is produced mainly by men who have had few advantages for intellectual discipline in early life, and few to make acquaintance with books at a later period. That portion of our literature is commonly stronger and more American, but it is often coarse and rude. The permanent literature is imitative; the other is rowdy. But we have now no time to dwell upon this theme, which demands a separate paper.

Mr Emerson is the most American of our writers. The idea of America, which lies at the bottom of our original institutions, appears in him with great prominence. We mean the idea of personal freedom, of the dignity and value of human nature, the superiority of a man to the accidents of a man. Emerson is the most republican of republicans, the most protestant of the dissenters. Serene as a July sun, he is equally fearless. He looks everything in the face modestly, but with earnest scrutiny, and passes judgment upon its merits. Nothing is too high for his examination; nothing too sacred. On earth only one thing he finds which is thoroughly venerable, and that is the nature of man; not the accidents, which make a man rich or famous, but the substance, which makes him a man. The man is before the institutions of man; his nature superior to his history. All finite things are only appendages of man, useful, convenient, or beautiful. Man is master, and nature his slave, serving for many a varied use. The results of human experience — the State, the Church, society, the family, business, literature, science, art—all of these are subordinate to man: if they serve the individual, he is to foster them, if not, to abandon them and seek better things. He looks at all things, the past and the present, the State and the Church, Christianity and the market-house, in the daylight of the intellect. Nothing is allowed to stand between him and his manhood. Hence there is an apparent irreverence; he does not bow to any hat which Gessler has set up for public adoration, but to every man, canonical or profane, who bears the mark of native manliness. He eats show-bread, if he is hungry. While he is the most American, he is almost the most cosmopolitan of our writers, the least restrained and belittled by the popular follies of the nation or the age.

In America, writers are commonly kept in awe and subdued by fear of the richer class, or that of the mass of men. Mr Emerson has small respect for either; would bow as low to a lackey as a lord, to a clown as a scholar, to one man as a million. He spurns all constitutions but the law of his own nature, rejecting them with manly scorn. The traditions of the churches are no hindrances to his thought; Jesus or Judas were the same to him, if either stood in his way and hindered the proportionate development of his individual life. The forms of society and the ritual of scholarship are no more effectual restraints. His thought of to-day is no barrier to freedom of thought to-morrow, for his own nature is not to be subordinated, either to the history of man, or his own history. "To-morrow to fresh fields and pastures new," is his motto.

Yet, with all this freedom, there is no wilful display of it. He is so confident of his freedom, so perfectly possessed of his rights, that he does not talk of them. They appear, but are not spoken of. With the hopefulness and buoyant liberty of America, he has none of our ill-mannered boasting. He criticises America often; he always appreciates it; he seldom praises, and never brags of our country. The most democratic of democrats, no disciple of the old régime is better mannered, for it is only the vulgar democrat or aristocrat who flings his follies in your face. While it would be difficult to find a writer so uncompromising in his adhesion to just principles, there is not in all his works a single jeer or ill-natured sarcasm. None is less addicted to the common forms of reverence, but who is more truly reverential?

While his idea is American, the form of his literature is not less so. It is a form which suits the substance, and is modified by the institutions and natural objects about him. You see that the author lives in a land with free institutions, with town-meetings and ballot-boxes; in the vicinity of a decaying church; amongst men whose terrible devils are poverty and social neglect, the only devils whose damnation is much cared for. His geography is American. Katskill and the Alleghanies, Monadnock, Wachusett, and the uplands of New Hampshire, appear in poetry or prose; Contocook and Agiochook are better than the Ilyssus, or Pactolus, or "smooth-sliding Mincius, crowned with vocal reeds." New York, Fall River, and Lowell have a place in his writings, where a vulgar Yankee would put Thebes or Pæstum. His men and women are American—John and Jane, not Coriolanus and Persephone. He tells of the rhodora, the club-moss, the blooming clover, not of the hibiscus and the asphodel. He knows the humblebee, the blackbird, the bat, and the wren, and is not ashamed to say or sing of the things under his own eyes. He illustrates his high thought by common things out of our plain New-England life—the meeting in the church, the Sunday school, the dancing-school, a huckleberry party, the boys and girls hastening home from school, the youth in the shop, beginning an unconscious courtship with his unheeding customer, the farmers about their work in the fields, the bustling trader in the city, the cattle, the new hay, the voters at a town-meeting, the village brawler in a tavern full of tipsy riot, the conservative who thinks the nation is lost if his ticket chance to miscarry, the bigot worshipping the knot hole through which a dusty beam of light has looked in upon his darkness, the radical who declares that nothing is good if established, and the patent reformer who screams in your ears that he can finish the world with a single touch,—and out of all these he makes his poetry, or illustrates his philosophy. Now and then he wanders off to other lands, reports what he has seen, but it is always an American report of what an American eye saw. Even Mr Emerson's recent exaggerated praise of England is such a panegyric as none but an American could bestow.

We know an American artist who is full of American scenery. He makes good drawings of Tivoli and Subiaco, but, to colour them, he dips his pencil in the tints of the American heaven, and over his olive trees and sempervives, his asses and his priests, he sheds the light only of his native sky. So is it with Mr Emerson. Give him the range of the globe, it is still an American who travels.

Yet with this indomitable nationality, he has a culture quite cosmopolitan and extraordinary in a young nation like our own. Here is a man familiar with books, not with many, but the best books, which he knows intimately. He has kept good company. Two things impress you powerfully and continually—the man has seen nature, and been familiar with books. His literary culture is not a varnish on the surface; not a mere polish of the outside; it has penetrated deep into his consciousness. The salutary effect of literary culture is more perceptible in Emerson than in any American that we know, save one, a far younger man, and of great promise, of whom we shall speak at some other time.

We just now mentioned that our writers were sorely

deficient in literary culture. Most of them have only a smattering of learning, but some have read enough, read and remembered with ability to quote. Here is one who has evidently read much, his subject required it, or his disposition, or some accident in his history furnished the occasion; but his reading appears only in his quotations, or references in the margin. His literature has not penetrated his soul and got incorporated with his whole consciousness. You see that he has been on Parnassus, by the huge bouquet, pedantic in its complexity, that he affronts you with; not by the odour of the flowers he has trampled or gathered in his pilgrimage, not by Parnassian dust clinging to his shoes, or mountain vigour in his eye. The rose gatherer smells of his sweets, and needs not prick you with the thorn to apprize you of what he has dealt in.

Here is another writer who has studied much in the various literatures of the world, but has lost himself therein. Books supersede things, art stands between him and nature, his figures are from literature not from the green world. Nationality is gone. A traveller on the ocean of letters, he has a mistress in every port, and a lodging-place where the night overtakes him; all flags are the same to him, all climes; he has no wife, no home, no country. He has dropped nationality, and in becoming a cosmopolitan, has lost his citizenship everywhere. So, with all Christendom and heathendom for his metropolis, he is an alien everywhere in the wide world. He has no literary inhabitiveness. Now he studies one author, and is the penumbra thereof for a time; now another, with the same result. Trojan or Tyrian is the same to him, and he is Trojan or Tyrian as occasion demands. A thin vapoury comet, with small momentum of its own, he is continually deflected from his natural course by the attraction of other and more substantial bodies, till he has forgotten that he ever had any orbit of his own, and dangles in the literary sky, now this way drawn, now that, his only certain movement an oscillation. With a chameleon variability, he attaches himself to this or the other writer, and for the time his own colour disappears and he along with it.

With Emerson all is very different; his literary culture is of him, and not merely on him. His learning appears not in his quotations, but in his talk. It is the wine itself, and not the vintner's brand on the cask, which shows its quality. In his reading and his study, he is still his own master. He has not purchased his education with the loss of his identity, not of his manhood; nay, he has not forgotten his kindred in getting his culture. He is still the master of himself; no man provokes him even into a momentary imitation. He keeps his individuality with maidenly asceticism, and with a conscience rarely found amongst literary men. Virgil Homerizes, Hesiodizes, and plays Theocritus now and then. Emerson plays Emerson, always Emerson. He honours Greece, and is not a stranger with her noblest sons; he pauses as a learner before the lovely muse of Germany; he bows low with exaggerating reverence before the practical skill of England; but no one, nor all of these, have power to subdue that serene and upright intellect. He rises from the oracle he stooped to consult just as erect as before. His reading gives a certain richness to his style, which is more literary than that of any American writer that we remember; as much so as that of Jeremy Taylor. He takes much for granted in his reader, as if he were addressing men who had read everything, and wished to be reminded of what they had read. In classic times, there was no reading public, only a select audience of highly cultivated men. It was so in England once; the literature of that period indicates the fact. Only religious and dramatic works were designed for pit, box, and gallery. Nobody can speak more clearly and more plainly than Emerson, but take any one of his essays or orations, and you see that he does not write in the language of the mass of men, more than Thucydides or Tacitus. His style is allusive, as an ode of Horace or Pindar, and the allusions are to literature which is known to but few. Hence, while his thought is human in substance, and American in its modifications, and therefore easily grasped, comprehended, and welcomed by men of the commonest culture, it is but few who understand the entire meaning of the sentences which he writes. His style reflects American scenery, and is dimpled into rare beauty as it flows by, and so has a pleasing fascination, but it reflects also the literary scenery of his own mind, and so half of his thought is lost on half his readers. Accordingly no writer or lecturer finds a readier access for his thoughts to the mind of the people at large, but no American author is less intelligible to the people in all his manifold meaning and beauty of allusion. He has not completely learned to think with the sagest sages and then put his thoughts into the plain speech of plain men. Every word is intelligible in the massive speech of Mr Webster, and has its effect, while Emerson has still something of the imbecility of the scholar, as compared to the power of the man of action, whose words fall like the notes of the wood-thrush, each in its time and place, yet without picking and choosing. "Blacksmiths and teamsters do not trip in their speech," says he, "it is a shower of bullets. It is Cambridge men who correct themselves, and begin again at every half sentence; and moreover, will pun and refine too much, and swerve from the matter to the expression." But of the peculiarities of his style we shall speak again.

Emerson's works do not betray any exact scholarship, which has a certain totality, as well as method about it. It is plain to see that his favourite authors have been Plutarch, especially that outpouring of his immense common-place book, his "Moral Writings," Montaigne, Shakspeare, George Herbert, Milton, Wordsworth, Coleridge, and Carlyle. Of late years, his works contain allusions to the ancient oriental literature, from which he has borrowed some hard names and some valuable thoughts, but is occasionally led astray by its influence, for it is plain that he does not understand that curious philosophy he quotes from. Hence his oriental allies are brought up to take a stand which no man dreamed of in their time, and made to defend ideas not known to men till long after these antediluvian sages were at rest in their graves.

In Emerson's writings you do not see indications of exact mental discipline, so remarkable in Bacon, Milton, Taylor, and South, in Schiller, Lessing, and Schleiermacher; neither has he the wide range of mere literature noticeable in all other men. He works up scientific facts in his writings with great skill, often penetrating beyond the fact, and discussing the idea out of which it and many other kindred facts seem to have proceeded: this indicates not only a nice eye for facts, but a mind singularly powerful to detect latent analogies, and see the one in the many. Yet there is nothing to show any regular and systematic discipline in science which appears so eminently in Schiller and Hegel. He seems to learn his science from occasional conversation with men of science, or from statements of remarkable discoveries in the common Journals, not from a careful and regular study of facts or treatises.

With all his literary culture he has an intense love of nature, a true sight and appreciation thereof; not the analytic eye of the naturalist, but the synthetic vision of the poet. A book never clouds his sky. His figures are drawn from nature, he sees the fact. No chart of nature hangs up in his windows to shut out nature herself. How well he says:

"If a man would be alone, let him look at the stars. The rays that come from those heavenly worlds, will separate between him and vulgar things. One might think the atmosphere was made transparent with this design, to give man in the heavenly bodies, the perpetual presence of the sublime. Seen in the streets of cities, how great they are! If the stars should appear one night in a thousand years, how would men believe and adore; and preserve for many generations the remembrance of the city of God which had been shown! But every night come out these preachers of beauty, and light the universe with their admonishing smile. . .

"To speak truly, few adult persons can see nature. Most persons do not see the sun. At least they have a very superficial seeing. The sun illuminates only the eye of the man, but shines into the eye and the heart of the child. The lover of nature is he whose inward and outward senses are still truly adjusted to each other; who has retained the spirit of infancy even into the era of manhood. His intercourse with heaven and earth becomes part of his daily food. In the presence of nature, a wild delight runs through the man, in spite of real sorrows. Nature says,—he is my creature, and maugre all his impertinent griefs, he shall be glad with me. Not the sun or the summer alone, but every hour and season yields its tribute of delight; for every hour and change corresponds to and authorizes a different state of the mind, from breathless noon to grimmest midnight. Nature is a setting that fits equally well a comic or a mourning piece. In good health, the air is a cordial of incredible virtue. Crossing a bare common, in snow puddles, at twilight, under a clouded sky, without having in my thoughts any occurrence of special good fortune, I have enjoyed a perfect exhilaration. Almost I fear to think how glad I am. In the woods too, a man casts off his years, as the snake his slough, and at what period soever of life, is always a child. In the woods is perpetual youth. Within these plantations of God a decorum and sanctity reign, a perennial festival is dressed, and the guest sees not how he should tire of them in a thousand years. In the woods, we return to reason and faith. There I feel that nothing can befall me in life,—no disgrace, no calamity (leaving me my eyes), which nature cannot repair. Standing on the bare ground,—my head bathed by the blithe air, and uplifted into infinite space,—all mean egotism vanishes. I become a transparent eyeball. I am nothing. I see all. The currents of the Universal Being circulate through me; I am part or particle of God. The name of the nearest friend sounds then foreign and accidental. To be brothers, to be acquaintances,—master or servant, is then a trifle and a disturbance. I am the lover of uncontained and immortal beauty. In the wilderness, I find something more dear and connate than in streets or villages. In the tranquil landscape, and especially in the distant line of the horizon, man beholds somewhat as beautiful as his own nature. . . . .

"The tradesman, the attorney, comes out of the din and craft of the street, and sees the sky and the woods, and is a man again. In their eternal calm he finds himself. The health of the eye seems to demand a horizon. We are never tired, so long as we can see far enough.

"But in other hours nature satisfies the soul purely by its loveliness, and without any mixture of corporeal benefit. I have seen the spectacle of morning from the hill-top over against my house, from daybreak to sun-rise, with emotions which an angel might share. The long slender bars of cloud float like fishes in the sea of crimson light. From the earth as a shore, I look out into that silent sea. I seem to partake its rapid transformations: the active enchantment reaches my dust, and I dilate and conspire with the morning wind. How does nature deify us with a few and cheap elements! Give me health and a day, and I will make the pomp of emperors ridiculous. The dawn is my Assyria; the sunset and moon-rise my Paphos, and unimaginable realms of faerie; broad noon shall be my England of the senses and the understanding; the night shall be my Germany of mystic philosophy and dreams."—*Nature*, pp. 9—10, 11—13, 21—22.

Most writers are demonized or possessed by some one truth, or perhaps some one whim. Look where they will, they see nothing but that. Mr Emerson holds himself erect, and no one thing engrosses his attention, no one idea; no one intellectual faculty domineers over the rest. Sensation does not dim reflection, nor does his thought lend its sickly hue to the things about him. Even Goethe, with all his boasted equilibrium, held his intellectual faculties less perfectly in hand than Emerson. He has no hobbies to ride; even his fondness for the ideal and the beautiful, does not hinder him from obstinately looking real and ugly things in the face. He carries the American idea of freedom into his most intimate personality, and keeps his individuality safe and sacred. He cautions young men against stooping their minds to other men. He knows no master. Sometimes this is carried to an apparent excess, and he underrates the real value of literature, afraid lest the youth become a bookworm, and not a man thinking. But how well he says:

"Meek young men grow up in libraries, believing it their duty to accept the views which Cicero, which Locke, which Bacon, have given, forgetful that Cicero, Locke, and Bacon were only young men in libraries, when they wrote these books. Hence, instead of man thinking, we have the bookworm.

"Books are the best of things, well used; abused, among the worst. What is the right use? What is the one end, which all means go to effect? They are for nothing but to inspire. I had better never see a book, than to be warped by its attraction clean out of my own orbit, and made a satellite instead of a system. The one thing in the world, of value, is the active soul. This every man is entitled to; this every man contains within him, although, in almost all men, obstructed, and as yet unborn. The soul active sees absolute truth; and utters truth, or creates. . . The book, the college, the school of art, the institution of any kind, stop with some past utterance of genius. This is good, say they,—let us hold by this. They pin me down. They look backward and not forward. But genius looks forward: the eyes of man are set in his forehead, not in his hindhead: man hopes: genius creates. Whatever talents may be, if the man creates not, the pure efflux of the Deity is not his;—cinders and smoke there may be, but not yet flame. . . . . .

"The world of any moment is the merest appearance. Some great decorum, some fetish of a government, some ephemeral trade, or war, or man, is cried up by half mankind and cried down by the other half, as if all depended on this particular up or down. The odds are that the whole question is not worth the poorest thought which the scholar has lost in listening to the controversy. Let him not quit his belief that a popgun is a popgun, though the ancient and honourable of the earth affirm it to be the crack of doom. In silence, in steadiness, in severe abstraction, let him hold by himself; add observation to observation, patient of neglect, patient of reproach, and bide his own time,—happy enough, if he can satisfy himself alone, that this day he has seen something truly. Success treads on every right step. For the instinct is sure that prompts him to tell his brother what he thinks. He then learns, that in going down into the secrets of his own mind, he has descended into the secrets of all minds. He learns that he who has mastered any law in his private thoughts, is master to that extent of all men whose language he speaks, and of all into whose language his own can be translated. The poet, in utter solitude remembering his spontaneous thoughts and recording them, is found to have recorded that which men in crowded cities find true for them also."—*Nature, Addresses, &c.*, pp. 85, 85—86, 98—99.

To us the effect of Emerson's writings is profoundly religious; they stimulate to piety, the love of God, to goodness as the love of man. We know no living writer, in any language, who exercises so powerful a religious influence as he. Most young persons, not ecclesiastical, will confess this. We know he is often called hard names on pretence that he is not religious. We remember once being present at a meeting of gentlemen, scholarly men some of them, after the New-England standard of scholarship, who spent the evening in debating "Whether Ralph Waldo Emerson was a Christian." The opinion was quite generally entertained that he was not: for "discipleship was necessary to Christianity." "And the essence of Christian discipleship" was thought to consist in "sitting at the feet of our blessed Lord (pronounced Laawd!) and calling him Master, which Emerson certainly does not do." We value Christianity as much as most men, and the name Christian to us is very dear; but when we remembered the character, the general tone and conduct of the men who arrogate to themselves the name Christian, and seem to think they have a right to monopolize the Holy Spirit of Religion, and "shove away the worthy bidden guest," the whole thing reminded us of a funny story related by an old writer: "It was once proposed in the British House of Commons, that James Usher, afterward the celebrated Archbishop of Armagh, but then a young man, should be admitted to the assembly of the 'King's Divines.' The proposition, if we remember rightly, gave rise to some debate, upon which John Selden, a younger man than Usher, but highly distinguished and much respected, rose and said, "that it reminded him of a proposition which might be made, that Inigo Jones, the famous architect, should be admitted to the worshipful company of Mousetrap Makers!"

Mr Emerson's writings are eminently religious; Christian in the best sense of that word. This has often been denied for two reasons: because Mr Emerson sets little value on the mythology of the Christian sects, no more perhaps than on the mythology of the Greeks and the Scandinavians, and also because his writings far transcend the mechanical morality and formal pietism, commonly recommended by gentlemen in pulpits. Highly religious, he is not at all ecclesiastical or bigoted. He has small reverence for forms and traditions; a manly life is the only form of religion which he recognizes, and hence we do not wonder at all that he also has been deemed an infidel. It would be very surprising if it were not so. Still it is not religion that is most conspicuous in these volumes; that is not to be looked for except in the special religious literature, yet we must confess that any one of Emerson's works seems far more religious than what are commonly called "good books," including the class of sermons.

To show what is in Mr Emerson's books and what is not, let us make a little more detailed examination thereof. He is not a logical writer, not systematic; not what is commonly called philosophical; didactic to a great degree, but never demonstrative. So we are not to look for a scientific plan, or for a system, of which the author is himself conscious. Still, in all sane men, there must be a system, though the man does not know it. There are two ways of reporting upon an author: one is to represent him by specimens, the other to describe him by analysis; one to show off a finger or foot of the Venus de Medici, the other to give the dimensions thereof. We will attempt both, and will speak of Mr Emerson's starting point, his *terminus a quo*; then of his method of procedure, his *via in quâ*; then of the conclusion he arrives at, his *terminus ad quem*. In giving the dimensions of his statue, we shall exhibit also some of the parts described.

Most writers, knowingly or unconsciously, take as their point of departure some special and finite thing. This man starts from a tradition, the philosophical tradition of Aristotle, Plato, Leibnitz, or Locke, this from the theological tradition of the Protestants or the Catholics, and never will dare get out of sight of his authorities; he takes the bearing of everything from his tradition. Such a man may sail the sea for ages, he arrives nowhere at the last. Our traditionist must not outgo his tradition; the Catholic must not get beyond his Church, nor the Protestant outtravel his Bible. Others start from some fixed fact, a sacrament, a constitution, the public opinion, the public morality, or the popular religion. This they are to defend at all hazards; of course they will retain all falsehood and injustice which favour this institution, and reject all justice and truth which oppose the same. Others pretend to start from God, but in reality do take their departure from a limited conception of God, from the Hebrew notion of Him, or the Catholic notion, from the Calvinistic or the Unitarian notion of God. By and by they are hindered and stopped in their progress. The philosophy of these three classes of men is always vitiated by the prejudices they start with.

Mr Emerson takes man for his point of departure, he means to take the whole of man; man with his history, man with his nature, his sensational, intellectual, moral, affectional, and religious instincts and faculties. With him man is the measure of all things, of ideas and of facts; if they fit man they are accepted, if not, thrown aside. This appears in his first book and in his last:

"The foregoing generations beheld God and nature face to face; we, through their eyes. Why should not we also enjoy an original relation to the universe? Why should not we have a poetry and philosophy of insight and not of tradition, and a religion by a revelation to us, and not the history of theirs? Embosomed for a season in nature, whose floods of life stream around and through us, and invite us, by the powers they supply, to action proportioned to nature, why should we grope among the dry bones of the past, or put the living generation into masquerade out of its faded wardrobe? The sun shines to-day also. There is more wool and flax in the fields. There are new lands, new men, new thoughts. Let us demand our own works and laws and worship."—*Nature*, pp. 5—6.

Again he speaks in a higher mood of the same theme:

"That is always best which gives me to myself. The sublime is excited in me by the great stoical doctrine, Obey thyself. That which shows God in me, fortifies me. That which shows God out of me, makes me a wart and a wen. There is no longer a necessary reason for my being. Already the long shadows of untimely oblivion creep over me, and I shall decease for ever."

"Wherever a man comes, there comes revolution. The old is for slaves. When a man comes, all books are legible, all things transparent, all religions are forms. He is religious. Man is the wonder-worker. He is seen amid miracles. All men bless and curse. He saith yea and nay only. The stationariness of religion; the assumption that the age of inspiration is past, that the Bible is closed; the fear of degrading the character of Jesus by representing him as a man; indicate with sufficient clearness the falsehood of our theology. It is the office of a true teacher to show us that God is, not was; that he speaketh, not spake."

"Let me admonish you, first of all, to go alone; to refuse the good models, even those which are sacred in the imagination of men, and dare to love God without mediator or veil. Friends enough you shall find who will hold up to your emulation Wesleys and Oberlins, Saints and Prophets. Thank God for these good men, but say, 'I also am a man.' Imitation cannot go above its model. The imitator dooms himself to hopeless mediocrity. The inventor did it, because it was natural to him, and so in him it has a charm. In the imitator, something else is natural, and he bereaves himself of his own beauty, to come short of another man's.

Yourself a new-born bard of the Holy Ghost,—cast behind you all conformity, and acquaint men at the first hand with Deity. Look to it first and only, that fashion, custom, authority, pleasure, and money, are nothing to you,—are not bandages over your eyes, that you cannot see,—but live the privilege of the immeasurable mind."—*Nature, Addresses, &c.*, pp. 127—128, 139—140, 141.

"Let man then learn the revelation of all nature, and all thought to his heart: this, namely; that the Highest dwells with him; that the sources of nature are in his own mind, if the sentiment of duty is there. But if he would know what the great God speaketh, he must 'go into his closet and shut the door,' as Jesus said. God will not make Himself manifest to cowards. He must greatly listen to himself, withdrawing himself from all the accents of other men's devotion. Their prayers even are hurtful to him, until he have made his own. The soul makes no appeal from itself. Our religion vulgarly stands on numbers of believers. Whenever the appeal is made,—no matter how indirectly,—to numbers proclamation is then and there made, that religion is not. He that finds God a sweet, enveloping thought to him, never counts his company. When I sit in that presence, who shall dare to come in? When I rest in perfect humility, when I burn with pure love,—what can Calvin or Swedenborg say?"—*Essays*, p. 243.

And again in his latest publication:

"The gods of fable are the shining moments of great men. We run all our vessels into one mould. Our colossal theologies of Judaism, Christism, Buddhism, Mahometism, are the necessary and structural action of the human mind."

"Man is that noble endogenous plant which grows, like the palm, from within, outward. . . . I count him a great man who inhabits a higher sphere of thought, into which other men rise with labour and difficulty; he has but to open his eyes to see things in a true light, and in large relations; whilst they must make painful corrections, and keep a vigilant eye on many sources of error."

"The genius of humanity is the right point of view of history. . . . For a time our teachers serve us personally, as metres or milestones of progress. Once they were angels of knowledge, and their figures touched the sky. Then we drew near, saw their means, culture, and limits; and they yielded their place to other geniuses. Happy, if a few names remain so high, that we have not been able to read them nearer, and age and comparison have not robbed them of a ray. But, at last, we shall cease to look in men for completeness, and shall content ourselves with their social and delegated quality."

"Yet, within the limits of human education and agency, we may say, great men exist that there may be greater men. The destiny of organized nature is amelioration, and who can tell its limits? It is for man to tame the chaos; on every side, whilst he lives, to scatter the seeds of science and of song, that climate, corn, animals, men may be milder, and the germs of love and benefit may be multiplied."

"The world is young? the former great men call to us affectionately. We too must write Bibles, to unite again the heavens and the earthly world. The secret of genius is to suffer no fiction to exist for us; to realize all that we know; in the high refinement of modern life, in arts, in sciences, in books, in men, to exact good faith, reality, and a purpose; and first, last, midst, and without end, to honour every truth by use."—*Representative Men*, pp. 10—11, 12, 38, 39—40, 284—285.

In this Emerson is more American than America herself—and is himself the highest exponent in literature of this idea of human freedom and the value of man. Channing talks of the dignity of human nature, his great and brilliant theme; but he commonly, perhaps always, subordinates the nature of man to some of the accidents of his history. This Emerson never does; no, not once in all his works, nor in all his life. Still we think it is not the whole of man from which he starts, that he undervalues the logical, demonstrative, and historical understanding, with the results thereof, and also undervalues the affections. Hence his man, who is the measure of all things, is not the complete man. This defect appears in his ethics, which are a little cold, the ethics of marble men; and in his religious teachings, the highest which this age has furnished, full of reverence, full of faith, but not proportionably rich in affection.

Mr Emerson has a method of his own as plainly marked as that of Lord Bacon or Descartes, and as rigidly adhered to. It is not the inductive method, by which you arrive at a general fact from many particular facts, but never reach a universal law; it is not the deductive method, whereby a minor law is derived from a major, a special from a general law; it is neither inductive nor deductive demonstration. But Emerson proceeds by the way of intuition, sensational or spiritual. Go to the fact and look for yourself, is his command: a material fact you cannot always verify, and so for that must depend on evidence; a spiritual fact you can always legitimate for yourself. Thus he says:

"That which seems faintly possible—it is so refined, is often faint and dim because it is deepest seated in the mind among the eternal verities. Empirical science is apt to cloud the sight, and, by the very knowledge of functions and processes, to bereave the student of the manly contemplation of the whole. The savant becomes unpoetic. But the best read naturalist, who lends an entire and devout attention to truth, will see that there remains much to learn of his relation to the world, and that it is not to be learned by any addition or subtraction or other comparison of known quantities, but is arrived at by untaught sallies of the spirit, by continual self-recovery, and by entire humility. He will perceive that there are far more excellent qualities in the student than preciseness and infallibility; that a guess is often more fruitful than an indisputable affirmation, and that a dream may let us deeper into the secret of nature than a hundred concerted experiments."

"Every surmise and vaticination of the mind is entitled to a certain respect, and we learn to prefer imperfect theories, and sentences which contain glimpses of truth, to digested systems which have no one valuable suggestion. A wise writer will feel that the ends of study and composition are best answered by announcing undiscovered regions of thought, and so communicating, through hope, new activity to the torpid spirit."—*Nature*, pp. 82—83, 86—87.

And again:

"Jesus astonishes and overpowers sensual people. They cannot unite him to history or reconcile him with themselves. As they come to revere their intuitions and aspire to live holily, their own piety explains every fact, every word."

"The inquiry leads us to that source, at once the essence of genius, the essence of virtue, and the essence of life, which we call spontaneity or instinct. We denote this primary wisdom as intuition, whilst all later teachings are tuitions. In that deep force, the last fact behind which analysis cannot go, all things find their common origin. For the sense of being which in calm hours rises, we know not how, in the soul, is not diverse from things, from space, from light, from time, from man, but one with them, and proceedeth obviously from the same source whence their life and being also proceedeth. We first share the life by which things exist, and afterwards see them as appearances in nature, and forget that we have shared their cause. Here is the fountain of action and the fountain of thought. Here are the lungs of that inspiration which giveth man wisdom, of that inspiration of man which cannot be denied without impiety and atheism. We lie in the lap of immense intelligence, which makes us organs of its activity and receivers of its truth. When we discern justice, when we discern truth, we do nothing of ourselves, but allow a passage to its beams. If we ask whence this comes, if we seek to pry into the soul that causes,—all metaphysics, all philosophy is at fault. Its presence or its absence is all we can affirm. . . . Perception is not whimsical, but fatal. If I see a trait, my children will see it after me, and in course of time, all mankind,—although it may chance that no one has seen it before me. For my perception of it is as much a fact as the sun."

"The relations of the soul to the Divine Spirit are so pure that it is profane to seek to interpose helps. It must be that when God speaketh, He should communicate not one thing, but all things; should fill the world with His voice; should scatter forth light, nature, time, souls, from the centre of the present thought; and new-date and new-create the whole. Whenever a mind is simple, and receives a divine wisdom, then old things pass away,—means, teachers, texts, temples fall; it lives now and absorbs past and future into the present hour."

"The soul is the perceiver and revealer of truth. We know truth when we see it, let sceptic and scoffer say what they choose. Foolish people ask you, when you have spoken what they do not wish to hear, 'how do you know it is the truth, and not an error of your own?' We know truth, when we see it, from opinion, as we know when we are awake that we are awake."

"The great distinction between teachers, sacred or literary; between poets like Herbert and poets like Pope; between philosophers like Spinoza, Kant, and Coleridge,—and philosophers like Locke, Paley, Mackintosh, and Stewart; between men of the world who are reckoned accomplished talkers, and here and there a fervent mystic, prophesying half-insane under the infinitude of his thought; is, that one class speak *from within*, or from experience, as parties and possessors of the fact; and the other class, *from without*, as spectators merely, or perhaps as acquainted with the fact, on the evidence of third persons. It is of no use to preach to me from without. I can do that too easily myself."

"The soul gives itself alone, original, and pure, to the Lonely, Original, and Pure, who, on that condition, gladly inhabits, leads, and speaks through it. Then is it glad, young, and nimble. It is not wise, but it sees through all things. It is not called religious, but it is innocent. It calls the light its own, and feels that the grass grows and the stone falls by a law inferior to, and dependent on, its nature. Behold, it saith, I am born into the great, the universal mind. I, the imperfect, adore my own Perfect. I am somehow receptive of the Great Soul, and thereby I do overlook the sun and the stars, and feel them to be but the fair accidents and effects which change and pass. More and more the surges of everlasting nature enter into me, and I become public and human in my regards and actions. So come I to live in thoughts and act with energies which are immortal."—*Essays*, pp. 23, 52—53, 53—54, 231, 237, 245—245.

"All your learning of all literatures would never enable you to anticipate one of its thoughts or expressions, and yet each is natural and familiar as household words."—*Nature, Addresses, &c.*, p. 209.

The same method in his last work is ascribed to Plato:

"Add to this, he believes that poetry, prophecy, and the high insight, are from a wisdom of which man is not master; that the gods never philosophize; but, by a celestial mania, these miracles are accomplished." *Representative Men*, p. 61.

Sometimes he exaggerates the value of this, and puts the unconscious before the self-conscious state:

"It is pitiful to be an artist, when, by forbearing to be artists, we might be vessels filled with the divine overflowings, enriched by the circulations of omniscience and omnipresence. Are there not moments in the history of heaven when the human race was not counted by individuals, but was only the Influenced, was God in distribution, God rushing into multiform benefit? It is sublime to receive, sublime to love, but this lust of imparting as from *us*, this desire to be loved, the wish to be recognized as individuals,—is finite, comes of a lower strain."—*Nature, Addresses, &c.*, pp. 201—202.

He is sometimes extravagant in the claims made for his own method, and maintains that ecstasy is the natural and exclusive mode of arriving at new truths, while it is only one mode. Ecstasy is the state of intuition in which the man loses his individual self-consciousness. Moments of this character are few and rare even with men like the St Victors, like Tauler, and Böhme and Swedenborg. The writings of all these men, especially of the two last, who most completely surrendered themselves to this mode of action, show how poor and insufficient it is. All that mankind has learned in this way is little, compared with the results of reflection, of meditation, and careful, conscientious looking after truth: all the great benefactors of the world have been patient and continuous in their work;

> "Not from a *vain and shallow* thought
> His awful Jove young Phidias brought."

Mr Emerson says books are only for one's idle hours; he discourages hard and continuous thought, conscious modes of argument, of discipline. Here he exaggerates his idiosyncracy into a universal law. The method of nature is not ecstasy, but patient attention. Human nature avenges herself for the slight he puts on her, by the irregular and rambling character of his own productions. The vice appears more glaring in the Emersonidæ, who have all the agony without the inspiration; who affect the unconscious; write even more ridiculous nonsense than their "genius" requires; are sometimes so child-like as to become mere babies, and seem to forget that the unconscious state is oftener below the conscious than above it, and that there is an ecstasy of folly as well as of good sense.

Some of these imbeciles have been led astray by this extravagant and one-sided statement. What if books have hurt Mr Oldbuck, and many fine wits lie "sheathed to the hilt in ponderous tomes," sheathed and rusted in so that no Orson could draw the blade,—we need not deny the real value of books, still less the value of the serious and patient study of thoughts and things. Michael Angelo and Newton had some genius; Socrates is thought not destitute of philosophical power; but no dauber of canvas, no sportsman with marble, ever worked like Angelo; the two philosophers wrought by their genius, but with an attention, an order, a diligence, and a terrible industry and method of thought, without which their genius would have ended in nothing but guess-work. Much comes by spontaneous intuition, which is to be got in no other way; but much is to precede that, and much to follow it. There are two things to be considered in the matter of inspiration, one is the Infinite God from whom it comes, the other the finite capacity which is to receive it. If Newton had never studied, it would be as easy for God to reveal the calculus to his dog Diamond as to Newton. We once heard of a man who thought everything was in the soul, and so gave up all reading, all continuous thought. Said another, "if all is in the soul, it takes a man to find it."

Here are some of the most important conclusions Mr Emerson has hitherto arrived at.

Man is above nature, the material world. Last winter, in his lectures, he was understood to affirm "the identity of man with nature;" a doctrine which seems to have come from his oriental reading before named, a doctrine false as well as inconsistent with the first principles of his philosophy. But in his printed works he sees clearly the distinction between the two, a fact not seen by the Hindoo philosophers, but first by the Hebrew and Greek writers. Emerson puts man far before nature:

"We are taught by great actions that the universe is the property of every individual in it. Every rational creature has all nature for his dowry and estate. It is his if he will. He may divest himself of it; he may creep into a corner, and abdicate his kingdom, as most men do, but he is entitled to the world by his constitution. In proportion to the energy of his thought and will, he takes up the world into himself."

"Thus in art, does nature work through the will of a man filled with the beauty of her first works."

"Nature is thoroughly mediate. It is made to serve. It receives the dominion of man as meekly as the ass on which the Saviour rode. It offers all its kingdoms to man as the raw material which he may mould into what is useful."—*Nature*, pp. 25, 30, 50—51.

Nature is "an appendix to the soul."

Then the man is superior to the accidents of his past history or present condition:

"No man ever prayed heartily, without learning something."—*Nature*, p. 92.

"The highest merit we ascribe to Moses, Plato, and Milton, is that they set at nought books and traditions, and spoke not what men said but what they thought. A man should learn to detect and watch that gleam of light which flashes across his mind from within, more than the lustre of the firmament of bards and sages."

"Kingdom and lordship, power and estate, are a gaudier vocabulary than private John and Edward in a small house and common day's work; but the things of life are the same to both; the sum total of both is the same. Why all this deference to Alfred, and Scanderbeg, and Gustavus? Suppose they were virtuous; did they wear out virtue? As great a stake depends on your private act to-day, as followed their public and renowned steps. When private men shall act with vast views, the lustre will be transferred from the actions of kings to those of gentlemen."—*Essays*, pp. 37, 38, 51—52.

Hence a man must be true to his present conviction, careless of consistency:

"A foolish consistency is the hobgoblin of little minds, adored by little statesmen and philosophers and divines. With consistency a great soul has simply nothing to do. He may as well concern himself with his shadow on the wall. Out upon your guarded lips! Sew them up with packthread, do. Else, if you would be a man, speak what you think to-day in words as hard as cannon-balls, and to-morrow speak what to-morrow thinks in hard words again, though it contradict everything you said to-day."—*Essays*, p. 47.

The man must not be a slave to a single form of thought:

"How wearisome the grammarian, the phrenologist, the political or religious fanatic, or indeed any possessed mortal, whose balance is lost by the exaggeration of a single topic. It is incipient insanity." —*Essays*, p. 280.

Man is inferior to the great law of God, which overrides the world; "His wealth and greatness consist in his being the channel through which heaven flows to earth;" "the word of a poet is only the mouth of divine wisdom;" "the man on whom the soul descends—alone can teach:" all nature "from the sponge up to Hercules is to hint or to thunder man the laws of right and wrong." This ethical character seems the end of nature: "the moral law lies at the centre of nature and radiates to the circumference. It is the pith and marrow of every substance, every relation, every process. All things with which we deal point to us. What is a farm but a mute gospel?" Yet he sometimes tells us that man is identical with God under certain circumstances, an old Hindoo notion, a little favoured by some passages in the New Testament, and revived by Hegel in modern times, in whom it seems less inconsistent than in Emerson.

This moral law continually gives men their compensation. "You cannot do wrong without suffering wrong."

"And this law of laws which the pulpit, the senate, and the college deny, is hourly preached in all markets and all languages, by flights of proverbs, whose teaching is as true and as omnipresent as that of birds and flies.

"All things are double, one against another.—Tit for tat; an eye for an eye; a tooth for a tooth; blood for blood; measure for measure; love for love.—Give and it shall be given you.—He that watereth shall be watered himself.—What will you have? quoth God; pay for it and take it.—Nothing venture, nothing have.—Thou shalt be paid exactly for what thou hast done, no more, no less.—Who doth not work shall not eat.—Harm watch, harm catch.—Curses always recoil on the head of him who imprecates them.—If you put a chain around the neck of a slave, the other end fastens itself round your own.—Bad counsel confounds the adviser.—The devil is an ass."

"There is no den in the wild world to hide a rogue. There is no such thing as concealment. Commit a crime, and the earth is made of glass. Commit a crime, and it seems as if a coat of snow fell on the ground, such as reveals in the woods the track of every partridge and fox and squirrel and mole. You cannot recall the spoken word, you cannot wipe out the foot-track, you cannot draw up the ladder, so as to leave no inlet or clew. Always some damning circumstance transpires. The laws and substances of nature, water, snow, wind, gravitation, becomes penalties to the thief."

"Neither can it be said, on the other hand, that the gain of rectitude must be bought by any loss. There is no penalty to virtue; no penalty to wisdom; they are proper additions of being. In a virtuous action, I properly *am*; in a virtuous act, I add to the world; I plant into deserts, conquered from chaos and nothing, and see the darkness receding on the limits of the horizon. There can be no excess to love; none to knowledge; none to beauty, when these attributes are considered in the purest sense. The soul refuses all limits. It affirms in man always an Optimism, never a Pessimism."—*Essays*, pp. 90, 95—96, 100.

By virtue of obedience to this law great men are great, and only so:

"We do not yet see that virtue is height, and that a man or a company of men plastic and permeable to principles, by the law of nature must overpower and ride all cities, nations, kings, rich men, poets, who are not."

"A true man belongs to no other time or place, but is the centre of things. Where he is, there is a nature. He measures you, and all men, and all events. You are constrained to accept his standard. Ordinarily everybody in society reminds us of somewhat else or some other person. Character, reality, reminds you of nothing else. It takes place of the whole creation. The man must be so much that he must make all circumstances indifferent,—put all means into the shade. This all great men are and do. Every true man is a cause, a country, and an age; requires infinite spaces and numbers and time fully to accomplish his thought;—and posterity seem to follow his steps as a procession."—*Essays*, pp. 57, 50.

Through this any man has the power of all men:

"Do that which is assigned thee, and thou canst not hope too much or dare too much. There is at this moment, there is for me an utterance bare and grand as that of the colossal chisel of Phidias, or the trowel of the Egyptians, or the pen of Moses, or Dante, but different from all these. Not possibly will the soul, all rich, all eloquent, with thousand-cloven tongue, deign to repeat itself; but if I can hear what these patriarchs say, surely I can reply to them in the same pitch of voice; for the ear and the tongue are two organs of one nature. Dwell up there in the simple and noble regions of thy life, obey thy heart, and thou shalt reproduce the foreworld again."

"The great poet makes us feel our own wealth, and then we think less of his compositions. His greatest communication to our mind, is, to teach us to despise all he has done. Shakspeare carries us to such a lofty strain of intelligent activity, as to suggest a wealth which beggars his own; and we then feel that the splendid works which he has created, and which in other hours we extol as a sort of self-existent poetry, take no stronger hold of real nature than the shadow of a passing traveller on the rock."—*Essays*, pp. 68—69, 239.

Yet he once says there is no progress of mankind; "Society never advances."

"The civilized man has built a coach, but has lost the use of his feet. He is supported on crutches, but loses so much support of muscle. He has got a fine Geneva watch, but he has lost the skill to tell the hour by the sun. A Greenwich nautical almanac he has, and so being sure of the information when he wants it, the man in the street does not know a star in the sky. The solstice he does not observe; the equinox he knows as little; and the whole bright calendar of the year is without a dial in his mind. His note-books impair his memory; his libraries overload his wit; the insurance office increases the number of accidents; and it may be a question whether machinery does not encumber; whether we have not lost by refinement some energy, by a Christianity entrenched in establishments and forms, some vigour of wild virtue. For every stoic was a stoic; but in Christendom where is the Christian?"—*Essays*, pp. 69—70.

But this is an exaggeration, which he elsewhere corrects, and justly says that the great men of the nineteenth century will one day be quoted to prove the barbarism of their age.

He teaches an absolute trust in God:

"Ineffable is the union of man and God in every act of the soul. The simplest person, who in his integrity worships God, becomes God; yet for ever and ever the influx of this better and universal self is new and unsearchable. Ever it inspires awe and astonishment. . . . . When we have broken our god of tradition, and ceased from our god of rhetoric, then may God fire the heart with His presence. It is the doubling of the heart itself, nay, the infinite enlargement of the heart with a power of growth to a new infinity on every side. It inspires in man an infallible trust. He has not the conviction, but the sight that the best is the true, and may in that thought easily dismiss all particular uncertainties and fears, and adjourn to the sure revelation of time, the solution of his private riddles. He is sure that his welfare is dear to the heart of being. In the presence of law to his mind, he is overflowed with a reliance so universal, that it sweeps away all cherished hopes and the most stable projects of mortal condition in its flood. He believes that he cannot escape from his good."—*Essays*, pp. 241—242.

"In how many churches, by how many prophets, tell me, is man made sensible that he is an infinite soul; that the earth and heavens are passing into his mind; that he is drinking for ever the soul of God? Where now sounds the persuasion, that by its very melody imparadises my heart, and so affirms its own origin in heaven? Where shall I hear words such as in elder ages drew men to leave all and follow—father and mother, house and land, wife and child? Where shall I hear these august laws of moral being so pronounced, as to fill my ear, and I feel ennobled by the offer of my uttermost action and passion? The test of the true faith, certainly, should be its power to charm and command the soul, as the laws of nature control the activity of the hands,—so commanding that we find pleasure and honour in obeying. The faith should blend with the light of rising and of setting suns, with the flying cloud, the singing bird, and the breath of flowers. But now the priest's Sabbath has lost the splendour of nature; it is unlovely; we are glad when it is done; we can make, we do make, even sitting in our pews, a far better, holier, sweeter, for ourselves."—*Nature, &c.*, pp. 132—133.

God continually communicates Himself to man in various forms:

"We distinguish the announcements of the soul, its manifestations of its own nature, by the term *Revelation.* These are always attended by the emotion of the sublime. For this communication is an influx of the Divine mind into our mind. It is an ebb of the individual rivulet before the flowing surges of the sea of life. Every distinct apprehension of this central commandment agitates men with awe and delight. A thrill passes through all men at the reception of new truth, or at the performance of a great action, which comes out of the heart of nature. In these communications, the power to see is not separated from the will to do, but the insight proceeds from obedience, and the obedience proceeds from a joyful perception. Every moment when the individual feels himself invaded by it, is memorable."—*Essays,* pp. 232—233.

"The nature of these revelations is always the same: they are perceptions of the absolute law."

"This energy does not descend into individual life, on any other condition than entire possession. It comes to the lowly and simple; it comes to whomsoever will put off what is foreign and proud; it comes as insight; it comes as serenity and grandeur. When we see those whom it inhabits, we are apprized of new degrees of greatness. From that inspiration the man comes back with a changed tone. He does not talk with men, with an eye to their opinion. He tries them. It requires of us to be plain and true. . . . . The soul that ascendeth to worship the great God, is plain and true; has no rose-colour; no fine friends; no chivalry; no adventures; does not want admiration; dwells in the hour that now is, in the earnest experience of the common day,—by reason of the present moment, and the mere trifle having become porous to thought, and bibulous of the sea of light."

"How dear, how soothing to man, arises the idea of God, peopling the lonely place, effacing the scars of our mistakes and disappointments!"—*Essays,* pp. 239, 240, 241—242.

He says the same thing in yet more rhythmic notes:

"Not from a vain or shallow thought
His awful Jove young Phidias brought;
Never from lips of cunning fell
The thrilling Delphic oracle;
Out from the heart of nature rolled
The burdens of the Bible old;
The litanies of nations came,
Like the volcano's tongue of flame,

Up from the burning core below,—
The canticles of love and woe;
The hand that rounded Peter's dome,
And groined the aisles of Christian Rome,
Wrought in a sad sincerity;
Himself from God he could not free;
He builded better than he knew;—
The conscious stone to beauty grew.

. . . . . .

"The passive Master lent his hand
To the vast soul that o'er him planned;
And the same power that reared the shrine,
Bestrode the tribes that knelt within.
Ever the fiery Pentecost
Girds with one flame the countless host,
Trances the heart through chanting choirs,
And through the priest the mind inspires."

Poems, pp. 17—18, 19.

If we put Emerson's conclusions into five great classes representing respectively his idea of man, of God, and of nature; his idea of self-rule, the relation of man's consciousness to his unconsciousness; his idea of religion, the relation of men to God; of ethics, the relation of man to man; and of economy, the relation of man to nature; we find him in the very first rank of modern science. No man in this age is before him. He demonstrates nothing, but assumes his position far in advance of mankind. This explains the treatment he has met with.

Then in his writings there appears a love of beauty in all its forms—in material nature, in art, literature, and above all, in human life. He finds it everywhere:

"The frailest leaf, the mossy bark,
The acorn's cup, the raindrop's arc,
The swinging spider's silver line,
The ruby of the drop of wine,
The shining pebble of the pond,
Thou inscribest with a bond,
In thy momentary play,
Would bankrupt nature to repay.

. . . . . .

"Oft, in streets or humblest places,
I detect far-wandered graces,

Which, from Eden wide astray,
In lowly homes have lost their way."

Poems, pp. 137, 139.

Few men have had a keener sense for this in common life, or so nice an eye for it in inanimate nature. His writings do not disclose a very clear perception of the beauty of animated nature; it is still life that he describes, in water, plants, and the sky. He seldom refers to the great cosmic forces of the world, that are everywhere balanced into such systematic proportions, the perception of which makes the writings of Alexander Von Humboldt so attractive and delightful.

In all Emerson's works there appears a sublime confidence in man; a respect for human nature which we have never seen surpassed—never equalled. Man is only to be true to his nature, to plant himself on his instincts, and all will turn out well:

"Build, therefore, your own world. As fast as you conform your life to the pure idea in your mind, that will unfold its great proportions. A correspondent revolution in things will attend the influx of the spirit. So fast will disagreeable appearances, swine, spiders, snakes, pests, mad-houses, prisons, enemies, vanish; they are temporary and shall be no more seen. The sordor and filths of nature, the sun shall dry up, and the wind exhale. As when the summer comes from the south, the snow-banks melt, and the face of the earth becomes green before it, so shall the advancing spirit create its ornaments along its path, and carry with it the beauty it visits, and the song which enchants it; it shall draw beautiful faces, and warm hearts, and wise discourse, and heroic acts around its way, until evil is no more seen. The kingdom of man over nature, which cometh not with observation,—a dominion such as now is beyond his dream of God,—he shall enter without more wonder than the blind man feels who is gradually restored to perfect sight."—*Nature*, pp. 94—95.

"Foolish hands may mix and mar,
Wise and sure the issues are."

He has also an absolute confidence in God. He has been foolishly accused of pantheism which sinks God in nature; but no man is further from it. He never sinks God in man, he does not stop with the law, in matter or morals, but goes back to the Lawgiver; yet probably it would not be so easy for him to give his definition of God as it would be for most graduates at Andover or Cambridge.

With this confidence in God he looks things fairly in the face, and never dodges, never fears. Toil, sorrow, pain, these are things which it is impious to fear. Boldly he faces every fact, never retreating behind an institution or a great man. In God his trust is complete; with the severest scrutiny he joins the highest reverence.

Hence come his calmness and serenity. He is evenly balanced and at repose. A more tranquil spirit cannot be found in literature. Nothing seems to fret or jar him, and all the tossings of the literary world never jostle him into anger or impatience. He goes on like the stars above the noise and dust of earth, as calm yet not so cold. No man says things more terribly severe than he on many occasions; few in America have encountered such abuse, but in all his writings there is not a line which can be referred to ill-will. Impudence and terror are wasted on him; "upstart wealth's averted eye," which blasts the hope of the politician, is powerless on him as on the piles of granite in New Hampshire hills. Misconceived and misreported, he does not wait to "unravel any man's blunders: he is again on his road, adding new powers and honours to his domain, and new claims on the heart." He takes no notice of the criticism from which nothing but warning is to be had, warning against bigotry and impudence, and goes on his way, his only answer a creative act. Many shafts has he shot, not an arrow in self-defence; not a line betrays that he has been treated ill. This is small praise, but rare; even cool egotistic Goethe treated his "Philistine" critics with haughty scorn, comparing them to dogs who bark in the court-yard when the master mounts to ride:

"Es will der Spitz aus unserm Stall
Mit Bellen uns begleiten;
Allein der Hundes lauter Schall
Beweist nur dass wir reiten."

He lacks the power of orderly arrangement to a remarkable degree. Not only is there no obvious logical order, but there is no subtle psychological method by which the several parts of an essay are joined together; his deep sayings are jewels strung wholly at random. This often confuses the reader; this want appears the greatest defect of his mind. Of late years there has been a marked effort to correct it, and in regard to mere order there is certainly a great improvement in the first series of Essays on Nature, or rather formless book.

Then he is not creative like Shakspeare and Goethe, perhaps not inventive like many far inferior men; he seldom or never undertakes to prove anything. He tells what he sees, seeing things by glimpses, not by steady and continuous looking, he often fails of seeing the whole object; he does not always see all of its relations with other things. Hence comes an occasional exaggeration. But this is commonly corrected by some subsequent statement. Thus he has seen books imprison many a youth, and speaking to men, desirous of warning them of their danger, he undervalues the worth of books themselves. But the use he makes of them in his own writings shows that this statement was an exaggeration which his practical judgment disapproves. Speaking to men whose chief danger was that they should be bookworms, or mechanical grinders at a logic-mill, he says that ecstasy is the method of nature, but himself never utters anything "poor and extemporaneous;" what he gets in his ecstatic moments of inspiration, he examines carefully in his cool, reflective hours, and it is printed as reflection, never as the simple result of ecstatic inspiration, having not only the stamp of Divine truth, but the private mark of Emerson. He is never demonized by his enthusiasm; he possesses the spirit, it never possesses him; if "the God" comes into his rapt soul "without bell," it is only with due consideration that he communicates to the world the message that was brought. Still he must regret that his extravagant estimate of ecstasy, intuitive unconsciousness, has been made and has led some youths and maids astray.

This mode of looking at things, and this want of logical order, make him appear inconsistent. There are actual and obvious contradictions in his works. "Two sons of Priam in one chariot ride." Now he is all generosity and nobleness, shining like the sun on things mean and low, and then he says, with a good deal of truth but some exaggeration:

"Do not tell me of my obligation to put all poor men in good situations. Are they *my* poor? I tell thee, thou foolish philanthropist, that I grudge the dollar, the dime, the cent I give to such men as do not belong to me and to whom I do not belong. There is a class of persons to whom by all spiritual affinity I am bought and sold; for them I will go to prison, if need be; but your miscellaneous popular charities; the education at college of fools; the building of meeting-houses to the vain end to which many now stand; alms to sots; and the thousandfold Relief Societies;—though I confess with shame I sometimes succumb and give the dollar, it is a wicked dollar which by-and-by I shall have the manhood to withhold." —*Essays*, p. 43.

Thus a certain twofoldness appears in his writings here and there, but take them all together they form a whole of marvellous consistency; take them in connection with his private character and life—we may challenge the world to furnish an example of a fairer and more consistent whole.

With the exceptions above stated, there is a remarkable balance of intellectual faculties, of creative and conservative, of the spontaneous and intuitive, and the voluntary and reflective powers. He is a slave to neither; all are balanced into lovely proportions and intellectual harmony. In many things Goethe is superior to Emerson: in fertility of invention, in a wide acquaintance with men, in that intuitive perception of character which seems an instinct in some men, in regular discipline of the understanding, in literary and artistic culture; but in general harmony of the intellectual powers, and the steadiness of purpose which comes thereof, Emerson is incontestably the superior even of the many-sided Goethe. He never wastes his time on trifles; he is too heavily fraught, and lies so deep in the sea that a little flaw of wind never drives him from his course. If we go a little further and inquire how the other qualities are blended with the intellectual, we find that the moral power a little outweighs the intellectual, and the religious is a little before the moral, as it should be, but the affections seem to be less developed than the intellect. There is no total balance of all the faculties to correspond with the harmony of his intellectual powers. This seems to us the greatest defect in his entire being, as lack of logical power is the chief defect in his intellect; there is love enough for almost any man—not enough to balance his intellect, his conscience, and his faith in God. Hence there appears a certain coldness in his ethics. He is a man running alone, and would lead others to isolation, not society. Notwithstanding his own intense individuality and his theoretic and practical respect for individuality, still persons seem of small value to him—of little value except as they represent or help develope an idea of the intellect. In this respect, in his writings he is one-sided, and while no one mental power has subdued another, yet his intellect and conscience seem to enslave and belittle the affections. Yet he never goes so far in this as Goethe, who used men, and women too, as cattle to ride, as food to eat. In Emerson's religious writings there appears a worship of the infinite God, far transcending all we find in Taylor or Edwards, in Fénélon or Channing; it is reverence, it is trust, the worship of the conscience, of the intellect; it is obedience, the worship of the will; it is not love, the worship of the affections.

No writer in our language is more rich in ideas, none more suggestive of noble thought and noble life. We will select the axioms which occur in a single essay, which we take at random, that on Self-reliance:

"It needs a divine man to exhibit anything divine."

"Nothing is at last sacred but the integrity of your own mind."

"The virtue most in request is conformity. Self-reliance is its aversion."

"No law can be sacred to me but that of my nature, the only wrong what is against it."

"Truth is handsomer than the affectation of love."

"Your goodness must have some edge to it."

"Do your work and you shall reinforce yourself."

"A foolish consistency is the hobgoblin of little minds."

"To be great is to be misunderstood."

"Character teaches above our wills."

"Greatness always appeals to the future."

"The centuries are conspirators against the sanity and majesty of the soul."

"If we live truly we shall see truly."

"It is as easy for the strong to be strong as it is for the weak to be weak."

"When a man lives with God, his voice shall be as sweet as the murmur of the brook and the rustle of the corn."

"Virtue is the governor."

"Welcome evermore to gods and men is the self-helping man."

"Duty is our place, and the merry men of circumstance should follow as they may."

"My giant goes with me wherever I go."

"It was in his own mind that the artist sought his model."

"That which each can do best none but his Maker can teach him."

"Every great man is an unique."

"Nothing can bring you peace but the triumph of principles."

His works abound also with the most genial wit; he clearly sees and sharply states the halfnesses of things and men, but his wit is never coarse, and wholly without that grain of malice so often the accompaniment thereof.

Let us now say a word of the artistic style and rhetorical form of these remarkable books. Mr Emerson always gravitates towards first principles, but never sets them in a row, groups them into a system, or makes of them a whole. Hence the form of all his prose writings is very defective, and much of his rare power is lost. He never fires by companies, nor even by platoons, only man by man; nay, his soldiers are never ranked into line, but stand scattered, sundered and individual, each serving on his own account, and "fighting on his own hook." Things are huddled and lumped together; diamonds, pearls, bits of chalk and cranberries, thrown pell-mell together. You can

> "No joints and no contexture find,
> Nor their loose parts to any method bring."

Here is a specimen of the Lucretian "fortuitous concourse of atoms," for things are joined by a casual connection, or else by mere caprice. This is so in the Orations, which were designed to be heard, not read, where order is the more needful. His separate thoughts are each a growth. Now and then it is so with a sentence, seldom with a paragraph; but his essay is always a piece of composition, carpentry, and not growth.

Take any one of his volumes, the first series of Essays, for example, the book does not make an organic whole, by itself, and so produce a certain totality of impression. The separate essays are not arranged with reference to any progress in the reader's mind, or any consecutive development of the author's ideas. Here are the titles of the several papers in their present order:—History, Self-Reliance, Compensation, Spiritual Laws, Love, Friendship, Prudence, Heroism, The Over-Soul, Circles, Intellect,

Art. In each essay there is the same want of organic completeness and orderly distribution of the parts. There is no logical arrangement of the separate thoughts, which are subordinate to the main idea of the piece. They are shot together into a curious and disorderly mass of beauty, like the colours in a kaleidoscope, not laid together like the gems in a collection; still less grown into a whole like the parts of a rose, where beauty of form, fragrance, and colour make up one whole of loveliness. The lines he draws do not converge to one point; there is no progress in his drama. Towards the end the interest deepens, not from an artistic arrangement of accumulated thoughts, but only because the author finds his heart warmed by his efforts, and beating quicker. Some artists produce their effect almost wholly by form and outline; they sculpture with their pencil; the Parcæ of Michael Angelo is an example; so some writers discipline their pupils by the severity of their intellectual method and scientific forms of thought. Other artists have we known produce the effect almost wholly by their colouring; the drawing was bad, but the colour of lip and eye, of neck and cheek, and hair, was perfect; the likeness all men saw, and felt the impression. But the perfect artist will be true to both, will keep the forms of things, and only clothe them with appropriate hues. We know some say that order belongs not to poetic minds, but the saying is false. In all Milton's high poetic works, the form is perfect as the colouring: this appears in the grouping of the grand divisions of the Paradise Lost, and in the arrangement of the smallest details in L'Allegro and Il Penseroso, and then the appropriate hue of morning, of mid-day, or of night is thrown upon the whole.

His love of individuality has unconsciously deprived him of the grace of order; his orations or essays are like a natural field: here is common grass, only with him not so common as wild roses and violets, for his common grasses are flowers—and then rocks, then trees, brambles, thorns, now flowers, now weeds, here a decaying log with raspberry-bushes on the one side and strawberry-vines on the other, and potentillas creeping among them all. There are emmets and wood-worms, earth-worms, slugs, grasshoppers, and, more obvious, sheep and oxen, and above and about them, the brown thrasher, the hen-hawk, and the crow—making a scene of beautiful and intricate confusion which belongs to nature, not to human art.

His marked love of individuality appears in his style. His thoughts are seldom vague, all is distinct; the outlines are sharply drawn, things are always discrete from one another. He loves to particularize. He talks not of flowers, but of the violet, the clover, the cowslip and anemone; not of birds, but the nuthatch, and the wren; not of insects, but of the Volvex Globator; not of men and maids, but of Adam, John, and Jane. Things are kept from things, each surrounded by its own atmosphere. This gives great distinctness and animation to his works, though latterly he seems to imitate himself a little in this respect. It is remarkable to what an extent this individualization is carried. The essays in his books are separate, and stand apart from one another, only mechanically bound by the lids of the volume; his paragraphs in each essay are distinct and disconnected, or but loosely bound to one another; it is so with sentences in the paragraph, and propositions in the sentence. Take for example his essay on Experience; it is distributed into seven parts, which treat respectively of Illusion, Temperament, Succession, Surface, Surprise, Reality, and Subjectiveness. These seven brigadiers are put in one army with as little unity of action as any seven Mexican officers; not subject to one head, nor fighting on the same side. The subordinates under these generals are in no better order and discipline; sometimes the corporal commands the king. But this very lack of order gives variety of form. You can never anticipate him. One half of the essay never suggests the rest. If he have no order, he never sets his method a going, and himself with his audience goes to sleep, trusting that he, they, and the logical conclusion will all come out alive and waking at the last. He trusts nothing to the discipline of his camp; all to the fidelity of the individual soldiers.

His style is one of the rarest beauty; there is no affectation, no conceit, no effort at effect. He alludes to everybody and imitates nobody. No writer that we remember, except Jean Paul Richter, is so rich in beautiful imagery; there are no blank walls in his building. But Richter's temple of poesy is a Hindoo pagoda, rich, elaborate, of costly stone, adorned with costly work, but as a whole, rather grotesque than sublime, and more queer than beautiful; you wonder how any one could have brought such wealth together, and still more that any one could combine things so oddly together. Emerson builds a rambling Gothic church, with an irregular outline, a chapel here, and a tower there, you do not see why; but all parts are beautiful, and the whole constrains the soul to love and trust. His manifold images come from his own sight, not from the testimony of other men. His words are pictures of the things daguerreotyped from nature. Like Homer, Aristotle, and Tacitus, he describes the thing, and not the effect of the thing. This quality he has in common with the great writers of classic antiquity, while his wealth of sentiment puts him with the classics of modern times. Like Burke he lays all literature under contribution, and presses the facts of every-day life into his service. He seems to keep the sun and moon as his retainers, and levy black-mail on the cricket and the titmouse, on the dawdling preacher and the snow-storm which seemed to rebuke his unnatural whine. His works teem with beauty. Take for example this:

"What do we wish to know of any worthy person so much as how he has sped in the history of this sentiment? [Love.] What books in the circulating libraries circulate? How we glow over these novels of passion when the story is told with any spark of truth and nature! And what fastens attention in the intercourse of life, like any passion betraying affection between two parties? Perhaps we never saw them before, and never shall meet them again. But we see them exchange a glance, or betray a deep emotion, and we are no longer strangers. We understand them, and take the warmest interest in the development of the romance. All mankind love a lover. The earliest demonstrations of complacency and kindness are nature's most winning pictures. It is the dawn of civility and grace in the coarse and rustic. The rude village boy teases the girls about the school-house door;—but to-day he comes running into the entry, and meets one fair child arranging her satchel: he holds her books to help her, and instantly it seems to him as if she removed herself from him infinitely, and was a sacred precinct. Among the throng of girls he runs rudely enough, but one alone distances him: and these two little neighbours that were so close just now, have learnt to respect each other's personality. Or who can avert his eyes from the engaging, half-artful, half-artless ways of school girls who go into the country shops to buy a skein of silk or a sheet of paper, and talk half an hour about nothing, with the broad-faced, good-natured shop-boy. In the village they are on a perfect equality, which love delights in, and without any coquetry the happy, affectionate nature of woman flows out in this pretty gossip. The girls may have little beauty, yet plainly do they establish between them and the good boy the most agreeable, confiding relations, what with their fun and their earnest, about Edgar, and Jonas, and Almira, and who was invited to the party, and who danced at the dancing-school, and when the singing-school would begin, and other nothings concerning which the parties cooed. By-and-by that boy wants a wife, and very truly and heartily will he know where to find a sincere and sweet mate, without any risk such as Milton deplores as incident to scholars and great men."

"The passion re-makes the world for the youth. It makes all things alive and significant. Nature grows conscious. Every bird on the boughs of the tree sings now to his heart and soul. Almost the notes are articulate. The clouds have faces as he looks on them. The trees of the forest, the waving grass and the peeping flowers have grown intelligent: and almost he fears to trust them with the secret which they seem to invite. Yet nature soothes and sympathizes. In the green solitude he finds a dearer home than with men."

"Behold there in the wood the fine madman! He is a palace of sweet sounds and sights; he dilates; he is twice a man; he walks with arms akimbo; he soliloquizes; he accosts the grass and the trees; he feels the blood of the violet, the clover, and the lily in his veins; and he talks with the brook that wets his foot."—*Essays*, pp. 142—143, 145, 146.

Emerson is a great master of language; therewith he sculptures, therewith he paints; he thunders and lightens in his speech, and in his speech also he sings. In Greece, Plato and Aristophanes were mighty masters of the pen, and have not left their equals in ancient literary art; so in Rome were Virgil and Tacitus; four men so marked in individuality, so unlike and withal so skilful in the use of speech, it were not easy to find; four mighty masters of the art to write. In later times there have been in England Shakespeare, Bacon, Milton, Taylor, Swift, and Carlyle; on the Continent, Voltaire, Rousseau, and Goethe; all masters in this art, skilful to work in human speech. Each of them possessed some qualities which Emerson has not. In Bacon, Milton, and Carlyle, there is a majesty, a dignity and giant strength, not to be claimed for him. Yet separating the beautiful from what men call sublime, no one of all that we have named, ancient or modern, has passages so beautiful as he. From what is called sublime if we separate what is simply vast, or merely grand, or only wide, it is in vain that we seek in all those men for anything to rival Emerson.

Take the following passage, and it is not possible, we think, to find its equal for the beautiful and the sublime in any tongue :

"The lovers delight in endearments, in avowals of love, in comparisons of their regards. When alone, they solace themselves with the remembered image of the other. Does that other see the same star, the same melting cloud, read the same book, feel the same emotion that now delight me? They try and weigh their affection, and adding up all costly advantages, friends, opportunities, properties, exult in discovering that willingly, joyfully, they would give all as a ransom for the beautiful, the beloved head, not one hair of which shall be harmed. But the lot of humanity is on these children. Danger, sorrow, and pain arrive to them as to all. Love prays. It makes covenants with Eternal Power, in behalf of this dear mate. The union which is thus effected, and which adds a new value to every atom in nature, for it transmutes every thread throughout the whole web of relation into a golden ray, and bathes the soul in a new and sweeter element, is yet a temporary state. Not always can flowers, pearls, poetry, protestations, nor even home in another heart, content the awful soul that dwells in clay. It arouses itself at last from these endearments, as toys, and puts on the harness, and aspires to vast and universal aims. The soul which is in the soul of each, craving for a perfect beatitude, detects incongruities, defects, and disproportion in the behaviour of the other. Hence arise surprise, expostulation, and pain. Yet that which drew them to each other was signs of loveliness, signs of virtue ; and these virtues are there, however eclipsed. They appear and reappear, and continue to attract; but the regard changes, quits the sign, and attaches to the substance. This repairs the wounded affection. Meantime, as life wears on, it proves a game of permutation and combination of all possible positions of the parties, to extort all the resources of each, and acquaint each with the whole strength and weakness of the other. For it is the nature and end of this relation, that they should represent the human race to each other. All that is in the world which is or ought to be known, is cunningly wrought into the texture of man, of woman.

"The person love does to us fit,
Like manna, has the taste of all in it."

"The world rolls; the circumstances vary, every hour. All the angels that inhabit this temple of the body appear at the windows, and all the gnomes and vices also. By all the virtues, they are united. If there be virtue, all the vices are known as such; they confess and flee. Their once flaming regard is sobered by time in either breast, and losing in violence what it gains in extent, it becomes a thorough good understanding. They resign each other without complaint to the good offices which man and woman are severally appointed to discharge in time, and exchange the passion which once could not lose sight of its object, for a cheerful disengaged furtherance, whether present or absent, of each other's designs. At last they discover that all which at first drew them together,—those once sacred features, that magical play of charms, was deciduous, had a prospective end, like the scaffolding by which the house was built; and the purification of the intellect and the heart, from year to year, is the real marriage, foreseen and prepared from the first, and wholly above their consciousness. Looking at these aims with which two persons, a man and a woman, so variously and correlatively gifted, are shut up in one house to spend in the nuptial society forty or fifty years, I do not wonder at the emphasis with which the heart prophesies this crisis from early infancy, at the profuse beauty with which the instincts deck the nuptial bower, and nature and intellect and art emulate each other in the gifts and the melody they bring to the epithalamium.

"Thus are we put in training for a love that knows not sex, nor person, nor partiality, but which seeketh virtue and wisdom everywhere, to the end of increasing virtue and wisdom. We are by nature observers, and thereby learners. That is our permanent state. But we are often made to feel that our affections are but tents of a night. Though slowly and with pain, the objects of the affections change, as the objects of thought do. There are moments when the affections rule and absorb the man, and make his happiness dependent on a person or persons. But in health the mind is presently seen again, its overarching vault, bright with galaxies of immutable lights, and the warm loves and fears that swept over us as clouds, must lose their finite character, and blend with God, to attain their own perfection. But we need not fear that we can lose anything by the progress of the soul. The soul may be trusted to the end. That which is so beautiful and attractive as these relations, must be succeeded and supplanted only by what is more beautiful, and so on for ever."—*Essays*, pp. 152—155.

We can now only glance at the separate works named above. His nature is more defective in form than any of his pieces, but rich in beauty; a rare prose poem is it, a book for one's bosom. The first series of Essays contains the fairest blossoms and fruits of his genius. Here his wondrous mind reveals itself in its purity, its simplicity, its strength, and its beauty too. The second series of Essays is inferior to the first; the style is perhaps clearer, but the water is not so deep. He seems to let himself down to the capacity of his hearers. Yet there is an attempt at order which is seldom successful, and reminds one of the order in which figures are tattooed upon the skin of a South Sea Islander, rather than of the organic symmetry of limbs or bones. He sets up a scaffold, not a living tree, a scaffold, too, on which none but himself can walk.

Some of his Orations and Addresses are noble efforts: old as the world is, and much and long as men are given to speak, it is but rare in human history that such Sermons on the Mount get spoken as the Address to the Students of Theology, and that before the Phi Beta Kappa, at Cambridge. They are words of lofty cheer.

The last book, on "Representative Men," does not come up to the first Essays, neither in matter nor in manner. Yet we know not a man, living and speaking English, that could have written one so good. The lecture on Plato contains exaggerations not usual with Emerson; it fails to describe the man by genus or species. He gives you neither the principles nor the method of Plato, not even his conclusions. Nay, he does not give you the specimens to judge by. The article in the last classical dictionary, or the History of Philosophy for the French Normal Schools gives you a better account of the philosopher and the man. The lecture on Swedenborg is a masterly appreciation of that great man, and to our way of thinking, the best criticism that has yet appeared. He appreciates but does not exaggerate him. The same may be said of that upon Montaigne; those on Shakspeare and Goethe are adequate and worthy of the theme. In the lecture on Napoleon, it is surprising that not a word is said of his greatest faculty, his legislative, organizing power, for we cannot but think with Carlyle, that he "will be better known for his laws than his battles." But the other talents of Napoleon are sketched with a faithful hand, and his faults justly dealt with, not enlarged but not hid—though, on the whole, it seems to us, no great admirers of Napoleon, that he is a little undervalued.

We must briefly notice Mr Emerson's volume of Poems. He has himself given us the standard by which to try him, for he thus defines and describes the poet:

"The sign and credentials of the poet are, that he announces that which no man foretold. He is the true and only doctor; he knows and tells; he is the only teller of news, for he was present and privy to the appearance which he describes. He is a beholder of ideas, and an utterer of the necessary and causal. For we do not speak now of men of poetical talents, or of industry and skill in metre, but of the true poet. I took part in a conversation the other day, concerning a recent writer of lyrics, a man of subtle mind, whose head appeared to be a music box of delicate tunes and rhythms, and whose skill and command of language we could not sufficiently praise. But when the question arose whether he was not only a lyrist, but a poet, we were obliged to confess that he is plainly a contemporary, not an eternal man. He does not stand out of our low limitations, like a Chimborazo under the line, running up from the torrid base through all the climates of the globe, with belts of the herbage of every latitude on its high and mottled sides; but this genius is the landscape-garden of a modern house, adorned with fountains and statues, with well-bred men and women standing and sitting in the walks and terraces. We hear through all the varied music the ground tone of conventional life. Our poets are men of talents who sing, and not the children of music. The argument is secondary, the finish of the verses is primary.

"For it is not metres, but a metre-making argument that makes a poem,—a thought so passionate and alive, that, like the spirit of a plant or an animal, it has an architecture of its own, and adorns nature with a new thing. The thought and the form are equal in the order of time, but in the order of genesis the thought is prior to the form. The poet has a new thought: he has a whole new experience to unfold; he will tell us how it was with him, and all men will be the richer in his fortune."—*Essays*, 2nd Series, pp. 9—11.

It is the office of the poet, he tells us, "by the beauty of things" to announce "a new and higher beauty. Nature offers all her creatures to him as a picture language." "The poorest experience is rich enough for all the purposes of expressing thought;" "the world being put under the mind for verb and noun, the poet is he who can articulate it;" he "turns the world to glass, and shows us all things in their right series and proportions." For through that better perception he stands one step nearer things, and sees the flowing or metamorphosis, perceives that thought is multiform; that within the form of every creature is a force impelling it to ascend into a higher form, and, following with his eyes the life, uses the forms which express that life, and so his speech flows with the flowing of nature." "The poet alone knows astronomy, chemistry, vegetation, and animation, for he does not stop at these facts, but employs them as signs."

"This insight, which expresses itself by what is called imagination, is a very high sort of seeing, which does not come by study, but by the intellect being where and what it sees, by sharing the path or circuit of things through forms, and so making them translucid to others. The path of things is silent. Will they suffer a speaker to go with them? A spy they will not suffer; a lover, a poet, is the transcendency of their own nature,—him they will suffer. The condition of true naming, on the poet's part, is his resigning himself to the divine *aura* which breathes through forms, and accompanying that.

"It is a secret which every intellectual man quickly learns, that, beyond the energy of his possessed and conscious intellect, he is capable of a new energy (as of an intellect doubled on itself), by abandonment to the nature of things; that, beside his privacy of power as an individual man, there is a great public power, on which he can draw, by unlocking, at all risks, his human doors, and suffering the ethereal tides to roll and circulate through him: then he is caught up into the life of the Universe, his speech is thunder, his thought is law, and his words are universally intelligible as the plants and animals. The poet knows that he speaks adequately, then, only when he speaks somewhat wildly, or, 'with the flower of the mind;' not with the intellect, used as an organ, but with the intellect released from all service, and suffered to take its direction from its celestial life; or, as the ancients were wont to express themselves, not with intellect alone, but with the intellect inebriated by nectar. As the traveller who has lost his way, throws his reins on his horse's neck, and trusts to the instinct of the animal to find his road, so we must do with the divine animal who carries us through this world. For if in any manner we can stimulate this instinct, new passages are opened for us into nature, the mind flows into and through things hardest and highest, and the metamorphosis is possible."—*Essays*, 2nd Series, pp. 28—30.

In reading criticisms on Emerson's poetry, one is sometimes reminded of a passage in Pepys' Diary, where that worthy pronounces judgment on some of the works of Shakspeare. Perhaps it may be thought an appropriate introduction to some strictures of our own.

"Aug. 20th, 1666. To Deptford by water, reading Othello, Moor of Venice, which I have heretofore esteemed a mighty good play, but having so lately read the Adventures of Five Hours, it seems a mean thing. Sept. 29th, 1662. To the King's Theatre, where we saw Midsummer Night's Dream, which I had never seen before, nor shall ever again, for it is the most insipid and ridiculous play that ever I saw in my life."

Emerson is certainly one

> "Quem tu, Melpomene, semel
> Nascentem placido lumine videris;
> Spissæ nemorum comæ
> Fingent Æolio carmine nobilem."

Yet his best poetry is in his prose, and his poorest, thinnest, and least musical prose is in his poems.

The "Ode to Beauty" contains some beautiful thoughts in a fair form:

> "Who gave thee, O Beauty,
> The keys of this breast,—
> Too credulous lover
> Of blest and unblest?
> Say, when in lapsed ages
> Thee knew I of old?
> Or what was the service
> For which I was sold?
> When first my eyes saw thee,
> I found me thy thrall,
> By magical drawings,
> Sweet tyrant of all!
> I drank at thy fountain
> False waters of thirst;
> Thou intimate stranger,
> Thou latest and first!
> Thy dangerous glances
> Make women of men;
> New-born, we are melting
> Into nature again."—*Poems*, pp. 136—137.

The three pieces which seem the most perfect poems, both in matter and form, are the "Problem," from which we have already given liberal extracts above; "Each in all," which, however, is certainly not a great poem, but simple, natural, and beautiful; and the "Sphinx," which has higher merits than the others, and is a poem of a good deal of beauty. The Sphinx is the creation of the old classic mythology. But her question is wholly modern, though she has been waiting so long for the seer to solve it, that she has become drowsy.

This is her problem:

> "The fate of the man-child;
> The meaning of man."

All the material and animal world is at peace:

> "Erect as a sunbeam,
> Upspringeth the palm;
> The elephant browses,
> Undaunted and calm;
> In beautiful motion
> The thrush plies his wings;
> Kind leaves of his covert,
> Your silence he sings.
>
> . . . .
>
> "See, earth, air, sound, silence,
> Plant, quadruped, bird,
> By one music enchanted,
> One deity stirred,—
> Each the other adorning,
> Accompany still;
> Night veileth the morning,
> The vapour the hill."

In his early age man shares the peace of the world:

> "The babe by its mother
> Lies bathed in joy;
> Glide its hours uncounted,—
> The sun is its toy;
> Shines the peace of all being,
> Without cloud, in its eyes;
> And the sum of the world
> In soft miniature lies."

But when the child becomes a man he is ill at ease:

> "But man crouches and blushes,
> Absconds and conceals;
> He creepeth and peepeth,
> He palters and steals;

Infirm, melancholy,
Jealous glancing around,
An oaf, an accomplice,
He poisons the ground."

Mother Nature complains of his condition:

"Who has drugg'd my boy's cup?
Who has mix'd my boy's bread?
Who, with sadness and madness,
Has turn'd the man-child's head?"

The Sphinx wishes to know the meaning of all this. A poet answers that this is no mystery to him; man is superior to nature, and its unconscious and involuntary happiness is not enough for him; superior to the events of his own history, so the joy which he has attained is always unsatisfactory:

"The fiend that man harries
Is love of the best;
Yawns the pit of the dragon,
Lit by rays from the blest.
The Lethe of nature
Can't trance him again,
Whose soul sees the perfect,
Which his eyes seek in vain.

"Profounder, profounder,
Man's spirit must dive;
To his aye-rolling orbit
No goal will arrive;
The heavens that now draw him
With sweetness untold,
Once found,—for new heavens
He spurneth the old."

Even sad things turn out well:

"Pride ruin'd the angels,
Their shame them restores;
And the joy that is sweetest
Lurks in stings of remorse."

Thus the riddle is solved; then the Sphinx turns into beautiful things:

"Uprose the merry Sphinx,
And crouch'd no more in stone;

She melted into purple cloud,
She silver'd in the moon;
She spired into a yellow flame;
She flower'd in blossoms red;
She flow'd into a foaming wave;
She stood Monadnoc's head."—*Poems*, pp. 8—13.

We pass over the Threnody, where "well-sung woes" might soothe a "pensive ghost." The Dirge contains some stanzas that are full of nature and well expressed:

"Knows he who tills this lonely field,
To reap its scanty corn,
What mystic fruit his acres yield
At midnight and at morn?

. . . . . .

"The winding Concord gleam'd below,
Pouring as wide a flood
As when my brothers, long ago,
Came with me to the wood.

"But they are gone—the holy ones
Who trod with me this lovely vale;
The strong, star-bright companions
Are silent, low, and pale.

"My good, my noble, in their prime,
Who made this world the feast it was,
Who learn'd with me the lore of time,
Who loved this dwelling-place!

. . . . . .

"I touch this flower of silken leaf,
Which once our childhood knew;
Its soft leaves wound me with a grief
Whose balsam never grew.

"Hearken to you pine-warbler
Singing aloft in the tree!
Hearest thou, O traveller,
What he singeth to me?

"Not unless God made sharp thine ear
With sorrow such as mine,
Out of that delicate lay could'st thou
Its heavy tale divine.

"'Go, lonely man,' it saith;
'They loved thee from their birth;

Their hands were pure, and pure their faith,—
  There are no such hearts on earth.

. . . . . .

" 'Ye cannot unlock your heart,
  The key is gone with them ;
The silent organ loudest chants
  The master's requiem.' "—*Poems*, pp. 232—235.

Here is a little piece which has seldom been equalled in depth and beauty of thought ; yet it has sometimes been complained of as obscure, we see not why :

TO RHEA.

"THEE, dear friend, a brother soothes,
Not with flatteries, but truths,
Which tarnish not, but purify
To light which dims the morning's eye.
I have come from the spring-woods,
From the fragrant solitudes ;
Listen what the poplar-tree
And murmuring waters counsell'd me.

"If with love thy heart has burn'd;
If thy love is unreturn'd ;
Hide thy grief within thy breast,
Though it tear thee unexpress'd ;
For when love has once departed
From the eyes of the false-hearted,
And one by one has torn off quite
The bandages of purple light ;
Though thou wert the loveliest
Form the soul had ever dress'd,
Thou shalt seem, in each reply,
A vixen to his alter'd eye ;
Thy softest pleadings seem too bold,
Thy praying lute will seem to scold ;
Though thou kept the straightest road,
Yet thou errest far and broad.

"But thou shalt do as do the gods
In their cloudless periods ;
For of this lore be thou sure,—
Though thou forget, the gods, secure,
Forget never their command,
But make the statute of this land.

As they lead, so follow all,
Ever have done, ever shall.
Warning to the blind and deaf,
'Tis written on the iron leaf,
Who drinks of Cupid's nectar cup
Loveth downward, and not up;
Therefore, who loves, of gods or men,
Shall not by the same be loved again;
His sweetheart's idolatry
Falls, in turn, a new degree.
When a god is once beguiled
By beauty of a mortal child,
And by her radiant youth delighted,
He is not fool'd, but warily knoweth
His love shall never be requited.
And thus the wise Immortal doeth.—
'Tis his study and delight
To bless that creature day and night;
From all evils to defend her;
In her lap to pour all splendour;
To ransack earth for riches rare,
And fetch her stars to deck her hair;
He mixes music with her thoughts,
And saddens her with heavenly doubts:
All grace, all good his great heart knows,
Profuse in love, the king bestows:
Saying, 'Hearken! earth, sea, air!
This monument of my despair
Build I to the All-Good, All-Fair.
Not for a private good,
But I, from my beatitude,
Albeit scorn'd as none was scorn'd,
Adorn her as was none adorn'd.
I make this maiden an ensample.
To Nature, through her kingdoms ample,
Whereby to model newer races,
Statelier forms, and fairer faces;
To carry man to new degrees
Of power, and of comeliness.
These presents be the hostages
Which I pawn for my release.
See to thyself, O Universe!
Thou art better, and not worse.'—
And the god, having given all,
Is freed for ever from his thrall."—*Poems*, pp. 21—24.

Several of the other pieces are poor; some are stiff and rude, having no lofty thoughts to atone for their unlovely forms. Some have quaint names, which seem given to them out of mere caprice. Such are the following: Mithridates, Hamatreya, Hermione, Merlin, Merops, &c. These names are not more descriptive of the poems they are connected with, than are Jonathan and Eleazer of the men thus baptized. What have Astrea, Rhea, and Etienne de la Boéce to do with the poems which bear their names?

We should think the following lines, from Hermione, were written by some of the youngest Emersonidæ:

"Once I dwelt apart,
Now I live with all;
As shepherd's lamp on far hill-side
Seems, by the traveller espied,
A door into the mountain heart,
So didst thou quarry and unlock
Highways for me through the rock.

"Now, deceived, thou wanderest
In strange lands unblest;
And my kindred come to soothe me.
Southward is my next of blood;
He has come through fragrant wood,
Drugg'd with spice from climates warm,
And in every twinkling glade,
And twilight nook,
Unveils thy form.
Out of the forest way
Forth paced it yesterday;
And when I sat by the watercourse,
Watching the daylight fade,
It throbb'd up from the brook."—*Poems*, pp. 153—154.

Such things are unworthy of such a master.

Here is a passage which we will not attempt to criticise. He is speaking of Love:

"He will preach like a friar,
And jump like a harlequin;
He will read like a crier,
And fight like a Paladin," &c.

Good Homer sometimes nodded, they say; but when he went fast asleep, he did not write lines or print them.

Here is another specimen. It is Monadnoc that speaks:

> "Anchor'd fast for many an age,
> I await the bard and sage,
> Who, in large thoughts, like fair pearl-seed,
> Shall string Monadnoc like a bead."

And yet another:

> "For the present, hard
> Is the fortune of the bard."
> "In the woods he travels glad,
> Without bitter fortune mad,
> Melancholy without bad."

We have seen imitations of this sort of poetry, which even surpassed the original. It does not seem possible that Emerson can write such stuff simply from "lacking the accomplishment of verse." Is it that he has a false theory, and so wilfully writes innumerous verse, and plays his harp, all jangling and thus out of tune? Certainly it seems so. In his poems he uses the old mythology, and in bad taste; talks of Gods, and not God; of Pan, the Oreads, Titan, Jove, and Mars, the Parcæ and the Dæmon.

There are three elaborate poems which demand a word of notice. The "Woodnotes" contains some good thoughts, and some pleasing lines, but on the whole a pine tree which should talk like Mr Emerson's pine ought to be plucked up by the roots and cast into the depths of the sea. "Monadnoc" is the title of another piece which appears forced and unnatural, as well as poor and weak. The third is called "initial, dæmonic, and celestial Love." It is not without good thoughts, and here and there a good line, but in every attribute of poetry it is far inferior to his majestic essay on Love. In his poetry Mr Emerson often loses his command of language, metaphors fail him, and the magnificent images which adorn and beautify all his prose works, are gone.

From what has been said, notwithstanding the faults we have found in Emerson, it is plain that we assign him a very high rank in the literature of mankind. He is a very extraordinary man. To no English writer since Milton can we assign so high a place; even Milton himself, great genius though he was, and great architect of beauty, has not added so many thoughts to the treasury of the race; no, nor been the author of so much loveliness. Emerson is a man of genius such as does not often appear, such as has never appeared before in America, and but seldom in the world. He learns from all sorts of men, but no English writer, we think, is so original. We sincerely lament the want of logic in his method, and his exaggeration of the intuitive powers, the unhappy consequences of which we see in some of his followers and admirers. They will be more faithful than he to the false principle which he lays down, and will think themselves wise because they do not study, learned because they are ignorant of books, and inspired because they say what outrages common sense. In Emerson's poetry there is often a ruggedness and want of finish which seems wilful in a man like him. This fault is very obvious in those pieces he has put before his several essays. Sometimes there is a seed-corn of thought in the piece, but the piece itself seems like a pile of rubbish shot out of a cart which hinders the seed from germinating. His admirers and imitators not unfrequently give us only the rubbish and probably justify themselves by the example of their master. Spite of these defects, Mr Emerson, on the whole, speaks with a holy power which no other man possesses who now writes the English tongue. Others have more readers, are never sneered at by respectable men, are oftener praised in the journals, have greater weight in the pulpits, the cabinets, and the councils of the nation; but there is none whose words so sink into the mind and heart of young men and maids; none who work so powerfully to fashion the character of the coming age. Seeing the power which he exercises, and the influence he is likely to have on generations to come, we are jealous of any fault in his matter, or its form, and have allowed no private and foolish friendship to hinder us from speaking of his faults.

This is his source of strength: his intellectual and moral sincerity. He looks after Truth, Justice, and Beauty. He has not uttered a word that is false to his own mind or conscience; has not suppressed a word because he thought it too high for men's comprehension, and therefore dangerous to the repose of men. He never compromises.

He sees the chasm between the ideas which come of man's nature and the institutions which represent only his history; he does not seek to cover up the chasm, which daily grows wider between Truth and Public Opinion, between Justice and the State, between Christianity and the Church; he does not seek to fill it up, but he asks men to step over and build institutions commensurate with their ideas. He trusts himself, trusts man, and trusts God. He has confidence in all the attributes of infinity. Hence he is serene; nothing disturbs the even poise of his character, and he walks erect. Nothing impedes him in his search for the true, the lovely, and the good; no private hope, no private fear, no love of wife or child, or gold, or ease, or fame. He never seeks his own reputation; he takes care of his Being, and leaves his seeming to take care of itself. Fame may seek him; he never goes out of his way a single inch for her.

He has not written a line which is not conceived in the interest of mankind. He never writes in the interest of a section, of a party, of a church, of a man, always in the interest of mankind. Hence comes the ennobling influence of his works. Most of the literary men of America, most of the men of superior education, represent the ideas and interest of some party: in all that concerns the welfare of the human race, they are proportionably behind the mass who have only the common culture; so while the thought of the people is democratic, putting man before the accidents of a man, the literature of the nation is aristocratic, and opposed to the welfare of mankind. Emerson belongs to the exceptional literature of the times—and while his culture joins him to the history of man, his ideas and his whole life enable him to represent also the nature of man, and so to write for the future. He is one of the rare exceptions amongst our educated men, and helps redeem American literature from the reproach of imitation, conformity, meanness of aim, and hostility to the progress of mankind. No faithful man is too low for his approval and encouragement; no faithless man too high and popular for his rebuke.

A good test of the comparative value of books, is the state they leave you in. Emerson leaves you tranquil, resolved on noble manhood, fearless of the consequences;

he gives men to mankind, and mankind to the laws of God. His position is a striking one. Eminently a child of Christianity and of the American idea, he is out of the Church and out of the State. In the midst of Calvinistic and Unitarian superstition, he does not fear God, but loves and trusts Him. He does not worship the idols of our time—wealth and respectability, the two calves set up by our modern Jeroboam. He fears not the damnation these idols have the power to inflict—neither poverty nor social disgrace. In busy and bustling New-England comes out this man serene and beautiful as a star, and shining like "a good deed in a naughty world." Reproached as an idler, he is active as the sun, and pours out his radiant truth on Lyceums at Chelmsford, at Waltham, at Lowell, and all over the land. Out of a cold Unitarian Church rose this most lovely light. Here is Boston, perhaps the most humane city in America, with its few noble men and women, its beautiful charities, its material vigour, and its hardy enterprise; commercial Boston, where honour is weighed in the public scales, and justice reckoned by the dollars it brings; conservative Boston, the grave of the Revolution, wallowing in its wealth, yet grovelling for more, seeking only money, careless of justice, stuffed with cotton yet hungry for tariffs, sick with the greedy worm of avarice, loving money as the end of life, and bigots as the means of preserving it; Boston with toryism in its parlours, toryism in its pulpits, toryism in its press, itself a tory town, preferring the accidents of man to man himself—and amidst it all there comes Emerson, graceful as Phœbus-Apollo, fearless and tranquil as the sun he was supposed to guide, and pours down the enchantment of his light, which falls where'er it may, on dust, on diamonds, on decaying heaps to hasten their rapid rot, on seeds new sown to quicken their ambitious germ, on virgin minds of youths and maids to waken the natural seed of nobleness therein, and make it grow to beauty and to manliness. Such is the beauty of his speech, such the majesty of his ideas, such the power of the moral sentiment in men, and such the impression which his whole character makes on them, that they lend him, everywhere, their ears, and thousands bless his manly thoughts.

HILDRETH'S HISTORY OF THE UNITED STATES.

The History of the United States of America, from the Discovery of the Continent to the Organization of Government under the Federal Constitution. By Richard Hildreth. In three volumes. New York: Harper & Brothers. 1849.

At the present day, the United States present one of the most interesting and important political phenomena ever offered in the history of mankind. England has planted her colonies in New Holland, in New Zealand, in the East and the West Indies, at Cape Good Hope, and at Labrador; at Mauritius, Gibraltar, and in the Islands of the Pacific. She has forced an entrance into China; she longs to get firm footing in Borneo and Nicaragua. Wheresoever her children wander, they carry the seed out of which British institutions are sure to grow; institutions, however, which never produce their like, but nobler and better on another soil. Omitting all mention of Ireland, abundantly treated in a previous article, America was the oldest of these colonies; the first to detach itself from the parent stem, and is, perhaps, the prophecy of what most of the others are destined to become.

It must be a vigorous tribe of men which can hold so vast a portion of the earth, while themselves are so few in numbers. Three hundred years ago, in the reign of Edward the Sixth, England was a third-rate power in Europe. Her population was less than three millions, her exports were trifling, and consisted of the raw materials of her clumsy agriculture, and her mineral treasures, which the Tyrians had traversed the ocean to purchase two thousand years before. Her soil could hardly raise a salad. Scotland was independent; Ireland not wholly subject to English rule; Wales had but lately been added to her realm. She was remarkable chiefly for the stormy seas which girt the Isle, and the chalky cliffs along her shore; for the fogs that cover it; for the rudeness of her inhabitants and the tough valour of her soldiers. Now, in three hundred years, England contains some seventeen millions of inhabitants; Scotland and Ireland, ten millions more. Russia, Austria, and France, are the only nations in Europe that outnumber her in population. Turkey, with nine millions, and Spain, with twelve, are powerless beside her. Her ships are in all the oceans of the world; the sun never sets on her flag; her subjects capture the whale at Baffin's Bay, and the elephant in India; they sport at hunting lions in South Africa. Her navigators, with scientific hardihood, explore each corner of the Northern Sea, or, locked in ice, wait the slow hand of death, or the slower sun of an arctic summer. She has climes too cold for the reindeer; climes too hot almost for the sugar-cane and the pine-apple; the lean larch of Scotland, and the banyan-tree of Hindostan, both grow in the same empire. Esquimaux, Gaboon, and Sanscrit, are tongues subject to Britain. At least an eighth part of the men now living in the world owe allegiance to the queen of that little island.

Her children came to America when the nation was in all the vigour of its most rapid growth. The progress of their descendants in population and in wealth has been without parallel. Two hundred and fifty years ago, there was not an English settler in the United States; now the population is not far from two-and-twenty millions; two-thirds of the people are of English origin. The increase of property has been more rapid than that of numbers. In fifty years, Boston has multiplied her inhabitants nearly five-fold, and her property more than twenty-five-fold in the same time. The increase of intelligence is very remarkable, and probably surpasses that of property.

The Americans are now trying a political experiment which has hitherto been looked on with great suspicion and even horror. Here is a democracy on a large scale; a church without a bishop; a state without a king; society (in the Free States) without the theoretical distinction of patrician and plebeian. What is more surprising, the experiment succeeds better than its most sanguine friends ever dared to hope. The evils which were apprehended have not yet befallen us. The "Red Republic," which hostile prophets foretold, has not come to pass; there are "red" monarchies, enough of them, the other side of the world, born red; doomed, we fear, to die in that sad livery of woe; but in America, the person of the citizen is still respected quite as much as in Austria and England; and nowhere in the world is property safer or so much honoured; the lovers of liberty here are lovers of order as its condition. Even Mr Carlyle, accustomed to speak of America with bitterness and contempt, and of the ballot-box with loathing and nausea, confesses to the success of the experiment so far as wealth and numbers are concerned. Indeed, it is a matter of rejoicing to warm-hearted men, that we have cotton to cover and corn to feed the thousands of exiles who yearly are driven by hunger from England, to seek a home or a grave on the soil of America. It is interesting to study the growth of the American people; to observe the progress of the idea on which the government rests, and the attempts to make the idea an institution.

This is one of the few great nations which can trace its history back to certain beginnings; there is no fabulous period in our annals; no mythical centuries, when

> Οἳ πρῶτα μὲν βλέποντες ἔβλεπον μάτην,
> Κλύοντες οὐκ ἤκουον· ἀλλ' ὀνειράτων
> Ἀλίγκιοι μορφαῖσι, τὸν μακρὸν χρόνον
> Ἔφυρον εἰκῆ πάντα, κοὔτε πλινθυφεῖς
> Δόμους προσείλους ᾖσαν, οὐ ξυλουργίαν·
> Κατώρυχες δ' ἔναιον, ὥστε ἀήσυροι
> Μύρμηκες, ἄντρων ἐν μυχοῖς ἀνηλίοις.

To be rightly appreciated, American history requires to be written by a Democrat. A Theocrat would condemn our institutions for lacking an established church with its privileged priesthood; an Aristocrat, for the absence of conventional nobility. Military men might sneer at the smallness of the army and navy; and æsthetic men deplore the want of a splendid court, the lack of operatic and other spectacles in the large towns. The Democrat looks for the substantial welfare of the people, and studies America with reference to that point. At present, America is not remarkable for her literature or her art; she has made respectable advances in science, but her industrial works and her political institutions are by far her most remarkable achievements hitherto. We are not sanguine enough to suppose that all the advantages of all the other forms of government are to be secured in this, but yet trust that the most valuable things will be preserved here. In due time, we doubt not, the higher results of civilization will appear, and we shall estimate the greatness of the nation not merely by its numbers, its cotton, its cattle, and its corn. But "that is not first which is spiritual." First of all, the imperious wants of the body must be attended to,—the woods are to be felled, the log-cabins built, the corn got into the ground, the wild beasts destroyed, the savages kept at peace. There must be many generations between the woodsman who erects the first shanty of logs, and the poet who sheds immortal beauty on logs and lumberers. Were there not ages between the wooden hut of Arcadian Pelasgos in Greece and the Parthenon? From mythical Cecrops to Aristophanes, the steps are many, each a generation. The genius of Liberty only asks two things—time and space. Space enough she has, all America is before her; time she takes possession of fast enough, only a second at once; and in the course of ages, we think she will make her mark on the world. Up to this time the achievements of America are, taken as a whole, such as we need not much blush at. Some things there were and are to be ashamed of—not of the whole. That dreadful blot of slavery remains yet, an Ireland in America; among the whites, on the one hand, causing the most shameful poltroonery which modern times can redden at, and, on the other, calling forth heroism, that seems almost enough to redeem the wickedness which has brought it to light. But, turning to that half of the nation free from direct personal contact with this sin of the state, forgetting for a moment the foolishness of "political sages," the cowardice of those leaders who never dare enact justice as a statute, but take the responsibility of making iniquity a law, and omitting the defalcation of men who forsake their habitual worship of a calf of gold, to bow down before a face of dough,—there is certainly a gratifying spectacle. Here are some fifteen millions of free men, trying the voluntary system in church and state, richer than any other people of the same numbers in the world, and with the aggregate wealth of the nation more equally distributed; a nation well fed, well clothed, well housed, industrious, temperate, well governed, and respecting one another and themselves; that certainly is something. In all that territory there are probably more muskets in the hands of private men than there are habitations, yet not one is kept for actual defence; and, through the Free States, no soldier walks abroad with loaded gun; only in the large towns is there a visible police. There are not two thousand soldiers of the state in all that territory, and they are as inoffensive to the citizens as the scarecrows in the field, only not so useful, nor so well paying for their keep. Of this population some three millions are in the public schools, academies, and colleges. Nowhere are churches so numerous, or so well attended; nowhere such indications of happiness, comfort, intelligence, morality among the mass of men. This, we repeat, is something. We have no very great men; we have never had such. An Alexander, a Cæsar, a Charlemagne, a Napoleon, we have not had. Perhaps we never shall; but it is hardly worth while to go into mourning yet for the absence of such. Great artists, poets, philosophers, men of letters, we have not had, hitherto. We have shown no great respect for such, to our shame be it spoken; but in due time we may trust that they also will come and shine for ages, with the halo of genius around their brow. However, it does seem a little remarkable that, in America, everything seems to be done democratically—by the combined force of many men with moderate abilities, and not by one man of Herculean powers. It was so in the early periods of the nation; so in the Revolution, and so now. It has always been so with the Teutonic tribes of men, much more than with the nations from the Shemitic stock. With them there comes a Moses, or a Mohammed, who overrides a nation for one or two thousand years, and its progress seems to be by a series of leaps; while the western nations, with less nationalism, and more individualism, accomplish less in that way, but slope upwards by a more gradual ascent. In the English Revolution, there was no one great man who condensed the age into himself, and created the institutions of coming generations, as Moses and Mohammed have done: spite of the great abilities and great services of Cromwell, no just historian will claim that for him. It was so in the American Revolution; so in the French. Washington led our armies, and Napoleon the legions of France, but neither gave the actors the idea which was slowly or suddenly to be realized in institutions.

It is an interesting work to trace the growth of the American people from their humble beginnings to their present condition; to discover and point out the causes which have helped that growth, and the causes which have hindered it. To a philosophical historian this is no unpromising field; the facts are well known; it is easy to ascertain the ideas out of which the general political institutions of America have grown; it is not difficult to see the historical causes which have modified these institutions, giving them their present character and form. None but a democrat can thoroughly appreciate that history. As the history of Christianity must be written by a Christian who can write from within, and the history of art by a man with an artistic soul, so must the history of America be written by a democrat—we mean one who puts man before the accidents of man, valuing his permanent nature more than the transient results of his history.

American history, up to the adoption of the Federal Constitution, forms a whole, and has a certain unity which is not obvious at first sight. The several colonies were getting established, learning to stand alone; they were quite unlike in their origin, form of government, ecclesiastical and other institutions. Very different ideas prevailed in Georgia and New Hampshire. Looked at carelessly, they seem only divergent, but when studied carefully, it seems as if there was a regular plan, and as if the whole was calculated to bring about the present result. No doubt there was such a concatenation of part with part, only the plan lay in God, not in the mind of Oglethorpe and Captain Smith, of Carver and Roger Williams.

Considering this history as an organic whole, to treat it philosophically, it seems to us it is necessary to describe the material theatre on which this historic drama is to be acted out; to describe the American continent, telling of its extent and peculiarities in general, its soil, climate, and natural productions, and its condition at the time when the white men first landed on its shores; this, of course, comprises a description of the inhabitants at that time in possession of its soil.

Then the historian is to tell us of the men who came here to found this empire; of their origin, their character, and their history in general. He is to tell the external causes which brought them here, or the motives which impelled them: and the ideas which they brought, as well as those which sprung up under their new circumstances. Next, he is to show speculatively by the idea, and practically by the facts, how these ideas worked under the new conditions of the people; how they acted on circumstances and circumstances on them, and what institutions came thereof. The historian very poorly performs his duty who merely relates the succession of rulers, the increase or diminution of wealth and numbers, the coming on of wars, and the termination thereof, the rise of great men, with their decline and fall, and the presence of institutions, without telling of the ideas they represented. Showing the continual growth of the ideas which create the institutions, is little more than the work of an annalist or chronicler.

If a great idea appears in human affairs, founding new institutions and overturning the old, it is part of the work of a philosophical historian to give us the story of this idea; to refer it back to its origin in the permanent nature of man, or the accidents of his development; to show the various attempts to make the thought a thing, and the idea a fact. Such is the case in American history: political institutions were set agoing here radically unlike any others in the world. True, we may find points of agreement between the American and various European governments. The trial by jury dates far back beyond the "gray goose" code, and has its origin in remote antiquity; the *habeas corpus* is doubtless of English origin, and its history may be read in Hallam, and elsewhere; the notion of delegates to represent corporations, or republics, may have originated with the early Christians, who sent their ministers and other servants (or masters) to some provincial synod; the idea of individual liberty, the sacredness of the person before the state, may be traced to the wilds of Germany long before the time of Christ. We know how much of American freedom may be found in Sir John Fortescue's Laudation of the laws of England, or in the books of Moses, if we will; but yet the American government, in nation, estate, and town, is an original thing. The parts are old, many of them, but the whole is the most original thing that can be found in the political history of the world, for many an age. Almost every special and true moral precept of the

New Testament may be found in some heathen or Hebrew writer before Jesus, but yet, spite of that, Christianity was an original form of religion, as much so as the statue of a goddess, which a Grecian sculptor gathered by a grand eclecticism from five hundred Spartan maids, corrected by the ideal in his own creative and critical mind.

You trace the secret cause of the American institutions far off in the history of mankind. Here it is a dim sentiment in the breast of the German in the Hercynian forest; then again it burns in the bosom of the Christian, and he tells the world that God is no respecter of persons, that Jew and Gentile are alike to Him. But it leads, at first, to no political consequences; even its ecclesiastical results are trifling, and its social consequences at first of small moment. It could not make St Paul hostile to personal Roman slavery. In the Middle Ages you trace the path of this idea. Sometimes it goes over the mountain side, and is seen amid the works of great men, but commonly it winds along in the low valleys of human life; a little path, known only to the people, and worn by their feet, not knowing whither it leads them; a by-path for the vassal, not the highway which the baron and prelate took care to have in order. The record of its existence is found in the song of the peasant or in the popular proverb; in some fabulous legend of unhistorical times,—times that never were,—or in the predictions of days to come. This idea has not a place in the pulpit of the minister; but in the silent cell of the devout mystic it has its dwelling-place, and gladdens his enraptured heart as a vision of the kingdom of heaven.

Now it waxes mighty, and contends against the oppression of tyrannical men, less in the state than in the church. Fast as it becomes an idea, men organize it as well as they can, now in little convents or monasteries, then in trading companies; then in guilds of mechanics; in cities and small states, as in Italy and in the Low Countries, in Switzerland, and the Hanse towns. At length this impulse — it was hardly an idea — puts all Europe into commotion. Men call for spiritual freedom. Under the guidance of that great spirit who stands as the water-shed between the Middle Ages and modern times, feeling the contradictions of a divided age, under Martin Luther, men break the yoke of ecclesiastical tyranny they have borne so long. Liberty of conscience was all mankind called for, but for that time they must put up with liberty of conscience limited on the divine side by the Bible, on the human side by the king. Strait and oppressive limits both proved to be,—bonds that approached nearer and threatened to crush the struggling soul. Still men were not satisfied; they wanted political liberty as well as spiritual, and of spiritual much more than they got. How rapidly the idea of a free state got abroad over Europe. Bodinus, in his Republic; Thomas More, in his Utopia; Bacon, in his New Atlantis,—very undemocratic men at the best,—are witnesses to the power of this demand. The sentiment had long been in men's hearts,—it was now rapidly becoming an idea. Kings and priests told men the less liberty they had the better; if they tried to go alone they would certainly fall. Was it not better to sit on the hearth of the king, their head under the apron of the church, than thus try to walk in the open air? There was good and bad scripture for such a course,—and of precedents the world was full. But men would not be satisfied; the king's hearth was warm, and the motherly apron of the church made the head easy and comfortable, but there was a divine soul in man which would break out into all sorts of peasant wars, of Jack Cade's rebellions, of Runymedes, and the like. At length the idea gets so fully set forth, as an idea, and so widely spread abroad by fanatics, and amongst sober men, that the chief question is, Where shall the idea first become a fact? Shall it be in Germany, where the ecclesiastical Reformation began and succeeded most? No, the feudal system had taken deep root in the Teutonic soil, and could not be pulled up for some ages to come; the Reformation had affected thought in all departments, in Germany, but politics suffered little change, and by that little it does not appear that the people were directly gainers, to any considerable degree. Could it be in France? There was a body of enlightened men taking the lead in European science and literature, but there was no intelligence in the people. They seemed subjects of authority, not subjects of reason, and, though they now and then gave indication of the sentiment for freedom, which has since become so mighty in that nation, yet then no idea of it swept through the land, stirring the tree-tops, and agitating the grass and the very dust. In France there was a gorgeous court; a wealthy king; nobles, rich, famous, and of long-renowned descent; there were soldiers with genius and skill; merchants and artists, and clergymen, from Abbé Jean to Cardinal Richelieu, but there was no people to appreciate or desire freedom. In Spain no one would think of free institutions; the mind of the nation, chained by the state and palsied by the church, had only life enough left for the mere external things, for gold and sugar; even her European possessions she could not hold against the vigour of Protestant Dutchmen. Italy had given lessons in commerce, arts, literature, religion, and politics to all the rest of Europe. In the Dark Ages she had kept the holy fire of science and of literature, covered in the ashes of her old renown, and when occasion offered raked the embers, with her garment fanning them to a flame, and sent little sparkles thereof to Scotland, Ireland, England, and to all the north. While despotism laid his iron rod on all the north of Europe, and the centre too, little commonwealths sprung up at practical Venice, at prudent Pisa, and at haughty Florence, as a poet calls them; green gardens were they in a snowy world, filled with many a precious plant. But these, too, had declined. Art, literature, science, "*la bella scienza*," the sweet art of poesy, had flourished there, but the nature of liberty craved another soil. The Reformation, which winnowed the nations with a rough wind, did not separate the wheat from the chaff in Italy. The priests were too powerful; the people too indolent; the chaff is so thick, and dry withal, that the poor wheat can germinate but slowly.

"Ay! down to the dust with them, slaves as they are,"

might well be said of Italy in the end of the sixteenth century. Other vineyards she had helped to plant, but her own she had not kept. The last service she did mankind was, perhaps, the greatest: she showed them a new and savage world beyond the fabled island of Atlantis in the West. Columbus and Amerigo, Verrazani and the Cabots, were pioneers of freedom for mankind. When Columbus turned his bark's head to the West, he little knew that he was leading the nations to universal democracy: but so it seems now.

The new idea must come across the water to make its fortune. To escape the persecution of the dragon with seven heads and ten horns, the man-child must flee with his mother into the wilderness and there sojourn, said our fathers, giving a "private interpretation" to a dark "prophecy;" at any rate, the American "earth helped the woman." Here, three thousand miles from their native land, out of the reach of old aristocratic institutions, the new nation could unfold its sentiment to an idea, could develope the idea into institutions; and, trying the experiment on a small scale at first, prepare to found a great empire on the American idea that all men are created equal, and endowed by their Creator with certain unalienable rights, and that it is the business of a government to preserve for each man the perfect enjoyment of all these natural rights, on the sole condition that he does the corresponding duties.

There are two great periods of human history. In the one men seek to establish unity of action, and form the individuals into tribes and states. This is commonly done to the loss of personal freedom: the state subdues the citizen, and he becomes the subject merely. In religion, the ante-christian forms represent this phase of men's affairs, and, in politics, it is indicated by aristocracies, monarchies, and despotisms. Then comes the second great period of history, in which men seek for personal freedom. In religion, this is represented by Christianity, not the Christianity of the Catholics or the Protestants, but the absolute religion of human nature; in politics, by a democracy, the government of all, for all, and by all. The settlers of America, in coming here, mainly escaped from the institutions of the former period of history; the institutions which once helped mankind, but at length hindered them. They brought with them the sentiments and ideas of the same period, imperfectly formed, and such helps and institutions as had previously come out of their sentiments and ideas. They came from a nation more vigorous in the arts of peace than any which the world had seen before. They came from that nation in the time of its greatest spiritual vigour. They brought with them the best treasures of the private spiritual earnings of the English nation—the common law, the *habeas corpus*, trial by jury, the form of representative government, the rich, noble literature of England, of its Elizabethan age. From the general spiritual treasures of the world, they brought Christianity and the experience of mankind for five or six thousand years. Virgin America, hidden away behind the Atlantic and Pacific oceans, is now to be married to mankind.

The first settlers came with different motives and expectations, driven by different forms of necessity. There came two types of men quite unlike in most important particulars—the settlers of the North and the South, the Puritans of New-England, the secular and more worldly planter of Virginia and the Carolinas. They came from different motives, for a different purpose; they founded different institutions, which produce the contradictory results we now see. The difference between South Carolina and Massachusetts in 1850, dates plainly back to the different origin of the two colonies. New-England was settled for the sake of an idea; Virginia and the Carolinas by men who reasonably thought to better their condition and make their fortune. M. Chevalier long ago pointed out the distinction between these two types, the Puritan and the Cavalier; only he finds a distinction in birth, wealth, and breeding, in favour of the Cavalier, which he would not have found had he known American history somewhat better. However, the difference between the secular and the religious colonies still continues in the descendants of the two. But these types unite, or will unite, as he says, to form a future national type, namely, the Western man.

Let us look at the volumes of Mr Hildreth. His work is divided into forty-eight chapters, and, beginning with the first voyage of Columbus, ends with the election of the first President after the adoption of the Federal Constitution. When so great a theme is to be treated in the small compass of three volumes, the author must needs be brief; accordingly, he despatches quite summarily the preliminary matter, relating to the discoveries of the continent by the Italian navigators, and briefly sketches a picture of the country and its inhabitants at the period when European colonization first began. The account of the Indians is short, occupying but about twenty pages, yet distinct and clear; for one so brief it is the best account we remember to have seen. The whole Indian population within the limits of the United States and west of the Rocky Mountains, he thinks never exceeded, if it ever reached, three hundred thousand; others make the number not far from one hundred and eighty thousand. The Indians have not yet received the attention which they demand from the historian and the philosopher; they are as remarkable monuments in the development of the human race as the fossils are in the history of the physical changes of this earth. But they are passing away; their institutions, manners, traditions, and language will soon be forgotten, and by and by it will be impossible to reconstruct the history of which they furnish so valuable a chapter.

Mr Hildreth speaks of the French settlements in America, and then comes to the history of the English colonization here. For a long time there is an apparent want of unity in the subject, which no historical treatment can wholly disguise. The reader is hurried from Virginia to New-England, then to New York, to Maryland, to the Carolinas, to Pennsylvania, to Delaware, and to Georgia. However, for a long time, Virginia and New-England are the objects of chief interest. We shall dwell chiefly on the latter, and call the attention of our readers to some things of considerable importance in the story of America. The character of the Puritans has been the theme of unqualified praise and unqualified condemnation; the Puritan of Hume, of Macaulay, and of Bancroft are quite different characters. Perhaps no one of these three great masters of the art of history has given us a fair and just likeness of the men. Mr Hildreth is not ambitious in his attempt to defend the fathers of New-England; he rather leaves their actions to speak for themselves. He thus speaks of them, however:—

"As the other traditions of the Church fell more and more into contempt, the entire reverence of the people was concentrated upon the Bible, recently made accessible in an English version, and read with eagerness, not as a mere form of words to be solemnly and ceremoniously gone through with, but as an inspired revelation, an indisputable authority in science, politics, morals, life. It began, indeed, to be judged necessary, by the more ardent and sincere, that all existing institutions in church and state, all social relations, and the habits of every-day life should be reconstructed, and made to conform to this divine model. Those who entertained these sentiments increased to a considerable party, composed chiefly, indeed, of the humbler classes, yeomen, traders, and mechanics, but including, also, clergymen, merchants, landed proprietors, and even some of the nobility. They were derided by those not inclined to go with them as *Puritans;* but the austerity of their lives and doctrines, and their confident claim to internal assurance of a second birth and special election as the children of God, made a powerful impression on the multitude, while the high schemes they entertained for the reconstruction of society brought them into sympathy with all that was great and heroic in the nation.

"The Puritans denounced the Church ceremonies, and presently the hierarchy; but they long entertained profound reverence for the Church itself, and a superstitious terror of schism. Some of the bolder and more ardent, whose obscurity gave them courage, took at length the decisive step of renouncing the English communion, and setting up a church of their own, upon what they conceived to be the Bible model. That, however, was going further than the great body of the Puritans wished or dared to follow, and these separatists remained for many years obscure and inconsiderable."—Vol. I. pp. 153—154.

There are certain peculiarities in the institutions they at first founded, which Mr Hildreth very properly dwells upon and exposes. We refer to the theocratical governments which they founded. No historian of America has so fully done them justice in this respect. He fears no man; he is not misled by any reverence for the Puritans; he shows no antipathy to them; extenuates nothing, adds nothing, and sets down nought in malice. We shall dwell a little on the theocratical tyranny which they sought to exercise. In 1629, John and Samuel Browne, at Salem, insisted on using the liturgy of the English Church, and set up a separate worship of their own, for that purpose. They were arrested as "incorrigible," "factious and evil conditioned," and shipped home to England.

In 1631, the government of Massachusetts decided that no man shall be admitted a freeman, that is, a voter, a citizen in full, unless he were a member of a church in the colony. The candidate for church membership must state his "religious experience" before the church, convince them of his "assurance" and "justification," before he shall be admitted as a member. Thus the road to the ballot-box led through the church, and lay directly in the range of the pulpit. Hence it was no easy matter to become a freeman. Mr Hildreth says not a fourth part of the adult population were church members. Baptism was the special privilege of church members and their "infant seed."

The clergy were aristocratic, in the evil sense of that word. They would not let the inhabitants of Newtown [Cambridge] remove to Connecticut in 1634, for "the removal of a candlestick is a great judgment, which ought to be avoided." Fines were imposed for absence from public worship; they aided the "Patricians" to carry "the point against the Plebeians."

Stephen Goldsmith was fined forty pounds, forced to make acknowledgment in all the churches (1636), and give bonds for a hundred pounds, because he said all the ministers in the colony, except Allen Wheelwright, and, "as he thought, Mr Hooker," "did teach a covenant of works." Men were forbidden to erect a dwelling more than half a mile from the meeting-house, says Mr Hildreth. The Puritan authorities became as arbitrary and unjust as the court of "High Commission," in England; and persecuted men, and women not less, for differing from the opinion of the theocratic officers. Stoughton was persecuted for political opinions, Williams for religious, and Mrs Hutchinson for philosophical notions on questions of the most subtle character. Baptists and Quakers were imprisoned, whipped, banished, or put to death.

No man was allowed to settle in the colony without a permit from the magistrate; a new comer must not have a house, and no man was suffered to entertain him more than three weeks, without permission. Before Massachusetts had been settled ten years, the synod at Newtown condemned eighty-two prevalent opinions as "false and heretical!" Wheelwright and Mrs Hutchinson were banished for unpopular opinions; freedom of worship was forbidden even to the like-minded, and "the lords brethren" became as tyrannical as "the lords bishops." An attempt was made, in 1639, to establish a church at Weymouth, on the principle of admitting all baptized persons without requiring a profession of faith or relation of experience. It was promptly suppressed; the minister concerned in the business was forced to make an apology; some of the laymen were fined from two to twenty pounds, one whipped "eleven stripes," and one disfranchised. Two persons once called the churches of Massachusetts "anti-christian," and were heavily fined and imprisoned for the offence. Governor Easton, of Rhode Island, it is alleged, once said, "the elect have the Holy Ghost and also the Devil indwelling." He had provocation for his conclusion. The judicial treatment of Mrs Hutchinson was infamous, and the conduct of the leading clergy was worthy of the darkest ages of popish bigotry. The misfortunes of that noble woman were attributed to "the hand of God." The treatment of Samuel Gorton and his coadjutors is nearly as disreputable. Did Dr Child and others petition for a change of laws, so that inhabitants, not church members, might have the rights of English subjects, it gave "great offence to many godly priests, elders, and others;" the petition was "adjudged a contempt," the petitioners were fined from ten to fifty pounds apiece. When the Doctor was about to embark for England, his trunk was searched for dangerous papers it might contain. Copies of two memorials were found in the study of Mr Dand, addressed to the Commissioners of Plantations, one of them signed by some "fishermen of Marblehead, profane persons," and by "young men who came over servants, and never had any show of religion in them," and by "men of no reason." "A young fellow, a carpenter," by the name of Joy, had been busy in obtaining signatures to the petition, and was kept in irons till "he humbled himself" and "blessed God for these irons upon his legs, hoping they would do him good while he lived." The offence of the men in whose hands the petitions were found was deemed "in nature capital," treason against the Commonwealth. Dand was kept in prison more than a year, and Child, with others, was heavily fined.

The magistrates of Massachusetts were long averse to having fixed laws—preferring an arbitrary government by men to the sober and dispassionate government of impartial statutes. The code made in 1649 contained some remarkable provisions: "Stubborn and rebellious sons," and children over sixteen "who curse or smite their natural father or mother," were punished with death.

Courtship must not be undertaken without the permission of the parents or guardians of the maid; or, in their absence, that of the "nearest magistrate," under penalty of fine and imprisonment. Blasphemy was a capital crime. Men were to be banished "for preaching and maintaining any damnable heresies, as denying the immortality of the soul, or resurrection of the body," or "that Christ gave himself a ransom for our sins," or "for declaring that we are not sanctified by his death and righteousness," or for denying "the morality of the fourth commandment," or the efficacy of infant baptism, or for departing from church at the administration of that ordinance. A few years later, a law was made punishing with fine, whipping, banishment, or with death, any persons "who denied the received books of the Old and New Testaments to be the infallible word of God." We know some persons who would be glad to revive these pleasant statutes at the present day. We are told it is not long since an attempt was made, in Massachusetts, to secure the indictment of a distinguished scholar for a learned article, published in a very respectable theological journal, in which he maintained that there was no prophetic passage in the Old Testament which was originally intended to apply to Jesus of Nazareth. It is not yet ten years since there appeared, in one of the leading secular newspapers of Boston, an article written by a venerable clergyman, calling for the arrest and punishment of a young man who had, in a sermon, spoken against the corruption of the Christian church at this day, and the doctrines that had no foundation in reason and the nature of things. Three years' confinement in the State's prison was the punishment demanded for the young minister!

Everybody knows the treatment of Baptists and Quakers in Massachusetts. The "great Cotton" declared that denial of infant baptism was "soul-murder," and a capital offence. When Obadiah Holmes was fined thirty pounds for being a Baptist, as he went from the bar he thanked God that he was "counted worthy to suffer for the name of Jesus." "Whereupon," says Holmes, "John Wilson [minister of 'First Church' in Boston] struck me before the judgment-seat and cursed me, saying: 'The curse of

God or Jesus go with thee.' " Holmes would not pay his fine, and was whipped thirty stripes with a three-corded whip, "the man striking with all his strength." But he "had such a spiritual manifestation that I could well bear it," says he, "yea, and in a manner felt it not, although it was grievous, as the spectators said." He told the magistrates, "you have struck me as with roses," and "I pray God it may not be laid to your charge." Two men came up after the brutal punishment was over, and shook hands with him, saying, "blessed be God." They were fined forty shillings, and imprisoned. Yet the Baptists continued to increase. Blow the fire, if you wish it to burn.

The town of Malden was fined for presuming to settle a minister without consulting the neighbouring churches, though there was no law to that effect. The General Court forbade the settlement of Michael Powell in the ministry, at the second church in Boston; he had been a tavern-keeper at Dedham, and though "gifted," was "unlearned." How humbly he submitted: "My humble request is, that you would not have such hard thoughts of me that I would consent to be ordained to office without your concurrence; nor that our poor church would attempt such a thing without your approbation." At his death, this "gifted" man left furniture to the value of fourteen pounds, and a library consisting of "three Bibles, a Concordance, with other books," valued at "two pounds."

In Massachusetts, men not members of the church were compelled to support the clergyman, and through her influence Plymouth, always before her sister in liberality, passed a law to the same effect. However, Williams, in his settlement at New Providence, could rejoice that we have not "been consumed with the over-zealous fire of the so-called godly ministers." Saltonstall writes to the New-Englanders: "First, you compel such to come into your assemblies as you know will not join you in your worship, and, when they show their dislike thereof, or witness against it, then you stir up your magistrates to punish them for such, as you conceive, their public affronts." Cotton and Wilson replied, "Better be hypocrites than profane persons," "we fled from men's inventions," and only compelled others to attend to "God's institutions,"—that is, to all the abominations of the Puritan creed and ritual.

"We content ourselves with unity in the foundation of religion and church order."

Never was the violent attempt to secure "unity in the foundation of religion" less successful. New-England was a perfect hotbed of heresy. "How is it," writes Sir Harry Vane, in 1653, "that there are such divisions among you, —such headiness, tumults, disorder, injustice? Are there no wise men among you,—no public self-denying spirits?"

A law was passed prohibiting the erection of a meeting-house without the consent of the freemen of the town,—who were all theocratically orthodox,—and the county court, or the consent of the General Court. It would be "setting up an altar against the Lord's altar." Quakers were banished or hanged. But all this was ineffectual in making men think alike. Baptists, Quakers, Antinomians, Ranters of all sorts there were, excited no doubt by the laws against freedom. The "hateful Episcopalians" at length got a church established, in 1686; the theocracy dwindled.

It is instructive to see the Puritans in New-England and the Jesuits in Canada, at the same time, contending to establish a theocracy, both for the same purpose, each by the same means,—the suppression of individual freedom in religion.

"Presbytery does but translate
The Papacy to a free state,"

said Butler, and with not a little truth. The laws of Massachusetts, which continued in force till the Revolution, provided that a "Popish priest," coming here, should be accounted "an incendiary, and disturber of the public peace and safety." He was to suffer perpetual imprisonment, and death, if he attempted to escape. But spite of the law against "Popish priests," the worst part of Papacy came here,—the spirit of intolerance and persecution.

Along with this intolerance of the churches, the old elements of feudal aristocracy were brought to America, and continued to live for awhile in the new soil. A distinction was carefully kept up between "gentlemen" and those of an inferior condition. Only the "gentlemen" were allowed the title "Mr;" their number was not very large. The rest rejoiced in the appellative "Goodman." In 1639, some "persons of quality" wished to come to New-England, and it was proposed to establish "a standing council for life;" in the Commonwealth there were to be two classes of men, namely, "hereditary gentlemen," to sit as a permanent senate, and a body of "freeholders," who were to send deputies to constitute a lower house. The magistrates and elders favoured the scheme, finding it conformable to the "light of nature and Scripture." The "great Cotton," an able man, with the soul of a priest, liked the scheme well; democracy was "not a fit government either for church or state;" monarchy and aristocracy "are approved and directed in Scripture," "but only as a theocracy is set up in both." "If the people are governors," says he, "who shall be governed?" Indignant Mr Savage, commenting on this measure, says, "the ministers were perpetually meddling with the regimen of the Commonwealth; and we have frequent occasion to regret that their references to the theocracy of Israel were received as authority rather than illustration." But how could it be otherwise, with such a theology? Calvinism naturally leads to an aristocracy on earth, as well as in heaven. The world—this and the next—is for the elect, and who shall lay anything to their charge? However, the people put an end to all talk about "hereditary gentlemen," who disappear from the history of New-England for ever. Had this ungodly proposition become a law, the state of things would have been a little different to-day! For a long time the law, however, recognized a distinction between the gentleman and the simple man. "No man," says a law of 1641, "shall be beaten above forty stripes; nor shall any true gentleman, or any man equal to a gentleman, be punished with whipping, unless his crime be very shameful and his career of life vicious and profligate." But in 1703, Paul Dudley thought Massachusetts a very poor place for "gentlemen;" meaning, says Mr Hildreth, "those who wish to grow rich on the labour of others." For some time there was no trial by jury in Connecticut; "no warrant was found for it in the Word of God." We find the democratic element active in New-England at the very beginning, continually increasing in strength. At first, it is more powerful in Plymouth than in Massachusetts. For eighteen years all the laws of Plymouth were made in a general assembly of all the people. The governor was only president of a council of assistants. The church had no pastor for eight years; Brewster, the ruling elder, and such members as had the "gift of prophecy," exhorted the congregations. On Sunday afternoons there was a free meeting; a question was started, and all spoke that saw fit. But gradually the theocratic spirit of Massachusetts invaded the sister colony. Still church membership was not required as a condition of citizenship. In 1631, the freemen in Massachusetts began to be jealous of the theocratic oligarchy which ruled the colony, and claimed the right of annually electing new assistants. The constitution of towns was democratic from the beginning, and has been changed but little since. The towns were then, as now, little republics, managing their own affairs, voting money, levying taxes, and choosing "selectmen," a town clerk, treasurer, and constable. The town system is an original New-England institution, and has proved of great value in the acquisition of political liberty. The freedom of the town helped overcome the tyranny of the church.

At first, the magistrates levied the taxes for the whole colony; but, in 1632, the people of Watertown considered that it "was not safe to pay moneys after that sort, for fear of bringing themselves and their posterity into bondage." It was a wholesome and a timely fear. The freemen determined to choose their governor and deputy governor. In 1634, the first representative court assembled; there were three deputies from each of the eight towns or plantations. Soon they demanded fixed and definite laws. It seems quite remarkable, but it is true, that while money was not the chief basis of social respectability, Boston was far before the country in point of liberality. Now, the opposite is true. Providence Plantation led the way in the establishment of liberty; for, in 1647, the government was declared "democratical," freedom of faith and worship was assured to all, "the first formal and legal establishment of religious liberty ever promulgated," says Mr Hildreth. In 1652, in Yorkshire (in Maine), and in some other parts of New-England, church membership was not necessary to citizenship. Toleration began to be demanded for the Church of England, and as the Puritans had established a theocratic tyranny as bad as what they fled from, so the Episcopalians became an humble instrument in promoting religious freedom in America. In 1662, the king demanded the repeal of the law which limited citizenship to church members, substituting a proper qualification instead, and the admission of all persons of honest lives to baptism and the Lord's Supper. For some years there were three parties in New-England: the theocratic party, which continually diminished; the Episcopalians, Baptists, and Quakers, who demanded religious freedom; and the moderate men, who mediated between the two extremes. The "halfway covenant" was adopted in 1659; a few years later a Baptist church was formally organized in Boston, and though persecuted for a long time survives to this day. After the revocation of the charter, the theocratic party was weakened still further, and their domination at length came to an end.

"A new school of divines, known as Latitudinarians, sprung up among the Protestants towards the conclusion of the previous century, had essayed the delicate task of reconciling reason with revelation. They not only rejected the authority of tradition, so highly extolled and implicitly relied upon by the Catholics and the English High Churchmen; they scouted, also, that special interior persuasion which the Puritans, after the early Reformers, had denominated faith, but which to these reasoning divines seemed no better than enthusiasm. They preferred to rest the truth of Christianity on the testimony of prophecy and miracles, of which they undertook to establish the reality by the application to the Bible history of the ordinary rules of evidence; by which same rules they undertook to establish, also, the authenticity and inspiration of the Bible itself."—Vol. II. pp. 249—250.

"They presently pushed the principle of the halfway covenant so far as to grant to all persons not immoral in their lives admission to the Lord's Supper; indeed, all the privileges of full church membership. Much to the mortification of the Mathers, who wrote and protested against this doctrine, the college at Cambridge presently passed under the control of the new party—a change not without important results on the intellectual history of New-England."—*Ib.* p. 250.

"In the century since its settlement, New-England had undergone a great change. The austere manners of the Puritan fathers were still, indeed, preserved; their language was repeated; their observances were kept up; their institutions were revered; forms and habits remained—but the spirit was gone. The more ordinary objects of human desire and pursuit, the universal passion for wealth, political squabbles with the royal governors, land speculations, paper money jobs, and projects of territorial and personal aggrandizement, had superseded those metaphysical disputes, that spiritual vision, and that absorbing passion for a pure theocratic commonwealth which had carried the fathers into the wilderness. Even Cotton Mather, such was the progress of opinion, boasted of the harmony in which various religious sects lived together in Boston, and spoke of religious persecution as an obsolete blunder.''—Vol. II. p. 306.

"Education and habit, especially in what relates to outward forms, are not easily overcome. Episcopacy made but slow progress in New-England. A greater change, however, was silently going on; among the more intelligent and thoughtful, both of laymen and ministers, Latitudinarianism continued to spread. Some approached even towards Socinianism, carefully concealing, however, from themselves their advance to that abyss. The seeds of schism were broadly sown; but extreme caution and moderation on the side of the Latitudinarians long prevented any open rupture. They rather insinuated than avowed their opinions. Afraid of a controversy, in which they were conscious that popular prejudice would be all against them, unsettled many of them in their own minds, and not daring to probe matters to the bottom, they patiently waited the further effects of that progressive change by which they themselves had been borne along. To gloss over their heresies, they called themselves Arminians; they even took the name of moderate Calvinists. Like all doubters, they lacked the zeal and energy of faith. Like all dissemblers, they were timid and hesitating. Conservatives as well as Latitudinarians, they wished, above all things, to enjoy their salaries and clerical dignities in comfort and in peace. Free comparatively in their studies, they were very cautious in their pulpits how they shocked the fixed prejudices of a bigoted people whose bread they ate. It thus happened, that while the New-England theology, as held by the more intelligent, underwent decided changes, the old Puritan phraseology was still generally preserved, and the old Puritan doctrines, in consequence, still kept their hold, to a great extent, on the mass of the people. Yet remarkable local modifications of opinion were silently produced by individual ministers, the influence of the abler Latitudinarian divines being traceable to this day in the respective places of their settlement."

"As the exalted religious imagination of New-England subsided to the common level, as reason and the moral sense began to struggle against the overwhelming pressure of religious awe, a party inevitably appeared which sought by learned glosses to accommodate the hard text of the Scriptures and the hard doctrines of the popular creed to the altered state of the public mind."—*Ib.* pp. 309—311.

"The modern doctrines of religious freedom and free inquiry have constantly gained ground, throwing more and more into the shade that old idea, acted upon with special energy by the Puritan colonists of New-England—deep traces of which are also to be found in every North American code—the theocratic idea of a Christian commonwealth, in which every other interest must be made subservient to unity of faith and worship."—Vol. II. p. 391.

At length, Unitarianism and Universalism came, after the Revolution, to bring things to their present condition. As Mr Hildreth says, of times soon after that, even "in New-England the old leaven of Latitudinarianism was still deeply at work among the learned, while, among the less educated classes, the new doctrine of Universalism began to spread."

Along with this bigotry of the Puritans, there was a hardy vigour, a capacity for doing and enduring, a manly reliance on God and their own arm, one acknowledged, the other not confessed, which are worthy of admiration.

The treatment of the natives has been remarkable. We have before spoken of the national exclusiveness of the Anglo-Saxon race;* it was never made more apparent than by the Puritans in New-England. It is difficult even for one of their descendants, at the present time, to understand the feeling of our fathers respecting the Indians. Dr Joseph Mede was a learned and enlightened man, but in 1634 he wrote to his friend, Dr Twisse, as follows:

"I think that the Devil, being impatient of the sound of the Gospel and Cross of Christ in every part of this old world, so that he could in no place be quiet for it, and foreseeing that he was like at length to lose all here, bethought himself to provide him of a seed over which he might reign securely; and in a place, *ubi nec Pelopidarum facta neque nomen audiret.*

"That accordingly he drew a Colony out of some of those barbarous Nations dwelling upon the Northern Ocean (whither the sound of Christ had not yet come), and promising them by some Oracle to shew them a Countrey far better than their own (which he might soon do), pleasant, large, where never man yet inhabited, he conducted them over those desart Lands and Islands (which are many in that sea) by the way of the North into America; which none would ever have gone, had they not first been assured there was a passage that way into a more desirable Countrey. Namely, as when the world apostatized from the Worship of the true God, God called Abram out of Chaldee into the Land of Canaan, of him to raise him a Seed to preserve a light unto his Name: So the Devil, when he saw the world

* See p. 121, *supra.*

apostatizing from him, laid the foundations of a new Kingdom, by deducting this Colony from the North into America, where since they have increased into an innumerable multitude. And where did the Devil ever reign more absolutely and without controll, since mankind fell first under his clutches? And here it is to be noted, that the story of the Mexican Kingdom (which was not founded above 400 years before ours came thither) relates out of their own memorials and traditions that they came to that place from the North; whence their God Vitzliliputzli led them, going in an Ark before them: and after divers years travel and many stations (like enough after some generations) they came to the place which the Sign he had given them at their first setting forth pointed out, where they were to finish their travels, build themselves a City, and their God a Temple; which is the place where Mexico was built. Now if the Devil were God's ape in this; why might he not be so likewise in bringing the first Colony of men into that world out of ours? namely, by Oracle, as God did Abraham out of Chaldee, whereto I before resembled it.

"But see the hand of Divine Providence. When the off-spring of these Runnagates from the sound of Christ's Gospel had now replenisht that other world, and began to flourish in those two Kingdoms of Peru and Mexico, Christ our Lord sends his Mastives the Spaniards to hunt them out and worry them: Which they did in so hideous a manner, as the like thereunto scarce ever was done since the Sons of Noah came out of the Ark. What an affront to the Devil was this, where he had thought to have reigned securely, and been forever concealed from the knowledge of the followers of Christ?

"Yet the Devil perhaps is less grieved for the loss of his servants by the destroying of them, than he would be to lose them by the saving of them; by which latter way I doubt the Spaniards have despoiled him but of a few. What then if Christ our Lord will give him his second affront with better Christians, which may be more grievous to him than the former? And if Christ shall set him up a light in this manner to dazle and torment the Devil at his own home, I will hope they shall not so far degenerate (not all of them) as to come in that Army of Gog and Magog against the Kingdom of Christ, but be translated thither before the Devil be loosed, if not presently after his tying up. And whence should those Nations get notice of the glorious happiness of our world, if not by some Christians that had lived among them?"—*The Works of the Pious & Profoundly-Learned* JOSEPH MEDE, B.D., *sometime Fellow of Christ's College in Cambridge*, &c., &c. London: 1677. pp. 800—801.

At Plymouth, the Indians were treated with more justice than it is usual for the civilized to show to barbarians. In 1633, legal provision was made in Massachusetts for such red men as should become civilized; but, with Anglo-

Saxon exclusiveness, they were to be formed into townships by themselves. Major Gibbons, at a later date, was admonished "of the distance which is to be observed betwixt Christians and barbarians as well in war as in other negotiations." It was with difficulty that Eliot obtained liberty to organize a church at Natick. Yet the threat was made by the praying Indians to the Wampanoags that, unless they accepted the gospel, Massachusetts "would destroy them by war." A sharp distinction was always made between converted Indians and other Christians; they were treated, in every respect, as an inferior race; restricted to villages of their own, and cut off by opinion, as well as law, from intermarriage and intercourse with the whites. No one was allowed to sell them horses or boats. It was proposed to exterminate them, as being of the "cursed seed of Ham." Thus causes were put in action which at length have brought the Indians to their present condition in Massachusetts.

At an early date, many of them were reduced to slavery, some in New-England; others were sent off as slaves to the West Indies, eight score at one time, though regular prisoners of war. There were Old Testament examples for this, and even worse treatment. Roger Williams once received "a boy" as his share of the plunder obtained at an Indian defeat. In 1712, Massachusetts forbade the further importation of Indian slaves; not from any moral scruples, but on account of "divers conspiracies, outrages, barbarities, murders, burglaries, thefts, and other notorious crimes and enormities, perpetrated and committed by Indians; being of a surly and revengeful spirit, rude and insolent in their behaviour, and very ungovernable." There seems to have been no moral objection to slavery in the great and general court at that time.

Outrageous cruelties were often practised on the Indians. It was once proposed by the commissioners for the colonies, that, in case of war, "mastiff dogs might be of good use." But we think the proposition was not carried out till nearly two hundred years later, then in a different latitude, to the amazement of the civilized world. Even the men of Plymouth loved bloody spectacles at the cost of the Indians. In 1622, Wituwamat's head was carried thither and set up on a pole, as a warning. It was in vain that pious Mr

Robinson wished they had converted some before they killed any. An order was once given to Endicott to put to death all the Indian men on Block Island, and make slaves of the women and children. He could not kill the men, so he stove their canoes, burnt their wigwams, and destroyed their standing corn. While the Rev. Mr Stone was once praying "for one pledge of love," to confirm the fidelity of the Indian allies, they came in with five such pledges, namely, five Pequod scalps. No doubt, he thought his prayer was "answered." In the war with the Pequods, in 1637, under Mason and Underhill, the colonists "bereaved of pity and without compassion," gave no quarter, and showed no mercy; not even to old men, women, and children. In the capture of an Indian fort they took only seven prisoners, seven more escaped, but hundreds were slain. Says Underhill, "Great and doleful was the sight, to the view of young soldiers, to see so many souls lie gasping on the ground, so thick that you could hardly pass along." But then "'twas a famous victory." On another occasion, in the same war, twenty-two Indian prisoners of war were put to death after they had surrendered; about fifty were distributed as slaves, not "to *every* man a damsel or two," but among the principal colonists. The scalp of Sassacus was sent to Boston. Heads and hands of Pequod warriors were brought in by other Indians! Even the savages thought the "war too furious, and to slay too many." But what can satisfy bigotry in the name of the Lord? Underhill refers to "the wars of David" for his precedent; and, for authority, says "we had sufficient light from the Word of God for our proceedings." Mason adds "that the Lord was pleased to smite our enemies in the hinder parts, and to give us their land for an inheritance." The New-Englanders commanded him to kill Miantonimoh, their captive and former friend; he did so, and ate a portion of the body, for which there was no scriptural warrant. If an Indian injured a white man, and the tribe did not give satisfaction, the offender might be seized and delivered to the injured party, "either to serve or to be shipped off and exchanged for negroes." The women of Marblehead once murdered two Indian prisoners; it was Sunday, and the murderers had just come out of church.

The most wholesale destructions of the Indians took place

during King Philip's war. More than two thousand were killed or taken in a single year. Witamo, the squaw-sachem of Pocasset, and friend of Philip, was drowned, but her body was saved, the head cut off and stuck upon a pole at Taunton, amid the jeers and scoffs of the colonists. Philip's dead body was beheaded and quartered; one of his hands was given to the Indian who shot him, and his head was carried in triumph to Plymouth, on a public day of thanksgiving (August 17, 1676). "Oh that men would praise the Lord," says Secretary Morton, "for his goodness and wonderful works unto them!" His wife and son were taken prisoners. What should be done with the lad, a boy nine years old? The opinion of the clergy was asked. Cotton of Plymouth, and Arnold of Marshfield, thought in general "that rule (Deuteronomy xxiv. 16) to be moral and therefore perpetually binding," and the crime of the parent did not attaint the son. Yet they say:

> "Yet, upon serious consideration, we humbly conceive that the children of notorious traitors, rebells, and murtherers, especially of such as have bin principal leaders and actors in such horrid villainies, and that against a whole nation, yea, the whole Israel of God, may be involved in the guilt of their parents, and may, *salva republica*, be adjudged to death, as to us seems evident by the Scripture instances of *Saul*, *Achan*, *Haman*, the children of whom were cut off, by the sword of Justice, for the transgressions of their parents, although, concerning some of those children, it be manifest, that they were not capable of being co-acters therein."—*Morton's Memorial, Davis' Edition*, p. 454, No. 1.

Increase Mather says:—

> "I should have said something about Philip's son. It is necessary that some effectual course should be taken about him. He makes me think of Hadad, who was a little child when his father (the chief sachem of the Edomites) was killed by Joab; and, had not others fled away with him, I am apt to think that David would have taken a course that Hadad should never have proved a scourge to the next generation."—*Ib.*, No. 2.

Keith, of Bridgewater, gave a milder counsel, which was followed. The boy was sold into slavery, and the money deposited in the treasury of the colony. Philip's wife also shared the same fate. The State of Massachusetts is so much richer at this day. We wonder the money arising from the sale, this price of blood, was not given to "The Society for propagating the Gospel among the Indians." In 1725, a premium of one hundred pounds was offered for each Indian scalp. It was estimated that each scalp, in the war of 1704, had cost one thousand pounds. The treatment the Indians receive at the hands of Massachusetts, at this day, is a terrible reproach to us.

There is another matter of a good deal of importance we wish to refer to, namely, the indented servants brought to New-England. Governor Bradford, in one of his poetical inspirations, thus alludes to them:—

> "Another cause of our declining here
> Is a *mixed multitude*, as doth appear.
> Many for *servants* hitherto were brought,
> Others came for gain, or new ends they sought;
> And of those, many grew loose and profane,
> Though some were brought to know God and his name."

"These servants," says Mr Hildreth, "seem in general to have had little sympathy with the austere manners and opinions of their masters, and their frequent transgressions of Puritan decorum gave its magistrates no little trouble." In 1622, Weston sent out nearly sixty of them; Gorges brought many the next year; Sir William Brewster sent several more in 1628; nearly two hundred came in 1629; Richard Saltonstall sent twenty in 1635. It was one of the offences of Morton, that his "merry mount" was a refuge for "runaway servants." At one time, a master received a grant of fifty acres of land for each servant he brought over. About two hundred servants were once set free on their arrival in New-England, in consequence of the scarcity of provisions in the colony!

In 1641, the law allowed any man to harbour servants flying from the tyranny of their masters, until the master could be judicially examined; notice must be given to the master and the nearest constable. A faithful and diligent service, for seven years, entitled the servant to a dismissal. He must not be sent off "empty-handed," says the humane statute, following the Mosaic code in this particular. If a master maimed or disfigured his servant, he was entitled to liberty and to damages also. Still, the law was not very precise in regard to the treatment of this anomalous class of persons.

In 1643, "the united colonies of New-England," forgetting the Old Testament when property was at stake, agreed to surrender runaway servants. In 1650, the law pursued such servants and arrested them at the public expense; they were required to make up, threefold, the time of their absence.

In 1665, the condition of servants in New York is remarkable.

"Under a provision borrowed from the Connecticut code, fugitive servants might be pursued by hue and cry at the public charge; but this was presently found too expensive, and the cost was imposed on the parties concerned. Runaway servants were to forfeit double the time of their absence, and the cost of their recapture. All who aided in concealing them were liable to a fine. Tyrannical masters and mistresses might be complained of to the overseers, and proceeded against at the sessions; and servants maimed by their masters were entitled to freedom and damages. During servitude, they were forbidden to sell or buy. Any master of a vessel carrying any person out of the colony without a pass was liable for his debts; and by a subsequent provision, *any unknown person travelling through any town without a pass was liable to be arrested as a runaway, and detained till he proved his freedom, and paid, by work and labour, if not otherwise able, the cost of his arrest.*"—Vol. II. p. 48.

The importation of this class of persons continued till after the middle of the eighteenth century.

"The colonial enactments for keeping these servants in order, and especially for preventing them from running away, were often very harsh and very severe. They were put, for the most part, in these statutes, on the same level with the slaves, but their case in other respects was very different. In all the colonies, the term of indented service, even where no express contract had been entered into, was strictly limited by law, and, except in the case of very young persons, it seldom or never exceeded seven years. On the expiration of that term, these freed servants were absorbed into the mass of white inhabitants, and the way lay open before them and their children to wealth and social distinction. One of the future signers of the Declaration of Independence was brought to Pennsylvania as a redemptioner. In Virginia, at the expiration of his term of service, every redemptioner, in common with other immigrants to the colony, was entitled to a free grant of fifty acres of land, and in all the colonies certain allowances of clothing were required to be made by the late masters."—Vol. II. p. 428.

The subject demands a distinct and entire treatise, for which we have no space at present; but the following document, copied for us by a friend, from the Court-records at Salem, throw some light on the age of which we have been speaking:—

"10 May 1654 Be it known unto all men by these presents that I George Dill, master of the ship Goodfellow; have sould unto Mr Samuel Symonds two of the Irish youthes I brought over by order of the State of England, the name of one of them is William Dalton, the other Edward Welch, to serve him, his heirs, executors or assignes for the space of 9 years, And the said Samuel in consideration hereof doth promise & engage to be paid unto the said master the sum of £26 in corn merchantable or live cattle at or before the end of October next, provided he give good assurance for the enjoying of them."

At the end of seven years the "two Irish youthes" ran away, or refused to work any longer. It was to recover the two years' service, or their value, that the action was brought in 1661. The following is their reply, or defence. It will be seen that their names do not agree with the names mentioned by the Captain.

"1661 To the Honoured Court & Jury now assembled the humble defence of Wm Downeing & Philip Welch in the action between them & their Master Wm Symonds; That which we say in defence of ourselves is that we were brought out of our own country, contrary to our own will & minds, & sold here to Mr Symonds, by ye Master of the ship, Mr Dill, but what agreement was made between Mr Symonds & ye said Master, was never acted by our consent or knowledge, yet notwithstanding we have endeavoured to serve him the best service we could these 7 compleat yeares, which is 3 yeares more than the Spirits * used to sell them for at Barbadoes, when they are stolen in England, And for our service we have noe calling or wages but meate & cloathes. Now 7 yeares' service being so much as is the

* "At the Court held in Whitehall, December 13th, 1682.

"Whereas it has been Represented to His Majesty that by reason of the frequent Abuses of a lewd sort of people called *Spirits* in Seducing many of His Majesty's Subjects to go on Shipboard, where they have been Seized & Carried by Force to His Majesty's Plantations in America, & that many idle persons, who have Listed themselves voluntarily to be Transported thither & have received money upon their entering into Service for that purpose have afterwards pretended they were Betrayed & Carried away against their wills & procured their friends to prosecute the Merchants who brought them," &c. &c.

practice of old England, & thought meet in this place, & we being 21 yeares of age we hope the Honored Court & Jury will seriously consider our conditions."

"The Testimony of John Ring.

"This deponent saith that he with divers others were stolen in Ireland by some of y[e] English soldiers in y[e] night out of their beds and brought to Mr Dill's ship, where the boate lay ready to receive them and in the way as they went some others they tooke with them against their consents & brought them aboard the said ship, where there were divers others of their countrymen, weeping & crying because they were stolen from their friends, they all declaring the same & amongst the rest were these two men, W[m] Downing & Philip Welch, & there they were kept until upon a Lord's day in the morning y[e] master set saile & left some of his vessels behind for haste as I understood.

"Sworne in Court 26 June 1661."

There were similiar servants in the other colonies. Of the hundred and five persons who settled in Virginia in 1606, forty-eight were "gentlemen," "brought up to esteem manual labour degrading. There were but twelve labourers, four carpenters, and four other mechanics, the rest were soldiers and servants." In 1608, one hundred and twenty men of the same sort arrived in Virginia; "vagabond gentlemen, unaccustomed to labour, and disdainful of it, with three or four bankrupt London jewellers, goldsmiths, and refiners, sent out to seek for mines." Governor Smith said of them, that it was better to send out thirty mechanics than a thousand such men! Servants were indispensable in such a community. In 1613, the Governor of Virginia had for his support a plantation cultivated by one hundred servants. In 1619, ninety young women, "pure and uncorrupt," were sent out to be disposed of as wives for the planters. The price was a hundred pounds of tobacco, about seventy-five dollars. A similar cargo, the next year, however, brought only about half that price. We think that was the last adventure of the sort sent to Virginia,—a woman for fifty pounds of tobacco was certainly too cheap.

About the same time, by the order of the king, a hundred dissolute vagabonds were taken from the jails and sent to Virginia, to be disposed of as servants. They were known by the name of "jail-birds." In 1643, the law forbade dealing with any servants without consent of their masters, and punished such as married without the master's consent. They once planned an insurrection in Virginia, which was detected beforehand; and the 13th of September, "the day the villanous plot should have been put in execution," was declared a perpetual holiday.

"Servants 'sold for the custom,' that is, having no indentures, if over nineteen years of age, are to serve five years; if under nineteen, till twenty-four—their ages to be adjudged by the county court. Masters are to provide 'wholesome and competent diet, clothing, and lodging, by the discretion of the county court;' nor shall they at any time give immoderate correction, nor 'whip a Christian white servant naked,' without an order from a justice of the peace, under penalty of forty shillings to the servant, to be recovered with costs, on complaint to a justice of the peace, 'without the formal process of an action.' Justices are bound to receive and investigate the complaints of all servants 'not being slaves.' Any resistance or offer of violence on the part of a servant is punishable by an additional year's servitude. Servants are guaranteed the possession of such property as may lawfully come to them by gift or otherwise, but no person may deal with them except by permission of their masters. In case of fines inflicted by penal laws, unless some one would pay the fines for them, servants are to be punished by whipping, at the rate of twenty lashes for every five hundred pounds of tobacco, or fifty shillings sterling—each stroke being thus estimated at about sixty cents. Women servants having bastards are to forfeit to their masters an additional year's service, unless the master were the father, in which case the forfeiture accrues to the churchwardens. In case the father were a negro or mulatto, other penalties are added, as by a law formerly mentioned. The provisions for the arrest of runaways, which are sufficiently stringent, apply equally to slaves and servants, except that outlying slaves might be killed, and irreclaimable runaways 'dismembered.'"—Vol. II. pp. 236—237.

Governor Thomas, of Pennsylvania, enlisted the servants, in 1740, into the army, and many of them never returned to their masters, whom the State indemnified for their loss. In 1756, the colonists were much offended because the English government authorized the enlisting of servants, though a compensation was given to their masters. In the revolutionary war, many of the soldiers, enlisted in the middle and southern States, were "redemptioners," or servants. It was proposed in Congress to direct a portion of their pay to compensate the masters for the loss of their services, but at the earnest request of Washington the plan was dropped, and the servants who enlisted were declared freemen. Since the Revolution, we think there have been no servants of this character.

Some curious anecdotes are preserved of the shifts resorted to by servants to escape from their condition. A citizen from Ireland was once "sold to pay his passage" to America, and bought by a farmer in New-England, as a servant. The farmer set him to read the Bible one Sunday. He held the book bottom upwards, and could not read. One day he was sent by his master into the woods to chop wood; at night, when he came home, he was asked how much he had cut; he said, "about a bushel." On looking, it appears he cut it up into slivers. When bade to replenish the fire, he did it with water. He was found of no value for any of the common work of the farm, and his master, who lived on the sea-shore, set him to tend the ducks and geese, to keep them from wandering or being destroyed, thinking it well, we suppose, to set a goose to watch a goose. At night, the servant came home with his charge, and complained that they must all of them be sick, for, he added, "they have not sucked their mothers once all day." His master considered him a fool, and finding him worthless, refused to keep him. The servant pretended that he was afraid somebody would kill him unless his master gave him a legal discharge, renouncing all claim upon him whatever. This was done; and within less than a week the foolish servant opened a school in the very town where he had been bought, and from the office of schoolmaster rose to high political stations in New-England, and founded a family still proud of his name.

We cannot pass over the matter of slavery, to which Mr Hildreth has directed much attention, and which is likely to be an interesting subject for some years to come. At the time of the settlement of America, the idea was beginning to prevail, that it was wrong to hold Christians in bondage, but this objection did not extend to heathens and infidels. It was prudently discovered that the negroes were the descendants of Ham, and the inheritors of the curse of the mythological Noah. Who so fit for bondmen as the negroes? It conduced to "godliness" to make them slaves, as well as to "great gain." The same year in which the Pilgrims came to Plymouth, twenty negroes were brought to Virginia as slaves for life, no doubt to the great comfort of the "gentlemen" there. It is not long before we find them in New-England; not long before Boston is concerned in the slave-trade, from which she is not yet become free; for while we are writing this paper, we learn that a ship from Boston, the "Lucy Anne," has lately been seized, loaded with five hundred and forty-seven slaves! Another vessel from the same port, the "Pilot," is also in British custody for the same offence. The actual seizure of five hundred and forty-seven slaves in Africa is by no means the most infamous part of the support which this city furnishes to slavery, only one of the obvious indications of a spirit well known to exist in Boston, and by no means confined to "illiterate and profane persons." The laws of Massachusetts, in 1641, justified enslaving "captives taken in just wars, and such strangers as willingly sell themselves or are sold unto us."

In 1662, Virginia revised the rule of the common law, and declared that children should follow the condition of their mother. All the Southern States have since adopted the same iniquitous provision. In 1663, Maryland made a law that the child of a free white woman shall follow the condition of the *father* if he be a slave: this was repealed a few years later; but a fine of ten thousand pounds of tobacco was imposed on the clergymen or the masters and mistresses who promoted or connived at the marriage of such persons.

In 1667, Virginia declared that Christianity was no bar to slavery—but the slave should not escape from bondage by communion and baptism; killing a slave was declared not felony. Indians "imported by shipping," and not Christians, might be slaves for life. In 1671, there were two thousand "black slaves" in Virginia, and six thousand "Christian servants;" of whom about fifteen hundred were imported yearly .In 1682, all negroes, mulattoes, or Indians, brought into the colony by sea or *land, Christians* or not, were declared slaves for life, unless they were of *Christian parentage or country*. In 1692, an "act for suppressing outlying slaves," declares that, if they resist, run away, or refuse to surrender, "they may be lawfully killed or destroyed with guns, or any other way whatever." The State was to indemnify the master for the loss, giving four thousand pounds of tobacco for a negro. A thousand pounds of tobacco were offered to any one who should kill a certain runaway—the "negro slave Billy." In 1705, laws were passed to prevent intermarriages between blacks and whites, and against emancipating slaves. Summary tribunals were established for the trial of slaves, "without the solemnity of a jury." They were to be kept in jail, "well laden with irons." Even in Pennsylvania, William Penn could not secure the right of equal marriage for slaves! As slaves increased—and about one thousand were annually imported into Virginia in 1720, and for some time after—the laws became more rigorous. It was made more difficult to set them free.

South Carolina has always been remarkable for the rigour of her slave laws. In 1670, the "fundamental and unalterable constitution" provided that every freeman "shall have absolute power and authority over his negro slaves." In 1704, we find one James Moore a "needy, forward, and ambitious man," kidnapping Indians to sell as slaves. Many others did the same in 1712, on a large scale, taking eight hundred at one time, and *re*-annexing Indian villages. A law was made the same year making it the duty of every person to arrest any slave found abroad without a pass, and give him "moderate chastisement." A slave guilty of petty larceny, for the first offence, was to be "publicly and severely whipped;" for the second, "one of his ears to be cut off," or "be branded on the forehead with a hot iron;" for the third, he was "to have his nose slit;" for the fourth, to "suffer death, or other punishment," at the discretion of the court. Any two justices of the peace, with three freeholders whom they might summon, formed a court for the trial of any slave, charged with any crime, from "chicken-stealing" to insurrection and murder; and was competent to sentence the accused to punishment, even if it were death, and have it executed forthwith, on their warrant alone! This mode of trial remains in force in South Carolina till this day. It was a capital crime for a slave to run out of the province, or for a white man to entice him to do so.

"Any slave running away for twenty days at once, for the first offence was to be 'severely and publicly whipped.' In case the master neglected to inflict this punishment, any justice might order it to be inflicted by the constable, at the master's expense. For the second offence, the runaway was to be branded with the letter R on the right cheek. If the master omitted it, he was to forfeit ten pounds, and any justice of the peace might order the branding done. For the third offence, the runaway, if absent thirty days, was to be whipped, and have one of his ears cut off; the master neglecting to do it to forfeit twenty pounds; any justice, on complaint, to order it done as before. For the fourth offence, the runaway, 'if a man, was to be gelt,' to be paid for by the province, if he died under the operation; if a woman, she was to be severely whipped, branded on the left cheek with the letter R, and her left ear cut off. Any master neglecting for twenty days to inflict these atrocious cruelties, was to forfeit his property in the slave to any informer who might complain of him within six months. Any captain or commander of a company, 'on notice of the haunt, residence, and hiding-place of any runaway slaves,' was 'to pursue, apprehend, and take them, either alive or dead,' being in either case entitled to a premium of from two to four pounds for each slave. All persons wounded or disabled on such expeditions were to be compensated by the public. If any slave under punishment 'shall suffer in life or member, which,' says the act, 'seldom happens, no person whatsoever shall be liable to any penalty therefor.' Any person killing a slave out of 'wantonness,' 'bloody-mindedness,' or 'cruel intention,' was to forfeit 'fifty pounds current money,' or if the slave belonged to another person, twenty-five pounds to the public, and the slave's value to the owner. No master was to allow his slaves to hire their own time, or, by a supplementary act, two years after, 'to plant for themselves any corn, pease, or rice, or to keep any stock of hogs, cattle, or horses.'"

"'Since charity and the Christian religion which we profess,' says the concluding section of this remarkable act, 'obliges us to wish well to the souls of men, and that religion may not be made a pretence to alter any man's property and right, and that no person may neglect to baptize their negroes or slaves for fear that thereby they should be manumitted and set free,' 'it shall be and is hereby declared lawful for any negro or Indian slave, or any other slave or slaves whatsoever, to receive and profess the Christian faith, and to be thereunto baptized; but notwithstanding such slave or slaves shall receive or profess the Christian religion, and be baptized, he or they shall not thereby be manumitted or set free."

"South Carolina, it thus appears, assumed at the beginning the same bad pre-eminence on the subject of slave legislation which she still maintains."—Vol. II. pp. 273—275.

At this day, no man in South Carolina can be elected as representative to the Assembly, unless legally seized and possessed of ten slaves in his own right.

At first, slavery was not permitted in Georgia; but many of the settlers of that province were taken from workhouses, from debtors' prisons, and even worse places; "selected from the most helpless, querulous, and grasping portion of the community," "broken traders and insolvent debtors;" men "found in the end as worthless as they were discontented and troublesome." "They were very importunate," says Mr Hildreth, "for permission to hold slaves, without whose labours they insisted lands in Georgia could not be cultivated."

"'Most of the early settlers were altogether unworthy of the assistance they received,' so says Stevens, a recent and judicious native historian of the colony, who has written from very full materials. 'They were disappointed in the quality and fertility of their lands; were unwilling to labour; hung for support upon the trustees' store; were clamorous for privileges to which they had no right; and fomented discontent and faction where it was hoped they would live together in brotherly peace and charity.' What wonder that men so idle, thriftless, and ungrateful, called loudly for slaves, whose unpaid labours might support them for life?"—Vol. II. p. 371.

So they had their slavery, and thereby Georgia attained her present condition and—prospects!

The gradual progress of liberty is remarkable in New-England. Hubbard, with the spirit of a priest, complains of the "inordinate love of liberty or fear of restraint, especially in matters of religion," which prevailed in 1647, and speaks of "all that rabble of men that went under the name of Independents—whether Anabaptists, Antinomians, Familists, or Seekers," with the same theocratic contempt now exhibited by sectarian bigotry and personal malice, which has not the power to bite, and only barks at the freemen of God, who go on their way rejoicing. There are in New-England two visible bulwarks of liberty—the free school and the free printing press. In 1639, the first printing press in America was set up at Cambridge. However it was kept under a strict censorship, and no other was for a long time allowed to be set up. The first three things printed are symbolical of New-England: the

"Freeman's Oath" was the proof-shot of the press, then came an "Almanac made for New-England," then the "Psalms turned into Metre," also "made for New-England," by men who knew how to

> "Crack the ear of melody,
> And break the legs of time."

The freedom of the press was not allowed, however, for a long time. Andros was to allow no printing in 1686; King William also forbade it in 1688. In 1719, Governor Shute objected to the printing of an obnoxious paper by the order of the General Court, declaring that he had power over the press, and would prevent it. The paper was printed; the Governor wished to prosecute the printer, but the Attorney-General could find no law on which to frame an indictment. This was by no means the last instance of an attempt by men "clothed with a little brief authority," to shackle the freedom of the press. The attempt has been repeated in Massachusetts in our own day, but what was once dangerous is now simply laughable. A donkey bracing himself against a locomotive is not a very formidable antagonist, yet he might have overturned the "Ark of Jehovah" when drawn by "two heifers" with no one to guide them.

In 1682, a printing press was established in Virginia, and the laws of that year were printed. But the governor, Culpepper, put the printer under bonds to print nothing till His Majesty's pleasure should be known. The next year, King James the Second forbade any printing press in the colony, and Virginia had none till 1729.

In 1687, the third printing press was set up at Philadelphia. The fourth was at New York, in 1692.

The first newspaper in America was established at Boston, in 1704, only containing advertisements and items of news; a regular newspaper, discussing public affairs, was begun here in 1722, conducted by James Franklin; but it perished for want of support," says Mr Hildreth, "ominous fate of the first free press in America!"

The records of Boston contain this entry, under date of April 13, 1635: "It was then generally agreed upon, that our brother Philemon Purmont shall be instructed to become schoolmaster for the teaching and nurturing of children with us." It does not appear that he kept a free school. In 1638, Harvard College was established. Private benefactors and public gifts helped endow this first collegiate institution in America. In 1642, the General Court passed a law making it the duty of the selectmen to see that every child was taught "perfectly to read the English tongue;" a fine of twenty shillings for each neglect was imposed. Thus was an attempt made to render education universal, and, in 1647, a law was passed making it also free; every town of fifty families was to have a teacher to instruct all the children in common branches, and each town of a hundred families was commanded to "set up a grammar school," where lads might be "fitted for the University." At that time, Massachusetts contained about twenty thousand inhabitants, and the entire property of the whole people, the valuation of the colony, could hardly amount to more than two or three millions of dollars. This is the first attempt in the world to provide by law for the public education of the people on such a scale. The Massachusetts system was soon adopted at Plymouth and New Haven. In this law, we find an explanation of much of the prosperity of New-England, and the influence she has exerted on America and the world.

Another important thing in our history is the trade of the country. New-England early manifested the Yankee fondness for trade and manufactures. In 1634, there were watermills at Roxbury and Dorchester, windmills in other places. Vessels were built, the "Blessing of the Bay," and the "Rebecca," and a trade began with New York, with Virginia, and the West Indies. In 1675, the little ships of New-England stole along the coasts of America, trafficking with Maryland, Virginia, Carolina, Antigua, and Barbadoes, or boldly stemmed the Atlantic wave, sailing to England, Holland, Spain, or Italy. The jealousy, the fear, and hate with which New-England enterprise, on land or sea, was met in Old England, by the merchants and the government of Britain, would be astonishing at this day, if we did not see the same bigotry and toryism reproduced in New-England itself at the present time. But we have not space to dwell on this theme.

It is curious to see how early the habit of self-reliance got established in New-England. Every man was a soldier, every church member a citizen in full. Soon, all men were able to read and write. Necessity at first forced them to rely on "God, and their own right arm." By and by, when the mother country interfered, she found a child not accustomed to submission.

But we must pass away from this theme, and pass over many other matters of interest touched upon by Mr Hildreth in this work, and speak of his book in general, and in special. It strikes us that, on the whole, the history of the colonial and provincial period is better and more happily treated than that of the Revolution. Everywhere we see marks of the same intellectual vigour which distinguishes the former writings of Mr Hildreth. There is a strength and freshness in his style. He writes in the interest of mankind, and not for any portion thereof. He allows no local attachment, or reverence for men or classes of men, to keep him from telling the truth as he finds it. He exhibits the good and evil qualities of the settlers of the United States, with the same coolness and impartiality. His work is almost wholly objective,—giving the facts, not his opinions about the facts. He shows two things as they have not been exposed before,—the bigoted character of the settlers of New-England, and the early history and gradual development of slavery in the South. His book is written in the spirit of democracy, which continually appears in spite of the author.

We must say something of its faults of matter and of form. The division into chapters, it seems to us, is not uniformly well made; sometimes this division disturbs the unity of the subject. He gives us too little of the philosophical part of history; too little, perhaps, of the ornamental. He lacks the picturesqueness of style which makes history so attractive in some authors. He does not give the student his authorities in the margin, as it seems to us he ought to do. His dates are not always to be relied upon. We notice some errors, the results of haste, which we trust he will correct in a second edition. Thus, in Volume I. p. 257, he says that Locke maintained that men's souls, "mortal by generation, are made immortal by Christ's purchase." It is well known that this was the opinion of Dodwell, who makes baptism a condition *sine quâ non* of immortality, but we have never found the doctrine in Locke;

In Volume II. page 397, *et seq.*, he omits some important particulars. The provincial troops, who comprised the entire land forces, were deprived of all share of the prize money, which amounted to one million pounds. The land forces were entitled to the greater part of it, but got none; the expense of these forces remained a long time a heavy burden on the colonies, and especially on Massachusetts. Commodore Warren, and the naval forces, kept the whole of the prize money, which was contrary to all law, usage, and equity.

On page 518, he calls Lord Grenville "Bute's chancellor of the exchequer." George Grenville was chancellor of the exchequer, but was never a lord. Bute was never in the ministry. George Grenville was not of the party called "king's friends," as Mr Hildreth intimates on page 533.

Volume III. page 58, Dean Tucker is called "author of the Light of Nature," which was written by a country gentleman rejoicing in the name of Abraham Tucker, with a literary *alias* Edward Search.

Page 62: "The private sentiments of Lord North were not materially different from those of Chatham." They differed in almost every material point,—as to the right of taxation, and the expediency of asserting it by force.

Page 66, the bridge spoken of was in Salem, not between Salem and Danvers; it was not a company of militia under Colonel Pickering, but a party of citizens.

Page 319, the praise of Arnold appears excessive. He was hardly "one of the most honoured [officers] in the American army." He was distinguished for courage more than conduct, and not at all for integrity.

Page 418, he speaks of an intercepted letter, which "seemed to imply a settled policy, on the part of France, to exclude the Americans from the fisheries and the Western lands." Mr Sparks, in his Life of Franklin, has successfully vindicated the French court from the charge of ill faith in these negotiations.

Page 419, he relies on John Adams' letter to Cushing, as authority for an odious sentiment ascribed to Mr Adams. This letter was a forgery, and was so pronounced by Mr Adams himself, in a letter written at the close of his administration, dated the 4th of March, 1801, and published extensively in the newspapers of that period. It is in the *Columbian Centinel.*

These are slight blemishes, which may easily be corrected in a new edition.

On the whole, this history must be regarded as a work of much value and importance. It is written in the American spirit, in a style always brief but always clear, without a single idle word. We look with high expectations for the volume which will bring the history down to our own times.

SOME THOUGHTS ON THE DIFFERENT OPINIONS IN THE NEW TESTAMENT RELATIVE TO THE PERSONALITY OF JESUS.

I. Let us first ascertain the opinion prevalent in the lifetime of Jesus himself, as the basis of our inquiry. It appears from the New Testament that the contemporaries of Jesus regarded him as the son of Joseph and Mary (Matt. xiii. 55, Luke iv. 22, John vi. 42). His brothers and sisters also are mentioned (*οἱ ἀδελφοὶ αὐτοῦ*), and Jesus is called the first-born son of Mary (*τὸν πρωτότοκον*), in some manuscripts, and the common editions (Matt. i. 25). In the third Gospel the author calls Joseph and Mary his parents (*οἱ γονεῖς αὐτοῦ*), and Mary herself is represented as calling Joseph his father. In the fourth Gospel Philip speaks of Jesus as the son of Joseph of Nazareth (John i. 45).

The genealogies still preserved, in the first and third Gospel, in curious contradiction to his divine origin, proceed on the supposition that Jesus had two human parents,— a mortal father, as well as a mortal mother. So, on the side of his father, his descent is traced back to Abraham in the one author, and to Adam in the other.

The Ebionites, who were the primitive Christians, it seems always adhered to the opinion that Jesus was a man, born and begotten in the common way, selected and anointed, and so becoming the Christ, not by his birth, but his selection and inspiration. It seems highly probable that this was the opinion of the earliest church at Jerusalem.*

* See Justin Martyr, Dial. cum Tryphone, cap. 49 (Opp. ed. Otto, Tom. II. p. 156), and Eusebius, H. E. Lib. III. 27 (ed. Heinichen, Tom. I. p. 252).

It seems that the celebrated Gospel according to the Hebrews regarded Jesus as a man born after the common way, and made his divinity commence only with the baptism by John: for after the descent of the Holy Spirit it is stated, "There came a voice from heaven and said, 'Thou art my beloved Son, *this day have I begotten thee.*'" Justin found this passage in the Memoirs of the Apostles extant in his time, † and it is still preserved, with many other curious and instructive readings, in the celebrated Cambridge manuscript, the *Codex Bezæ* (Luke iii. 22).

These monuments very plainly refer us to a period when it may reasonably be supposed that the prevalent opinion among the followers of Jesus was, that he was a man born after the common way, of two human parents, and subsequently became the Christ, the Hebrew Messiah. This is the nature and this the office assigned him. Such is the basis on which successive deposits of speculation have been made and continue to be made. It is no part of our present concern to determine what the Christians at first thought of his history, of his miracles, and of his resurrection, for we limit our inquiry to the nature and office of Jesus.

II. In the first and third Gospels, as they now stand in manuscripts and editions, it is taught that Jesus was the son of Mary and a holy spirit (Matt. i. 18, and Luke i. 35, it is in both cases πνεῦμα ἅγιον, not τὸ πνεῦμα ἅγιον). He was miraculously born, with no human father. He is also the Christ, the Hebrew Messiah, predicted in the Old Testament. He is called the Son of God (ὁ υἱὸς τοῦ Θεοῦ). He is endowed with miraculous powers, is transfigured, returns to life after his crucifixion, and is to come back yet once more. Such is the highest office, and such is the highest nature assigned him in the first and third Gospel.

There is, however, one curious passage in Matt. xi. 27, and Luke x. 22, in which Jesus is represented as saying, "All things are delivered to me by my Father, and no one knows who is the Son, except the Father, and who is the Father, except the Son, and he to whom the Son is pleased to reveal him." This passage may possibly mean only that

See also Schwegler, Nachapostolische Zeitalter (Tubingen, 1846, 2 vols. 8vo), B. I. p. 90, *et seq.*

† Dial. cum Tryphone, cap. 88 (Tom. II. p. 308). See, too, Epiphanius Hæres. xxx. 13, and Schwegler, *l. c.* B. I. p. 197, *et seq.*

Jesus is the complete possessor of his Messianic powers, and he alone knows who is the Messiah, and alone understands the character of God. But to us it seems to have a different meaning, and to stand in plain contradiction to the general notion of Jesus entertained in these two Gospels. It will presently appear to what a different class of speculations this verse seems to belong.

The second Gospel calls Jesus a son of God, (*υἱὸς Θεοῦ*, not *ὁ υἱὸς*, except iii. 11, &c., where uninformed persons speak), but is not quite so definite in its statements as the two other Gospels already referred to; but it does not seem probable that the author designed to set forth a distinct theory of the nature and office of Christ peculiar to himself, only to avoid difficulties by silence. The omission of the miraculous birth of Jesus, however, is characteristic of the third Gospel, which often compromises and steers a middle course between the Hebrew and the Hellenistic Christians. This omission (as well as the neglect to mention the Galileans, with whom Jesus stands in such entirely opposite relations in the first and third Gospels) was probably a part of the author's plan.

Thus, then, we find that a miraculous birth, with only one human parent, is the deposit of the first and third Gospels, the addition they have made to the earlier Christology.

III. Let us next examine the Epistles attributed to Peter, James, and Jude, with the Apocalypse—books which indicate the tendency of the Jewish party among the Christians.

In the so-called Epistle of James, which is rich in dogmatic peculiarities, and a valuable monument in the history of the development of Christianity, there is no peculiar and characteristic Christology which requires mention here.

In the First Epistle of Peter, so called, it is said the spirit of Christ was in the prophets of the Old Testament, who foretold his sufferings and glory (*τὸ πνεῦμα Χριστοῦ*, 1 Peter i. 11); Christ was pre-appointed before the foundation of the world (*προεγνωσμένος*); with his precious blood the Christians are redeemed from their foolish course of life, inherited from their fathers (*ματαίας ἀναστροφῆς πατροπαραδότου*, i. 18, 19), that is, from the Jewish form of religion. He also bore the sins of Christians in his own body on the cross, and died, the just for the unjust, that he might conduct the Christians to God (ii. 24, and iii. 18).

After his death, he went to the departed spirits who had not believed in the time of Noah. He is now gone to heaven, and is on the right hand of God. Angels, and authorities, and powers are subject to him (iii. 22).

The Second Epistle attributed to Peter, and that to Jude, are without any peculiar Christological significance for the present purpose.

In the Apocalypse, Christ is the "first-born of the dead, and the ruler of the kings of the world" (i. 5); he is the "beginning of the creation of God" (ἡ ἀρχὴ τῆς κτίσεως τοῦ Θεοῦ, iii. 14). He has the same functions as in the Epistles mentioned above,—he redeems the Christians by his blood.

Here the new matter added to the previous Christology is this: His spirit had previously existed; he was pre-appointed before the foundation of the world, was the beginning of creation, redeems man by his blood, is the first-born of the dead, ruler of the kings of the world, and has preached to the souls of men who lived before the flood.

IV. In the four Epistles ascribed to Paul, whose genuineness, we think, has not been questioned,—those to the Romans, Corinthians, and Galatians, we find a Christology unknown to the three Gospels and the other writings we have referred to above. As the Pauline Christology becomes more complicated than its predecessors, it is necessary to consider its elements separately; so we will speak first of the nature, and then of the function of Jesus.

In these Epistles, as in those Gospels, Jesus is the Christ of the Hebrew Scriptures—crucified, and risen from the dead. This is the point of generic agreement between the Christology of these four Epistles and those three Gospels. But in the Epistles there appear these peculiarities: The Christ had a pre-existence before he appeared in the personal form of Jesus; he was with the Israelites in the wilderness, a spiritual rock that followed the people in their wanderings, and from which they all drank the same spiritual drink—meaning, we take it, the same spiritual drink which the Christians drank in Paul's time, contradictory as it may seem; but the Christ could not change. This pre-existence is taught by the common text in Galatians iii. 17, which says that the covenant of God with Abraham, more than four hundred years before Moses, was made by God, through the mediation of Christ (ὑπὸ τοῦ

Θεοῦ εἰς Χριστόν); but as the best copies omit the reference to Christ, this passage cannot be fairly used at the present time, as an authority. However, a single genuine passage, if clear and distinct, is as good as many.

In 2 Cor. viii. 9, it is said that Christ had been rich, but had impoverished himself (ἐπτώχευσεν) for mankind. Of course, he could only have been rich in a state of existence before he took the personal form of Jesus.

Thus he was not merely a man and Messiah—having had a pre-existence in the latter capacity, at least—but God is immanent with him in a peculiar sense; for it is said (2 Cor. v. 19), "God was in Christ reconciling the world to himself." By the text of the common editions, he is once called "God over all, blessed for ever" (ὁ ὢν ἐπὶ πάντων Θεὸς εὐλογητὸς εἰς τοὺς αἰῶνας, Rom. ix. 5); but as the word God is of doubtful authority, the text ought not to be pressed into the service of any opinion as if it represented the undisputed sense of Paul. However, in passages beyond dispute, he is called God's power, and God's wisdom (Θεοῦ δύναμιν καὶ Θεοῦ σοφίαν, 1 Cor. i. 24), and is once called absolutely the Spirit (τὸ πνεῦμα, 2 Cor. iii. 17).

His resurrection is distinctly declared, but no allusion is made to his miraculous birth, or miraculous deeds.

Such is Panl's opinion of the nature of Christ, but he says more of the office and function of Christ than of his nature. He was the final cause, the scope or object aimed at in the law of Moses (τέλος νόμου, Rom. x. 4, and τέλος τοῦ [νόμου] καταργουμένου, 2 Cor. iii. 13). The Jews did not understand this, and so there is a veil on their understanding while they read the Old Testament, but it will be removed when they are converted to Christianity.

He is the instrument by which God is to judge the world; all are to appear before his tribunal; he is to rule the living and the dead (Rom. ii. 16; 2 Cor. v. 10).

Christ intercedes (ἐντυγχάνει) for men with God (Rom. viii. 34), he is the paschal sacrifice for the Christians (1 Cor. v. 7), men who were not just before and are not just now, are to be accounted just before God, on account of their faith in Christ, and by means of the ransom he has paid (Rom. v. 22—24; v. 18, *et seq.*, *et al.*). This ransom is paid for all men, and not merely for the Jews; he is the new Adam, who brings life to such as are dead (1 Cor. xv.

21, 22). Once, Paul had been ignorant of this fact, and knew Christ after the flesh, as the Saviour of the Jews alone, but now not after the flesh, but the Christ and Saviour of all (2 Cor. v. 16).

He is the proximate and efficient cause of all things, as God is the ultimate cause thereof (δὶ οὗ [Χριστοῦ] τὰ πάντα, 1 Cor. viii. 6), though elsewhere God is the ultimate, the efficient, and the possessory cause of all things.*

In these four Epistles, following their undisputed text, and neglecting the passages where the text is doubtful, Paul goes no higher in his description of the nature and function of Christ. He is a man, born of a woman; the first-born among many brethren; he had a pre-existence, distinct, and apparently self-conscious. He is the proximate cause of all things. His coming is the fulfilment of the law, which is now repealed, null, and void. He is the Saviour of all men, through a sacrifice on his part, and faith on their part.

The peculiar addition which Paul makes to the Christology of his predecessors, is this: A more distinct statement of his personal pre-existence and function as minister of the Abrahamic covenant, and as sustainer of the Israelites in the wilderness; a generalization of his function to that of a universal Christ and Saviour, and the destruction of the Mosaic law.

V. In some of the other Epistles ascribed to Paul, though with a disputed certainty, we find the personality of Christ goes still higher. Passing over the passages in the Epistle to the Ephesians, which are vague in their character or uncertain in their text, we come to the Philippians, and find there more remarkable expressions. Thus it is said that Jesus was in the form of God, though not equal to God, as we understand it (ἐν μορφῇ Θεοῦ, ii. 6, 9—11). He descends from this eminence and receives the form of a servant (μορφὴν δουλοῦ), but has since received "the name above every name;" all beings, subterranean, earthly, and super-celestial, are to do homage to him.

In Colossians, Christ is "an image of God, the invisible" (εἰκὼν τοῦ Θεοῦ τοῦ ἀοράτου), "the first-born of all creatures,

* Ἐξ αὐτοῦ, καὶ δι αὐτοῦ, καὶ εἰς αὐτὸν τὰ πάντα, Rom. xi. 36. These words seem to denote respectively the *ultimate* cause (or ground) of all things; the *proximate* or *efficient* (instrumental) cause thereof; and the *owner* of all things, whose purpose they were to serve.

for in him (*ἐν αὐτῷ*) were made all things in heaven and upon the earth—the seen and the unseen; all are made by him and for him" (*δὶ αὐτοῦ καὶ εἰς αὐτόν*), by him, as instrument, and for him, as possessor. "He is before all, and all things continue to subsist by him." "He is the beginning, that in all respects he might be the first, for in him it has pleased [God] that all the fulness [of the Deity] should dwell (i. 15—20). "All the fulness of the Deity resides corporeally in him" (*Πάντα πλήρωμα τῆς θεότητος σωματικῶς*, ii. 9), and he is "all in all" (iii. 11), the absolute.

The same Christology appears substantially in the Epistle to the Ephesians, which is, indeed, little more than an expansion of that to the Colossians, only the doctrine is not quite so clearly set forth, and there is some discrepancy in the readings of the manuscripts in important passages.

The other minor Epistles ascribed to Paul are not important in respect to their Christology, and so we pass them by. But, in the important Epistle to the Hebrews, remarkable additions are made to the Christology of the early age. Here, the Christ is "appointed heir of all things;" the agent by whom God made the *aeons* (*αἰῶνας*), "a reflected image of his [God's] glory and stamp of his substance" (*ἀπαύγασμα τῆς δόξης καὶ χαρακτὴρ τῆς ὑποστάσεως*); and sustains all things by the word of his power. He sits "at the right hand of the majesty above." He is the "word of God" (*ῥῆμα Θεοῦ*), he is the "first-born;" is superior to the angels, and, in the Old Testament, has been called "God's Son;" the angels serve him; the Old Testament is referred to as calling him by the title of the true God (*ὁ Θεός*), and his authority is eternal (i. 8, 9). It is Christ who, "in the beginning, established the earth;" the heavens are the work of *his* hands. The universe will perish, but Christ will remain the same for ever, and his years will have no end. The angels are to worship him, for they exist only for the sake of mankind, while Christ is the ultimate object and final cause of all creation. Yet, notwithstanding this exaltation of nature, he was made a little lower than the angels, so that he might suffer death for the sake of all mankind. In his human form, he became perfect by temptation and suffering.

Such is his nature; his function is commensurate with it. He is a priest for ever; by his own blood has obtained eternal redemption and superseded all sacrifices. He has appeared once to remove sin, and will come again to bring such as wait for him to salvation. He took the form of flesh and blood that he might by death destroy the devil, who had the power of death (ii. 14), and deliver mankind, who were subject to fear thereof. He is the "cause of eternal salvation to all that obey him," and in all his achievement is the preserver of mankind (v. 9). He is a priest, not according to a temporary enactment, but in virtue of the power of indissoluble life (vii. 16). The old law is set aside, and its priesthood at an end; for there has come a high priest, holy, free from evil in his nature, blameless in his life, thereby separated from sinners, and become higher than the heavens. He is the mediator of an everlasting covenant, in which the law will be that written eternally on the heart of man.

In these Epistles, it is plain a much higher dignity is claimed for the nature and function of Christ. All the fulness of God resides in him; he is even called God, *the* God; still, he is man also, wholly a creature, and dependent on God for existence.

VI. There still remain the Johannic writings, so-called, Epistles and Gospels. The Second and Third Epistles ascribed to John have no Christological value, and require no examination. The First Epistle and the fourth Gospel represent another addition made to the Christological strata already deposited, not wholly, we fear, in tranquil seas. Here we find the continuation and development of ideas found in the doubtful works attributed to Paul.

But before we speak of the Johannic Christology, we must say a few words by way of preface. The Christians and Jews had, amongst others, this point of ideal agreement: a common reverence for the Messiah, the Christ; but this point of ideal agreement became a point of practical disagreement and quarrel; for the Christians affirmed that Jesus of Nazareth was that Christ, while the Jews declared that he was only a malefactor. The attempt was made by Paul to bring the Jews to attach their reverence for the ideal Christ to the concrete person, Jesus of Nazareth; then discord between the Christians and Jews would end.

Plato had taught, in well-known passages, that God

could not come into direct communication with man. Philo, at Alexandria, an older contemporary of Jesus, was of the same opinion. But Philo, though a Platonist in his philosophy, continued also a Jew in the form of his religion, and believed that God did actually come into communication with men; according to his Platonic theology, it must be by mediators, beings between the finite man and the infinite God. At the head of these was the Logos, whom Philo calls a god and god junior (Θεὸς and Θεὸς δεύτερος). He found a preparation for his doctrine of the Logos in the figurative language of the Old Testament, and Apocrypha, in the personified wisdom of God (Σοφία τοῦ Θεοῦ) and word of God (Λόγος τοῦ Θεοῦ). But in the Old Testament and Apocrypha, this Logos, wisdom or word, does not appear detached from God, but still attached to him: we think it is still the same with Philo, the Logos is not completely detached from God and become a distinct personality, though this may be thought doubtful. All this has been abundantly discussed of late years, and requires no further examination here.

In this manner, he found a point of agreement on the one hand with the Jews, and on the other with the philosophers; so the Jew could accept much of the Platonic philosophy without giving up his form of religion, and his Platonic contemporaries might find Judaism itself dignified into a philosophical scheme. Thus the Platonists and the Jews had a point in common, namely, the Logos, which belonged to the current philosophy of the time, and which Philo had found in the Old Testament. In this way a preliminary step was taken to promote a reconciliation between the philosophers and the Jews; between the representatives of science, voluntary reflection, on the one side, and the representatives of inspiration, passive recipients of God, on the other side. It seems the attempt was not wholly unsuccessful; the Philonic doctrine of the Logos had great influence in the development of philosophy.

We have mentioned already the point of agreement which the Christians had with the Jews, and the point of difference. The first controversy of the Christians with others related to the Messiahship of Jesus. To make out their case, the Christians were forced to alter the features of the expected Messiah a good deal, to make the ideal of prophecy fit the actual of history. This they did by a peculiar manner of interpreting the Old Testament. Specimens of a most remarkable perversion of its language, in order to prove that Jesus of Nazareth was the Hebrew Messiah, appear in abundance in the New Testament. The Jews rejected the Christian doctrine that Jesus was the Messiah, and along with it the Christian mode of interpreting the Messianic prophecies. In eighteen hundred years, little progress has been made in turning the point of difference between them into a point of agreement.

The new Christians had numerous points of general agreement with the monotheistic believers about them, and Paul finds an argument in the inscription on an altar and in a verse from a heathen book. The Christian and the Platonic philosophers agree in this, that there were mediators between man and God. But the author of the Johannic Gospel finds an important and special point of agreement with the Alexandrian philosophy in particular. He accepts the doctrine of the Logos; Christians in general might have done so, as indeed they did, with no detriment to their Christianity. But we find a new and vital doctrine common to Christianity and philosophy—CHRIST IS THE LOGOS.

This author has two important doctrines to set forth, along with many others, namely: the generic doctrine of all Christians, that Jesus was that Christ of the Old Testament (this was addressed to the Jews, and of small consequence to the heathens, who had not heard of the "promise" until they were told of its fulfilment;) and also his peculiar dogma, that Christ was the Logos. If the Jews rejected the first doctrine, as indeed they did, the heathens might accept the other, which really came to pass in due time. We are not, however, to suppose that the author of this scheme wrought with a distinct consciousness of the work he was doing, and of its relation to the thought of mankind.

In philosophy, as in nature, nothing is done by leaps. In the Hebrew literature, in the Old Testament, and Apocrypha, there had been a gradual, but unintentional, preparation for the Philonic idea of the Logos, and a similar preparation is visible in the heathen literature. In the successive elevations of the person of Jesus, which we have already seen in the three earlier Gospels and the Epistles, there was a preparation for the still further elevation of his person. It would have been abrupt, sudden, and unnatural, if Jesus had been called a God in the Gospel according to the Hebrews; it is not surprising at all in the Epistle to the Hebrews. There had been a gradual sloping up, from Jesus considered as the son of Joseph and Mary to Jesus considered as the Maker of the worlds, from the man to the God. If extended over many years, the ascent is not violent—it is not *per saltum*, but *gradatim*, that the difficulty is overcome. *Vires acquirit eundo* is true of more than fame. The first Life of Ignatius Loyola, published by Ribadaneira, his friend, fifteen years after Loyola's death, records no miracle; the enlarged edition, some twenty years later, contains no miracle. But at his canonization, more than two hundred miracles were claimed for him, and the depositions of six hundred and seventy-five witnesses were used in the process.

The Christology of the fourth Gospel is quite remarkable. The author states his design, at the end of what has been thought the genuine portion of the book: "These things are written that you may believe that Jesus is the Christ—the Son of God; and that believing you might have life in his name" (xx. 31).

He begins with the Logos: "In the beginning was the Logos, and the Logos was with God, and the Logos was God." These are some of the powers ascribed to the Logos (we will still use the word in the neuter gender, and speak thereof as IT): All things were made (*ἐγένετο*) by it; life was in it, and the life was the light of men; it enlightens every man; it was in the world, but not known thereby; to such as received it, it gave power to become children of a God (*τέκνα Θεοῦ*); such persons had their origin from a God (*ἐκ Θεοῦ*), not from man (*ἐκ θελήματος ἀνδρός*). It alone had seen God; it only brought him to the knowledge (*ἐξηγήσατο*) of men. It was in the bosom of the Father.* At length, the Logos was made flesh (*σὰρξ ἐγένετο*), and dwelt amongst men, in the person of Jesus of Nazareth.

* Clement, of Alex., defines the Κόλπον τοῦ Θεοῦ: *τὸ δ' ἀορατόν καὶ ἄῤῥητον. Βαθὺν αὐτὸν κεκλήκασιν ἐντεῦθέν τίνες, ὡς ἂν περιειληφότα καὶ ἐγκολπεσάμεκον τὰ πάντα.*

CPSIA information can be obtained
at www.ICGtesting.com
Printed in the USA
LVHW100513130422
716029LV00002B/96

9 783752 589955